A LADY'S CODE OF MISCONDUCT
BookPage Top Pick in Romance

"Political intrigue drives a captivating historical romance . . .
a smart love story, peopled with complex and absorbing
characters."

—*BookPage*

"*A Lady's Code of Misconduct* is chock-full of emotional
depth, passion, and compassion. Duran delivers a wonderfully crafted romance with an intriguing historical back-
drop, and characters readers will hold in their hearts."

—*Publishers Weekly*, starred review

"Although Duran has written a novel as layered as an onion,
the characters are well-drawn and the plot flawlessly executed. Add in some very steamy sex, and the fifth install-
ment of Duran's Rules for the Reckless series can't help but
delight. This book weaves its spell so thoroughly that the
most fortunate reader will be the one who has time to read
the entire thing in one sitting. A masterful tale of suspense,
forgiveness, and love."

—*Kirkus Reviews*, starred review

LUCK BE A LADY
RT Book Reviews Top Pick

"Flawless novel . . . These intelligent, multilayered characters embody the best aspects of this wonderfully indulgent
series."

—*Publishers Weekly*, starred review

"A powerful story with emotional punch. . . . A joy to read."
—*The Romance Dish*

AT YOUR PLEASURE
RT Book Reviews Top Pick
A *Romantic Times* nominee for Most
Innovative Romance of 2012
An American Library Association Shortlist selection

"Unforgettable. . . . Rich in texture."
—*Romantic Times* (4½ stars)

"Fast-paced, heart-pounding . . . a wonderful read!"
—*Fresh Fiction*

A LADY'S LESSON IN SCANDAL
RT Book Reviews Top Pick
A Desert Isle Keeper for *All About Romance*
An American Library Association Shortlist selection

"Compelling, exciting, sensual . . . a nonstop read everyone will savor."
—*Romantic Times* (4½ stars)

"Top-notch romance."
—*Publishers Weekly*

WICKED BECOMES YOU
RT Book Reviews Top Pick

"Witty, often hilarious, sensuous, and breathlessly paced."
—*Library Journal*

"Sexy, inventive, and riveting, it's hard to put down and a joy to read."
—*All About Romance*

ALSO BY MEREDITH DURAN

MEREDITH DURAN

THE SINS OF LORD LOCKWOOD

POCKET BOOKS

New York   London   Toronto   Sydney   New Delhi

Pocket Books
An Imprint of Simon & Schuster, Inc.
1230 Avenue of the Americas
New York, NY 10020

This book is a work of fiction. Any references to historical events, real people, or real places are used fictitiously. Other names, characters, places, and events are products of the author's imagination, and any resemblance to actual events or places or persons, living or dead, is entirely coincidental.

First Pocket Books paperback edition March 2018

POCKET and colophon are registered trademarks of Simon & Schuster, Inc.

For information about special discounts for bulk purchases, please contact Simon & Schuster Special Sales at 1-866-506-1949 or business@simonandschuster.com.

The Simon & Schuster Speakers Bureau can bring authors to your live event. For more information or to book an event, contact the Simon & Schuster Speakers Bureau at 1-866-248-3049 or visit our website at www.simonspeakers.com.

Manufactured in the United States of America

10 9 8 7 6 5 4 3 2 1

ISBN 978-1-5011-3904-8
ISBN 978-1-5011-3905-5 (ebook)

This book is for all the people who reached out over the past ten years to ask me about Lockwood, thereby persuading me that his story should be told. Without you, he might always have remained in the dark.

ACKNOWLEDGMENTS

For a decade now, I've been thanking my editor, Lauren McKenna—but with each book, I have learned more from her, while being amazed anew by her talent and skill (and charm). No writer could ever hope for better.

My thanks as well to the rest of the team at Pocket, including Sara Quaranta, Melissa Gramstad, and others behind the scenes, for your hard work, support, and unflagging patience with dilatory writers.

A grateful curtsy to my agent, Holly Root, and Taylor Haggerty, also of the Root Agency, who solve problems while I'm still scratching my head in befuddlement over what the problems might be.

Above all, my bottomless gratitude to my family: my extraordinary parents, the gorgeous fam in Washington, my sister S. J. Kincaid, my in-laws (who graciously took the pup when I desperately needed sleep), and my husband, who specializes in the defusing of writerly angst with a grace and good humor that keep me smitten and awed by my miraculous fortune in finding him.

PROLOGUE

August 1857

He had never lost a fight before. He was built like his forefathers, long and lean and quick of foot, but with fists like hams and an insensitivity to pain. Childhood brawls with his cousin, scraps on the playing fields at Eton, one moonlit assault by ruffians on the road to Oxford—he had always emerged the victor. He had become a legend among his friends. He had the instinct, they joked, of an assassin.

But he had never fought while in chains.

The chains choked him. They closed around his feet. He stumbled to his knees, blood thick in his mouth. A foot struck his temple. He fell hard on his belly, the wind knocked out. He could not see his assailants in the darkness. His eyes were still blinded by the noonday glare above deck.

Not three hours ago, he had been dragged topside, flogged in the harsh sunlight for causing trouble below. Then the captain had ordered him strung out over the bow, so the salt spray from the churning waves had spattered his wounds, a venom that even now burned.

His assailants surrounded him and aimed again.

A heel drove into his skull. Howls and hoots rose from the darkness. "Teach 'im!" someone cried. "Teach 'is bloody *lordship*!"

Raucous laughter. A fist slammed into his back. Then another foot struck his chin.

Deep in his brain, something seemed to pop free. He floated into a deeper darkness, and a strange peace diffused through him, softening the world into mist.

When his eyes opened again, a dim light pervaded the thick, dark stench of the holding cell. Hellfire trembled over the mass of packed bodies, the single barrel dedicated to the prisoners' waste. It had long since overflowed. The sludge glittered.

He made some movement and pain lanced through him. The floorboards sucked at his wet clothing.

"Shh. Lie back now." The voice came from nearby—coarse, thick with mucus. "Best give what broke time to knit."

Something itched inside his throat. It took him a moment to register that it was laughter, black and curdled, stillborn in his mouth.

He was the fifth Earl of Lockwood. He had been abducted onto a prison hulk. He was chained and bound for the Australian colonies.

What was not broken? The world had gone mad.

He gingerly turned his head, looking for the advice giver. A hundred men packed the room; he saw hunched shoulders, heads, limned by lamplight. Lamps were forbidden. But he understood, seeing eyes glitter from darkness, that the risk was worth it. The sight, at last, of a face twisted with compassion—of hooded eyes meet-

ing his squarely, from a face lined with age—returned
him to himself abruptly.

He sat up, damned be to the pain and broken parts.
"Listen," he said hoarsely. "You must believe me—"

The old man's face changed. Flattened into indifference.

Liam felt the withdrawal like a knife in his belly. He
fell silent, waiting with breath suspended, battling with
the last shred of pride not to beg the man to look upon
him kindly again.

He, the Earl of Lockwood. Desperate for a convict's
kind look.

"Doesn't matter what I believe," the old man said at
last. "What matters is, you want to live or not."

Did he want to live? Above deck, strung over the
waves, he had been wrapped in rage, throttled by it, his
single aim to loosen the bonds and hurl himself into the
water below.

Five days ago, the urge would have seemed nonsensical. Five days ago, arrayed in silk with his new bride on
his arm, Liam had seen nothing but her face, and the
future.

But both were gone.

His breath caught. He held himself still beneath the
cascading weight of that thought.

Both were gone.

This was not a nightmare. This stinking pen, the jail-
ers, the cruel blue shoreless sea he had glimpsed above—
this was real.

Some last childish piece of him still balked. It took
hold of his tongue. "There was a mistake—"

"Aye, we all heard it," the old man said. "Again and

again. Kidnapped and traded for a real criminal. You see what it's got you, this tale. They don't like lunatics here." The old man smirked. "And they like lords even less. So either way, lad, you'd best change your story."

Either way. The truth did not matter: that was what the old man meant.

Astonishment leached through him. The old man was right.

There was no hope.

"The Crown's a fine instrument," said the old man. "There's a lad over in the corner, no older than fifteen, sentenced for stealing handkerchiefs. I ain't going to defend the law, you see. It's the hand of the powerful, no justice in it. But one thing I will say—that hand does the bidding of those what can pay it. Ain't no rich man ever sentenced by accident, or transported by mistake."

Somewhere across the room, the lamp guttered out.

Hisses and curses filled the darkness. Liam stared into nothing.

It had not happened by accident. Those men had been waiting for him on the wharf.

As for the other possibility . . . "It was no mistake," he said softly.

Of course it had not been a mistake.

How had he not realized this already? Peers of the realm did not get abducted by mistake, traded for true prisoners by mistake, transported by mistake.

"Aye, well, then you've got enemies." The old man sounded reassured. "Better than being a lunatic, to be sure."

This rising tide of fury was not better. It was apocalyptic. This nightmare was by design. Someone had plotted it for him.

He knew who had plotted it. He had only one enemy.

My God. What must Anna be thinking? For all she knew, he had disappeared of his own volition. Was she weeping at this moment? Was she raging against him?

From the darkness came a vision of her at the altar, her face alight with joy. *Freedom tastes sweet*, she had whispered as they'd kissed.

Freedom was what they had promised each other. Not love. He had not dared speak of love to her, though he'd wanted to, badly. *Later*, he'd told himself. *On the honeymoon. In Paris, at sunset.*

The ship shuddered. Groans and gasps filled the pen as the floor abruptly tilted.

"God save us," muttered the old man.

"A storm is coming." Liam could offer this. Above deck, he had caught the crew's mutterings, their fear, which they had then exorcised, violently, on his body.

This would not be the first transport ship to be sunk in a storm, if God willed it.

But God clearly had no interest in men's affairs.

"First test," said the old man. "First of many to come, I expect. Count yourself lucky. Young lad like you. Young lad with enemies—the strongest kind."

"Strongest." He was bound in chains, stripped of his name, kicked and beaten like a dog. He had never felt weaker.

"Strongest," the old man confirmed. "Ain't no cure for lunacy, lad. But an enemy—oh, that can be fixed."

Liam did not want to think of his cousin. But Stephen's face came to mind, regardless.

The hatred did feel stronger than despair. It boiled through him, caused his battered hands to clench.

"Yes," the old man muttered. "A man can learn to live for revenge."

CHAPTER ONE

London, spring 1861

Anna had never set foot inside her husband's London townhouse. They had met and fallen in love in the north of Scotland; he had wed and then abandoned her in Edinburgh. But she felt as though she knew the house from top to bottom. The newspapers were full of florid descriptions. The *Times* particularly admired the Moorish touches that Lockwood had added to the salons. The *Telegraph* preferred the stately dignity of his Louis XIV dining room. Everybody agreed that the Earl of Lockwood had laudable taste. Nobody mentioned that this taste was funded by Anna's money. The earl had been broke as a fishmonger when she'd married him.

Since she had paid for Lockwood's furnishings, she felt no compunction at going to explore them, regardless of the hour, regardless that her husband had no idea she was in town. Then again, after years spent traveling only heaven knew where, he had not bothered to inform *her* of his return. So why should she prove more polite?

Indeed, did he even know she was alive? Had he

bothered to check? How much more of her money had he spent this week? Would he guess that she was armed, and not in case of brigands?

These questions made fine games as she watched London pass, the streets wet and dirty. The hired coach was moving at a good clip, but the interior smelled musty. Had the city outside it not smelled worse—a fetid mix of coal smoke and sewage—she might have opened the window.

It was nine in the evening. Beggars gathered around burning cans of rubbish to keep warm. Respectable folk strode past them, mufflers drawn against the spring chill, no tenderness in their faces as they looked through their starving brethren. A faint suggestion of lilac sunset still clung to the rim of the English sky.

"This city's *huge*," murmured the girl across from her. Jeannie's eyes were wide with wonder.

Anna spared a moment's pity for her. Jeannie had been raised on romances. She believed that all the filth might be hiding something interesting.

As they passed Westminster Abbey, Jeannie sat straighter. "I know what that is! I've seen it in books!"

"You read the wrong books," Anna said. She had tried to train Jeannie into assisting with her experiments, but the girl's literacy proved strangely changeable: when science was involved, Jeannie forgot how to read. She made a passable lady's maid, though; her favorite magazines included extensive discussions of au courant hairstyles.

"And there!" Jeannie laid a finger to the glass. "Is that the Tower, where they killed poor Nan Boleyn?"

Jeannie also enjoyed history, but only the gruesome bits. "No. But it would not surprise me if every inch of this city were haunted by unfortunate wives." At Jeannie's skeptical look, Anna shrugged. "Englishmen make very poor husbands."

Jeannie grimaced. She was petite, with a doll-like, heart-shaped face, peaches-and-cream skin, and striking black curls. Gentlemen on the train had stared. Jeannie's mother, suspicious of her daughter's enthusiasm for this trip, had begged Anna to make certain she didn't elope with a Sassenach.

"Not *all* of them, surely!" Jeannie said. "Some Englishmen must be—"

"All of them."

Jeannie slumped.

The sights out the window changed, grew cleaner and more orderly. The hackney driver had lifted his brows at the address Anna had given, and now she saw the reason for it. Mayfair looked a different species of city from the environs they had passed: clean and well-swept pavements, smooth roads, and manicured parks around which large houses with bright-striped awnings marched in orderly lines.

The coach slowed, drawing up at the curb beside a house lit from top to bottom. Anna cracked the window. The faint strains of a jig flavored the night air.

The newspapers had also spoken of her husband's penchant for parties. He used these glamorous gatherings to introduce his friends to new artists. Apparently one such party was under way tonight.

She was not dressed for it. Her wool cloak was travel stained, and beneath it she wore a walking dress of brown taffeta on which Jeannie had sloshed tea not three hours before. If somebody mistook her for a maid . . . She loosed a slow breath.

A fine anger had been brewing in her for days now.

She had good reasons for her trip to London, and only one of them concerned her husband. Nevertheless, what a waste if she did not get to hit somebody! Preferably it would be Lockwood, but in a pinch, any of his friends would serve.

Jeannie saw her temper. The girl was clever when it came to people. She caught Anna's wrist as the driver opened the door for them. "A hotel?" she suggested. "The guidebook recommended several. We could dress your hair, and change into something more . . . fitting? The English are very formal, you know."

"Are they, indeed? What an expert you are." Marvelous, too, how Jeannie's accent kept changing to match their surroundings. In Newcastle, she'd dropped her *r*'s; by the time the train had passed Peterborough, she'd lost her lilt. "Tell me," Anna said. "How does a girl raised by Loch Lomond sound more English now than the Queen?"

Jeannie blushed. "Oh, ma'am. I have always wanted to visit London. You know it!"

"I do know it. And I warn you, if I catch you humming a *single* bar of 'Rule, Britannia!' I'll leave you behind when I go home."

Jeannie sniffed and flounced out of the cab. The poor goose had grown up dreaming of sparkle and lace. Hoping for luxury, she'd leapt at the chance to work as a lady's maid, just as her mother had once done for Anna's mother. But what a disappointment she'd found in her mistress's households! Wool instead of silk, mud in the carpets, whisky in tin cups instead of champagne.

Nevertheless, Anna had promised to supervise and educate her, and she would continue to do her best at it. "I am the mistress of this house," Anna said after joining Jeannie on the curb. "However I dress is precisely how

I am meant to dress. It is the guests who will feel themselves inappropriate. Do you understand?"

The girl opened her mouth to argue, then evidently thought better of it. With a hike of her chin, she followed the driver around back to oversee the removal of the luggage.

Anna adjusted the hem of her cloak, straightened her shoulders, and marched up the steps to bang the knocker.

The door creaked open. Somebody had left it ajar. Somebody was getting sacked tonight. Anna did not pay for incompetence in her staff.

She stepped into the entry hall, a rectangular space paved by checkerboard marble, topped by a curving split staircase, also of marble. The English had no restraint: they piled ancient statues into every nook and cranny, and managed to find ways to make staircases expensive. That bronze balustrade had probably cost her a year's interest on her harvest profits in the lowlands.

From behind her came some noise. She turned and found herself locking eyes with a squat, barrel-chested man whose bald skull gleamed in the gaslight.

"Guest?" he croaked—then frowned as his gaze ran down her bedraggled cloak. "Servants around the back," he said, and shot a stream of tobacco juice into a spittoon standing behind the door.

Anna snorted. *The English are very formal, are they?* "I am no servant." Whereas Jeannie's accent had smoothed, her own had grown new burrs with every southbound mile they'd traveled. She now sounded like one of the islanders, and the little man frowned in consternation.

"What?" he demanded. "Speak English."

She stepped toward him. He looked startled by his own retreat, and moved his hand into his jacket—a threatening gesture that she acknowledged with a lift of one brow.

"Go ahead," she said. "Brandish a weapon at your master's wife."

His jaw slackened. She caught a glimpse of the tobacco packed into his mouth. "You aren't," he said uncertainly.

She smiled.

She had not been born beautiful, like Jeannie. Her cousins teased her that her pale green eyes were witchy, her copper hair the color of devil's flames. But she had been born with a talent for smiling: with the mere curve of her mouth, she could make men stumble and gape, or quail in momentary fear, for reasons they would never manage to explain to themselves.

The brute was not immune. He let go of his weapon, his eyes widening. "You *are* the countess."

She narrowed her eyes. What an odd remark. Had Lockwood been *describing* her to his staff? "Naturally. And your name, sir?"

"Danvers. But, ma'am, his lordship ain't . . ." His gaze shifted past her. Jeannie was staggering across the threshold, a trunk sliding from her grip.

"Assist Miss Galbraith," Anna said. "And have our rooms aired and readied. Which way is Lord Lockwood?"

The man made a helpless grunt. Then he lifted his finger to point down the darkened hall. "But, ma'am— my lady—I'll warn you—"

She did not accept advice from rogues. Besides, what news could he impart of her husband that she did not already know? It took an utter blackguard to abandon his newlywed bride on her wedding night, and to disappear for three years without a word, much less to let her discover his return, months delayed, by a headline in the newspaper.

"Help Miss Galbraith," she repeated coolly, and turned on her heel to find her errant husband.

The noises of the party drew her around the corner, and to doors that opened into a long gallery. Pausing there, she beheld a scene of complete debauchery: gentlemen in shirtsleeves with waistcoats flapping, women powdered and painted, feathers sagging from their hair. A stray dog or two frolicked amid scraps thrown by cheeky boys. Violinists were wandering among the crowd, sawing out street ditties—multiple ditties, none of them in tune. One wore a monkey on his shoulder. The creature was lifting his little hat in time to the music.

Out the windows that lined one side of the gallery, torches lit a lawn filled with couples. Half of them appeared to be dancing, but to no uniform rhythm or step. Pieces of clothing littered the grass—and glittering shards of broken glasses—and bodies, intertwined.

"Goodness," she murmured. But her own voice was lost in the din of chatter and discordant tunes and the sudden explosion of a bottle hurled into the wall. "Watch for the paintings!" somebody cried.

It was then that she noticed the other wall of the gallery.

The paintings there showed scenes of slaughter.

After a moment, when her pulse slowed, she realized that these must be the Ashdown paintings. She had read about them in a newspaper she'd purchased at the platform in Peterborough. Her husband was a patron of the artist Miss Aurora Ashdown, and had hosted an exhibit recently for the titillation of his English friends.

Patron. She wondered if that was a polite euphemism, and Miss Ashdown was his mistress. Otherwise, why would he promote such nightmarish scenes? The artist had talent, but taste . . . ?

She averted her eyes from the paintings. The people cavorting beneath them hardly made a better sight. Gritting her teeth, she picked up her skirts and shoved her way into the crowd, using her elbows to clear a path for herself.

"Hey! Watch yourself—"

"Oi, sweetheart! What's your hurry?"

She pivoted sharply at this last remark, catching the startled eye—and then, between her thumb and forefinger, the ear—of a lad who looked barely old enough to shave.

"What was that?" she asked sweetly. "Whose sweetheart am I?"

He blinked, his reddened eyes and chinless, sallow face lending him the look of a snared rabbit. "I—I—I reckon you're nobody's, ma'am!"

Not the cleverest retraction, but the sentiment served. Anna released him, wiped her hand on her skirts, and resumed her progress.

It did occur to her, as glass crunched under her boot and she spied the salon ahead, that she might not recognize Lockwood. Three years and eight months, after all. She herself had changed, so she liked to think. She had far better taste now than to trifle with bankrupt English lordlings, particularly those who had no better use for her money than the despoiling of decency and common sense—

There he was.

She drew up a foot inside the salon, watching through narrowed eyes as William Alexander Knollys Devaliant, fifth Earl of Lockwood, extricated himself from a sofa heaped with three scantily clad women, his balance clearly unsteady.

A pair of hands clung to him as he rose. Those hands belonged to a woman whose hair had been dyed a brassy false red. Lockwood, stepping forward, looked surprised to find himself caught. Looking down and discovering the hands that held him, he pulled them free, lifting one of them to his mouth for a kiss.

On occasional Tuesdays, Liam opened his doors to the crème de la crème of London society. On occasional Sundays, his staff made the invitations.

The contrast never failed to amuse him—particularly now, as some unnamed drug swam through his brain and lent him a novel perspective. Last Tuesday, some five hundred well-heeled Londoners—members of Parliament and gentlemen farmers and lords—had winced before Miss Ashdown's paintings. Her images of the violent insurrection in British India had seemed to those guests like accusations. Society folk had murmured among themselves, then fled to the ballroom to guzzle champagne.

Tonight's crowd, on the other hand, cavorted beneath those same paintings, admiring but not shocked. Working people—servants and barmaids, factory men and honest criminals—saw nothing unusual in such graphic depictions. Violence and power were but two sides of the same coin; this crowd knew it.

Liam had kept the ballroom closed. The music room stood locked as well, the interior burned after more recent festivities. Tonight, the musicians wandered freely, and the dancing took place on the lawn outside. The grass proved a novelty for this crowd, to whom London's finest parklands stood closed.

In the salon, he'd gathered the small number of men whom he'd invited personally. They were penned there by Liam's footmen, who had stationed themselves in postures of servitude but who nevertheless managed to loom in a manner that discouraged guests from pushing past them. Few of the celebrants noticed this, much less wondered if it was deliberate. Half of them were drunk, a quarter more dazed, like him, by the toxic tarry substance that Colthurst had brought to smoke.

Liam's cousin was sober, though. Stephen Devaliant had accepted the invitation, delivered this afternoon in the reading room at White's, very casually, as though there was nothing unusual in it. He was doing a very good job of pretending he had not tried to have Liam killed four years ago, much less that the greatest shock of his life had not been to learn of Liam's return, this past autumn, and not in a casket—for Liam, despite his cousin's best efforts, had survived.

Liam walked over to the sofa, his mere approach causing Stephen's conversation with a courtesan to fracture into stuttering syllables. "More champagne?" he asked his cousin. Stephen's glass had remained empty for an hour now. Hunted creatures could not afford to muddle their brains.

Stephen glanced up. He was Liam's elder by eighteen months, with a full head of brown hair and a lineless face. Had he spent three years battling starvation, however, he might have looked different. His hair might have been bleached, his cheeks hollow, and his crow's-feet deeper, to match Liam's.

"How kind of you," he said. "No, I'm entirely content." His smile looked fixed; no doubt he was racking his brain for a reason to leave. Stephen aspired to public office—a seat in Parliament would go·far to effacing the commercial stain of his wealth—and to that end, he cultivated a pious reputation. He sponsored charities. He paid newspapers to publish his homilies on Christian virtue. He volunteered as churchwarden in the parish where London's most powerful men prayed.

To be seen at this raucous party would do him no favors. But he accepted all of Liam's invitations. He could not afford to do otherwise. He was not yet certain if Liam knew what he had done.

"But it's very fine champagne," Liam said. The finest that money could buy—a fitting slogan for everything in this house. In the last eight months, he'd spent vast amounts of money refurbishing his London property. The glitter now gave him a headache, but it made excellent camouflage. Blinded by his opulent good taste, nobody ever bothered to look too closely at *him*. "Come," he told his cousin. "Just a glass."

"Just a glass," echoed the courtesan on a giggle—she was one of Colthurst's, a long-limbed beauty with a lisp and dyed scarlet hair.

Her hair annoyed Liam. He had told Colthurst not to bring redheads. He considered hunting down Colthurst and gutting the man—an image so vivid and pleasurable that he abruptly reconsidered the wisdom of trying Colthurst's drugs.

Stephen's mouth was tightening. This game was a delicate one; push him too far, bully him in any way, and he would find a credible reason to withdraw. "I'm certain it's very fine champagne," he said. "I order it occasionally myself, when the Lafitte is not available."

Liam laughed. "Of course," he agreed, "you would only drink Lafitte." He felt kinder now to the courtesan, who must have been annoying Stephen, to set him so on edge as to allude to his own wealth. For a time, this had been Stephen's great advantage—his only solace for having been born to a second son, and thereby deprived of the earldom.

That trick of birth had been the greatest tragedy of Stephen's life to date. Liam meant to correct that, but he was taking his time. Revenge made an excellent hobby.

Stephen rose, drawing himself as straight as possible to diminish the difference between their respective heights. "A lovely evening," he said. "I'm afraid I must be going."

"Of course." Liam straightened, looking down his nose, and Stephen's mouth pinched. By their next meeting, no doubt, he'd be wearing lifts in his shoes. "Shall I walk you out?"

"I believe I can find the way," Stephen said stiffly. "If you'll recall, I once lived here myself."

Ah, yes. The old reminder of their shared boyhood. After Stephen's father had died, he had come to live with Liam's family for a time. "Of course!" Liam clapped his cousin on the shoulder, *just* as a brother would, and felt the man flinch.

He had several advantages over Stephen, in fact, the earldom being the least of them. Thanks to Stephen, he had learned a great deal about torture, and come to grasp that the usual methods—floggings and starvation and terror—were not useful. Pain stripped a man of his humanity. What remained became bestial and wild: it could not be controlled. Common tortures were useless, then, unless one intended to put down the animal directly.

The subtler tortures held a world of possibility, though. To invite a man over and ask him to drink, to smile at him in one's club, to clap him on the back—to keep him startled, second-guessing, dreaming of poison, his paranoia ever-growing: it made a fine game, far better than the brief satisfaction of a bullet in the brain.

"Perhaps I'll drop by tomorrow," he said into his cousin's ear. "You can catch me up on the world of commerce."

Stephen recoiled from this murmur and threw a hunted look over his shoulder as he hurried away.

"What's so funny?" The courtesan wound her arms around Liam, the cloying scent of her lavender perfume tickling his nose as she pulled him down onto the sofa beside her.

"A great deal." Laughter escaped Liam, though he no longer felt amused. The laugh felt like an animal, clawing and wrestling out of his throat. *Stop it.* The sound of the chatter intensified all around him, rattling and buzzing like bees.

Foul drug. Colthurst should know better. Liam wanted a numbing, not a false enlivening. He needed a quiet place to wait this out. He stood again, realizing belatedly that the courtesan still clutched on to him. He pried away her wrists, dropping a casual kiss on her knuckles when she protested.

"Find someone else," he told her with a smile. He did not like being touched, but there was no need to advertise it.

The woman, perhaps hard of hearing, misunderstood the kiss as an invitation. "I'll put you in a better mood," she said, twining herself around him.

"I will not pay for *that*," came a woman's voice from the doorway.

The gaslights seemed to flicker. His heart missed a beat. Liam found himself abruptly nauseated, mouth dry.

"Are you all right?" asked the courtesan, her eyes wide with concern.

A mirror hung on the wall beyond her. Liam did not let himself focus on it. He would not like what he saw. These were not feelings he could feel.

His mouth still held the semblance of a smile. He widened that smile as he pivoted from one redhead toward the other.

She filled the doorway completely. She was taller than he remembered, her jaw squarer. Her lips were full, wide, sneering. He had remembered the feel of them better than the look.

Ah, but this drug was wicked. It caused her to intensify into impossible vividness, a vision in copper and green and cream. In all the lands he had crossed to come home, there had been no shade like her eyes: leaves were not vibrant enough, grass was too dark. Her hair was blazingly bright, the color of freshly polished pennies. The world behind her was breaking apart, swimming in little colored dots, like schools of fish.

"You should not be here," he said to her. God above, not now. Sober would serve them both better.

Her smile gutted him. He had forgotten the trick of that smile—how it could spark a light inside a man that made him feel untethered from the earth, or gut him more deeply than a blade. "And you should be in hell," she said. "Alas, few of us end up where we belong."

CHAPTER TWO

*T*hree years and eight months made a *great* deal of difference. In that space of time, Anna had cut romance out of her heart completely. She could look across the room now at what was, objectively, a very handsome man, his chiseled lips turning into a slight and impenetrable smile, and feel nothing but irritation.

He looked older. His gold-brown hair remained thick, his body still tall and leanly fashioned. But new crow's-feet bracketed his eyes. Wherever he'd adventured, he'd squinted at the sights. And the look in his eyes . . .

His eyes had always dazzled her. The color of dark honey, of fine Scottish whisky, they had glimmered across rooms at her, caused her breath to come short. But they looked flat now, empty. They watched her with the inhuman, steady focus of a wolf.

The scarlet-haired woman was gawking. Anna spoke crisply. "We have business to discuss."

He appeared at last to recollect himself. Straightening, he offered her a bow that was too deep to be anything but mockery. "Won't you join us?" he said with a sweep of his hand toward the sofa he'd just vacated.

For a moment, she remained stock-still, stinging beneath a wave of realization:

He was not ashamed.

He was not embarrassed.

He did not even seem surprised to see her, much less *glad*.

In reply, she turned and strode for the exit.

Moments later, he passed her, moving with a swiftness that belied his earlier loss of balance. "Follow me," he said casually over his shoulder.

From this angle, she could see that he'd fleshed out through the shoulders, put on bulk to suit a stevedore. He moved with swinging, athletic strides, and the crowd parted before him, crowing and cheering his passage.

Was he trying to outrun her? He'd be disappointed: she walked for two hours each day, and rode for two more besides. He was not the only one with muscle.

He led her out of the gallery through a hidden door that opened into a gaming room. The leather-paneled cave reeked of stale tobacco. A raffish young man with auburn hair and freckles was sleeping atop the snooker table, a cue draped across his belly.

She folded her arms and waited. It took Lockwood a good shove to wake the interloper. The youngster sat up, blinking sleepily, then set aside the cue and scratched his head. Bits of cue chalk scattered from his hair onto the green nap of the table.

"Party's over, Wilkins," said her husband.

"Right," said the boy, then staggered to his feet and lurched out.

She hugged herself more tightly. "Who are these

people?" A sad and pathetic lot, to be sure! "Are you running a hostel for the soused?"

Lockwood laughed—a strange sound, unsteady and abruptly over. "Oh, that's good." Leaning back against the closed door, he closed one eye and squinted at her. "If you had written ahead of your visit, I might have gathered a company more to your taste."

Was he drunk? "That would require you to understand my tastes, and your knowledge on that count is outdated."

He nodded amiably. "Been a while."

Her disbelief felt almost hysterical. "You've been in London for eight months now. Eight months! *You* might have written. But I suppose that would have ruined the fun!"

He lifted a dark brow. "Fun?"

She would not yell. She took a long breath. "I discovered your return through a newspaper headline. Fun is *one* way to put it." *An unconscionable and shameless dereliction of your marital duties* was another.

But she would not say that, either. She had not come to shriek and rail at him; that would suggest she cared.

"Ah, I . . ." He threw a distracted glance toward the wall, from which came a thump as somebody on the other side presumably kicked it. "I thought you would be on the island."

If he was drunk, he did not sound it. She'd forgotten the arrogant tenor of his mannerisms, the irksome cut-glass precision of his accent—all still fully intact. "So I was."

"You once told me that no post reaches Rawsey in winter."

"It was a mild winter," she bit out. "And behold: it is almost *May*."

The journalists were correct, his fashions were the definition of au courant. His dark suit fit him so closely she could see the bulge of his muscled shoulder as he shrugged. "I meant to write," he said. "Besides, you keep so busy there. I imagined I had until June at the least."

The way he phrased it! As though she were some kenneled animal, safely ignored until summer! She opened and closed her mouth before recovering her aplomb. "Well, it's good to confirm it with my own eyes. Your dreadful cousin kept insisting you were dead. I hope you have put *that* to rest. He harassed me terribly."

Something violent flickered over his face. For the first time, she had the startled sense that he was not nearly as calm as he seemed. "What do you mean, he harassed you?"

"Precisely what it sounds like. He seemed to labor under the impression that this"—she waved a hand around the room, the leather gaudily trimmed in gilt—"belonged to him now. And my properties as well, though as I had my lawyers explain to him, even if you *were* dead, the Scottish estates belong to *me*." She rolled her eyes. "These little English brains can hardly compass it, the idea of properties entailed through a woman."

"Do you have any of his letters still? Those in which he said I was deceased?"

"Why should I save kindling? But you can hardly blame him, Lockwood. Three years without news— even *I* was tempted once or twice to bury you."

He slumped against the door again, his smile lopsided, designed to charm. "How good of you to refrain."

"Yes, well, I know your character better than your cousin does. Stephen's mistake was to overestimate you; he felt certain you'd never run away for years on end. I informed him that running away had been your plan all along. I said, why, Lockwood never promised to stay at all! He married only so somebody else would fix up his estates."

She paused briefly.

He made no denial.

You are a fool, she told herself.

"I'll confess, though—" She pushed out a light laugh. "I *did* expect you to make it through the honeymoon. Especially since it promised to play to your strengths! Drinking and lounging and loafing, and not much else."

Another man, *any* man with some pride in him, would have objected. But again, his only reply was a long, mildly quizzical stare. He looked the very picture of a dissolute rake: all chiseled bones and full lips, no brains whatsoever.

Her discipline began to fray. She bit her tongue hard, but could not stop herself. "You're not even going to *apologize*, are you?"

Unblinking, he replied: "For what? As you say, we had a bargain."

Snap went her temper. "You shameless fool. I *did* think you were dead, near the end. That money you took must have run out. What else was I to think? How dare you not write me a letter, cable a single line!"

"My apologies." His own tone sounded very mellow. "I should have written, yes. But my travels took me to some very . . . remote corners of the world." This appeared to amuse him; a faint smile played over his lips. "The money stretched farther than I'd expected. The telegraph wires did not."

"Then you should have made a detour." Her hands were fisted; she fought the urge to stalk him down, to slap some real emotion, some proper regret or repentance, into that handsome face. But the effort would be wasted, obviously.

"Well," he said, flipping his hand to prompt her to continue. "Was there something else? As you saw, I have guests."

She marveled at him a moment. "I don't recall you being such a jackass."

He laughed, a low, husky sound. "I don't recall you cursing like a sailor."

"Then it's true, time *does* reveal all. On that note, I will be in residence for the remainder of the spring, so I expect—"

"Alas, no." He pulled open the door to the hall. "I will send to Claridge's to book you a suite."

"You will not. I am staying here."

He turned back, looking puzzled. "I'm afraid it won't be possible."

"I paid for every furnishing in this house."

"And you have exquisite taste," he said solemnly, and then laughed again.

She glared. At least he was amusing himself. "Regardless of my *taste*, I intend to enjoy what I have purchased."

"But there's no room," he said genially. "Guests, you know."

"Expel them."

He hesitated, sighed, then closed the door, giving her his full and apparently earnest attention. "Lady Forth. It seems I must explain to you—"

"South of the border, I am known as the Countess of Lockwood, I am *very* sorry to say."

He did not seem to register the barb. "I must explain how unsuitable the company is. You cannot stay here.

Not tonight, at any rate." He tipped his head, looking thoughtful. "Perhaps not tomorrow, either."

He was not drunk, but something was addling him. As she advanced on him, she saw that his pupils had nearly disappeared; his amber irises were huge and unnervingly bright. "Did somebody hit you very hard on the head?" If so, she could not blame them. "I am here. I am certainly staying. If the company doesn't suit, then it is the *company* that must change."

He blinked several times—seeming confused by how closely she suddenly loomed. For she was not a small woman; on her tiptoes, she was nearly eye level with him, which gave her an opportunity to deliver him a fulminating glower.

"Now," she said as her hand landed on the doorknob. One swift tug sent him stumbling off the door past her, though he recovered with grace, swinging back as his own brows began to lower into a proper scowl. "Get rid of the company," she said as she stepped through the doorway. "At *once*."

He opened his mouth to reply. She shut the door in his face to spare him the effort.

A hammer was knocking on Liam's skull.

"My lord."

And now came the hiss of rings across the curtain rod, and an unbearable scalding light that caused him, with a groan, to drape his arm over his eyes.

"Your lordship."

He was not going to move for another hour. "I am dead," he said. "Go away."

The floorboards squeaked. "Lock, it's your—"

Eyes closed, he reached out, seizing the oncoming hand before it could shake him awake. Then, on a hard breath, he forced himself to face the full light of day.

Hanks was staring down, rheumy eyes wide in amazement. "That's a fine trick," he said. "I'll never know how you do it."

"Magic." Dropping the man's wrist, Liam closed his eyes again. "Now you try some. Disappear."

"She's downstairs," came Hanks's apologetic voice. He was, nominally, Liam's valet. It was not a role that came easily to him; ironing and folding, yes, but the fussy proprietary hassling of a typical valet, no. "She's questioning the staff. Has us lined up, introducing ourselves, explaining what purpose we serve."

Jesus bloody—

He made himself sit up, wincing as the hammer transformed into a dagger that lanced his right eye. What in God's name had Colthurst given him last night?

Whatever the substance, it was useless: it had not blurred his memory by a fraction. He stared blindly at a pool of sunlight on the Persian carpet, reliving in an instant the entire disaster.

His wife was here.

She was here, and famously and gorgeously in form. She had not changed a whit.

Worse, she intended to stay.

"I think she means to sack Tommy," Hanks said.

He looked up. "What?"

Hanks gave a mournful tug of his gray beard. He was the only one of them who had not gone clean shaven at the first opportunity, but he spent an hour each night trimming and grooming his facial hair. The others had a name for his beard—"the poodle," for how wildly it curled, and how lovingly Hanks tended to it. "Nobody was attending the front door last night," he said. "And she ran into Tommy inside, and so takes him for the porter, and means to sack him for not minding his business."

Liam gingerly rose, and was relieved to find that the floor remained steady beneath him. "I'll take care of it."

Hanks, brightening, hurried to fetch the clothing he'd laid out.

Liam sighed. "Paisley," he said. "What did we decide about paisley, Hanks?"

The old man hesitated, considering the pile in his arms. "Ah—doesn't go with stripes?"

"Doesn't go with stripes," Liam confirmed. Sometimes, very occasionally, and not without a feeling of disloyalty, he did wish he'd kept on his old valet. Morris had spent three years here sitting on his arse, cheerfully drinking his way through the cellar, skills rusting—but he had not been color-blind, and he had known what to do with paisley.

Alas, Morris would *not* have known what to do with his master's new body. Liam stripped off his nightshirt, and Hanks did not so much as blink at what was exposed. Hanks had seen it done to Liam; that was the difference. All the men in this house knew more about him than he might have wanted—and he knew just as much of them.

That was why Hanks, and not Morris, now served as Liam's valet.

Also, Liam had no idea what else to do with the old man.

He dressed quickly, Hanks fluttering around him with hands too palsied to be of use. When Liam started for the door, Hanks came up hard on his heels, and between the headache and premonitions of the disaster below, it was all Liam could do to keep from snapping.

Instead, on a deep breath, he sidestepped and waved Hanks ahead of him.

Hanks, oblivious, hurried onward. To imagine that he'd once been convicted of thieving sheep! He couldn't have caught a sheep had one been placed before him in a state of advanced decomposition.

On the staircase, Liam got his first glimpse of the problem below. His wife had the staff lined up like a regimental formation—unaware, of course, of how much she asked. The chambermaids and the housekeeper—all of whom had been on holiday yesterday—looked to a woman very pleased by this crisis. No doubt they had dreamed of a mass sacking for months now.

The men looked torn along a spectrum from rage to bewilderment. Henneage, a squat Northman who'd been transported for leading a riot, looked red faced and indignant enough to rally a new mob. Scrawny Wilkins was weaving on his feet, barely supported by the combined efforts of Gibbs and Riley, who were muttering ominously.

"What nonsense is this?" came a strident female voice. As Liam hurriedly took the last few steps, his wife came into view. She was pacing the line, her hands clasped at her back, her lavender woolen walking gown fittingly garnished with black epaulettes and military braids. She stopped in front of Wilkins, peering down her Roman nose. "Did your nap on the snooker table last night not leave you sufficiently refreshed, sir? And to think I'd imagined you a guest! Instead, it seems, you are . . . Well? What, precisely, *is* your role here?"

"He's the other porter," said Matthew Dunning, a

naval mutineer. His sly smile dissolved when he noticed Liam's approach.

"Ah." The countess nodded, the jeweled comb in her copper hair winking in the morning light that fell from the skylight above. "Then with Danvers you will go." She pointed a long finger toward the corner, where Tommy Danvers huddled miserably.

Liam hesitated.

It was a delicate situation, to be sure—for as his wife had pointed out last night, and *he* remembered all too clearly, her money *did* fund this household. And although they had been married in the Church of England, her fortune was Scottish—which made it subject to laws that granted ladies a good deal more control over their wealth than did sensible English patriarchy. Liam would not want to test it in a court, at any rate.

In short, the countess could probably make his life quite difficult if he countermanded her authority in front of the servants.

He chose instead to clear his throat and say, "Good morning."

Her shoulders stiffened, and her posture drew impossibly straighter, before she faced him.

"This household is an abomination of order," she said crisply. Her brief, increasingly dour survey of his figure suggested that he, too, was a piece of the mess. "Were you aware that your cook has no eggs? That your porter—both of them, evidently, though why you should require two, I can't imagine—*both* your porters abandoned their posts for a night of carousing. And your footmen, sir, I found loitering with their feet on the chairs in your drawing room!"

"Ah, yes." He'd hoped that some inspiration would

come to him before he finished drawling that first bit, but nothing did, so he helpfully added, "*Our* drawing room, you mean."

She opened her mouth, then closed it, looking nonplussed. "I—yes. *Our* drawing room, with the very expensive cushions paid for by *me*. So you will understand if I mean to make changes here."

It was peculiar how good he'd gotten at never thinking about her. Looking at her now, listening to her, felt surreal, as though beholding in the flesh some long-forgotten fantasy from boyhood. Her lips, for instance, were much plusher and pinker than he recalled.

He'd wanted her so badly. She'd never known just how much he wanted her.

"Change is a fine thing," he said. Change was all he had to offer. She was looking at *him* as though she knew him, when in fact the boy she'd married was dead now.

She thought that boy had abandoned her. Marvelous! He felt pity for the sap. That stupid boy had nursed grand plans for their marriage, wild and romantic hopes, while all the while his bride had held him in secret contempt—or so it seemed to Liam now. For why else would she have been so ready to believe him capable of deserting her?

She was scowling. Did his replies seem off? He did not feel quite sober, though he didn't think Colthurst's poison was to blame any longer. Looking at her rather nauseated him. It made him feel as though the world were tilting. No handholds, nothing to arrest the fall.

He took a deep breath. It would have been wiser to plan for her reappearance. But he'd imagined he had until mid-June. And thinking of her rather felt like grinding a burr into his brain; pleasanter to avoid.

"I am glad we're in agreement," she said. "The porters will need to be sacked, the footmen placed on a period of probation—"

Her voice died as he caught her elbow. "Alas, I haven't yet had coffee." With his hand at the small of her back, he urged her toward the corridor. "Let's talk of this over breakfast, shall we? Dismissed," he said casually over his shoulder, and pretended not to see the disappointment in the maids' faces and the relief in the men's.

Once in the hallway, he released her, his palm burning oddly, as though the wool of her gown were somehow toxic to him. Well, no doubt it was; certainly some kind of black magic was involved here, to bring her back to life so suddenly, a dead man's dream.

She had turned pink, and was not meeting his eyes. "You should go back to Scotland," he told her. "For your own comfort." And for his. He felt disoriented, strange in his skin, with her so nearby. It was a dead man's skin, a dead man's role, which her presence forced him to adopt. "At least until I've straightened out the staff."

"It isn't all disastrous. The chambermaids appear satisfactory."

"How good to hear." He pushed open the door to the dining room, allowing her to precede him. "I rather like the chambermaids myself."

She gave him an odd sharp look, but he forgot it in the next second as he drew up in amazement.

A full breakfast lay spread on the table. With china plates!

"No eggs," said the countess bitterly. "Can you believe it?"

No eggs, to be certain—but rashers and potatoes and sausages, O divinities! And those plates—he'd felt certain that Beauregard had stolen and sold them weeks ago.

"This took more than two hours from the time I rang for it," the countess continued, seating herself opposite. "Can you imagine? What was Cook doing down there? I'll wager you that he had no food whatsoever, and had to send the scullery maids out to buy it all."

He sank into his chair, then nodded gratefully as she lifted a silver pot.

The coffee was steaming hot. "You are invited to harass the cook whenever you like," he said. He hadn't known old Beauregard had it in him to lay a proper table. Toast and oatmeal, he'd thought, were the whole of it.

"Thank you, I will." She sipped her own coffee, then wrinkled her nose and reached for the cream. "Now, as for the question of hiring replacements—"

"I'm afraid I can't let any of the men go," Liam said. "But if you wish to reassign them to positions that better suit their strengths, by all means, do so."

She stared. Some trick of the slanting morning light lit the tips of her long red lashes, and illuminated her eyes so they glowed like peridots.

With a jolt, he realized she was not staring but *glaring*, and quickly made an apologetic grimace.

Christ, he had no idea what face to show her. He was doing his best here to play the affable boy she'd known, but he would slip up; it already felt like a parody somehow. "Forgive me," he said. "I know it's inconvenient. But when you come back—say, in the autumn—"

"Oh no, it's a fine idea." She took a measured sip of her coffee. "Do tell me, what positions here best suit incompetence and drunkenness?"

He stopped a sigh. Those were the least of the men's sins. The thieving, gambling, and brawling were at least commonplace flaws. But Hanks, left to his own devices, often dissolved into tears, and refused to leave his bed till dusk. Henneage went into rages: he had broken several chairs a week ago after one of the maids had called him a lazy toad.

He had done it only after the maid left, though, which Wilkins had argued was in his favor. Wilkins was forever speaking up for others, but had no ability to defend himself. Indeed, Liam had once caught him drawing in the flesh of his own arm with a razor, but after a severe discussion, Wilkins had not done it again.

These would look like vices to her. But they were not. They were the relics of survival. At the height of it, Elland had held ninety prisoners. Forty, besides Liam, had survived to the end. Six had died of injuries before leaving Australia, and four more had perished of the cholera in Singapore. Twelve had dropped off later, in ports that welcomed newcomers with vague histories. Of the twenty who had reached England, twelve had returned to their former lives, and the remaining eight, lacking family or resources, lived here—where, as long as they limited their deviancies to those things that harmed nobody else, they were free to remain.

His wife, of course, would not understand any of this. His wife, being a piece of sheltered innocence bred on privilege and swaddled in money, had every reason to expect perfection—in her staff, in her surroundings, in her husband.

"I've an idea," he said pleasantly. "Separate households. Quite fashionable now, actually. The duchess of Buckminster—"

Her teacup slammed into its saucer without a drop being shed. "How free you are with money. One might almost think it were in limitless supply."

It very nearly was, in her case. But he did not think she would appreciate the observation. "Then hire your own staff," he said, his voice only slightly frayed by his effort to remain charming, charming, blandly charming: young Lord Lockwood had been a bright-eyed optimist, after all, for whom the whole world had seemed a grand adventure.

"A shadow staff, like the shadow ministries?" Her laughter was sharp. "What a ridiculous idea."

Young Lord Lockwood, that naïve and rosy-cheeked idiot, would never have pointed out to his wife that her presence here was her own doing, and if she did not like it, she could leave. Nor would he have observed that their marriage made her money into his, and if Scottish laws wanted to protest, then English courts would crush them.

Young Lord Lockwood had been a fool. He had rested on his laurels, imagining the future would only bring more of them. He had extended endless olive branches to Stephen, mindful of his cousin's pride, sympathetic to the difficulties of Stephen's inferior position. He had believed that best intentions would triumph, always.

That callow, idealistic idiot had probably deserved what was coming to him.

"How long do you intend to stay, then?" Liam asked.

"I haven't yet decided. I have business to settle here— the MacCauleys, idiots, leased the beach that my islanders use to access Rawsey. I offered to buy it outright, but the railway company that leased it . . . oh, it's complicated. At any rate, I've no idea how long it will take to settle the matter. It may go to court."

"I'm sorry to hear so." Her skin remained as smooth and creamy as the day he'd first seen her, but her freckles had multiplied. Her freckles had always fascinated him. He had tried to count them once, but she'd been wearing too many clothes.

The memory hit like a fist in his gut.

He found himself staring at her, abruptly transfixed. Transformed, brain evacuated by a fierce, full-bodied, singular pulse of hunger.

Christ. He had forgotten what desire felt like. He'd imagined his appetite permanently blunted by hunger—pain—and now, Colthurst's toxins.

He'd been wrong.

His senses expanded. He could feel her skin beneath his fingertips, a memory made tactile. He could smell her from across the table: soap, skin, the musk of her. He *wanted*.

"Lockwood?" She tipped her head. "Are you . . . all right? You look rather . . ."

He clamped his hands on the edge of the table, pressed his fingertips into the embroidered linen. Coffee was what he smelled. Rashers, sausage. He would not touch her. He could not.

"Certainly," he said. "A bit tired, perhaps."

Without remark, she refilled his empty cup.

"The men I have hired." His voice sounded hoarse. God save her—she thought the staff rude, rough, and unkempt? His body would make a lesson for her. But she would never see it. "I will keep those men. I'm afraid I must insist on it. If you choose to add to their number, that's your own affair."

Her cheek hollowed, as though she were biting the interior to stem her protest. "Fine," she said at last, very curtly.

One freckle sat directly between the peaks of her upper lip. That freckle was a taunt.

He lifted his coffee, bent his face into the cup. Bitter, dark, hot. *Breathe.*

How many times had young Lord Lockwood passed up the opportunity to touch her? He had imagined himself honorable for waiting. He'd believed there would be endless time to explore her. He had forgone the chance to kiss her once more, to stroke the curve of her waist, to trace the vein that wound down her chest and disappeared beneath the neckline of her lavender gown, to rip that gown apart and bare her body, to suck the peaks of her nipples and then pull her into a dark corner and lift her skirts and take her.

Honor had demanded that he wait.

Liam bolted the remainder of his coffee.

He would have reached back in time and throttled that other man, if only he were able.

"I may insist on removing them from public roles," she said.

"Of course." He laid down his cup, not knowing or caring to what he'd just agreed.

"As for the business of your estates," she said, "I hope you have reviewed the improvements I made. While *you* were on holiday, I undertook a catalog . . ."

He watched her mouth as her voice faded from his ears. It had not all been a waste. He had not been entirely monkish. He remembered:

The heat of her, the hot wet depths of her mouth, the heavy weight of her breasts, her nipples peaking as her plump soft thighs yielded—

"Where are you going?" she asked.

He had risen from his chair. She looked surprised, but not shocked. She would look shocked in truth if he came to her tonight.

No, not shock. When he bared his body, she would be horrified. He could imagine that look. He held it fixed in his mind, for it killed his desire quicker than any drug.

"Out," he said as he turned for the door.

"Were you always so charming?" came her sharp voice. "Four years—heaven knows I can't remember what I saw in you."

He closed the door with effortful care, then leaned against it, taking a deep breath of air unscented by her.

If she truly did not remember, then how fortunate she was.

CHAPTER THREE

Four years earlier

"They say he was sent down from Oxford for wenching," said her cousin Moira.

"I heard it was gambling—and the man he fleeced was a don!"

"He set a fire in the Bodleian." This from Helen Selkirk. "They lost dozens of books, and expelled him. He disappeared for a year afterward; even his own father didn't know where he'd gone."

Anna had been listening with half an ear, her attention on the dance floor. She liked a reel, the stomp and spring of it, but this orchestra had clearly been given orders to the contrary. The hostess, Mrs. Cameron, was determined to bring her daughter's suitor up to snuff, and apparently believed that four waltzes in a row would do the trick.

"Anna, he was asking after you, you know."

Anna glanced over. Helen Selkirk was a terrible gossip, but also a discerning one; she did not carry tales that turned out to be false. "Who said so?"

"I heard him myself, speaking with your auntie May. Imagine it—she said you didn't like to dance!"

The other girls groaned. Anna glanced to the far corner, where Aunt May was whispering furiously into her son Daniel's ear. Daniel looked miserable, his broad, handsome face contorting into grimaces as he furiously shook his head.

Poor Daniel. He was a sweet, decent fellow, who thought of her as a sister, and who loved a girl from Glasgow whose father was a clerk. His parents wanted more for him. They wanted him to wed Anna, to be precise.

They were not alone in that effort. All the aunts had plans for Anna. During her childhood, they had passed her around more quickly than a hot potato, despairing of her as an ungainly, graceless tomboy. But now she was grown, every one of them had a son or nephew that they knew would make a perfect match for her.

Happily, ungainly tomboys did not grow up to be easy marks.

"Poor Lord Lockwood," purred Moira. "How downcast he must feel, to think you don't wish to dance with him."

"Fortune hunter," Anna said dismissively.

"Oh, Anna!" This from Fiona Shaw. "He's very handsome. And quite popular in London, I believe. If he only wanted a fortune—"

"I don't wish to be introduced."

The others gasped, their fans fluttering harder. "What? You can't mean it," said Moira.

"But I do." Anna did stand in need of a husband. Otherwise, she would never have consented to an entire spring of incessant house parties up and down the country. She would much rather be on the island, for spring was very beautiful on Rawsey, the waves feisty and sparkling, the light strong and clear.

But to have the island, she must first acquire a husband.

He would not be an Englishman, though. An Englishman would, quite reasonably, expect his wife to spend time in England. Anna had no interest in that. She had refused all encouragement to make her debut in London. What was the point? To make a life in Scotland, she required a Scot.

Moira still looked aghast. "You mean to say that if he approached to ask your hand, you'd refuse him?"

"Precisely," said Anna. "I congratulate you on your keen wit, Moira."

"He's the Earl of Lockwood, coz! You can't cut him!"

Anna shrugged. "English titles don't impress me."

"He owns eighty thousand acres!"

"In England," said Anna.

"All of it gone to seed," Helen put in slyly.

Moira bridled. "Is *he* to blame for that? He only just came into the title."

Anna smiled. "It rather sounds as though *you* fancy him."

"Who wouldn't?" Moira blushed. "Have you seen him?"

Anna had seen him. Any woman with a pulse had noticed him. He was tall, broad shouldered, with a warm laugh that traveled the length of a room. He had a strong, chiseled face and he waltzed like an athlete. Those long, flying strides had been wasted on his other dance partners tonight, but Anna could have matched him turn for turn.

Alas. "I've no interest in jackanapes," she said.

"Oh ho!" Moira's voice was growing heated. "And here I thought you were looking for a man with spirit."

"I've no objection to spirit—or gambling, as you say, or wenching, either, as long as the wench is willing. But a man who sets fire to a library?" Anna snorted. "That's base idiocy at best, wanton malice at worst."

"Base idiocy," came a smooth, low voice from behind her. Moira gasped. Anna, looking into her cousin's reddening face, was left with no doubt as to who owned that voice—which matched his laugh, intriguingly warm and husky, despite the clipped vowels that marred it.

She fanned herself, and did not turn. She did not speak to eavesdroppers. "Fiona, is that genuine ratafia, or did the Davis boys manage to slip in some spice?"

Fiona glanced helplessly from the eavesdropper to her cup. "I—" She cleared her throat, then continued primly, "I'm sure I couldn't say."

Anna rolled her eyes. The moment an English title came sniffing about, her friends began to posture like nuns. "I'll go find out." She pushed through the others, cutting across the dance floor for the refreshment room.

It did not entirely surprise her to realize that he was following her. From the corner of her vision, she caught Aunt May's concerned frown: that was her first clue. The second, rather more blunt, was when he caught her elbow in the hall.

As she swung to face him, she stepped backward, freeing herself of his grip and causing her white muslin skirts to bell wide, which in turn left him no choice but to quickly back away from her circumference.

"You're as rude as a potboy," she said—rather less crisply than she would have liked, for she was startled to find him laughing at her, his hands raised in mock surrender.

"True," he said. "What else can one expect from an idiot who sets a library on fire?"

To follow her bespoke a confidence born of arrogance. But to mock himself suggested the opposite quality. The intention to put him in his place briefly wavered. He *was* very handsome, which counted against him. On the other hand, he could laugh at himself, a rare quality.

"You really did set the Bodleian on fire?"

He gave a rueful tug of his mouth. "If I told you the truth, it would seem like a lie to save face. So I'll own the sin, and ask you only to believe that if I'd truly intended to burn a book, I would have positioned myself in the Latinate stacks, rather than chemistry."

Struck, she opened her mouth—then closed it, suspicious. A fortune hunter, indeed. He had done his research on her. "I suppose," she said dryly, "that you have a passionate interest in the sciences."

"Not passion, but genuine interest, yes—unsupported by any discipline." He smiled again. "There: I have confessed my greatest failing."

He had a dimple in his left cheek, and amber-colored eyes that seemed more alive than other men's. She found herself avoiding them, lest she surrender to the impulse to stare.

He stepped closer. "I wished to make your acquaintance," he said. "I suppose you've heard so already."

He was a few inches taller than her. She was not accustomed to being overshadowed, but the temptation to step backward felt too much like retreat. He wore cologne, a rather womanish affectation—but no woman would have chosen such a woodsy, clean scent. She caught herself inhaling, and expelled the breath in annoyance.

"Yes," she said, "but I barely remarked it. Any number of men ask to make my acquaintance, particularly once they have learned how well I might enrich them."

His eyes opened wide, and then he laughed again, an open-throated sound of true amusement. "Touché." He raked a long-fingered hand through his brown hair, leaving the sun-lightened tips standing astray. No pomade—his countrymen would judge him. "You are, indeed, a plainspoken woman."

"Yes. Worse yet, Lord Lockwood, I speak not only plainly, but as often as I like."

He nodded. "Professor Arbuthnot had told me so, but only now do I perceive it was a warning."

She blinked. "Professor . . ." She could not have heard right. Professor Arbuthnot would waste no time on book burners. "I beg your pardon," she said coolly. "A warning?"

"A warning to buffle-headed young men. I will have to use my brain in this conversation, and I confess, I may be out of practice at it."

She stared, uncertain if she had been complimented or insulted. "How do you know Professor Arbuthnot?"

"I studied with him at Oxford."

"Before or after you burned down the library?"

"A dozen books," he said evenly. "But the professor was quite disappointed in me. And I, in turn, was distraught to have lost his confidence. You'll understand, then, when I tell you what a compliment it was to be entrusted with your manuscript."

Her breath caught. "*What?*"

"He has reviewed it quite thoroughly, he says, and scribbled all through the margins. I did not read it," he added quickly, again lifting his hands in a sign of truce.

She noticed calluses on his palms, not a typical sight in an English gentleman. "But I did promise to ferry it to you, since he knew my path led me north for the spring."

A queer buzzing filled her ears as she compassed how deeply she had misjudged this situation. "I see." She cleared her throat, then, to her horror, felt her lips twitch. "I . . ." She needed to apologize. But suddenly, with him marveling at her, it struck her as absurdly amusing. "I'm sorry," she managed through a sudden irrepressible giggle. "How dreadfully rude of me—but I thought—"

"You thought a penniless English earl saw an opportunity." Before she could deny it, he flashed a lopsided grin, boyish, which somehow mocked himself and her, too. "Yes, well, don't think it didn't cross my mind. We penniless earls must look for love in high places, particularly with all those crumbling castles to pay for. But that was before I knew your opinion of wenching."

Her face felt afire now. He had overheard *that*? On a deep breath, she brazened through it. "I see. I hope this doesn't mean that you disregard whether the wenches are willing."

"Oh no," he said, then leaned forward, close enough that his breath warmed her cheek as he murmured, "The wenches are always willing. But I could never court a lady who doubted it."

As he drew back, her heart skipped a beat. She rather believed he was right about the wenches.

But she would not give him the satisfaction of knowing so. "It must be your vanity that impresses them."

"It is very large," he said solemnly, "but I've not yet had complaints."

She sputtered on a scandalized laugh. Good heavens. Surely he didn't mean . . . ?

He dimpled as though in answer, and she felt herself blush. "You're a rogue," she said.

"Entirely."

"And unashamed of it, too."

He laughed, an easy and relaxed sound. "You would be surprised at how far roguery can take a man. Behold: I've had you to myself for five minutes now. Can any other man here claim such good fortune?"

It was not like her to fall for flattery. But she felt the odd urge to preen.

In the space of her hesitation, he continued in a more formal tone. "I did not bring the manuscript with me tonight. But I'll have it sent over tomorrow, if that suits you."

"Yes." A smile bloomed on her lips as she fathomed the implications of his errand. "He read it, you say?"

"He did."

"And he liked it?"

"The professor would not waste his opinions on me. But judging by his manner when he handed me the manuscript, I would guess he liked it very much."

Now she felt purely dizzy, as though the floor were floating away. "How marvelous," she murmured. And then, catching his gaze on her, she felt herself flush again. The light in his eye left no doubt that he was admiring her.

Well, at the least, he was a man of fine judgment, then.

She smiled at him, deliberately this time, and did not miss how his breath caught. Her smile was her greatest beauty; everyone always said it.

"Do send it," she said. "Or better yet, bring it your-self, but only if you're in the mood for a walk."

"Delightful." He bowed and turned away. But before he stepped out of view, she called after him.

"You'll need to arrive before daylight if you want to join us."

She caught his glance toward the nearby grandfather clock. It was already half past midnight. "Ambitious," he said.

"Quite. And if you arrive too late, I'll be forced to conclude that you're afraid of heights, and looked for an excuse not to come."

The interest on his face was unmistakable. "I've no fear of heights. But which heights, exactly, do you mean?"

"The highest one," she said. "We are climbing Ben Nevis. Don't be late."

Liam had anticipated a pastoral frolic. The proof of his misjudgment was now plain in his own ragged breath as he labored up the woodland path. In college, he'd con-quered the cricket fields. At university, no rower could outpace him. But Anna Winterslow Wallace, Countess of Forth, was built of some strange mettle, the same no doubt as steam trains, so steadily she chugged along.

He was at risk of falling behind.

His recent routine was to blame for it. Gone were the mornings of disciplined exertion. For the past few months, he'd been on a tour of sorts—a survey of likely heiresses up and down the British Isles. He was a bach-elor with a title: everywhere he went, he was welcomed and feted and flirted with. But this campaign entailed a great many late nights, and bottles of wine and rich food. Now, in his laboring lungs, he found evidence of his own dissipation.

Lady Forth, meanwhile, was rumored to be on a campaign of her own—Professor Arbuthnot had said as much when handing over the manuscript. *Don't get any ideas, lad. She'll be looking for a husband of substance, not a book burner.* But since Scottish flirtations evidently entailed scaling mountains, Lady Forth's desirability had turned her into an athlete.

Liam wanted to tell her now that the professor's spectacles were as thick as windowpanes: on that fateful night in the Bodleian, he'd mistaken Liam's attempt to beat out the flames for an effort to fan them. But it seemed rather late to launch his self-defense. Getting tossed out of Trinity had led to some grand times abroad, and so Liam had never minded the rumors, nor imagined a time when they might irk him.

For that matter, he'd never foreseen himself laboring to keep up with a woman, much less struggling to impress her. Why, as recently as last night, he'd gone to sleep quite content. Countess Forth was attractive, clever, and prickly enough to make it interesting. Wealthy enough, too, to solve his problems, which was the reason he'd bothered in the first place. He'd envisioned this walk as a chance to evaluate her—not to be evaluated. For what rich young heiress, denied a season in London and kept sequestered in the north, would look on a gentleman such as himself, and *not* think of the fun they could have?

The answer: Anna Winterslow Wallace, who, despite his best and most charming discourse over the last hour of walking, seemed thoroughly unimpressed by tales of

London, Rome, Geneva, Madrid—and not at all out of breath, either, though the slope continued to steepen.

He was shamefully grateful when she drew up by a waterfall, a sparkling ribbon that danced down the granite flank of the mountain. "You've certainly traveled a great deal," she said. Usually these words came lofting on a warm current of admiration, but her tone was arid.

Of course, there had been other pretty young women at the Camerons' last night—all of them seeming excited to make his acquaintance. Perhaps one of *them* had money. He looked up the path, but their companions had taken a half hour's head start. "We had been waiting for an hour already," Countess Forth had told him when he'd arrived, "and they went ahead, fearing it would rain."

He'd overslept. It was one of his vices.

Lady Forth crept near to the falls to refill her canteen. The other women—he had caught sight of them above, as the trail twisted sharply—were dressed in sensible but respectable woolen gowns. The countess, in all her scientific glory, was wearing split skirts, the hems of which she had tucked into tall boots. Nor, he suspected, was she wearing a corset. She looked like a Zouave soldier; all she lacked was the mustache and medals.

Troubling, then, that he found himself staring at her backside. She had a narrow waist, and magnificently broad Scottish hips. He was perverse. The experience of failing to charm a woman was somehow seducing him.

"Should we try to catch up with the others?" he asked when she sat down on a mossy rock and began to drink. "They may be waiting for us."

It was only water that she was drinking—water no doubt flavored by deer droppings. But she swallowed it with such obvious relish that he felt a stirring in his groin, and that, paired with the hoarseness in his breath, was too much for his vanity.

She was as tall as a man, and wearing trousers. No matter that she had two hundred thousand pounds to her name, or that her hair looked brighter than the fire in the Bodleian that night. He had standards to keep.

She glanced up, her green eyes cool. "No," she said, "they won't be waiting. After all, it was *I* who invited you on this walk. It is not *their* responsibility to see to your comfort." Her gaze dropped significantly to his boots. "Are your feet all right?"

"Brilliant," he said. These boots were the height of fashion. They had started pinching a mile ago. He would have sliced off his toes before admitting it.

"I see." She paused. "I had thought you were limping. My mistake!"

He bit back a rueful smile. She had standards as well—and he clearly did not meet them.

She rose and set out without a backward glance. He was reminded, as he trailed her, of equally miserable adventures as a child—crammed between his mother and cousin in some carriage, his head aching from the rattle of the windows and jostling of springs, while Stephen delivered some ingratiating monologue on the historical sights ahead, to Liam's parents' encouragement—*Tell us more, Stephen; how clever you are*—while all the while Liam tried not to vomit, praying the journey would end before he disgraced himself.

The memories faded as he caught up with Lady Forth, leaving melancholy in their wake.

He missed his parents.

They had never taken him to Scotland. It had not

been in fashion in his youth. But his mother would have adored these surroundings—the path bedecked by green ferns and shoots of heather, and below, in the shadow cast by the mountain, foothills studded by alder and birch trees whose bright leaves rippled in the wind.

She would have liked the Countess of Forth, too. His mother had been hot tempered, elegant, strong willed. She had loathed a sidesaddle, and spoken fondly of her youth, when women had sometimes stepped out wearing only a single petticoat, and had "the full use of their limbs," as she'd put it, allowing them to tramp for hours across hill and dale.

He missed her. He missed her even more now than in the year immediately following her death. While his father had still lived, they had remembered her together, so often and so openly that she had seemed still to hover between them. But now, with both parents gone, Liam felt truly alone.

An image came to him suddenly, vivid and frightening: his own figure, reduced to slightness by the looming debts, the crumbling estates, the hungry and hollow-cheeked tenants staring toward him in search of hope.

The Countess of Forth would not be his solution. But he needed to find one quickly. For while life could be a grand adventure for a gentleman born to his station, money was the trick—and without it, this adventure would quickly become far more unpleasant, not only for himself.

"Are you thinking of England?" asked the countess.

Startled, he lied: "No." Then, with a frown—could she also be a witch?—he asked, "Why do you wonder?"

"You had a very grim look on your face." She cut him a mischievous look, and then laughed.

He found himself startled again. One moment she seemed like a plain gorgon. The next, her wit flashed out, dry and clever, and when humor lit her face, she abruptly seemed beautiful.

He cleared his throat and fixed his gaze on the trail. If she was not the solution, then she was at least his temporary hostess on this mountain, and he would treat her with respect.

Not with leers. He would reserve those for the solution, he hoped. His father had not strayed, and had not raised Liam to do so, either.

"England's beauty is less dramatic," he said, "but no less remarkable. Surely you've visited the Lake District?"

"I have never been south of the border." His unconcealed surprise made her laugh again. "Is that so unimaginable?"

"Most ladies of your station do spend a season in London, at least."

She shrugged. "I never saw the use."

A thousand objections sprang to mind. What kind of cramped and calloused soul proved indifferent to the lure of strange places, distant cities?

But he was determined to be pleasant for the remainder of their walk. "Was it here, then, that you met Professor Arbuthnot?"

"Yes, at his lecture in Edinburgh. Every scientist of note passes through that city eventually, and when I am in residence, I attend all the engagements."

For a woman of such broad mind, it seemed very odd that she did not wish to explore the world. "You must have impressed him a great deal," Liam said. "He took far less interest in *my* work as an undergraduate."

"Oh, I privately suspect that the good professor has a weakness for redheads." She winked at him.

His jaw nearly dropped. "I . . . see."

"I approached him after his lecture, inquiring about his work on the spectroscope. I was having some trouble reproducing his results, you see. He was tremendously kind to take the time to explain my error. And later he proposed a most ingenious way to simplify the whole business, which proved useful for little fingers."

His glance dropped down to her hands; she gave him a sideways smile.

"Not *my* fingers." She held them up. "*These* hands I have heard my own aunt call paws. 'Manly paws,' to be precise."

His denial was automatic: "Nonsense." But in truth, her hands matched the rest of her: uncommonly large for a woman.

She snorted. "Flattery only appeals when rooted in truth." She stretched her hands to their full span and beamed at them. "Far from little! But I've dozens of cousins with children of their own, and *their* hands still have growing to do."

He realized he was smiling. Women often took opportunities to slight themselves in order to invite his compliments. But Lady Forth looked visibly pleased with, even fond of, her own supposed flaw. His reassurances would be superfluous. "So the children assist your experiments, then?"

"Of course." She looked startled. Was she blushing? Some marvelous glow spread across her skin, darkening the freckles on her plump, rosy cheeks. "Did you imagine that I . . . Goodness!" Now she grinned, a toothy and entirely unself-conscious expression of delight, girlish and deeply charming. "You were imagining me as a true scientist, weren't you? Presiding over experiments of my own design!"

She sounded delightfully gratified. He said, "I confess, the vision held appeal."

"Alas! Perhaps if I'd been born a man. Or born a Nightingale, even!" She shrugged. "I'm no true scientist, sir. I took an interest for the sake of my estates—it seems that every day brings some new revolution in agricultural chemistry. But from there, I kept reading. We live in such a marvelous, modern age—I like to keep abreast of new discoveries."

"And to keep your small cousins abreast as well."

"It does entertain them. And when all of them are under the same roof, you would not believe how useful it proves."

"Oh, I believe it." For part of the journey, he had shared a train carriage with an apologetic matron and her five small boys. *The nanny gave sudden notice*, she had said weakly to him, as the boys ran riot over the benches. "That must make a pretty picture, all the children gathering to assist you."

"Not pretty in the least," she said cheerfully. "We get very dirty in our experiments. Once or twice, somebody has blown something up."

"How fearsome."

"Oh, we've only lost one eye and two fingers to date."

Her delivery was so deadpan that it took him a moment to realize she was joking. She laughed at him again.

"And the manuscript," he said, smiling back. "Is it a memoir of these misadventures?"

"Who would want to read *that*? No, it's a book in the style of Mrs. Marcet and Mrs. Lowry. They were the great heroes of my youth, writing tales of science that even a little girl could understand."

"Not only little girls." He had adored Mrs. Marcet's volumes as a boy. He could still recall their exact placement on the little bookshelf, which he'd insisted on keeping directly next to his bed. "I found those primers tremendously interesting."

The countess nodded. "Chemistry and geology, the animal kingdom and the wonders of plant life . . . Mrs. Marcet and Mrs. Lowry retired, of course, but science has kept marching onward. For my cousins' sake, I decided to take up their banner."

"I think that's marvelous," he said sincerely. How lucky that she had not taken a liking to him—he would not have known what to do with such a talented wife. He would have ruined her.

The vegetation was thinning now, and as the path twisted around a scree-covered slope, one side abruptly dropped away, the rocky bank sloping at a deadly angle into a gully far below. The sun slipped behind clouds, the temperature beginning to drop. They walked in silence for several long minutes until a thin layer of mist began to rise around them.

"Oh dear," said the countess.

Was there some cause for concern? He opened his mouth to inquire, and the chill abruptly became icy. In the space of a moment, the mist reached them and solidified, rising to form a freezing and impenetrable wall.

The countess came to a stop, and he nearly bumped into her.

"Ah, Ben Nevis," she said, an affectionate scolding note in her voice. "This is its greatest trick, you know— blind the walker, so he plummets to his death off a cliff."

"How cheerful," he said dryly. "Shall we take shelter until the mist clears?"

"No need. I've done this walk a hundred times."

But he hadn't. "Very well," he said, unwilling to be outdone by her.

She adopted a slower pace, but not slow enough for his liking; his brain remained acutely aware of the sudden drop to his right and shrieked at his stupidity as he blundered forward, regardless. He had never seen mist so thick, save in the worst London pea soupers, which certainly concealed runaway carriages and open sewers, but no cliffs, a fact for which he now realized he should be grateful.

A voice floated down to them. "Anna!" it cried. "Anna, can you . . ."

"That's Moira," exclaimed his regrettably plucky guide. "Moira!" she bellowed—directly beside his ear, causing him to wince. She had missed her calling as an opera singer. "Moira, are you at the summit?"

They waited silently in a milky white haze for a reply that never came. "Did she sound distressed?" asked the countess, her former blitheness nowhere in evidence. "I hope somebody hasn't twisted an ankle."

He bit his tongue lest he remind her that she had mentioned darker possibilities not minutes ago. "If they're coming down, surely the wisest thing is to wait."

"She needs help," the countess snapped. "Otherwise, why would she have called for me?"

"To check on *your* welfare?"

The notion appeared to surprise her. "No," she said. "Moira wouldn't—she knows I'm fine."

A peculiar insight: Lady Forth's assurance came with a price. Nobody ever checked on her.

"You wait here," she said. "I'll go on up, quickly, and I—"

"To hell with that." He regretted the curse a second too late, but she did not seem to notice it. "Splitting up is a very poor idea. If we but wait—"

She ripped free of his grip—only then did he realize he'd grabbed hold of her. "Stay here," she said, and in the next second, she had moved into the mist and disappeared.

Now he did curse deliberately. *He* didn't know the trail. But to wait here meant leaving her alone on the path, with a deadly fall looming on one side. Following was unwise, but not following was unchivalrous.

He listened hard, and caught the sound of her footsteps crunching on small rocks ahead. He slowly walked toward the sound—realizing, with each deep and steady breath, that there was a reason he'd forgone that excursion into the Alps last year. Heights were not his strength.

"Moira!" She was calling out, her voice still nearby. "Moira, can you—"

Her gasp did not sound intentional.

"Countess." He called out sharply—even smacked at the mist like an idiot, as though it would somehow dissolve beneath the wave of his lordly hand. "Countess!"

Silence.

Damn it to hell. He shuffled forward faster, and called out again. "My lady—Anna! Can you—"

"Here," came a strained whisper.

He stopped. That whisper came from very close. He squinted into the field of consuming white. "Where? Speak again."

"I am here," she muttered. A little to the left, a pace

or two ahead— "Don't follow," she groaned. "I went over the . . . edge."

His body froze. Muscles congealed, bones stiffened. He stood very still. "You're—you've got hold of something?"

"A root." Her voice was growing tighter. She was struggling, he realized, to remain calm. "It's . . . not very . . . strong. What an idiot I am!"

He dropped to all fours, the rocky soil digging into his palms and knees. "Keep speaking," he said. "Hum, if that's easier."

The first weak, ragged bars of "Rule, Britannia!" hit his ears. He swallowed a laugh, half hysteria, half amazement. Not the choice he'd expected of her.

The sound led him forward. With one hand, he made wide, sweeping arcs—found the edge of the path, the drop beyond it. But he could not feel her.

Her humming abruptly ceased. "Oh," she said, almost inaudible. "It's giving way. It's break—"

He lunged forward on a prayer, thrusting his hand blindly into the ether, thanking God when his grip closed on her forearm.

Sporting might prove useless in walking competitions against a Scotswoman, but it did aid in pulling. With a mighty heave, he hauled the countess up, and she tumbled atop him into the dirt.

For a long moment they lay pressed together, dazed, panting, as the mist iced around them. From somewhere nearby came the stray peep of a snow bunting, and the angry flutter of wings.

She felt shockingly warm against him, her breath burning his ear like a brand. She was very tall for a woman. But he was taller. She fit against him perfectly.

" 'Rule, Britannia'?" he asked in a whisper.

"Horrid song," she whispered back. "But I thought your last memory of me should be pleasant for you."

The force of his sudden laughter proved contagious. She joined in as she rolled off him, and they lay side by side in the white mist, giggling like loons.

When at last he sobered, he heard himself say, "I did not set that fire in the library."

"Oh?" She still sounded amused, breathless and giddy. "Then who was it?"

"Makes no difference. What matters is that you know it wasn't me."

She pushed herself up on one elbow, smiling down at him. Her eyes were a green not found elsewhere on the earth, luminous and pale, more vibrant than spring leaves. "And why should that matter to me?"

He stared up at her, gripped by some premonition that felt sweet and powerful and altogether new.

"Because you have no truck with book burners," he said. "So you should know beforehand: you have no cause to turn away."

A line appeared between her russet brows. But her mouth was still smiling. "Turn away from what?"

"From me," he said, "when I kiss you."

"Kiss me!" She drew back, wide-eyed. "And when will you try *that*?"

"I'm still deciding."

The smile kept toying with her lips, slipping and changing shape, as though she was torn between amusement and disapproval. "Is it customary," she said, "for Englishmen to announce their kisses beforehand?"

"Only when at the edge of a cliff, with a lady strong enough to give a good shove."

The laughter escaped her in a bright, happy cascade. *There* was the sign. He moved more quickly than he ever had on any playing field—sitting up, slipping his hand through the heavy silk of her hair, and pulling her mouth to his.

Her lips were soft, full, a glorious shock.

She sighed into his mouth, and did not pull away.

CHAPTER FOUR

London, 1861

The club cultivated the atmosphere of a tomb, hushed and stagnant. In this refined atmosphere, lent force by thick-pile Persian carpets and tasseled curtains that blocked out the sun, even whispers carried. His cousin's shout, then, drew outright stares.

"Here you are!" Stephen drew up by his table, broadcasting what was no doubt intended to be a thoroughly intimidating glare.

Liam bent the newspaper to peruse the headline—which was the cause, no doubt, of Stephen's foul temper—before sitting back and giving the man his full attention.

"Where else should I be?" he asked.

Stephen narrowed bloodshot blue eyes. "Indeed. Your seat in the Lords must be buried in dust by now. You leave it to your friends to carry out the real work in Parliament."

Liam allowed himself a brief smile—far too brief to fully convey his enjoyment of his cousin's trembling, red-faced fury.

Stephen had done a fine job in the first few months of pretending joy in Liam's return. Then had come whey-faced stolidness. Now, having seen his empire begin to crumble, the man was verging on full-blown rage—which was exactly what Liam wanted.

Come at me, he willed his cousin. *Come out from hiding, you cowardly bastard, and show me the knife in your hand.*

"Parliament," he said, then aped a shudder. "Hot and tedious business, to be sure! I *did* think to take my seat again, but those benches give such a backache, don't you find? Oh, forgive me"—this added with a wince— "I expect you haven't had cause to sit on them. One day, coz—one day, you'll manage to win an election!"

Had he been standing, he would have added a manly slap of camaraderie. Instead, he slumped deeper into his wing chair and waved a hand toward the seat opposite—an invitation that Stephen pointedly ignored.

"Forgive me," Stephen said icily. "I suppose you know nothing of the bill that just passed—is that what you mean to say?"

That bill promised to make Stephen's life as a railway baron considerably harder. Until now, Parliament had adjudicated all matters of compulsory purchase for lands needed for new railroad routes. The new law dispersed that authority among more local forms of government, while also granting landowners the right to challenge any sale or leasing agreement, should information emerge that proved a railway company had undervalued the land.

Liam had already reached out to several landowners who had done business with Stephen's railways. In all those cases, Liam's own richer offer on the land would

serve as proof that Stephen's company had undervalued it.

"Goodness," he murmured. "Is it really politics that
has you so unkempt?"

"It will not fly," Stephen growled. "The Commons
would never have passed that bill without assurance that
the Lords would put an end to it. Auburn thinks he has
routed me—but he will learn otherwise. The Commons
will not tolerate the suppression of—"

"A radical!" Liam lifted his finger to a passing server.
"Two brandies," he told the boy. "My cousin and I will
toast the coming revolution."

"You mock me," Stephen bit out. "But I warn you, I
know what you're about."

"Pardon?" Despite himself, Liam could not resist un-
coiling from his seat. Was the moment on them at last?
Was the rat coming out of his hidey-hole? "What on
earth do you mean?"

Stephen stared, a muscle ticking in his jaw. "'Blessed
are they which are persecuted for righteousness' sake,'"
he muttered. "'For theirs is the kingdom of heaven.'"

Liam frowned. "Are you persecuted? Only name the
villain, Stephen, and I will show him what comes of
troubling an innocent man."

Stephen drew a hissing breath, then looked away,
visibly struggling for composure. His assurance had always relied on his fortune—he'd inherited a great deal,
and worked hard through conspiracy, corruption, and
glad-handing to increase it. But what of it? Corruption
was the way of the world. His wife's charity bazaars, his
endowment of an orphanage here and there, his public
professions of virtue, had distracted the world from his
private practice.

Recently, though, he'd no doubt noticed a sea change. His friends were deserting him. His companies were facing a great challenge, dozens of local bureaucracies to placate. And starting tomorrow, his creditors—for he'd borrowed heavily for his newest railway—would come knocking at his door, their faith shaken by this development . . . and by Liam's murmured concerns, in their earshot, about his cousin's faltering fortunes.

The turmoil was beginning to tell. Stephen's handsome thick hair was somewhat disarrayed, and his Savile Row suit, while still the height of fashion, no longer fit him as exquisitely as it had when he'd been measured for it. Anxiety whittled a man away, and Stephen's shoulders were shrinking.

He still looked healthy enough, though. He still looked as though he could never imagine himself falling onto his knees to beg.

"You know," he told Liam stonily, "what you have done."

"Goodness—you mean to say *I* am working against you? But whyever should I do that? You know how little I care for politics these days. And how much I value family! Why—we were raised as brothers, you and I!"

So close . . . He all but saw the haze that settled over Stephen's vision. But at the last moment, his cousin remembered wisdom: to accuse Liam of menacing him, he must understand the cause for their enmity. And that he could not admit to knowing.

"That bill will not stand." Spittle beaded at the corners of Stephen's lips. "There is a precedent, and it will not be undone."

"If I were in the railway business, I should be much

relieved to know so," Liam said. "Ah, here comes our brandy—won't you join me?"

Stephen turned on his heel and stalked out, his vigorous exit collecting marveling looks from others in the reading room.

Liam watched him go. That spot between Stephen's shoulder blades—that was where he would stick the knife. Stephen already felt the tip of it. But he did not yet know the pain of being gutted.

When the server arrived with the tray, Liam said, "Carry that to the Waterloo Room. I believe my guests should be arriving shortly."

"The passing of that bill makes him toxic." Crispin Burke spoke with amusement as he reached across the table for the sugar bowl. "If he catches fire on the steps of the Exchange, not a man will waste water to throw at him." He dropped a cube of sugar into his brandy glass.

"Bravo," Liam murmured from his position by the wall. He had booked this private room for its thick walls, locking doors, and the full bar in the corner, which spared them the need for servers who might eavesdrop.

But the absence of assistance had clearly left Burke deranged. In addition to sugar, he was now adding milk. "That's a profanation," Liam said. "Jules? Do you see this?"

Julian, seated opposite Burke, was shaking his head, horror apparent on his tanned, chiseled features. "Word of that gets out, you'll never be PM."

"What, this?" Burke leaned back in his chair, lifting his drink to dramatically relish the fumes. The public knew him as a ruthless and mercenary politician, whose aggressive championship of the railway bill had proved instrumental in its passage. In private, however, Burke showed a different face—genial, relaxed, ever ready to laugh at himself. "It's brandy milk punch," he said. "Perfectly respectable drink."

"For grandmothers with toothaches," Liam agreed. "And wretches who fermented their brandy in a bucket."

Burke reached for another lump of sugar, no doubt to provoke them. But Julian snatched away the bowl. "Have some respect, man. That batch was bottled for Napoleon."

Burke laughed. "Then I'll make my toast to Wellington, shall I?"

"And to politics," Liam said as he raised his glass.

The other men followed suit. Mention of Wellington felt fitting, for they had gathered today to celebrate the first victory in their own campaign: the public destruction of Stephen Devaliant.

"I had word that the creditors are already calling on Devaliant," Julian said. The Duke of Auburn, one of society's leading lights, he had taken up where Burke left off, seeing the bill through the Lords with a few well-placed murmurs. That was Jules's way: he wielded his power with subtlety and charm.

Burke, on the other hand, had rammed the bill through the Commons with a fiery speech that had received four inches of space in the newspapers. "A dirty game," he said now, his smile spreading, "but never a boring one."

"And here I've been telling everyone that you've turned a new leaf," Julian remarked.

"Oh, I have done. But my wife allowed me a brief relapse: when it comes to drowning pigs, she said, one must naturally dabble in mud."

"And no pig has ever drowned more artfully. That line in your speech about caterwauling . . . !"

The two men fell into an amused exchange about the debates they had steered. Liam, watching, felt himself suddenly at a remove—as though a transparent wall of glass had risen between him and the other men.

He leaned hard against the wall, taking a deeper drink of the liquor. These fits came and went. They settled over him without warning, like a cold and numbing fog, and when he was alone, he would smash his fist into a wall in order to feel, but he could not do that in company. He forced himself to listen to the joking conversation, but it was difficult to grasp the humor, to turn his mouth into a smile at the appropriate moments. His heart was pounding. Why? It bore no relation to his emotions, which felt curiously inaccessible—as though, like a candle, he himself had snuffed out.

Once, this place of remove had been his greatest refuge. Alone in the hole, as night had passed into day, as the heat grew deadly and his stomach rebelled on bile, Liam had found this place and clung to it, desperate never to leave.

But then he had escaped. Why, then, had this place followed him? Why did it swallow him without warning, even in the company he liked best? These men were rare friends, who had gone out of their way to assist his efforts with Stephen. Burke had been the one to discover the plot behind Liam's abduction; he was sharp, sly witted, an invaluable coconspirator. Jules had been Liam's friend since boyhood. Surely, of all times and places, *here* he should most feel himself.

Silence had fallen. With a start, Liam realized his reply was wanted. "Indeed," he said, and bolted the contents of his glass before refilling it. He drank that down, too, then poured out two fingers more.

As he carried the glass to the table, he caught frowns on the other men's faces. He drank a great deal these days, but no surprise that they hadn't realized so until now. Liquor no longer seemed to affect him. It took stronger toxins to wrestle down his unruly brain.

"You look very alike when you scowl," he told them.

This remark was received with polite but unpersuaded smiles. Both men were tall, dark haired, and celebrated for their looks. Julian's skin held a golden cast, against which his green eyes looked startling. Burke, in turn, was black eyed as the devil, which seemed fitting. His wife might have reformed him, but most of England had yet to believe it.

"What's soured your mood?" Julian asked. "I saw Devaliant leaving as I came in—did you have words with him?"

"I did." The memory acted like a tonic, pulling him back into the moment and allowing him to smile with genuine pleasure. "Very cross words. But he caught himself before he lost his temper, more's the pity."

"Baiting makes a dangerous game," Burke murmured. "Push him too far, and he'll come after you."

Liam shrugged. "What else is the point, Burke? Do you imagine I want a trial for him?"

Burke cast an uneasy look toward Julian. "I thought you wanted justice—for your men, as well as yourself. We still don't know how he met Marlowe. If he came after you now—"

"Then I would put a bullet in his brain," Liam said. "But yes, it would not help us to discover the rest."

For Stephen had arranged for Liam's abduction by using the services of Harold Marlowe, a mad inventor who had owned and operated the prison camp from his home here in England. Marlowe had accepted bribes from rich men to dispatch their enemies abroad. But how had he known Stephen? In eight months, neither Liam nor his friends had uncovered a connection between the two men.

Increasingly, it seemed that Marlowe had employed some intermediary in soliciting his clients. That man, too, deserved a bloody justice.

"We need to expand our search," Julian muttered. "The middleman might be anyone in high circles."

A needle in a haystack might be easier to locate.

Restlessness drove Liam to his feet. He paced the length of the carpet, finishing his own drink and then appropriating Burke's as he passed.

"Christ." Grimacing, he returned the drink to Burke. "You should be flogged for that."

"Acquired taste," Burke said. "Sophisticated palates appreciate it."

"Perhaps the key lies in those who died," Julian said. He drummed his fingers in thought. "Lord Sadler and Sir George Davin—both of them were political at one time, were they not?"

Burke set his glass down heavily. "Sadler?"

"I thought you knew," Julian said.

"No. I thought—he was lost at sea, when the *Pacific* sank."

"No," Liam said. "He was baked to death, in a very deep hole."

A shocked silence filled the room. That detail Julian had not known, either.

Murder was not amusing. But the stricken faces of men who rightly considered themselves jaded—that could be considered a mild diversion.

Christ. No, there was nothing humorous about it—not to anyone with a normal brain. Liam took a long breath. He felt very few emotions nowadays, and none of them worth trusting: irritation, anger, twisted amusement . . .

And lust. As of this morning, he would add lust to the list. His flesh was not dead, after all: his wife had proved so. He had sat across from her and felt the rise of a desire so powerful and dark that it felt devouring, dangerous to her.

Fortunate, then, that he could not have her. He would not impose his body on her. She had not agreed to marry *that*. And he had no interest anyway in seeing her reaction to it—the horror, or worse, the pity.

Burke spoke of justice. But justice was not reparation. Reparation was impossible.

"Perhaps there's a clue in who survived," Burke suggested. "All commoners—barring you, Lockwood. If it was intended to be a death camp only for a few, it might tell us—"

"No." A bright blot of sunlight illuminated the pastel carpet, worn threadbare by generations of boots. Men accustomed to such carpeting, men who thought this finery their birthright, rarely had experiences of true hardship. If they encountered it, it was always only by mistake. "It tells you that the upper classes are soft," Liam said. "Nothing more. We were all intended to die eventually."

Another beat of silence. No doubt his friends were wondering to what depths Liam had sunk in order to survive where his peers had not managed.

But when he lifted his gaze, he saw no evidence to substantiate his imaginings. Burke was scribbling something, and Julian looked merely weary.

"I'll ask around about Davin," said Julian. "See if I can figure out who might have wanted him gone."

Burke glanced up. "And I'll speak with Sadler's family—I know them well." He gathered his notes and rose. "I would not blame you," he told Liam, "nor turn a hair, should Devaliant end up dead in a gutter. But from what I see, you have a care for these men who came back with you. So I hope you'll continue to have patience until we can nail the bastard who assisted him."

They shook hands, and Burke let himself out. Julian, however, loitered behind, eyeing Liam closely. "Is all well? You seem . . ."

"What?"

Julian shrugged. "A bit ragged, forgive me for saying it."

Liam felt the possibility open between them of an honest discussion. Had he felt inclined to bare his soul, no one else would have served but Jules. They had been close from boyhood—had sported and fought together from their first day at Eton, when they had thrashed some callow gang who'd imagined Julian's Indian ancestry made him an easy mark.

But what would he say, if he decided to confide? *Half the time, Jules, my brain is like a child's, inventing causes for panic in the cheers of a crowd, a sudden noise, a breaking glass, a sound in the dark.*

And asleep—in his own bed—memories slipped into dreams, dreams twisting into nightmares, so that he woke up midbattle, trying to claw his way out of the hole, and discovering the room ablaze, once or twice, from a lamp he'd knocked over.

If he confessed all this, how would Julian be able to help him?

Julian did not speak of what *he* had survived during the Indian Uprising. Liam knew that during that bloody conflagration, Julian had saved the life of Emma Martin—a woman better known to society as the artist 'Aurora Ashdown.' At a recent ball where Liam had showcased her paintings, Julian had looked stricken, like a man encountering a ghost—but he'd shared no explanation for his dark mood or odd behavior afterward.

There were some kinds of grief that did not profit from being spoken, and that never were cured. Julian knew that as well as he.

And so Liam said only, "I slept poorly."

"Ah."

"Also"—no use in concealing what was soon to be public—"the countess is in London."

Julian stepped back a pace. "The—your *wife?*"

"Quite." Liam crossed to the door, pulling it open to forestall the inevitable questioning.

"But—by God, Liam. When did she—"

"A few days ago. I expect you'll see her shortly."

"I should hope so," Julian murmured. "Have you plans this evening?"

"None," Liam said. "Perhaps dinner? You can tell me how Miss Martin fares."

At the mention of her name, Julian's curiosity vanished beneath a bland smile. "Alas, I have another engagement. But soon, yes, certainly." And without further remark, he stepped out the door, ignoring Liam's mocking laughter as he led the way down the hall.

"I still can't believe you're here. In London!"

"Yes, well, if you pinch me again to prove it, you'll get a bop in reply, directly on your nose." Anna spoke impatiently as she leaned around her cousin to consider the gathering.

A dozen women had crammed into the airless little salon, most of them very familiar to Anna. Lady Dunleavy's house was the center of Scottish society in London. For years, Anna's friends had returned from their southern seasons with tales of parties here: the luxury, the conversation, the latest French styles!

Nobody had mentioned the backaches, though. Lady Dunleavy's furniture was overstuffed horsehair, designed to force the sitter to her feet after a scarce five minutes of discomfort. The baroness also kept the drapes closed against sunny afternoons, and Anna found herself squinting through the gloom. The walls loomed, full of dark, gloomy paintings of biblical trials.

All in all, the effect was Calvinist, and therefore supremely Scottish. Anna felt at home.

"You're staring," Moira whispered into her ear. "Who at?"

"Barbara Devaliant." Her husband's cousin's wife was a handsome matron in a pinstriped afternoon dress trimmed with silver lace. The footman had announced her minutes ago. "I called on her recently, but had no reply."

"The cheek!" Moira sat forward, blue eyes wide. "You rank well above her—she should have been honored. Who else have you called on?"

"Everybody." Two days ago, after her husband had fled breakfast, she'd found herself alone and miserable and furious about it. But she was far from friendless, even in England. Having commandeered Lockwood's finest coach—a predictably ornate and hedonistic vehicle, upholstered in mauve velvet with silver trimmings—

she'd spent four hours circling Mayfair and Belgravia, sending Lockwood's least raffish footman scrambling up and down steps from Belgrave Square to Park Lane.

Her efforts had been rewarded yesterday afternoon. Starting at four o'clock, every well-born Scot in the capital had returned her call. Nobody could resist a chance to tour the house of the famous Lord Lockwood, patron extraordinaire of the arts.

Anna was not a natural hostess. But her tirades in the kitchen had paid off nicely: the cook, Beauregard, a hairy behemoth who reeked of cigar smoke, had produced passable cakes and cucumber sandwiches. The tea had arrived, if not hot, then at least lukewarm. And Anna had dodged all the questions about her husband with sufficient grace to quell curiosity.

Of course she'd always intended to join him for the season; alas that business had prevented her from coming earlier! Yes, everybody was invited to his next soiree; their invitations to the last one must have been lost in the post. Yes, he'd been traveling extensively for years now. Why, he was the most prized member of the Travellers Club, where his obligations kept him busy for days on end.

In truth, Anna had no idea where her husband had gone after bolting out of the dining room. She tried very much not to care or wonder. She had extensive practice, after all, in being deserted by him. He should be the least of her concerns at present.

"I want to speak with Mrs. Devaliant," Anna told her cousin. "Come, make an approach with me. Look casual, or else she might flee."

"Flee!" Moira looked positively delighted by the hint of scandal. She made a quick survey by fingertips of the

state of her dark curls, then nodded and clutched on to
Anna's arm. As they progressed across the room, smiling
right and left, she conducted a whispered interrogation.
"Why flee? What have you done? Did you insult her
somehow? Anna, you *must* guard your tongue here; we
aren't in Scotland any longer."

"I haven't done a thing." Not to Mrs. Devaliant,
at least. She *had* written to Mrs. Devaliant's husband,
but her request had been very simple—and quite mundane, between cousins-in-law. Stephen Devaliant was
a railway baron. Anna had a question about a railway
company—a company that seemed not to exist, save in
its control of a piece of land very dear to her.

Of course, this was not the *first* letter she had ever
written to Stephen. Three years ago, after Stephen
had gotten wind of Lockwood's traipse abroad, he
had graciously offered to assume the management of
Lockwood's properties. Equally graciously, Anna had
declined his offer. In turn, Stephen had *insisted* on it. He
had also dispatched lawyers to Scotland to investigate
her property deeds—thinking, mistakenly, that they had
become Lockwood's on marriage.

On hearing the gossip from the general register's
office—that English lawyers had come poking about,
wanting to see the sasines—Anna had cabled her solicitors. Sir Charles Kent had proceeded to correct Stephen's misunderstanding, and to ungently instruct that
he find a new hobby for himself.

Scots knew how to overlook small family tiffs. Alas,
Englishmen's familial loyalties seemed more brittle. Stephen had ignored her most recent letter. His wife, perhaps, could help smooth over matters.

"Lady Dunleavy!" she exclaimed as she stepped boldly

into the ongoing conversation between the baroness and her guest. "Had I known what delights awaited me in London, I would never have hesitated so long to enjoy them."

The baroness, a stout old bat with a gimlet eye and an iron hand welded to the social pulse, nodded smugly. But Mrs. Devaliant began to melt away, which Anna arrested by turning to her and saying, "Cousin! What a lovely surprise to see you here. I hope you received my invitation to dinner."

Barbara Devaliant was a pale blonde with thin colorless brows, which she arched now as she looked down her long, sharp nose. "Yes, it was very kind. Did you not receive my reply? I felt certain I'd given it over to post. Alas, we have a prior engagement."

"Then the night afterward, perhaps?"

Lady Dunleavy harrumphed. It was very rude, of course, to put a prospective guest on the spot in this manner.

But Mrs. Devaliant was Anna's family by marriage, so such courtesies could be overlooked—although the lady herself looked utterly indifferent to the prospect of a dinner *en famille*. "Alas. The season keeps us very busy."

As Anna opened her mouth again, she felt Moira squeeze her arm—a warning she ignored. "If there were some date when you *would* be available, I would be glad to rearrange my schedule."

Mrs. Devaliant made a moment's study of her. Then, with a deliberate smile, she said, "No, Countess. Pray don't trouble yourself."

Lady Dunleavy's jaw dropped.

"Oh dear," Moira said quickly. "I forgot the milliner. My appointment, Anna—we must rush. Lady Dunleavy, if you'll forgive us . . ."

Once outside on the curb, Anna felt her blush begin to cool. "What charming family my husband has."

"She was dreadfully rude," Moira burst out. "But why does she dislike you so?"

"I've no idea." But Anna now felt certain *she* was not the cause. Lockwood had given offense somehow, and she would know the whole story. A woman of science did not do well with mysteries.

CHAPTER FIVE

$\mathcal{A}$t home, Anna discovered that her husband had emerged from hiding, and was working—so Wilkins informed her—in his study.

Wilkins was not wearing livery, but his dark suit looked respectable, if a touch too loose on his scarecrow frame. His auburn hair had been neatly pomaded. "Very good," Anna informed him as she handed over her cloak. "Mind you, next time I return, you should not volunteer information until I *request* it. But otherwise, I am pleased: you opened the door promptly, and you appear to be sober."

The boy beamed so vigorously that she found herself momentarily startled by how young he looked. "Thank you, ma'am. I'm trying, I swear it!"

His accent was curious; she could not place it. "Where are your people from, Wilkins?"

"Lincoln, ma'am."

"Your accent doesn't sound northern to me."

"Oh—no, ma'am. My parents were from Lincoln, but I was born in New South Wales."

Jeannie had started up the stairs, and Anna caught her maid's shocked glance from the landing above. This was, indeed, a notorious origin.

Clearing her throat, she said gently, "You will not bandy that abroad, Wilkins. Some ignorant visitor might mistake you for the child of convicts."

Wilkins looked taken aback. "I—well, ma'am, I . . ." Frowning, he nodded and clasped his hands behind him. "I'm from Lincoln," he said firmly. "Only Lincoln."

"Quite right." Cheered by her salubrious effect on the staff—which only highlighted the pathetic nature of Lockwood's failure to intervene with them earlier—she turned on her heel and made for the study.

She opened the door without knocking. Lockwood was at his desk, scribbling something. "I thought you were off to Tiger Bay," he said absently.

"Tiger Bay? A curious name."

The sound of her voice worked a change on him. As he looked up, she saw how the ease went out of him, the line of his shoulders subtly stiffening.

A strange pang ran through her. They had not been enemies. Their marriage had been, in the broadest outlines, one of convenience—but they had liked each other very much.

Liked, ha! That had not been the word she'd used privately, in the days leading up to their wedding.

But she'd been a fool. And then he'd proven so: he'd abandoned her.

She reminded herself of that, reaching by habit for her anger, which made a durable shield against any stray whims that wished still to grieve. To grieve, one must lose something real—and she had not lost anything but her own illusions about him.

"Good afternoon," he said, laying down his pen but not rising from his seat. "Was there something you needed?"

"Yes. An appointment with your cousin Stephen. Preferably a dinner, or something friendly and casual in appearance."

His smile faded. "My cousin."

"Yes."

"For what purpose?"

Irritation prickled through her. "We have a business matter to discuss."

"Concerning?"

"Why do you care?"

He rose. "Why do you hesitate to answer?"

His soft voice sent a peculiar chill through her. Not understanding it, she frowned.

"How remarkable," she said. "You spent three years traipsing the world without a care for your properties. Not a single letter, not a line of inquiry. But now you wish to know all the details?"

His lips turned, but it was a dead smile, not to be trusted. "I am reforming," he said as he came near. The wolf's look was back in his eyes, flat and cold.

She found herself taking a step backward to seize hold of the door handle, though she could not follow why her instincts were suddenly screaming at her. "Well, that's very good of you. But you may limit your reform to your own business, not mine. If you don't wish to answer me, I will simply write to him myself—"

He slapped the flat of his hand against the door behind her, boxing her in place. She stared at him in mute astonishment.

"Tell me," he said, "why you need to speak with him."

Her heart was tripping. She dragged a breath in through her nose. "A simple question, that's all."

"Go on."

"Some railway company has leased a stretch of land that includes Clachaig—the beach my islanders use to come and go from Rawsey. They're advertising a new railway, and I need assurances that the route won't cut off my islanders' access to the beach. Otherwise the nearest harbor will put them half a day farther from market, and I'll lose half the farmers to the mainland."

"Ah." He slouched, his posture becoming raffish. "Rawsey. Of course."

"*Yes*, Rawsey. Some of us stick by our commitments."

"And you think Stephen is involved in this railway?"

"No," she said. "It's some man named Roy. But Stephen *is* in the railroad business. And this company—I can't actually locate Mr. Roy, or anyone save the stockbrokers who are selling shares in it. I thought your cousin might know him. Does that satisfy you?"

He stared at her for a long moment, as though— infuriating thought!—judging whether she was truthful. "I'll ask him about the railway," he said finally. "But you will not write to him, or seek him out in public. Do you understand?"

"Oh, won't I? What on earth is *wrong* with you?" She slipped out from beneath the bracket of his arm, side-stepping deeper into the room. "First you propose separate households, then you disappear for two days, and now you fly into a jealous rage when I propose to meet a man? Your own cousin, no less! If you think you can dictate my doings, you've run mad, Lockwood."

Their eyes locked. A muscle ticked in his square jaw; he raked his hand through his brown hair, leaving the bleached ends mussed. And then, on an audible exhalation, he dropped his hand and said, "Forgive me." Now came the other smile in his arsenal, wide and lopsided and charming and—all at once—as unconvincing as the other one. "We can certainly invite him to dinner, if you like. It would be . . . *delightful.*"

His moods were more mercurial than a Scottish spring day. What was his real face? She felt certain that she had not seen it since her arrival. None of his smiles were genuine.

But his dark mood, a moment ago . . . his bizarre, leashed rage . . . *that* had felt real.

He seemed to catch the flavor of her uneasy regard, for his effort to persuade her intensified. All cheerful ease, he fell into a nearby chair, adding a generous wave to indicate its partner. "Sit," he said. "Tell me of your day."

She did not want to sit. A new possibility seized her brain: mercurial moods. False faces. These abrupt shifts in personality. The sudden disappearance.

Madness could account for all of it. Had his mind somehow snapped on their wedding day?

He'd seemed quite sane when he'd left the cabin—furious, but in full possession of his faculties. But perhaps, on deck, something had happened. He had hit his head, or . . .

"What is it?" he asked. No doubt her face made a strange picture.

"Why did you go that night?"

He sat back, his smile fading. "Which night?"

"You know which night."

"Ah." He gave a one-shouldered shrug. "Must we retread old ground? It's rather tedious."

"We never tread it in the first place." Her voice sounded shaky. She cleared her throat. Why this was so difficult to ask, she could not say, but she felt as though she were flaying off pieces of her own skin as she forced herself to speak of it. "You left me. Without a note. Without a word. In the middle of the night."

"Yes," he said after a pause. "Dramatic timing."

Here was why it hurt. His flippancy, his casual mockery of a matter that had caused her more hurt than any wrong ever done to her before or since—

No. She took a deep breath. She would not let him hurt her. He didn't deserve that power. "Yes," she said flatly, "dramatic timing. But tell me: what prompted it? We quarreled, I know—"

His laughter rasped. "That is one way to put it."

"But to leave as you did—" She swallowed. "Do you know, I thought you had gone overboard. I—" Did he truly deserve to know this? "I ordered the captain not to leave the harbor. He tried to refuse, but I made such a scene—I screamed, I railed . . ."

He was staring at her fixedly, his face impassive. "Most impressive, I imagine."

This knot in her throat would not be swallowed. She recognized it. In the weeks after his disappearance, it had nearly choked her to death. First it had been grief. Then it had turned into humiliation, then rage.

She finally sat. Her legs trembled. She looked at her hands, knotted together in her lap. Her knuckles were white. She'd thought she had gotten over this bit. This . . . sense of betrayal.

And shame.

"What a fool they must have thought me," she said, making her voice hard and bright. "Making them circle the harbor for hours. We finally docked again—the other passengers were complaining. And then we got the news. You were spotted leaving the ship before we ever sailed." She made herself look up at him.

A queer surprise thumped through her. His eyes glittered as though—as though—

But no, it was only her imagination. For he gave her a smile, cool and sharp, and she realized that she was still, in some small way, that stupid foolish naïve little girl who had imagined this man capable of warmth, of real laughter, of the possibility of love, or at the least, human feeling, perhaps even tears.

But the man before her had dry eyes, and malice in his smile.

"What a fuss," he said. "I am sorry to have caused it. A boy's pride, you know. In retrospect, I should not have left the ship."

These regrets should have meant more to her. They bordered on the apology she had so desperately, furiously wanted.

But they were not enough. She felt parched inside, bruised and dry. "So where did you go," she asked dully, "when you left?"

He took a long breath. "To the tavern on the quay. I was angry. I thought a whisky would soothe my temper."

"And then?"

He scratched at the knee of his trousers. "And then, what?"

She ground her teeth together. He was not as dull witted as he was playing. "Then, was it the first whisky or the second that made you think, 'Why, I shan't go back. I will leave my newlywed bride on that ship, and go on a separate adventure of my own.'"

He flattened his hand on his knee, the movement abrupt and somehow violent. "Do you care?"

"What do you mean?" She sat forward, all but hissing. "You *deserted* me. How could I not care? Was I meant to go on, by myself? To sail without you, to not wonder what had happened, to simply say, 'Oh dear, I seem to have lost my husband somewhere. Tra-la-la, Paris will be lovely!'"

He did not move a muscle. "Is that not what you did?"

"No! Are you not listening? I did not go to Paris! I did not sail with the ship! How could you imagine—"

"Then where did you go?"

She caught her breath. "Where else? To the island."

"To the island," he said quietly. "Not, say, to the authorities. Not to the police. You went to *Rawsey*. Yes, I see how heartbroken you were."

Why, he was accusing her. How dare he! "Oh yes," she said. "I *did* think of going to the authorities. Imagine it: me at the police station. 'I seem to have misplaced my husband.' And the inspector: 'Why, where was he last seen?' And my reply: 'Storming off the ship, in a temper, with a letter of credit giving him access to *my* accounts, which he had used not hours before to withdraw five hundred pounds sterling!'"

He smirked. "Quite a speech."

"Isn't it? What a pity I didn't share it. They could have laughed me out of the station, and then run to the newspapers, where some cartoonist might have drawn a picture of a cow carted to slaughter, the bucket of milk having already been drawn!"

"God save your pride," he murmured.

"You are a beast! Do not try to paint *me* the villain. You were the one who left. You were the one who took a quarrel and turned it into a feud. I won't apologize for not having prostrated myself. Your estates are in the black now:

you should be on your knees thanking me for not having razed and salted the lands, to show you how much I care."

A silence fell, in which her loud breathing, and his utter stillness, seemed painfully vivid counterpoints. At last he looked away from her, to his hand on his knee, which tapped out some silent rhythm, ragged and quick.

"All right," he said. "I think that's enough."

"No. You were going to tell me why you ran like a coward. I am still waiting."

His gaze sliced up, glittering. "Very well. What would you prefer to hear?"

"*The truth.*"

He sighed. "The truth is never satisfying. The truth is either too plain to make sense, or too bizarre to be believed."

"What does that mean? Just tell me why you left!"

He stared at her a long moment, in which she saw the pulse ticking in his throat. His eyes, those eyes that had caught her attention across a crowded room in Fort William one night, were lambent gold, like honey held to the light, darkly and thickly lashed, beautiful, a liar's eyes: they could seem fevered and fierce even when behind them lay only falsity, shallowness, and cheap calculation.

"I was attacked," he drawled. "Ambushed. Bundled off the quay. Taken south. And placed on another ship, bound for New South Wales."

For a moment, the ticking of a nearby clock filled her ears as his words played and replayed in her head. With each pass, the tone of his voice—indifferent, casual, somehow bored—became more significant.

Even *he* was tired of his lies.

She rose. "Well. Yes. That would be pleasant to believe."

He laughed. "Pleasant? Why not say amusing?"

She crossed her arms. "You had a better sense of humor once. Or do I misremember? But I should pity you for—"

"No," he spat, startling her—but then, when he stood, he was smiling again, and she decided she had mistaken his tone. "Pity, darling, is the very last thing I look for. I can assure you of that."

"Contempt, then? May I offer that, in exchange for your gammon?"

He spread his hands, a conciliatory gesture. "Come up with a better story, and I'll gladly sign my name to it."

She nodded tightly. "This is impossible. I see it now."

"What is impossible?"

"Attempting to find some way to get on with you."

He shoved his hands into the pockets of his trousers, rocking slightly on his feet. "As I said, separate households can be arranged."

"No." She took another deep breath. "There are two reasons I came to London, the first being business. The second—well, I would not call it pleasure. Another piece of business, then, but one that involves *you*." She had tried to put it out of her mind, hoping that they would find some way to rub along together first, some more pleasant foundation on which to proceed.

But clearly that would not happen. So, like no doubt many of her female ancestors, she would suffer through the task with teeth gritted.

"And what might that be?" asked her husband, his head tipping slightly, allowing a boyish lock of blondish-brown hair to slip across his brow.

She hesitated.

His properties could go to the Devil from now on. But her own she would not bequeath to her nearest cousin. Gerald Wallace was a naïve and citified clergyman, who would entrust the estates entirely to paid stewards, who might plunder them and leave the tenants starving.

As the Countess of Forth, what she needed was an heir of her own body, whom she could raise and train in the proper care of the family's legacy.

As a woman, she wanted a child. She wanted a child more than anything; someone of her own, who would always be hers.

Alas, the rub: her marriage had been conducted according to English law, which had recently made divorce far easier. No longer did a man require parliamentary dispensation to cast off his wife. All he required was proof of her adultery and a judge's approval.

Lockwood would not have her properties in a divorce, for they were entailed to the earldom of Forth. But it seemed to her that the courts might grant him a good chunk of her fortune. After all, every judge in the world was a man.

Indeed, only one way clearly existed to get an heir, *and* to ensure that she retained the moneys to provide for a child, and her properties, and the tenants thereon.

"A separate household won't suit," she said. "Not until you've given me an heir."

He blinked. "An heir."

She felt her face flame. "It's like talking to a parrot! Yes, a *child*, Lockwood! Must I remind you of the specifics of our union? I did not marry you simply to get hold of Isle Rawsey. I require an *heir*, and alas that I cannot get my own self with babe—a man *is* sadly necessary!"

A peculiar look came over his face. His lips twitched, and he reached up to touch his mouth, as if to confirm that yes, he was trying not to laugh. "Still blunt," he said, but she barely heard him through the sudden roar in her ears. *Amuse* him, did she?

She grabbed the back of her chair, because she needed something to throttle and it would serve in lieu of his throat. "Listen to me!" She pounded the chair legs in time to each syllable: "You—are—useless. I would do better to advertise in a public tavern for a sire!"

His smile faded. For a moment, she thought she had gotten through to him.

But then, with a shrug, he said: "As you wish."

She goggled, truly shocked. "Don't think I haven't considered it!" If only the divorce laws had not changed, she would have gladly gotten herself bellyful, long ago! Not every man proved as eager to run from her as *this* one.

But she would not explain his advantage to him. "I could never bring an illegitimate child into the world." His smirk made her narrow her eyes. "It is your *duty*, Lockwood."

He laughed, an incredulous sound, and raked his hand through his hair. "Never in the history of womanhood—"

He fell abruptly silent as she stepped around the chair and grabbed his wrist. Beneath his undone shirt cuff, a dark inky pattern encircled his wrist.

"What is this?" she asked.

He was tremendously tense. She could feel the fine tremors racing through his body, the fierce flexed force of his resistance to them. Deeply puzzled, she peered up into his face.

His expression was full of some terrible intensity, instantly veiled as his lashes lowered. "It's a tattoo," he said. "What else?"

A tattoo! "Where on earth did you get it?"

He pulled free of her. "Elsewhere."

He no longer wore cologne. But this close, she recognized the smell of his skin. It made her heart trip.

God above. This was the second time now that proximity to him had caused her belly to stir. Her standards should have been higher. But the old attraction yet lived.

Well, it would make things easier.

She released him and strode to the door. But as she opened it, another thought occurred. "I will not have a drunkard for my child's father," she said as she turned back. "Nor will I risk disease. You will not bed another woman, or drink to excess, until the deed is accomplished. Do you agree?"

His lips parted. Why, she had astonished him into silence. Good!

"To that end," she said crisply, "since I can hardly trust you *not* to run off again, *much* less to refrain from your natural deviancies, I mean to know your whereabouts at all hours of the day—starting now. Are we agreed?"

A smile started at the corner of his mouth—a dark smile that spread very slowly. "On one condition," he murmured.

She would not let him see how that smile unnerved her. "What condition? Let me hear it."

"In the bedroom," he said, "I set the rules."

Her grip tightened on the door handle, the brass carving cutting into her palm. "I—I require a child," she said. "I will not tolerate any oddities that do not lead to that end."

His laugh was soft. "Good, a challenge. I like that."

CHAPTER SIX

*H*is wife had taken her dinner in her apartment; so Hanks informed him, when Liam dismissed him for the evening. Liam himself had no appetite, even though Beauregard had produced a half-passable approximation of cordon bleu. Nor did he feel particularly inclined to humor the countess's evident plan for him: to play the aggressor, and seek her out in order to grant her the bedding that she herself had demanded.

Oh, he had thought of nothing but it, for hours now.

But he would not give her an opportunity to imagine herself a martyr. If she wanted him, she would come find him.

And so, eventually, she did. At half eleven, the door to the salon opened. He did not look up from his book, though he had read the same page a dozen times, and still had no clear notion of what it entailed.

She stood silently for a full two or three minutes, a stubborn standoff that she lost when she finally said, "I was in the mood for tea. Is that still warm?"

He tilted his head toward the teapot. "Fresh as of eleven."

She poured herself a cup, then sat down on a settee opposite his wing chair. He turned the page of his book, glancing up only once, long enough to discover that she was immersed in the serious business of stirring and restirring the contents of the cup, and that she still wore the high-necked mauve gown from this afternoon. She was scowling.

He bit his cheek to stop his smile, and turned another page. She had *absolutely* expected him to come to her rooms, at which point that gown would have sent the clear message of her reluctant compliance.

Her spoon rattled now against the rim of her teacup. He heard the creak of springs in the settee as she shifted. "This tastes like bohea," she said stiffly. "But Mrs. Dawson's ledgers show the purchases come from Twining's. Somebody is switching out the tea, I think."

No doubt. Beauregard was an entrepreneur. "I will speak to Cook in the morning."

"No, that is the housekeeper's place. I will speak to Mrs. Dawson."

"Smashing." He turned another page.

More squeaking, another clatter of her spoon. "You seem curiously resigned to the dishonesty of your staff. I still think you should sack the lot of them."

"Oh?" Liam looked up and caught her biting her lip. She instantly released it, and sat straighter. She was gripping the teacup very tightly: the veins in her hands stood out.

She was nervous. How novel. Some old, rusted instinct instructed Liam to make an idle remark, something that would amuse her or put her at ease.

The larger part of him took a twisted pleasure in watching her strangle her cup. That part was not old; it belonged to the man he now was.

He could resist these dark urges, or castigate himself for them—but why bother? Reform was not his aim. Reform suggested some goal beyond it, a purpose for one's rehabilitated life. But he could see no purpose for himself save the crushing of his cousin, and perhaps—if he managed to keep patient—some unknown bastard who had played the go-between for Marlowe.

But after that?

Nothing. He had no ideas. He would continue to collect art, perhaps. And, if the woman before him had her way, he would also play the paterfamilias: an icy figure in the distance, occasionally dispensing praise or censure, as need be. God knew he would not take a direct hand in raising his offspring, lest he accidentally shape them into something resembling himself.

For look at him now: it was not fair, nor becoming, to sit across from his wife and be amused by how her hands shook as she sipped her tea. But his anger, alas, was a wild beast, barely leashed—or else a scattershot weapon that found targets everywhere, not least in those who had been spared . . . *everything*.

She claimed to have suffered. But she did not know the meaning of the word.

No, *no*, he knew that was wrong. What had happened to him had also disarranged her life. But . . . she had assumed the worst of him. She had not gone to the authorities. Instead she had gone back to that island, precious Rawsey, which had always been her first and only love.

And yet—*yes*, he had given her *every* reason to suspect he would abandon her. The terms of their marriage contract. His haste in discharging his debts, the very morning of their wedding. Their quarrel that night, fierce and terrible. And she had been young, and hot-headed, and God knew that what had *actually* happened to him on that quay would have been beyond her imagination, or anyone's.

So, yes, of course she had gone back to Rawsey. Of course she had told no one of his disappearance. Of course she had imagined his departure voluntary. He could not blame her for it.

He could not blame her; this was at once a fact he accepted and also another cause for his anger. For at the least, at the bloody *least*, he should feel free with his blame.

But no, she deserved none of it. She was guilty of nothing.

Yet he watched her fidget and said nothing to put her at ease. For she was ordinarily so completely self-assured. Why should she be otherwise? Nothing in this life had ever given her cause for discomfort. So let her enjoy the novelty of it. Let her fret.

He was staring. He realized it even as her gaze broke from his, shied away toward the wall, climbed . . .

"Good God," she gasped.

Ah. He reached for the dish of biscuits at his elbow. The first bite was overly sweet, cloying. "That is Miss Martin's painting," he said. "Or—pardon me, Miss Ashdown is the name she signs to them."

She looked pale. "So it really *is* a woman who made those paintings."

"Oh yes. Why do you ask?"

She shook her head, continuing to study the painting. It did make for a riveting view. The looming soldier filled the canvas entirely, his face a rictus of murderous lust. Such was the force and genius of the brushstrokes, of the perspective, of the vivid realism, that he seemed a moment away from reaching through the canvas to throttle the viewer.

"I don't know why it surprised me," she said softly. "Of course the artist is a woman. I'm sure this is a view that many of us have endured."

Her glance at him now felt like an accusation. And to his amazement, he flinched.

Christ, it would not be like *that* between them. Was that what she thought? He opened his mouth to reassure her—then closed it on a fresh wave of amazement.

Why, perhaps he retained some humanity after all.

Perhaps *she* was the key to it.

No. That burden was so unfair that even he would not thrust it upon her.

Nor, however, would he remain silent on this matter. "It is not a sight any woman should endure," he said flatly. "And if I encountered the man in that painting, I would see him hanged."

Her mouth twisted. Was she pressing back a relieved smile, or words of censure for his bloodlust? He could not say, for she looked into her teacup, concealing her expression.

Her hair was no less riveting than the painting. He found himself studying a ribbon of strawberry blond that snaked through the waves of copper and auburn.

Even Miss Martin could not have painted her hair. It was a natural miracle, inimitable. A single strand of it had slipped loose from her chignon, and curled past the shell of her ear.

Curious that ears were so often neglected by poetry. Hers put him in mind of a seashell. He had sucked on it once, and the sweet taste of her skin came back to him now, filling his mouth.

He was going to devour her.

"I didn't see that painting before," she said. "In the gallery."

"No." His voice sounded hoarse. He cleared his throat. "Those others had been sold, and were awaiting transport. This one, I kept."

For this admission, he received a glance of mingled horror and amazement. "But why?"

He considered his reply as he crumbled the rest of the wretched biscuit. One temptation, from the moment of her appearance in London, had been to tell her everything. But it felt much like the urge he'd had as a boy to place his hand in the flames in the fireplace—knowing it would hurt, knowing the burn would throb for days afterward, but drawn nevertheless.

Tell her and be done with it.

Tell her soberly, so she cannot doubt it; show her the proof, and watch her repent her anger—her flight to Rawsey—her care for her own pride, which kept her from raising the alarm that night.

It would be the quickest way to have the upper hand over her. Guilt, after all, was a crippling toxin.

And yet the urge never to tell her was far more powerful. Was that to his credit? He thought so. To *move on*, damn it: was that not the point, even if he could not see where to aim for? After all, why else had he survived, if not to repossess his rightful life and eventually, somehow, abandon the nightmare of his past?

That would not be achieved by an explanation. But the truth, if explained, certainly would transform how she looked at him. Her current looks, full of anger and contempt and bewilderment, were bearable, even amusing. They did nothing to blur the memories of how she had looked at him before—on Ben Nevis, on Rawsey, in Edinburgh. Those looks had been his nourishment in his early days of captivity. He had remembered them so often and so intensely that he had burned them into his soul.

But if he ever saw pity on her face . . .

It would efface all the rest. One offered pity to cowed animals and helpless children. Not to a man.

Her pity was the single thing he did not know if he could survive.

Thus, sitting across from her, having her so near, intending to draw her nearer yet, felt like living with a blade at his throat. And, like a man at knifepoint, he proceeded carefully.

"The painting shows a truth," he told her. "That in itself is a very rare accomplishment, and makes it worth the keeping."

She frowned. "It's a work of great power, I won't deny it. But I wouldn't like to dwell on it, day in and day out."

"We can have it moved, if you like. It needn't be in your line of view every day."

"But you would keep it in yours," she said slowly. "Why?"

He smiled, and she abruptly paled, so that he was forced to wonder what his expression telegraphed to her. "You ask clever questions," he said by way of explanation for whatever she saw that troubled her. "You always did know which would be the most interesting questions to ask."

The remark did not seem to calm her; the rapid rise and fall of her chest suggested quite the opposite, in fact. "You used to answer my questions. Now you merely dance around them."

He could not deny it. "I suppose, once upon a time, I thought you might have some use for my answers. But now, as you've said, you want nothing from me— pardon me: nothing, that is, that requires words."

She caught his meaning, and flushed. "I . . . There is no need to be vulgar."

"Was I vulgar?" He flicked a crumb from his fingers. "Fucking doesn't require speech: that seems a simple statement of fact."

She gawked as though he had sprouted another head. "Goodness. I don't know that word. But I believe I can follow its meaning. How glad I am that I expected no seduction!"

He laughed softly. There was her warrior's spirit. It had just taken a good shove to emerge. "Oh, I do mean to seduce you, Anna. But I had planned to begin that upstairs. The doors to this salon do not lock."

Her freckles were all but lost in the fierceness of her blush. "Upstairs will serve," she said faintly. "But you are proving my point. You are trying to scandalize me so you won't have to explain the appeal of the painting."

He laughed again, genuinely amused. She was so bloody clever, and self-possessed even when flustered— qualities that had not changed. "You're right, of course." He rose and held out his hand. "Shall we get to it? Unless you're in the mood for more sparring, of course."

She hesitated only a moment before squaring her shoulders and rising. She did not take his hand, instead using her own to smooth down her skirts—an unnecessary gesture that he found perversely touching, much in the vein of a condemned queen fixing her coiffure before mounting the block.

"My rooms or yours?" she asked stiffly.

He considered it. Her maid, he believed, slept in her dressing room. "Mine."

This was not the answer she'd wanted. He saw her fight a frown before she nodded. "Fine. I will meet you there in half an hour."

With these words, she marched out.

An optimist would assume she was hastening to bedeck and perfume herself. But Liam remembered her better. He would count himself lucky if she had not hurried off to tuck a weapon beneath his bed.

Anna was annoyed with herself. She was a sensible Scotswoman who spent half the year on a rocky spur off the southwestern coast whose survival depended on the copulation of sheep. She had played the bawd for old rams that had one more go to give. She was neither ignorant nor missish about what was required for conception. But all night—and most unforgivably, downstairs in Lockwood's salon—she had blushed and fretted like a schoolgirl about the coming event, as though *she* had not been the one to demand it.

After a firm, silent scolding to herself, she knotted her wrapper at the waist, checked to make sure that Jeannie was sleeping soundly on a cot in the dressing room, and then walked without knocking through the door that connected her bedroom to Lockwood's.

The bedchamber was warm, hushed, the bed curtains drawn back to reveal a mattress of gargantuan proportions. The tasseled maroon canopy matched the heavy quilts, and contrasted elegantly with the gold and navy patterning of the thick French rug that cushioned her footfall.

Lockwood was kneeling by the grate, poking at

the fire, and did not seem to notice her entrance. His dressing robe—some luxuriously glossy swath of dark silk—molded over his body, revealing the breadth of his shoulders and well-developed back, the narrowing of his waist, the firm high mounds of his flexed buttocks.

She crossed her arms and made herself stare. *Let* herself stare, perhaps. Even kneeling, with his back turned, he made a magnificent sight. His travels had left him with the build of a laborer, heavily developed through his upper body, taut and chiseled through his legs. She knew this, because his kneeling position had caused the hem of his robe to fall away, showing the distinct bulk of his flexed calf. His foot, braced behind him as he balanced on one knee, was long and elegant.

His leg hair was as light as the tips of the hair on his head: she had not known that. She acknowledged and dismissed as irrelevant the blush that crawled over her face. These were things a wife should know. She was four years overdue, and the advice her aunts had given her before the wedding—that the marital duty was not always pleasant, but with luck, yielded rewards—came back to her, renewing her courage.

He laid down the fire iron and rose in one easy, fluid movement. He showed no surprise to discover her standing behind him. "Warm enough?" he said.

He'd built the fire to leaping, and it outlined his figure, lending a devilish looming aspect to his posture. His expression was somewhat obscured by the trick of the light, but she sensed some air about him of repressed, disciplined energy. It was late, and she had taken longer than promised to join him in his rooms—but he seemed neither tired nor irritated, only deeply alert, and focused entirely on *her*.

"Certainly." She cleared her throat to eradicate the

huskiness in it. "Several degrees warmer than it properly ought to be—but I suppose Englishmen are not accustomed to a healthy chill."

He smiled as he came toward her. The robe slipped like dark liquid over his thighs, leaving no doubt that they, too, were magnificently bulked. She felt a grudging approval for that, for the industrious exertion it suggested. He had not spent her money while sitting on his arse, cream tea and bonbons in hand.

He stopped a pace away, looking her over with a thoroughness that put her in mind of a man at a horse auction. She lifted her chin. Her own robe, of soft but bulky flannel, did not seek to impress him. Impressing him was hardly necessary.

"Unbind your hair," he murmured.

She stiffened. She had braided her hair into a single plait, which seemed the neatest way to proceed. "We will make this brief, I hope."

His soft laughter raised gooseflesh on her arms. "Turn around, Anna."

"It needn't take longer than a few minutes." That was generous, she thought; sheep required sixty seconds, no more. "What I mean is, I've no interest in—"

"Hush."

Hush? "I beg your—"

His hand slipped around her nape, the warmth of his palm startling her. "Or keep talking," he said casually as his thumb lightly stroked over her pulse, the sensation sending a curious tremor through her belly. "Either way, you agreed to my terms."

Curious to realize that nobody had ever touched her there before—save him. The neck was not thought to be a particularly private area, yet as he studied her, his thumb slipped back and forth so lightly over her skin that she felt dizzied by it. In the firelight that filled the room, his amber eyes were dark pools, unreadable.

"Speaking of terms," he said quietly. "I do invite you to speak your mind. Should something displease you, tell me so."

An unsettling tremor quivered through her belly.

Tremors often presaged a collapse.

She crossed her arms. "Very well. Whatever you require to perform."

Another soft laugh: the jab to his manhood didn't bother him. He circled behind her, out of sight, and she hugged herself more tightly.

Light touches and tugs on her braid, then his hand slipped down it, toying with the ends. These sensations, so faint, had an outsized effect. The muscles in her neck and shoulders seemed to melt like butter.

"Your hair," he murmured, "is the eighth wonder of the world."

She scowled at the fire. Flattery was not wanted when it was false. "I suppose you would know. Is that where you went? To tour the other seven?"

Her pulse tripped as he stepped into her from behind, the sudden hard warmth of his body pressing against her from nape to knees. "Do you want to discuss that?" he whispered in her ear. "Or shall we get to it?"

Quite right. She closed her eyes. He smelled . . . familiar. How had the smell of his skin remained so vivid after so many years? Some distinctive and inimitable blend of soap and salt and musk and maleness, it cast her back to the time when she had hungered for him. When she had fallen asleep dreaming of this night, and expediency had not been what she hoped for.

"Yes, get to it," she managed. The words slipped out of her unsteadily, borne on a wave of realization: there was no good reason, no advantage, in failing to enjoy this. She wanted to lie with him for what it might bring her. What difference if the process felt pleasurable?

The decision lifted a burden from her, causing her to sag a little as he unbraided her hair. His broad palms stroked over her shoulders, and she bit down on a smile. How good his hands felt as they traced her arms through the thick layer of flannel.

But he could have had her long ago. Why should she feel gleeful and grateful for what should have been hers four years before? He had abandoned her on their wedding night. This, his clever light touches along her body, meant so little to him that he had not bothered to enjoy them before he left.

No. She would think on that tomorrow. Tonight, it would do her no good.

She turned in his arms, her eyes closed so she would not have to see his expression when she cupped his face and pulled his mouth to hers. She remembered how to kiss him. She remembered all of it.

Only through her fingertips, which bracketed his face, did she sense his surprise at her aggression: a momentary stillness, no longer than a heartbeat. Then he stepped into her again, so his chest brushed her breasts, and kissed her back.

His lips were still clever, shaping lightly, persuasively, over hers. But this kiss quickly turned bolder than any he'd ever offered. He opened her mouth with his lips and tasted her. The touch of his tongue made her head swim. It was . . . declarative: he had the right to go inside her now. And where their hips pressed together, she felt the instrument by which he would do it. He was hard, and very large.

The ewes never seemed to enjoy the rams' attention.

She pulled backward suddenly, out of his touch. He stared at her, his lips shining in the firelight, shining from the moisture of her mouth. But he did not speak. And the ferocious intensity of his look suddenly unnerved her.

She cleared her throat. "All right. Well—" She walked to the bed on legs that felt rusted at the joints, then lay down with mechanical stiffness. "On with it."

He came and sat on the edge of the mattress, looking down at her for a moment, some opaque calculation working through his face.

Frustration welled in her. She wanted him—and resented him. She wanted this over—she wanted him to kiss her again.

With an angry jerk, she unknotted her robe and threw it open. But he did not look down at her. He remained studying her face, his gaze speculative.

"Take off your robe," she said through her teeth, "and get *on* with it. Sheep, you know, only require a minute."

"Very well." He reached into the pocket of his robe and pulled out a white cloth. "First," he said, "tie this around your eyes."

She scrambled to a sitting position, her indignation as clear and loud as a yowl. "I beg your pardon?"

He had anticipated objections. Anna Winterslow Wallace Devaliant had not been fashioned in a mold of compliance. "We had an agreement." His voice was marvelously, miraculously calm. It did not belong to the beast pulling at the chains inside him, inflamed by the feel and scent of her.

He had not kissed a woman since he'd last kissed this one. He'd not bedded a woman since *she* came into his life. He had wondered, once or twice since his return, if he should hire some demimondaine who could be paid to keep quiet, some compliant and willing woman to prove he was still a man.

But his interest never lasted long enough to act. What could his body prove, after all? It had been the instrument of his degradation. For the rest of his life, it would tell the story of how he'd been broken. Pleasure, bodily pleasure, no longer had a place.

Or so he'd thought. Only now did he realize the depth of his error. His appetite had not been killed. Rather, it had built in secret, in some subterranean chamber unknown to his conscious mind. The pent-up force of four years' abstinence now roared through him. He was trembling with the effort to control it.

But, oh, how calm he looked to her. His voice, sweet honeyed deception, set her at ease, causing her to overlook how his muscles tensed, how his hands fisted on the urge to seize her. "You want a child," he murmured. "I will give you one. But you will allow me to set the terms of how it is done."

"I—" She looked between the cravat and his face. "I see no reason I must be *blinded* while you do it!"

Her robe was hanging open. She had forgotten to tie the sash. He would not remind her of it by staring. But his brain imprinted the sight in one flashing glance: the full, heavy sway of her breasts, the soft mound of her belly. *His.*

"There's no harm in it." Now his rough voice would

not have convinced an ingenue, much less his thorny, self-possessed wife. "The choice is yours."

"But—*why?*"

He cleared his throat. "I will also need to tie your hands to the headboard."

Her eyes flew wide. In that moment, he felt deviant in truth. It would take a powerful evil to drive this woman to cower.

Then she scowled and lifted her chin. "You're mad," she said. "Do you know it? Utterly deranged."

"Perhaps." Better a madman than a spectacle. He knew what his body looked like now. The scars were extensive, and as distinct as braille.

Christ help him, if she did not put on this blindfold he was going to have to find some way to make himself stand and walk away. "You have full rein to stop the proceedings. Only say the word, and it will end."

She snorted. "Tied up, blinded—why on earth should I believe you would stop?"

She was biting her lip now. It begged to be sucked. His entire body was a single pulse of need, and his brain was not functioning.

Her question—he forced himself to concentrate on it. He could hardly ask her to proceed on trust. In her view, he deserved none.

Schooling his breath, he turned to the small table by the bed. He kept a knife in the drawer there—also a pistol, and a set of cast-iron knuckle-dusters. But the knife would serve. She knew knives. "Keep this within reach." He folded it into her hand, wrapping her slim fingers around the hilt. The pleasure of touching her felt drugging. He slowly let go. "If I fail to listen, cut yourself free. Stab me, if you like."

She inspected the long, wicked blade. "Perhaps I should stab you right now," she muttered. "A widow would be free to find another father for her children."

His laugh startled him. It seemed astonishing that humor might break through this fierce grip of need.

But why not? From the moment she'd appeared in his salon last Sunday, he'd remembered instantly why he'd married her. What man could have resisted her? On the rare occasions she checked her thoughts before speaking them, it was a grave loss to the world, and a wasted opportunity to marvel at her.

"Have at it," he said, and flopped down onto his back, tipping his head to bare his throat to her.

She came over him, her long red hair brushing his chest and tickling his chin, her expression contorted in disbelief. "You did run mad," she muttered. "You know I'm not going to gut you." Her hand went to the sash of his robe.

He caught it in a firm grip. He could feel the thrumming of her pulse. He lifted her wrist and licked it, tasting the salted cream of her skin. Christ God.

Her breath caught audibly. "Lockwood . . ."

"First the blindfold," he whispered.

Her brows drew together. "Are you *shy*, Lockwood?" Taking his strained smile as affirmation, she sat back in clear amazement. "But this is absurd. You, bashful! Come now, open your robe."

He sat up. A blue vein wound down her throat, disappearing beneath the ruffled collar of her robe. It was his guide. A lure. "Lie back," he murmured. He would trace that vein. He would rip that robe off her to reveal it. One sharp tug was all it would take.

His fists clenched. *Not yet.* Not until she could not

see, could not reach out for him. "Lie back," he repeated roughly.

She shook her head slightly in bewilderment. "I can't . . ."

He took a hard breath through his nose. Another man would pretend not to hear. He was her husband, damn it.

But without choice, touch was naught but defilement.

"Very well." It was better this way, no doubt. This was no normal need. He could remember the fumblings of his youth. His desire had not felt like this—like a savage bottomless starving need that might well rip apart his body and hers before he managed to sate it.

Stand up. Walk away.

She was staring at him. "Why?" she whispered. "Why must it be like this?"

He could not move. Could not retreat. He stared back at her. "You said you wanted a child." *Anna. Let me. Anna.* "The choice is yours."

Her lips flattened. "I am not letting go of this knife," she said, and lay back.

His breath, his heart, stopped. For a moment, the wonder of her consent was so total that it blotted out everything.

Then he swallowed hard, schooling his expression. This bland mask he donned for her, the slight amused smile of a gentleman on a lark—he must not let it break, or she would see the truth and go flying.

And he might not let her go. That was what frightened him most.

"You need only tell me to stop," he said, and reached for the cravat. Hands shaking, he fitted it over her eyes, knotting it gently.

"You're depraved," she whispered. Her lips—he

leaned down and licked them, and she made a startled noise.

"Yes," he said into her mouth. Ah God, the taste of her—he was so hard that it was painful. But so much remained to be done. "But so are sheep," he continued unsteadily, "if you think on it. Now clutch the headboard."

"Sheep?" She sounded distracted as he bound her wrists with the other cravat. "Sheep are animals, Lockwood; they are sensible creatures who get this business accomplished in a minute flat, without any nonsense about—"

He kissed her lips again, the better to stop her objections. She submitted, then began to kiss him back—a hesitant but willing kiss. His wife, his wife's lips, and he poised over her, holding himself away, barely daring to breathe as he kissed her: this was real, this was happening, this was *now*.

Ambrosia, the flavor of her. Intoxicant. The more he tasted, the more frantic he felt. *Slow. Slow, now. You can have her. She cannot see, touch. You will have her soon enough.*

He tracked down her chin and throat, then forced himself to linger there, to sip her pulse, to persuade her to relax.

"Oh," she said softly, as he nuzzled her. "That's . . ."

Lightly, he warned himself. He skimmed his hand over her collarbone, delicate fragile architecture, never battered, never broken. How had he resisted having her before their wedding? Fool. He parted the robe, exposing her—pale and curving, rounded full hips, a soft belly like a provocation, God help him. He watched his trembling hand brush over her breast. Her nipple was a blushing pink. Nothing else in nature matched the color.

A strange fear coursed through him. Such unblemished perfection. She had no idea who touched her. He did not deserve this.

She sighed. Her nipple, beneath his thumb, stiffened. "Go on," she whispered.

Your wife.

He gritted his teeth hard against the urge to—

Bite her, crush her down into the mattress, hold her there, keep her there, do not let her move an inch.

He blew out his breath.

She doesn't know, she cannot see, she is not leaving, this is yours.

No call to rush. He would not rush.

He took her nipple into his mouth, and she gasped.

Gentleness, yes: this was what she expected of her husband. Gentle touches. Gentle lips, soft flicks of the tongue. Here he was, working a deceit on her as he moved over her body, kissing her quivering belly now—he had forgotten to acknowledge her freckles. A gentleman would have done so.

With a great effort, he forced himself to move up her body, back to her face. He kissed her again, licking that sunspot between the peaks of her lip. She kissed him back, arching against him, soft and warm, so soft.

Who did she see, in the darkness behind her blindfold? The other Liam—young and callow and self-assured—would not have braced his hand against the headboard to stop its trembling. That Liam had been no virgin. He had known how to kiss a woman, to grasp her breast and palm her hip, without fearing that his own release would come on him without warning, before the deed had even been done. But the man he was now . . .

He kissed her savagely, plundering her mouth. She

made a raw noise, and kissed him back with teeth and tongue, rolling her hips against his. *Too much, too much.* He went rigid against her, breathing hard into her mouth. *Gentle.* Here was his deceit, to be worked on her like a spell: he was harmless. He was the man she had known.

Her body was beginning to believe it. She lay relaxed and accommodating beneath him, and her arms, which he glanced at every few seconds to gauge their comfort, sagged into the mounded pillows.

As he settled back against her, he heard her long ragged breath. Her hips canted into his, and his breath hissed out before he could catch it. *Not yet.* He twisted his pelvis away, inwardly cursing. Even as a virgin, he had not felt so clumsy, so unsure of his own body. So close to the edge, so ready to spill.

She twisted restlessly, her small noises like demands. But he could not yet press against her again. Not until she had been readied to take him.

A fine deceit, then, a pretense at control, restraint; at patience, gentility, goodness. He sipped his way down her body once more, suckling her breasts until she groaned.

But the deceit was its own punishment: a thousand nights or more he had rehearsed this in his dreams, those dreams that had taken him from the nightmares of his waking hours. No terrors in his sleep at Elland—those had come later. In Elland, in crippling heat, in agonizing pain, he had dreamed only of her, and of that make-believe hour of their wedding night—an hour forever denied them. That other Liam had planned to seduce her—slowly, coaxingly, persuading her to realize the promise that had always leapt between them: the rapport of their bodies, the desire like electricity on Ben Nevis, on Rawsey, in Edinburgh. He had planned nothing else, for the charge upon him had felt grave and weighty. The raw current between their bodies was rare—the other Liam had known it. It could be ruined if he did not take care. On his wedding night, he'd vowed, he would be the most careful man alive. They would have years, decades, all the time in the world, to explore and sate and inflame each other, but on their wedding night, she would be educated into anticipating it as he did. He would show her the way. He would be the best husband alive.

Now, dreams collapsed into reality. The hair on her mound was exactly as he had imagined—wiry and red, glinting in the dim firelight, soft beneath his combing fingers. Her breath stuttered audibly in her throat— there was curiosity in the syllable she whispered, *yes*, and he gripped his cock to hold it away from the plump sweetness of her thigh, desperation singing along his nerves, torturous little pricks as she pushed her body against his, ah God, she was wet. He stroked between her lips and found the spot that would bring her joy. He was shaking now, violently. Gentleness was no longer his native skill. But all she would feel was the steady rhythm of his fingers, their gentle probing against her, the coaxing, insistent stroke.

This was not his wedding night. He was not that other man. His wife was blindfolded and tied so she could not touch or see him. There was some weird grief that wanted to fill him—desperation could tip so easily into despair—but when he bent his head to taste her, all else washed away. He licked into her and she groaned. She groaned and it was music. His ravaged body could do this. It did not betray him.

He licked and suckled her, increasingly confident as she bucked beneath him. Another way, then—different from what he'd rehearsed as a cocksure boy prepared for happiness. A woman did not only wish to be wooed. Sometimes, God be praised, she wanted to be taken.

He coaxed her with his tongue until her hips twisted violently—but no, she would not break free of him. He gripped her to hold her still, and her thighs clamped around his ears, her scent enfolding him.

"Oh—wait—" She struggled more fiercely. The flash of the knife pulled up his head.

He pressed the length of his palm against her quim to remind her what she was missing, and reached up with his other hand to grip her hand that held the knife.

Words were almost beyond him. He forced them out in a growl. "Do you want to stop?" He ground his palm against her wetness and she shuddered.

"I—want to see—"

"Pick one. Sight or"—he rolled his palm again—"*this*."

Her whisper sounded like a defeat: "This." Her grip opened. The blade fell from the bed.

He lowered his head again. No gentleness now. She tightened beneath him, and then cried out. He pushed his fingers inside her, and she moaned.

Now.

A red haze settled over him. As much blinded now as she, he groped up her body, feeling his way by instinct as he fitted his cock to her. Ah God, anything had been worth this, even the worst nights—it was true, all the fevered dreams had saved his life, but none had come close to how this felt. He pushed into her and felt her full-bodied flinch, and then heard her small noise, surprise and perhaps, perhaps wonder.

It did not take long. So many years alone. This was not love but an exorcism. One stroke—two—she was taking him, he was inside her, her body was hot and wet and soft and her legs wrapped around him to draw him closer and he was, for one moment outside time, no longer himself, twisted and scarred, but the man she had wanted, who had known he could please her—

The orgasm overtook him.

He collapsed atop her. Powerless, emptied. Oblivion: what no drug had ever given him. Breathing her, his hand planted in her hair, he felt . . . at rest. Not an exorcism, after all.

A homecoming.

After a long minute, she stirred beneath him. Fretted at the restraints.

He could not stay.

A strange grief leached through him, more violent and horrible than the numbness—full of feelings he could not name. Too much feeling. God save him, he had to move.

"Untie me," she whispered.

On a hard, deep breath, he shoved himself off her body and threw on his robe. His body felt strange to him, heavy and clumsy, his reflexes blunted, his skin still hungering for hers. The air too sharp, her skin the only cure.

As he unknotted the restraints at her wrists, her blindfolded face tipped up toward his, silent, patient. *Trusting*. The gesture sank some sweet deadly arrow through his heart. Her trust was so much more than he deserved. Hadn't she learned not to trust him?

Dizziness rocked him. He sat down heavily on the mattress. The blindfold emphasized the strong bones of her face, a sturdy square frame for her pretty mouth and bold nose. But her eyes were marvels. With a shaking hand, he pushed the blindfold over her head. She blinked at him, her glorious hair spilling in fiery disorder over her bare shoulders, her mouth bruised looking.

She blushed as she smiled at him. "Well," she said. "That was . . . overdue."

He was home. But *she* smiled at a stranger, and she did not even realize it.

He leaned back against the headboard for balance, breathing deeply. Her glance dropped down his body, and her smile dimmed. He was dressed, and she found it odd. She had questions. She had hopes he could not fulfill.

"You're shaking," she said.

"No." The denial was automatic. A request for her to disbelieve her own eyes. What else was the blindfold but that request made into an order? *Do not look at me.* Or, more accurately: *do not see me.*

See him, the man I once was.

The thought nauseated him. He would not invite such a charade. But what else was it when he showed her the bland, smiling face that best comforted her?

"Are you all right?" she asked, frowning now.

Had he rued his own ability to feel? It was turning on him in spades. Tenderness, gratitude, bottomless grief—this violent tumult of feelings was causing the room to spin. "I'm perfectly well." He could not quite breathe. The tightness in his throat would not be swallowed. "You'll want to sleep in your own bed. Shall I escort you back to your rooms?"

She stared up at him for an interminable moment, her puzzlement plain. Then she slipped to her feet.

"No," she said, then knotted her robe before walking away.

She wanted an heir from him. That was her right, and his duty. The rest of it—ugliness, all ugliness—he would rather cut his own throat than reveal to her. He watched her walk away, tall and slim, her shoulders thrown back in a dignified posture. His hand wrapped around the bedpost, tightened, to keep himself steady. Ten seconds, nine . . . Once she was gone, then he could confront this.

At the door, she turned back. *Just go*, he willed her, but she studied him another moment before saying something.

He could barely hear her through the roar of his panic. But he nodded as though he'd understood. "Quite," he said.

The door closed behind her, and he sank down onto the carpet, pulling his knees to his chest, his back jammed hard against the bedstead. Eyes closed, he waited for this to pass. It was an illusion. There was air enough to breathe. Hard earth was not packing down on him, crushing the life from his body. He had escaped the hole, made it back from Elland. This panic was an illusion. He was free.

His eyes opened, and he covered his mouth with his hand to choke a noise.

He had escaped. But he had not returned home— not until tonight.

Her words suddenly clarified in his brain, dim but distinct:

It was nothing like sheep, she had said to him.

CHAPTER SEVEN

Four years earlier

Anna had no future with an Englishman, but that did not mean she couldn't amuse herself. That evening, as the entire walking party reconvened in the Camerons' raftered hall for an indulgent dinner of a dozen courses, she found herself staring down the table at Lockwood, not bothering to glance away when he caught her eye.

His skin was too tanned to reveal if he blushed, but she rather suspected he wasn't the blushing type. He'd had experience with women; his kiss had made that clear. Such a kiss! Not clumsy and fumbling, but slow and clever and altogether too brief. When he'd pulled away after a scant moment, this afternoon on the mountain, her heart had been pounding, and all the bruised corners of her body had buzzed with curiosity.

A wise woman would have taken that as cause to avoid him. The rest of their party had found them not minutes afterward, and in the happy chatter of those who had reached the summit before the mist closed in there had been ample excuse to drift away from him, or to distract herself by amazing the group with her tale of near death.

But some odd compunction had kept her silent about the accident. Not pride—though her pride should have smarted. The fact of sharing a secret with him felt seductive and intimate, and he, too, had held his tongue. She'd felt his gaze follow her as she'd led the way down, arm in arm with Moira.

He did not blush, but she did. Tonight, when he caught her gazing at him down the long table, she blushed and did not look away.

The others liked him. Respected him, even. Eavesdropping, Anna heard him once again trot out tales of his grand tour—but this time, one of the men, Colin Cameron, mentioned an essay that Lockwood had published concerning the pre-Raphaelites. "I heard John Ruskin himself praised that piece," Colin said. "You take his side, then? You don't think Millais blasphemes with his art?"

Tension settled over the table as their hostess, Lady Cameron, scowled.

Lockwood, noticing this, replied smoothly: "I think the clergy best equipped to decide what is and is not blasphemy. For laymen such as us, the question is different. Should blasphemy, by definition, lie beyond art's scope?"

"I should say so." Lady Cameron snorted.

Lockwood inclined his head to her. "But if so, that leads to another quandary: we have looked on painting as the highest form of representation precisely because its scope appears universal. But if it cannot grasp and represent blasphemy—why, then its power appears much diminished, and perhaps not worthy of our study."

As he finished this clever speech, which neatly forced Lady Cameron into a puritanical position, a murmur ran over the table, and he caught Anna's eye.

She felt struck. He spoke of art as though it were a science; he had even concocted a hypothesis to test its value.

"Perhaps Lady Forth does not agree," he said.

She ducked her head and shrugged, not trusting the steadiness of her voice to carry her reply.

Moira noticed all this, of course. She caught Anna at the end of the night, as they all made their way to their rooms. "Did you quarrel with Lord Lockwood today?"

"No, of course not. Why do you ask?"

"The way you kept staring at him—I felt certain he'd offended you. And you didn't exchange a word all night."

But they had been communicating, regardless. She felt breathless from the messages they'd exchanged, through silent looks across the room.

"He's very charming," Moira continued dubiously. "I know you don't like charm. You've often said it conceals something."

It concealed, in his case, callused hands, and the strength to pull a woman to safety. Rueful awareness of his own faults, and shameless candor when he wanted to kiss someone.

"I don't mind him," Anna said. "He's not so bad."

Moira looked amused. "*You* like an Englishman? Quick, to the windows: are pigs flying?"

That night she lay awake for a time wondering at herself, at the temptation upon her: to invite him to join the group for the next stage of its journey, a planned excursion to Rawsey for May Day. It was risky—no, foolish—in a manner she'd never expected of herself. She wanted him nearby to stare at, and perhaps to touch. This was no way to find a husband. It was a way to ruin herself.

She would not invite him, she decided.

But the next morning, when he came down to breakfast freshly washed and dressed in plain clothing that he must have borrowed from another gentleman in the party—commonplace and rugged clothing quite at odds with his fine-tailored suits to date—she felt her resolve weaken.

He looked like a man who belonged on the island, broad shouldered and fit, able to pull a woman to safety with the strength of a single hand.

And so, at the station later that afternoon, when the others moved to bid their farewells to him, she found herself saying, "Or you could come with us."

And when his reply came immediately and just as casually, she knew she had not been the only one hoping to continue this adventure.

"That sounds pleasant," he said. "If there's room for me, I might be able to rearrange my plans."

Rawsey was reached by stages: first train, then carriage, and at last, by boat. A journey of two days, and the last bit, the most beautiful. Anna kept her distance, congratulating herself on her restraint, until the last hour on the sea, when she found Lockwood alone at the bow, apart from the others who were huddled beneath shawls and blankets, sharing nips of whisky from one of the Davis boys' flasks.

"The water suits you," she said. For his color looked

healthier than the others', and he stood solidly, braced with athletic grace against the churning of the waves that rocked the boat.

"I've sailed since boyhood," he said, "but never in such chop. Is that a whirlpool leeward?"

She was pleased by his sharp eye, which had spotted what centuries of men had missed, to their misfortune. "Aye, Wallace's Deep."

"It's larger than any I've seen."

She nodded. "It's kept the island safe from more than one invading army. You can still see the bones of the shipwrecks on the south beach. We'll take a tour, if you like."

"Vikings," he said.

"And a few Englishmen." When he turned, brows raised, she smiled at him. "It was suggested, though never proved, that some of my family were Jacobite sympathizers, and sheltered many a Highlander on this island before dispatching them off to America."

"So I'm sailing into enemy territory."

"Oh, I think you've been in it for some time now."

Their gazes caught, held.

"A wise man, thus caught, would be planning his retreat," he said.

"Yet here you are. Perhaps it's victory you foresee."

"Adventure is a victory of its own."

She laughed. "Well, there is plenty of adventure to be had on Rawsey. Who knows? You may even have the chance to rescue a sheep from the cliffs. Cliff rescues are your specialty, I think."

The island was drawing into view now, a long stretch of deceptively rocky ground, the manor concealed by a sheer thrust of stony cliff. In the valley behind it grew long grasses for grazing, fed by peaty brown runoff from the shallow loch above. But from this vantage, the isle looked barren.

She found herself testing him. "Lovely, no?"

He paused. "Wild," he said. "Scrubbed, scoured, and magnificent."

"Yes." She felt herself relax. "That it is."

"And you truly spend the winter here? Lady Moira said there was no coming and going in the winter, thanks to the whirlpool."

"The whirlpool isn't the main cause; that can be avoided if the captain has skill. It's the tides, and the shape of the harbor, and the roughness of the seas." She paused. "But yes, I've spent most winters here since childhood. My gram owned this island, you see. It was a wonderful place to roam free as a child—scrapping and racing and exploring, with no chaperones to scold me."

"Scrapping with your 'dozens of cousins'?"

He was quoting her own words back to her. He listened closely, which she liked. "Yes, sometimes," she said. "And sometimes the islanders' children. But usually it was only me and Gram."

Something changed in his face, a softening that looked too close to pity. "I see."

"I wanted to be here," she said forcefully. It had been far better than being tossed from aunt to aunt—forced to master new rules, and learn how not to disappoint—only to discover, as soon as she'd grown comfortable, that soon she'd be living elsewhere. "My father . . . After my mother passed, he became a wanderer. A dozen estates of his own, but he found no peace in any of them. He was a traveler by nature."

"Ah. I know the type."

She remembered what Helen Selkirk had said the night of the Camerons' party. "You're a wanderer, too," she said. "Did you really disappear for a year, without word to anybody?"

He shrugged. "I had a long list of artworks I was determined to see—it took a year to find them all. And I knew my family would oppose it."

"So you were chasing after art," she said with a smile. Most grand tours, from what she gathered, were not nearly so wholesome. She would not have figured him for a kind of scholar. "Why should your family have opposed that?"

He took a deep breath. "Well, at first, I thought to . . ." He offered a sheepish sideways smile. "I went to Rome to train," he said. "As a painter. And that, my father found appalling."

"Ah." Yes, she could see how a peer of the realm would not fancy his son running off to become an artist. "At first, you said? What happened?"

His smile widened into a grin. "I lacked all talent."

She laughed. "No!"

"Oh yes. But I discovered something else—a skill for looking. I hadn't known it could be a skill, until I realized in Rome that I could spot talent where others overlooked it." He gave a rueful tug of his mouth. "And I could spot its absence, too, in my own wretched work."

"So you went on a tour of looking."

"Precisely." He glanced beyond her, toward the coast. "I never wanted it to end."

There was something open and wistful in his expression that moved her. "You'll travel again, I'm sure."

"No doubt. But my father's passing left . . . responsibilities," he said. "A great deal of property, not in good repair. And I must address those needs first. Then, perhaps, I'll take back to the road."

"While all I want to do is to remain here. All year, if I could."

"You wouldn't grow tired of it?"

She shook her head. "I think there are many kinds of journeys. One can have grand adventures without ever leaving a place. My father, though—he was like you. A perpetual guest by temperament."

"So this truly is home for you."

"Yes," she said. "This is home."

A cry came from behind them, joyous and rowdy: the group was toasting the sight of the harbor, now drawing into view as the boat cut a wide berth around treacherous rocks.

"A village," said Lockwood.

He was generous to give that small cluster of thatched huts the dignity of such a title. "Ninety souls," she said, "where once there were four hundred."

"It's not a life to everyone's taste, I imagine."

"They left after my gram passed. Until then, it was a proper settlement." But her father had paid no care to the islanders' needs. "The flocks are flourishing—there's profit to be made here. If there were a schoolhouse, a proper schoolmaster, we could lure the young ones to return, set up households of their own. That's the first thing I'll do as soon as . . ."

"As soon as . . . ?"

She took a long breath. "We Scots are a superstitious lot. And there's said to be a curse on this island, which Gram believed too well. Any maiden who owns it outright will become the island's own guardian spirit, and never marry. She herself did not inherit until she was wed."

"How very . . ." She saw him pick diplomatically through the possibilities. "Interesting."

Her thin smile spoke agreement to the dryness in his voice. "Infuriating, more like. The island is held in a trust; I can't do a thing to change or alter it until I'm married."

"Ah." Now he looked away, concealing his expression, and his voice was carefully neutral as he went on. "I'm sure there are a dozen Scotsmen who stand ready to assist you with that problem."

"Hundreds, to be blunt. Isn't a man on earth who isn't drawn to the glimmer of an heiress."

He laughed, as she'd expected him to do. She was coming to count on his easy acceptance of her frankness. Peculiar how she could speak more freely with him, a man she'd known for less than a week, than many of her friends. It was his lack of judgment, the rogue in him, that made it possible, she supposed. "Then I assume that the schoolhouse will be built shortly," he said.

"Well, there is a trick to it." She found herself speaking more slowly, picking her words with care. "A husband is easy to find, but a man who will let me live as I like—there's the rub."

"You fear he would keep you from the island," he said quietly.

She nodded. "Yes, but that's only the start. I told you my father was a traveler. But he did take me along for the harvests. He had old-fashioned notions of what a daughter should learn, so I never had Latin or Greek. But lacking a son, he also saw fit to train me in the keeping and care of the estates. And I formed a taste for it—making those decisions, moving when and where I liked, giving orders rather than answering to them. It's no ordinary man who will see fit to let me keep on in that routine, even if it's my money that funds his airs."

He held silent for so long that she became aware of her own bated breath, how anxiously she awaited his coming reply.

"You'll want a husband," he said finally, "who has his own aims in life. Unconnected from your wealth and your properties."

Her heart tripped once. "Yes."

"Someone whose aims might lead him in a different direction, and be glad that he needn't be saddled with your duties as well."

"Precisely." She swallowed. "For I'm quite skilled at the management of estates. I could manage a dozen more, I think, without trouble."

Now he faced her, the wind ruffling his hair, the faint smile on his face sending an arrow of heat straight to her belly.

"It's an unusual demand to fill," he said. "You may have to look outside of Scotland for this man."

She had not lied to him until now, but she spoke the falsehood so easily that it felt, in the speaking, like truth: "The thought had certainly occurred to me."

The manor house on Rawsey seemed to have grown by centuries of organic accretion. The guest quarters were located in a modern wing built of plastered stone, with high ceilings and long windows that overlooked a valley where sheep grazed in fields of wildflowers. But from the stony spur above the house, which Liam had climbed this afternoon with a dozen other guests—many of whom had arrived days before their hostess—he saw that the manor bent like an L, with the original building belching smoke from its medieval chimneys despite the mild weather that prevailed.

It was in that older portion of the house, wooden beamed and raftered, that the company gathered this evening for an early supper. The long tables had been set for more than a hundred: it transpired that the countess annually extended a broad invitation to Rawsey's May Day celebrations, not only to her friends but also to the community that lived by the harbor. On either side of the room, fires blazed in hearths large enough to roast two pigs speared snout to tail—and in her welcoming speech, the countess assured them all that such had been done, though not for fifty years or more. "Only try to transport a hog across these seas yourself," she told them, laughing, "then see if you've still any appetite for pork."

The gathering, for its size and the mixed nature of the crowd, felt oddly familial. Liam watched as scions of great Scottish families rose, tankards of frothy ale in hand, to wander from table to table, making friends and trading jokes with the plain-dressed guests who called the island their home. The countess herself led that by example, returning only rarely to try bites of the rich courses that came out of the kitchens in endless procession. Liam himself was the object of great coaxing from ladies who wished a companion for their strolls of the room, but he—who would usually be counted the likeliest butterfly in such a crowd—found himself content to sit at his place and watch the countess.

The fascination had come on so quickly that it felt

like a sickness. One moment, on Ben Nevis, he'd been in full possession of his wits. The next, he'd been in feverish thrall.

Studying her did not cure him. Her aubergine wool gown was plain in comparison to the lace and jewels her friends wore. She was not more beautiful than some of the others, ladies who cast him flirtatious glances as they nibbled their lamb chops or tipped their tankards against his. Nor was her wealth so very far superior as to make her utterly incomparable.

But she was. As she joked with her tenants, as she met and matched the bawdy shouted remarks of her cousins, as she lifted her tankard to propose toasts and caused the entire crowd to drink to the dregs, he realized that he recognized her—but from myth, not real life. She was a figure from that distant feudal past in which great ladies had kept and defended lands while their lords went off to slay dragons. This was her island. This was her demesne. In her element, she glowed in a way that could not be reduced to the creamy perfection of her blushing skin, or the brilliance of her peridot eyes, or the flushed plumpness of her lips, much less the flame-colored twists of her hair.

Christ, he was a sap. But he couldn't mind. He drank another mug of ale, and another. By the time the food was removed and a few of the islanders pulled out pipes to play, he was near to drunk, and full of dangerous ideas.

As though she sensed it, the countess approached, sitting down beside him and then making him flinch with her sudden shout of approval for a couple taking the floor: "Aye, a reel! Stomp loud now, Moira! Spin her properly, Samuel! So," she continued at a softer level as she turned to him. "Do we bore you terribly, Lord Lockwood, in comparison to Geneva and Paris and London?"

He grinned. Impossible to take offense at the gentle mockery in her voice. He had certainly been bragging during their walk up Ben Nevis. Prating to her of the foreign wonders he'd seen, seeking to remind her of the superior adventures he might offer her.

"Rawsey does not admit comparisons," he said. "And if it's bagpipes you want, the Continent will disappoint. But a week in Paris wouldn't bore you, Lady Forth. Even *you* must admit that it might possibly be a small bit entertaining."

She laughed, an easy and husky sound, relaxed pleasure infused with ale. "Yes, I suppose, provided I had an *expert* guide such as you. Or Baedeker," she added dryly after a beat. "A Baedeker guidebook would be cheaper by half."

"A great deal more than half. Let's be clear: I make a very expensive companion."

She laughed again, and their eyes locked. "But an amusing guide," she said softly. "I don't doubt that in the least."

The freckles scattered across her face seemed to form a map, or a language that he would manage to decipher, if only given the opportunity and leisure to study them.

He made himself look away, to prove that he could. But her freckles' configuration, the clusters on the crests of her cheeks, and those two in particular on the border of her upper lip, remained before him, like lights burned into his vision, even as he watched the dancers' numbers increase.

On the floor below, a dark-haired beauty caught

his eye and winked before she was spun back into the crowd.

"Lady Moira has taken a fancy to you," said his hostess. She sounded amused, which did not precisely please him.

"She's a lovely girl," he said. "Your cousin, yes?"

"That's right."

"She told me her forebears were great cattle raiders, and no doubt owed me restitution."

"Oh, indeed. Moira is *immensely* propertied."

He glanced at her and caught the sardonic smile on her lips, which she bit back as she continued. "Very wealthy. A fine target for you, Lockwood."

"Target," he repeated, amused now himself. "Lady Forth, I believe you misunderstand: in such matters, I do not need to aim."

"Oh?" She arched one russet brow. "Indeed, I suppose you are like catnip, and all the felines swarm you whenever you pause to catch your breath."

He bit the inside of his cheek to keep a straight face. "It would be ungentlemanly to confirm it, of course."

"No need, I have heard my fill about your popularity." She looked rather cross now herself. "It was all I heard, in fact, for the entire week leading up to the Camerons' ball. News of your attendance made any *interesting* conversation impossible. For a time, I wondered if you might not be torn limb from limb by the ravening crowd before you ever got the chance to set foot on the dance floor."

He laughed despite himself and heard the robustness of it, and made himself set aside his tankard. For Lady Forth, he would require his wits. "I see. And so we finally have the truth: it was self-preservation, rather than bibliophilism, that caused you to refuse my hand in a dance. You were afraid of falling casualty by proxy."

She met his eyes squarely. "You misremember, Lockwood: you never asked me to dance."

"By God." The oversight amazed him in retrospect. "Well, let me remedy that." He rose, holding out his hand. She looked from it to his face, a mischievous light entering her eyes.

"It would be unwise to assent," she said apologetically. "You see, four men already requested the honor of my first dance tonight. I said yes to all of them."

He laughed again. "You did not."

She shrugged. "I did not plan to dance. And now I cannot, lest I provoke a brawl."

"Four men?" He was torn between amusement and a creeping displeasure that felt, to his horror, like jealousy.

"Hmm." She tapped her lips in thought. "Perhaps five?"

He seized her hand and tugged her to her feet. "Which men might these be? Let me know so I can keep a lookout for my enemies."

"Oh, they're all your enemies, if you mean to dance with me. Or do anything else, for that matter." Her hand turned in his, her fingers warm—did she mean to deliver that soft stroke down his palm? Ridiculous, laughable, that such a light touch could cause his groin to stir. But she was looking into his eyes, her smile sly and knowing, and he felt the sudden barbaric urge— blame this medieval atmosphere—to sweep her into his arms and bundle her away from all other men's regard.

"Be honest," he said, his voice coming out fiercely. "Do you favor one of them? If so, tell me now."

She was a vixen whose smile widened as she studied

him, and who then turned away toward the crowd, to give the men there a considering survey. "Angus Stewart offered for me at Michaelmas," she said. "But I told him no, I thought his friendship too dear. In fact, what he requires is a hostess to advance his political career, and I cannot be bothered to wait hand and foot on a man, much less play hostess in Edinburgh. Now, Alex Carson"—her slender finger pointed out a muscular blond—"asked twice, the last time on Ash Wednesday, but he's the sort to expect a wife to ask permission every time she goes to market. I told him, what a time to propose! Alex, I said, you must keep your mind on your Lenten vows. And Thomas Sutherland, there, has tried to screw up his courage several times now, but he clings so fiercely he would never let me come here alone—" She broke off to stare at Liam with wide eyes, then looked down to their joined hands. "Your grip will not change those facts," she murmured, "though I am certainly impressed by the strength of it."

Startled and embarrassed, he loosed her hand. God save him, acting like a green-eyed boy.

She laughed softly, enjoying his fluster. She was accustomed to the upper hand.

But so was he. "Alas," he said, taking her hand again and lifting it for a kiss that made her breath audibly catch. "I've not had any proposals, myself." With his free hand, he took her waist, as though to turn her into the first step of a dance, and subtly urged her backward a pace. "I suppose that ladies, being trained in a subtler art, cast their lures more covertly."

"Oh yes," she said. "We ladies are very devious, and could not speak plainly even if we had to spell every word."

He laughed. She was a fine champion for her sex. He nudged her another pace backward. "If you wish to call me an ass, Lady Forth, go ahead and say it. My vanity will survive—it's quite robust, you see."

She nodded, aping concerned sympathy. "That is not uncommon among men."

"And among women such as yourself?" She did not seem to notice that their next step together moved them behind one of the broad wooden pillars that supported the ancient scaffolding of the roof. "Have you no flaws, no vanity born of your charms?"

She opened her mouth, then at last took note of their position: tucked out of sight, sheltered from the rest of the crowd. For a moment, as her lashes fluttered rapidly, he prepared to make a graceful retreat, to let her escape—but she took a deep breath and leaned back against the pillar and smiled at him.

He placed his hand over her head, leaning close. "Answer," he murmured. "What is your flaw, Lady Forth?"

"Pride," she said softly. "I know exactly what I want, and I will not consent to anything less, or otherwise."

He studied those two freckles, nestled so perfectly against the crest of her mouth. "That sounds very rigid," he murmured. "What you want may surprise you."

He pressed his mouth to hers.

The kiss on the mountain had been sweet but brief. Brief as a lightning flash: just long enough to illuminate what had been hidden, unseen, not guessed at.

This kiss aimed for what the other had discovered, but not managed to explore.

Her hands found his face, her fingers cool and soft. With a gentle nudge to her chin, he tilted her head back and sipped her. She tasted like ale and honey, and the inside of her mouth was warm and wet and her tongue was clumsy at first, but quickly cleverer.

On the dance floor, a drum joined the pipes, and as he kissed her, it seemed to Liam that the drum was his heartbeat, quickening and quickening as her arms came around him, as his palm traveled the unexplored length of her spine, tracing the buttons and ridges and seams of this garb that separated them, though their bodies now crushed together, all at once. His hand, braced hard on the post, was the only thing that kept their balance as she wrapped around him like a vine. God, but she was hot, her mouth and her grasping hands and the sweet cinnamon scent of her enfolding him as he devoured her. This moment, the taste of her, the stomp of the dancers and the beat of the drum and the air heated by fire, lifted him outside himself as they kissed.

When they broke apart, he felt heavy again, rooted, transformed. They stared at each other, her ragged breath as loud as his, and then she clapped her hand to her mouth and laughed.

No more beautiful sound in the world. He would make her laugh like that forever, given the chance.

He cleared his throat. Hunted for some clever line, when what he wanted to propose was an adjournment to a dark room—but no, Christ save him, ruining her was not his aim. He knew his aim now. It was clear.

He caught her hand, kissed each knuckle as she stared at him, eyes shining. "Now," he said hoarsely. "Will you dance?"

"No," she said. "In fact, I would like to rectify a failure of my sex. Lord Lockwood." Her hand turned in his, taking control of the grip. "You are a man who wishes the freedom to travel, and requires money. I am a woman who requires a husband, and wishes the freedom to live as I like. Do you see a match here?"

He blinked again. Surely she could not mean . . . "I beg your pardon?"

She gave a wry tug of her mouth. "If *this* is how men react, I begin to understand why ladies cast lures instead. But listen carefully, if you please: do you agree that we are perfectly suited for each other's purposes? Under no illusion of love, but with a great deal to gain from each other, and no aim to be a spouse who limits the other's freedom and choice."

He *was* understanding her. "Are you *proposing*, Lady Forth?"

Her eyes narrowed. "Do not expect me to go down on one knee," she said. "I could have done it on the mountain, but not in *these* skirts."

He began to smile, but it turned into a laugh, which he smothered by pulling her to him and kissing her again.

CHAPTER EIGHT

London, 1861

*A*nna woke alone, well into the morning. Jeannie teased her for it as she helped Anna dress. "London ways, ma'am. You're keeping the devil's hours now, up all night and abed till noon!"

It was, in fact, not yet ten o'clock. But in Scotland, Anna would have been up since dawn. "Perhaps Londoners know better than I do," she told Jeannie. She felt wonderful for the rest, and the mirror reflected back an unusual radiance, and a readiness at the corners of her lips to twitch toward smiles.

Very well, her husband was deviant. So, too, it seemed, was she—for she had enjoyed herself thoroughly by the end, and had gone to bed amazed and mildly indignant that once had been enough for him.

She would not be shy about it. That pleasure she'd had was four years overdue. And it had a very worthy goal.

As though to reward her, happy news came by post from her solicitor: while he had not yet located the chairman of the railway company, the lease of the beach might yet be revoked. The owners, the shiftless MacCauleys, were complaining that the company had not yet issued payment for its use of the land. *If the company continues to delay payment,* Sir Charles wrote, *we may persuade the MacCauleys to sue for breach of contract. I have offered to serve as their agent at no fee to them, should they agree.*

As Anna made her way downstairs, she kicked her feet on the stairs and reached overhead to feel the pleasant burn of stretching muscles. The good news had put her in mind of Rawsey—what a fine morning it would be there, with her mare at hand for a gallop through the fields! She had not felt the wind in her hair for two weeks now.

In the hall, she found Lockwood conferring in low tones with two unfamiliar men. Her appearance put an end to their conversation; they tipped their bowler hats to her as they passed, but did not meet her eyes. Something in their square, capable postures, and the economical briskness of their strides, made her pause and look after them.

"Early business," Lockwood said as he came toward her. He caught her hand and lifted it to his mouth, his grip warm and dry, and she was startled by her own impulse to flutter—such an old, forgotten reflex, which very few men but he had ever managed to trigger.

They smiled at each other. "You look well," he said.

She felt daring. "Blindfolds suit me, it seems."

She heard him catch his breath. His grip tightened on hers briefly before he kissed her knuckles again and released them. "How fortunate for me."

Distracted by his husky tone, she realized only belatedly that he did not look as well rested as she. Shadows were smudged beneath his eyes, and his gaze briefly broke from hers to follow the path his visitors had taken. He was distracted by something. "I hope your morning's business was not bad news?"

"Oh no. Merely some trifle to do with Miss Ashdown."

His smile and tone were persuasive, but she was not sure she believed them. The look of those men had been better suited to guarding a bank than settling artistic disputes. "What ails her?"

"A sensitivity to criticism," he said with a wink. "Which puts me in mind of the rest of them, fretting and stewing at Lawdon. It's been a fortnight since I visited—I should go settle their nerves."

Lawdon was his estate nearest to London; Anna had overseen its operations from Scotland, but since the harvest, she'd not had any correspondence from Mr. Pike, the steward there. "You're housing artists there now?"

"Yes, I've opened the house to a few of them. Perhaps you'd like to visit with me?"

A quick pang rippled through her. They had planned to visit Lawdon after their honeymoon. Lockwood had been raised there. But she had never seen it.

She had certainly paid for it, though. Alone of Lockwood's estates, it had been in good repair, but half the fields had been devoted to potatoes, and therefore vulnerable to blight. She had conducted quite a fierce argument with Mr. Pike, via letters and cables for three months, before he had finally agreed to diversify the crops.

Lockwood's father had also left behind a very fine and expensive stable at Lawdon. She bit her tongue now against mention of how much those horses had cost her before she'd found a market for the stallions' services—it would quite sour the mood.

"I should love to come," she said. She would have her satisfaction of that stable: country air and a ride through the fields were precisely what she craved.

Lawdon's bucolic location made it quicker to reach by road than by rail, and so Anna's first glimpse of the property came three hours later, through the glass window of the coach, as they turned into a drive lined by oak and elm trees. Lockwood had kept her amused during the drive with tales of the artists in residence—among them a former butcher with a genius for capturing the everyday rhythms of the countryside and a Frenchman who only painted housemaids, much to the housemaids' irritation. "He begs them to pose in the middle of dusting and sweeping, so nothing gets cleaned. I've had to double their pay to keep them satisfied," Lockwood said with a laugh.

These tales prepared Anna for some monument to bohemianism, but Lawdon Hall made no outward display of its mischief: the red-bricked manse was surprisingly modest, distinguished only by neat rows of tall, shining windows, and a scalloped trimming of gray stone.

"Prepare for admiration," Lockwood warned her as he helped her out of the carriage. "The profits from last year's harvest have kept the staff in wax candles all winter. I expect every member of the household will tug a forelock for you."

She laughed. "It *was* a handsome profit here last year."

"It was a handsome profit on every one of the estates," he said. "Four years running now, and all your doing."

She had wondered occasionally if he'd bothered to look to his business since returning. Now she had the answer. "I did promise to bring them into the black," she said softly.

"Yes. So you did." He hesitated on some syllable, then shrugged and led her up the steps, where a slight chill seemed to envelop them—the ghosts of his own broken promises, perhaps.

But she would not poke at those ghosts today. The sun was bright, the sky clear, the clean air scented by grass and fragrant pollen. She would enjoy herself. With an effort, she smiled as they stepped into the hall.

Lawdon's senior staff queued to introduce themselves. These were the thoroughly conventional counterpoints to the London household: a butler grayed and stooped with age, a housekeeper grown fat and jolly on the authority of her jingling key ring, and the steward, Mr. Pike, who clasped Anna's hand like an old friend and expressed his earnest thanks on the double-furrow plough she'd sent.

"I don't know where we would be without her ladyship," Mr. Pike told the room at large. "No idea, none indeed. I hope you'll have a moment to see that plough's results before you go."

"Of course," she said. "In fact, I've been meaning to chase down rumors of a new technology come out of the Midlands, which employs a double tackle and a self-propelled engine."

"Oh! You're a saint, my lady."

"So we've heard," Lockwood said dryly. "Countess, you have been nominated for sainthood several times in my hearing—it begins with oats, and now ends with engines."

"Goodness, may it never end!" exclaimed Mr. Pike, to laughter from everyone.

The housekeeper, Mrs. Bradley, offered a tour of

the hall while Lockwood went off to see to his artists. As Anna followed the woman from room to room, a strange feeling crept over her, surreal and disorienting. Here was the welcome she had envisioned four years ago. She walked in the footsteps of another Anna, who would have passed through these rooms as a new bride, blushing and contented by her honeymoon.

That other Anna would have found no cause for discomfort at Lawdon. In contrast to the townhouse, Lawdon's furnishings were quiet, tasteful, and worn by long use. They suited her far better than the gaudy and outrageously expensive gilt in which Lockwood had smothered his London home.

In an airy salon that overlooked the parkland, Anna paused to admire the view: rolling fields stretched away to a lake, on the far shore of which stood a small Roman folly. Nearer by, an ancient oak tree sheltered a fanciful little castle, two stories high, topped by a miniature turret and ramparts.

"That was the children's playhouse," Mrs. Bradley said in answer to her question. "His lordship's father then turned it into a schoolroom, in the hopes it might encourage a love of study."

"And did it?"

Mrs. Bradley laughed. "Well, young Mr. Devaliant never had to be dragged to his desk. But his lordship . . ." She mimed buttoning her mouth shut.

Anna smiled. One hand resting on the worn damask of a stuffed armchair, she gazed out again at the lake, the sunlight glimmering on the waters, as a sense of serenity came over her.

Why, she might have felt at home here. Here, in *England*.

"It's a lovely view, no?" Mrs. Bradley seemed cheerfully oblivious by nature, but perhaps that was only a mask for kindness—for Anna felt tears pricking her eyes, and would not have known how to explain them.

She cleared her throat and firmly pushed away all thoughts of the other Anna. "Yes, it's wonderful."

"This was the favorite room of our late countess. She often took her breakfast here, to watch the sun come up over the lake."

She would have adored you, Lockwood had once told her of his mother. *She also had strong opinions, and the knowledge to support them—and the temper, too.*

What had gone wrong, between that conversation and the night he'd left?

"It is very good," the housekeeper suddenly blurted, "to see you here, m'lady. We have been waiting ever so long for your visit."

"Indeed," Anna murmured. "It is very fine to be here, Mrs. Bradley."

Minutes later, as they mounted the stairs, Anna caught conversation overhead, from one of the artists no doubt: "Ain't fit for fine company," grumbled a man in a thick northern accent. "They'll laugh me out of the house."

"Every artist is nervous on the eve of discovery." This was Lockwood's voice, pitched in a gentle and soothing register. "But I will not allow you to discount your artwork as trifling. You have a genius, Mr. Jobson."

That strange melancholy twisted through her again. When had he last spoken to her with such patience and approval and warmth?

"Genius, ha!"

The housekeeper had already crested the stairs. Anna

hurried after her, and they emerged into the upstairs hall, where she spotted the object of Lockwood's persuasion: a plain-faced, sandy-haired man with a bulbous, speckled nose. He was tugging at his collar as though it strangled him. "I paint farmers and their flocks, my lord. When your city friends laugh me out of your house—"

"London society trusts my taste. If I say your work is fine, then it is—and the city will agree."

"This was a mistake," Jobson moaned. "I swore never to show again."

Lockwood clapped the man on the shoulder. "You will thank me before month's end; that, I promise you."

He spoke with easy confidence, like a man who had never been judged. But Jobson was not impressed. "I was drunk, or you'd never have persuaded me to it. Please, my lord, it's still not too late—"

"Come." Lockwood discarded charm for a more athletic approach. Seizing Jobson's arm, he hauled him off down the hall. "You'll look square at your work right now, and we'll see if you still dare insult it."

"I don't need—"

"Chin up, man. If the applause won't please you, then the offers will. You'll have three hundred pounds in your pocket by August."

"Three hundred?" Jobson's voice cracked. "Surely you're joking . . ."

As their voices faded, Anna spied the housekeeper smiling to herself.

"That's the fifth time I've heard that speech," she told Anna. "I never met an artist before his lordship began to lodge them here. But they're a nervous lot, aren't they? He always gets their feathers smoothed, though."

What an image! Lockwood fussing over clackish artists like a mother hen.

"This here is your office," said Mrs. Bradley, nodding toward an open door. "Been waiting for you for some time."

"My office?" Frowning, Anna stepped inside.

The room did not resemble any typical study. No carpet had been laid over the gleaming floorboards, and in place of a desk stood a sturdy oak table that nearly ran the length of the room, its shape mirrored exactly by the skylight overhead. Cloudy light gleamed over cushioned benches and bookshelves that lined the walls, full of . . .

Journals. Agrarian, geological, biological, chemical . . .

Scientific journals. As she stepped forward to examine them, she noticed their dates. "All from 1857," she murmured. This lot of journals was four years old.

He must have built and stocked this space directly before their wedding.

"We ran out of space for the newer ones," Mrs. Bradley said. "They are downstairs, in the library proper."

Wordless, she nodded. One volume was thicker and more handsomely bound than the rest. She picked up the book, brushing her fingers over the tooled leather cover. When she opened it, her heart turned over.

This was her manuscript. He'd had it bound, like a real book.

She sank onto the nearby bench and shut the book, gripping it so hard that the leather bore the marks of her fingernails when she finally let go.

Why had he done this?

Why had he built this place for her, if he had never intended to stay?

"Shall I leave you for a bit?"

The housekeeper's words seemed to come from a great distance. Anna nodded, barely hearing her retreat.

She opened the book again with trembling hands. Here was her inscription to him:

Promise me never to burn a book again!
AWW 1857

A noise drew her gaze up to the doorway, where Lockwood stood. She caught a strange look on his face before he offered an abrupt half smile. "You never published it," he said.

So he knew which book she held. Her bewilderment felt dizzying. "I sent it to publishers. But nothing came of it."

He stepped inside. "I can't believe there was no interest."

"Markham and Macallister wanted it. But they would not consent to anonymity. They wanted to send me around to give lectures."

His head tipped. "Why didn't you? It's a fine piece of work, Anna. You should have been proud of it."

Hating to ruin this fragile truce between them, she spoke in an apologetic voice. "It would have drawn notice to me. Markham had a campaign planned, advertisements for the 'Lady of Science,' the 'Scientific Countess,' all manner of nonsense. People naturally would have begun to wonder about my husband—where you were, why you'd gone. And I . . ." Feeling awkward, she gave a little shrug. "Well. I had no desire to be known as the bluestocking whose mannish interests drove her husband away."

She braced for his defense. But he offered none, his gaze opaque as he considered her. "Mannish?"

She flushed. "You *know* how people are."

"Idiots, for the most part."

Relieved that he hadn't bridled, she pushed out a short laugh. "So they would have been wrong, then? It *wasn't* my mannish interests that drove you away?"

The joke was poor, and her voice did not manage to carry it. Nor did he bother to muster a smile.

"No," he said. "Your intellect was—is—one of your beauties."

Surprise fluttered through her. She had no notion of how to respond to his compliment, much less whether it would make her a fool to seem to believe it. After all, for all her 'beauties,' he had left her.

In lieu of a reply, she looked around the room—and felt a startled laugh catch in her throat when she spotted the painting on the wall high above. She had never seen it, but she recognized it all the same. "Is that the 'Wretched Folly'?"

He followed her glance, then winced. "Is that what I called it?"

"Yes." He had begun the painting at her joking insistence, to 'prove' his lack of talent, and kept her apprised of its 'monstrous progress' in each letter he sent. But somewhere along the line, it had become something more than a silly lark. Her teasing encouragements had led him to discuss more honestly his old ambitions, and the pain and growth inherent to realizing his own inaptitude. *The first time I'd truly failed at something*, he'd said of his time in Rome. *My father had predicted it, but he never spoke a word in smugness. He told me to look elsewhere for my gifts. And so I did.*

He stepped back now, squinting at it. "*Wretched* might have been too kind."

She walked over to join him. "What was it titled?"

She knew the answer, of course. But she wanted to hear proof that he remembered as clearly as she did.

" 'The Lady at the Window,' " he said softly. "I should have painted a blonde. There was never any hope of capturing your hair."

The woman's hair was indeed a rather unlikely scarlet, interspersed with clumsy dashes of orange and yellow. But he was not *entirely* talentless, even when trying to be so: the view was recognizable as the parkland seen from the window of the morning room.

She remembered his vow to make the lake look as it had to his eyes as a child, when he'd been tossed in by a footman in order to learn to swim: endless, impossibly deep, large as the ocean.

Her lips twitched as she considered the results. "Is that a tidal wave coming toward us?" The wave rose so high that the trees beyond it looked dwarfed, three feet tall at most.

He slanted her a laughing look. "Precisely—a sweet promise that the viewer will be put out of her misery in a few moments."

She bit the inside of her cheek to keep a straight face. "Come now. It's . . . remarkable." Remarkably awful, in fact. The clouds looked as though they were melting out of the sky.

"Remarkable," he mused. "How . . . politic of you."

"The point was not to become Michelangelo, if you'll recall—or even to produce something averagely accomplished. I challenged you to paint terribly. In fact, I made you *promise* that you would only paint rubbish."

He arched a brow. "And evidently I obeyed. But what a waste of Prussian blue!"

"You enjoyed every moment of it. I still have the letters somewhere to prove it." She knew exactly where they were: in the chest at her Edinburgh townhouse. "You said that angels were rejoicing as you laid the final brushstroke, and that your next work would dazzle the Royal Academy into a collective fit of apoplexy."

His laughter was so robust and full throated that she wondered if he had ever laughed genuinely until now. "You'll notice I did not sign my name to this atrocity."

Her laughter slipped free, joining his. Some part of her looked down from a distance, marveling at this wondrous bizarre sight: the two of them joking together as of old.

The moment was over too soon, but it left her feeling lighter than air, as though her next step might launch her floating into the sky. Perhaps it was not too late for them, after all. Perhaps . . .

His gaze dropped to the book she held—she realized she had clutched it to her chest, a posture that suddenly seemed too revealing. Quickly she turned away, carrying the book back to the shelf, then sat again. What she wanted was some remark that might keep them in a casual, merry mood—but as she groped for it, he spoke first.

"You could publish it now," he said. "It's worthy of an audience."

"Yes, I suppose." She stared at him. None of this made sense. "You built this for me. This room."

"It was to be a wedding present."

"I wish . . . you had stayed to give it to me."

His head tipped, some complicated thought working

across his face. She could not hope to decipher it, but he seemed to resolve it for himself: with one sharp nod, he stepped toward her and caught her hand.

"I am giving it to you now," he said as he tugged her to her feet. "With apologies for the delay," he added against her mouth, then kissed her.

Her eyes closed. A pulse of pleasure beat through her at how softly he kissed her—a light molding of lips, tentative, almost innocent. This was an unfamiliar species of kiss. It bore no relation to the strange hot passion of last night. She relaxed, sighed into his mouth. How safe she had once felt in his arms—not simply protected and admired, but also, more crucially, ever free to pull away.

The memory caused her to sway into him. The hard warmth of his chest, the press of his hips . . . His grip on her chin, quick and clever and firm, tilted her face upward, giving him deeper access to her mouth. She opened to him, and swallowed the growl from his throat—

The kiss changed all at once. He crowded against her, pushed her back against the wall, an animal ferocity, almost a desperation, in how deeply he kissed her. She gripped his shoulders for balance, thrilling at the crush of his body—the flexing breadth of his shoulders beneath the soft nap of his jacket. His stubble rasped her skin. His hand found her buttocks through her skirts, palmed her, pulled her against him so she felt his readiness for her.

Her body clenched. Desire was a hard, insistent pulse, thrumming through all the spots he'd addressed so expertly last night. Her body knew its due now: it ached to be bared, to be handled and filled. She bit his lip, dug her fingers into his back.

Some rough noise came from him—he pulled her without warning away from the wall and lifted her onto the table. His palm cradled her skull as he laid her across it and pressed down over her. His fingers speared through her hair—a dozen stabbing pains along her scalp, pins popping free, the discomfort somehow magnifying the pleasure of his weight against her, his pelvis rocking into hers. She thrust upward against him. *Yes.* Pleasure beat through her now like a drum.

His palm found her calf, gripped it and squeezed. Possessiveness: it should have frightened her. But it didn't. *Take me*, she thought.

His hand smoothed up her leg, to the back of her knee, her thin stocking translating the rough, warm feel of his palm. She rolled against him, wanting these clothes gone, wanting his skin against hers. He thrust against her, but her skirts interfered. She reached down blindly, trying to claw them up. Her crinolines, her petticoats, trapped her. On an impatient noise, she tried to wrestle free.

Bright light spilled over them, falling through the skylight: the sun had broken free of the clouds.

He went still, his breath rasping into her mouth. And then, abruptly, he pulled away.

His withdrawal felt as shocking as ice water. She reached out to pull him back and caught a peculiar look on his face: pale and almost shocked.

He sidestepped her grip and turned away.

She sat up, bewildered. Her body felt abandoned— raw, throbbing, exposed. He was buttoning his coat, smoothing out his trousers. "What is wrong?"

He faced her, and the blank look on his face made her feel chilled. Gone, all evidence of tenderness and laughter. Of lust, or of any human feeling at all. "Nothing," he said.

"Then why . . . ?"

"We're in public."

Public? The door stood closed. The sight of it, of their undisputed privacy, caused some chemical shift inside her, tipping passion into embarrassed temper. "Nobody can see."

"I'm flattered by your eagerness." He inspected his shirt cuffs, smoothing them between thumb and forefinger. "But you will have to wait until tonight."

Her mouth opened. *She* would have to wait? He made her sound like some blowsy tart!

He glanced up. Heaven knew what she looked like. It caused him to take a deep breath.

"*You* started this," she said.

His jaw squared as he stared at her. "Very well," he said at length. "Lie back and I'll finish it for you, if that will improve your mood."

Did he mean . . . ?

She scrambled to her feet. Moments ago, she had felt brazen and bold. Now he made her feel judged for it—a pathetic, desperate strumpet. "Spare me your *kindness*."

"Good. Tonight, then." He turned for the door.

"But I won't be blindfolded."

He paused but did not turn back.

"Or"—even saying it made her flush—"tied. It's not decent." If this 'public' setting was not decent in *his* view, then neither were restraints in *hers*. "I won't tolerate that again."

He turned back, lifting one shoulder in an elegant shrug. "As you wish. Perhaps once will have done the trick anyway."

The way he said it! As though bedding his wife were some onerous duty to be endured with teeth gritted! But he had not seemed repelled just now. Not until he'd pulled away and stared at her as though *she* were the deviant between them.

"We must hope so," she said coldly. "For I won't submit to your depravity again."

His brows lifted. And then he laughed very softly. "Yes. I am depraved. I cannot argue it."

How had this turned so suddenly? She felt miserable, but it was not *she* who owed an apology. Indeed, it was never she—yet somehow *she* was the only one who seemed to care.

"I have business with one of the artists," he said. "You can entertain yourself, I hope?"

She knocked the wrinkles from her skirts. "You may look for me in the stables. Take *all* the time you need."

CHAPTER NINE

Four years earlier

"*I* don't understand why you're in such a hurry, Anna." Moira pulled back her club and let fly. The ball popped into the air and landed not a foot away from its original position, and Moira let out a groan.

A damp breeze whipped over them, stirring the grass and shoving clouds swiftly across the darkening sky. It had started out a fine day for golf at Muirswood Links, but Anna expected them both to be drenched within the hour. No matter: victory would have come long beforehand. Moira was a terrible golfer.

Anna retrieved the gutty, one of the newfangled gutta-percha productions, painted white, more resistant to dampness than the old leather balls stuffed with feathers. She ordered them from a factory in Glasgow by the thousand. "Try again. More slowly this time. Keep your eye on where you mean to aim."

Sighing, Moira repositioned the ball. "What I mean is, why not let him court you properly? A summer of romance, then the autumn to plan a wedding."

"There's no need to wait."

"This is about Rawsey, isn't it?" Moira looked up. "The island has been there—"

"Eye on your target, coz."

Moira rolled her eyes and obeyed. "The island has stood for thousands of years. I believe it will survive *one* more winter without your improvements."

Anna sighed. None of her cousins seemed to understand that Rawsey was not Rawsey without the islanders. That community, its decent, rough-spun kindness and honest industry, had been as much her family during her youth as any of her cousins. She could not fail them, nor could she love Rawsey without them. It fell to her to find them a way to make a living there, and that task couldn't wait.

But there was no point wasting her breath once more on explanations. "It's done," she said. "Oh, bravo!" For Moira had at last sunk her ball.

With their caddy, a young towheaded boy, on their heels, they strolled to the next putting green. "What do you mean, it's done?" Moira asked.

"I put out an advertisement yesterday for a schoolmaster and a builder. All that remains is to acquire the lumber."

"Anna!" Moira looked exasperated. "You know Uncle Peter is watching like a hawk. He'll be so grumpy if he finds out. Do you want a four-hour lecture?"

Smirking, Anna took a fresh ball from the caddy. Their uncle's trusteeship of Rawsey would remain in place until the hour Anna was wed, and Uncle Peter was a man of old-fashioned convictions who would rant terribly if he discovered her conniving. More to the point, he spat terribly when he spoke, and every member of the family under forty had a tale to tell of being boxed into a corner and soaked by his scolding. "He won't find out, though." She swung her club, and the ball rolled obediently into the hole.

"How do you *do* that?"

"The hole is ten yards away, Moira. It really isn't difficult. Now, if we were on the men's course—"

"What if Lockwood changes his mind, Anna? What will you do then?"

Anna laughed. "He won't."

"How can you be so sure? He's practically a stranger. And an Englishman, at that."

Anna handed her club to the caddy and put her hands on her hips. "What's all this sudden concern? *You* were the one who encouraged me to dance with him that night at the Camerons'."

Moira blew a dark strand of hair out of her eyes. The wind, picking up, blew it right back. "And *did* you dance? Because if so, I never noticed. In fact, from what I saw, one moment you were ignoring him, the next you were engaged!"

"Then you weren't watching closely enough."

But Moira had worked herself up into a lather and paid no heed to this remark. "And this nonsense with the marriage contract!" She whacked her ball off into the hedgerow, and the caddy, with laudably straight-faced restraint, set another down for her. "Mama says you're bringing a *dowry* to him. She says it's practically medieval."

Anna would not call it a dowry, more like a wise investment. His accountants and solicitors had met with hers, and proposed that twenty thousand pounds would clear Liam's inherited debts.

But why simply clear them? His estates consisted of

THE SINS OF LORD LOCKWOOD

some of England's richest agricultural lands. Why not equip them to turn a profit? Anna had instructed her solicitor to counter with a more appropriate figure—thirty thousand, to be paid in several installments, a third of it earmarked for agricultural improvements.

"I have no idea what Auntie Liz means," she told Moira.

"She says you have a clause requiring that neither of you may constrain each other's free movement, nor accuse each other of abandonment."

Auntie Liz had been eavesdropping at the study door. "Yes, well, I don't want a husband who complains when I disappear to Rawsey."

"Mama says a marriage can't work when it's treated as a business deal."

Anna snorted. "Oh, so she thinks me *unromantic*. Yes, I'd forgotten what an idealist Auntie is!"

Moira caught back a laugh. Her mother knew how to pinch a shilling till it shrieked, and had informed Moira that she would not be allowed to fall in love with anybody worth less than ten thousand a year. "Touché. But Anna, really—why are you so certain of *this* man? So soon? I thought you wanted to marry a Scot."

From over the hedges came a masculine hoot. Anna put her finger to her lips, and Moira, wide-eyed, nodded. The ladies' links converged with the gentlemen's course here, by the high hedgerows that boxed in Traitor's Corner.

They listened hard as the dim voices resolved into conversation: Anna caught her cousin David's voice, cheerful and lilting, explaining the origin of the Corner's name to Lockwood. "Here's the spot where the bastard Roger Johns betrayed Bonnie Prince Charlie's invasion plans to an English spy. Some say he was brought back here to be hanged, but that happy rumor hasn't ever been confirmed."

"Alas," came Lockwood's dry reply. "So what you mean to say is, I should have brought roses to leave in homage."

"Oh ho!" David sounded scandalized.

Moira, for her part, cast Anna a scowl. "Plenty of Scots," she muttered, "would let you go where you please. No need to settle."

"Lockwood's only teasing." Anna hiked up her skirts and clambered onto a nearby boulder. "Hullo there!"

Moira's brother's head shot up over the hedgerow. "Hark! The traitor's ghost!"

A moment later, Lockwood's head joined David's, his amber eyes crinkled in a smile. "How goes it in the ladies' links?"

"Tedious," she said, and ignored Moira's sniff. "All putting green, no chance to drive."

"Sounds well suited to Lockwood." This from David, grinning. "The lad couldn't hit a ball if his life depended on it."

"Lies," Lockwood said calmly. "I can hit them well enough. It's sinking them that's the problem."

"Meanwhile, I'm eight for eight," David gloated.

"I'll believe *that* when I see it," Moira said.

Anna clapped. "A splendid idea! Give us one minute—we'll join you."

"No, we won't," said Moira, and the caddy, clutching his hat in his hands, added his own objection:

"No ladies on the gents' course, strict orders of the club keeper."

Anna snorted. "The club keeper used to feed me bottles

of milk when I was too small to walk," she told the boy, "and to spank me when I was misbehaving as a toddler. He's welcome to try it again, but he'll have to catch me first."

The boy looked peaked as he clawed a hand through his corn silk hair. "My lady, I'll be sacked if I let you on that course."

"Then pretend you've lost us," Anna said. "Take our clubs, too, with half a sovereign for your trouble."

That made the boy perk up. "You want me to take the clubs?"

"That's right. We'll use the gentlemen's."

"You won't be able to lift 'em—even my putter," David predicted.

"You'll eat those words," Anna said. "Send away your caddy, with a half sovereign for him as well."

"You'd best pay me back for that!"

"I will." She seized Moira's arm, tugging her cousin down the length of the hedgerow, then shoving her, despite Moira's protest, through a narrow patch worn by the passage of deer.

The gentlemen's course was several times larger, an endless rolling field dotted with sandy bunkers and gentle hillocks, that spilled uninterrupted to the cliffs fronting the Firth of Forth. Anna took a moment, breathing deeply of the salt air, to admire the view: sunlight glimmering on the water, a distant ship passing beneath the low clouds, its white sails unfurled and billowing.

Then she turned smiling to face the others. Moira, arms crossed, was casting anxious glances down the links toward the distant clubhouse. But the other holes stood empty of players, and the caddies were scampering toward each other, leaping and crowing over their profits, so Anna felt it unlikely they would betray their benefactors.

"A foursome," she decided. "Ladies against gents? Or will the siblings march together to their doom?"

"I will play with my brother," Moira said over David's guffaw. "That way, you might get to know your *fiancé* better."

Lockwood, catching Anna's eye, lifted a brow in silent question: Moira's tone had been pointed. She shook her head in reply. "Very well," she said. "Who will go first?"

"Losers first," David said instantly, and handed Lockwood a driver.

Alas, defeat was all but inevitable. As they worked their way down the course, a light misting rain staining the grass an emerald green, Moira played the spoilsport by ceding all her shots to her brother—"Women aren't allowed on this course! I am only following the rules!"— while Lockwood, for all his raw power, demonstrated the rank flaw of all beginners: he could not aim.

"That one's gone into the water," Anna said, shielding her eyes as she tracked the flight of the gutty into the horizon. "Remarkable! Four hundred yards, would you say?"

"Perhaps longer," David allowed.

"Given practice, Lockwood, you could be a marvelous—"

"A pity your army didn't have your aim," David interrupted, his taunting smile directed at Lockwood as he lined up his next shot.

Anna kicked his ball away. "How many times have

you played golf, David? Lockwood had never lifted a club until today."

"No, let him have his fun now," said Lockwood with a grin. His errant aim did not seem to have dampened his mood, which made him the first man Anna had known who did not sulk when losing. "Tomorrow, we go shooting—we'll see then whose aim is better."

"At least David will be less insufferable," Moira muttered. "He is *far* less saucy when his opponent is armed."

David's next stroke was a piece of beauty, the ball arcing in a strong clean line toward the next hole, landing only yards short of the green. Everybody applauded, and then Moira complained of the distance to walk— "I much prefer the ladies' links, this course goes on *forever*"—and David hauled her up and tossed her over his shoulder, causing her to squeal and beat him about the head as he stalked onward.

Lockwood, for his part, was carrying both bags of clubs—no inconsiderable weight. Yet he readjusted them as if they weighed nothing, in order to offer his arm to Anna. They strolled onward over the wet grass, his bearing as elegant as though he escorted her at a ball.

"You make a fine beast of burden," Anna remarked. "Were you athletic at university?"

"I fenced and rowed for my college. Still do row, when I have the chance."

"I'll let Moira know. She was worried our sons would be sickly, thanks to the English blood."

"Our sons," he murmured. His gaze caught hers, and the heat in his look made her blush. "I doubt any son of yours would be less than strapping, Lady Forth. When I saw you drive that last ball, I realized why they have a separate course for ladies: you showed up your own cousin."

She grinned. David had made no remark on that shot, but she'd outdone him by fifty yards. "Yes, well. Oats and haggis are my secret weapons."

The air was darkening, the mist thickening into true rain. A drop splattered the tip of her nose, and Lockwood leaned forward and kissed it away.

Her stomach fluttered. "On a golf course?" she murmured. "Bold of you."

"Anywhere," he said huskily. "I am . . . deranged by you."

Ahead, David dropped Moira without care or warning, and his sister's outraged shrieks split the air as she staggered to catch her balance. "I'm done with this!" she cried. "It's raining now, and I refuse—oh! Oh! It's Murray!"

Anna turned to follow her pointing finger. Sure enough, the club keeper was running across the field toward them, shouting with fist upraised.

"Run!" cried David, and grabbed Moira's arm, dragging her shrieking toward the split in the hedges.

Anna could not breathe for laughing. Old Murray had not run so hard in thirty years. "We'll be—expelled," she managed. "And knowing Murray—bullwhipped beforehand."

"First he has to catch us." Settling the straps of the golf bags more securely around his shoulder, Liam seized her hand—but she resisted, tugging him in the opposite direction of her cousins.

"This way," she said. "We can hide, then circle around and slip back to the clubhouse."

Anna's father and uncles had golfed at this club throughout her childhood, and there was not an inch of the parkland she did not know. At the edge of the woods stood a shed where the groundskeeper kept his tools. The door swung open beneath her shove, admitting them into a cool, dry space mounded with sacks of soil and shovels and hoes. Rain pounded now on the tin roof, a thundering clatter that softened as Lockwood pulled the door shut.

He laid down the bags of clubs, then joined her at the small window, where she was watching Mr. Murray shove his way through the hedgerow.

"Oh, they're caught," she said with a wince as the old man dragged David back through the hedges by the scruff of his shirt. "Ha! He still treats us all as though we were children."

"Did that man really spank you when you were little?"

She slanted Lockwood a laughing look. "Why? Do you imagine him too kind, or *me* too well behaved?"

"Neither," he said, smiling.

"Quite right, on both counts."

"But I do think it odd that your father would have let him raise his hand to you."

She stepped back from the window. A sack stuffed with netting made a soft makeshift stool, which she sank onto with a sigh. "My father let anybody parent me who wanted to. He wasn't very good at it himself, you know. So he was always glad of the help." She smiled. "And I *was* awful. I still remember—he'd left me behind in the clubhouse while he went to play his rounds, and I was sulking awfully about it. So I pulled down the display of trophies, thinking that would force him to come back. You can't blame old Murray for losing his temper."

He crouched down before her, an easy athletic grace to the steadiness of his balance on the balls of his feet.

She envied men their clothes. Her own skirts were sodden and heavy, but the rain had rolled right off his waxed trousers.

"Perhaps not," he said. "But . . . your father left you there alone. Was that a commonplace habit?"

A single raindrop clung to his brow. As she watched, it dropped onto the high point of his cheekbone, then began a slow, luxuriant slide down the hollow of his cheek. He had beautiful bones. Full, chiseled lips. It was a wonder no English girl had snagged him already. Thank God nobody had snagged him.

What had he asked? Ah, yes: her father. "He was out of his depths," she said. "My mother died in childbirth, you know. He hardly knew what to do with a little girl. But he made do, and struggled on, though I was not the easiest child by any estimation."

"You loved him," he said softly. "Very much."

"Yes. And I was glad he took me wherever he went. When I was little, at least." Then, harassed about the seemliness of toting his little daughter to golf courses and clubs, he'd chosen a different tack. "Anyway, he sent me off to the aunts soon thereafter."

"The aunts? Which aunts? Lady Moira's mother?"

"Sometimes my aunt Elizabeth, yes." She smiled. Poor Auntie Liz. Her daughters, Moira and Celia and Laura, had not prepared her for a girl of Anna's temperament. "It was a kind of joke in the family—who could manage to keep me longest. I didn't make it easy."

"It seems rather . . . lonely for a child, to be passed around. Never to have a steady home."

She hesitated. "It was sometimes lonely. But I grew accustomed to it. It . . ." She took a breath. "It was hard when *he* left. But I never minded the aunts."

His kiss on her cheek was softer than a whisper. "You will never be left again," he said. "Not unless you choose it."

The promise opened some unsteady pit in her stomach. That was not what their marriage contract had been drawn up to guarantee.

As their gazes held, the silence between them felt abruptly weighted—liable to collapse into a conversation that would feel dangerous, exposing.

He'd made a casual comment, spoken without forethought. He probably didn't mean it as a promise.

But perhaps he did.

Perhaps she *wanted* him to mean it.

Marry, first. She swallowed. *Marry, before you test it by asking.*

"I could always count on Gram, though," she said with forced brightness. "Winters in Rawsey were my favorite." She made herself smile. "And now, thanks to you, I'll be able to count on Rawsey whenever I like."

For a moment, his regard remained serious and frowning. She touched his lips, gently urging them up at the corners. "Smile," she whispered.

He kissed her fingertips, then caught her palm and held it to his mouth, breathing deeply of her. "Rawsey will be yours." His lips moving against her skin raised goose bumps, caused her stomach to flip. "And anywhere else you might like. Whenever, wherever."

"Yes." That, he had promised in the contract. He would not interfere with her freedom of movement.

"Will you come to Rawsey?" she heard herself ask. "In the winter sometime?"

This laugh sounded genuine. "I could think of better climates for the winter."

Her stomach sank.

No, *no*, his reply should not disappoint her. Their marriage was not designed for companionship, but to free each other from burdens: he, from the debts that crippled his estates and restricted his travels, and she, from legal impediments to her ownership of the island, and from the societal expectations that constrained unmarried women.

But she'd felt so sure, a moment ago, that he wanted differently . . .

She took back her hand. "Of course you'll want to be in Nice or Rome, somewhere south."

"Better weather, yes. But not better places, if you aren't there." And before she could even think to check her smile, he leaned forward and kissed her.

They had kissed a good deal in the eight weeks since they'd left Rawsey. He'd gone back to England for a fortnight, but since his return, they'd found dozens of opportunities to meet. Spring was a festive time in Edinburgh. They met in ballrooms, over dinner tables, at musicales and garden parties. Anna's aunt Elizabeth, her nominal chaperone, was suffering from her annual headaches, and could not muster the energy to chase and scold her. "You're a mad girl who will do as you please," Auntie Liz had told her the afternoon she'd emerged from the Stromonds' garden with leaves in her hair. "Mind you don't drag Moira into your nonsense— that's all I ask."

And so they flirted their way through the New Town and Old Town, and slipped into empty boxes at the opera to kiss in the dark. Anna felt as though she had been walking through a dream this season, fevered and magical. But not until now, in this tin-roofed shed with the rain beating down, had she truly found herself alone with him.

Anything could happen.

She lay back on the floor and pulled him down atop her. He smelled so good, like an enchantment, though each note of his scent was very ordinary—soap and pomade gotten from a high-street chemist, starch from the laundry, sweat from their outdoor exertions. She breathed in deeply and felt her head swim. He bit her lower lip and she squirmed against him, wishing away her clothes, wishing she could imprint his skin on hers, carry that sweaty soapy musk with her, to sniff at odd moments when she found herself bored or fatigued in company. It was better than coffee to make her senses leap and sharpen.

He kissed divinely. It got better and better. He used his lips to open her mouth wider, then angled his head and did something clever that sealed her lips to his. They kissed long and deep as she squirmed beneath him, wanting . . . something . . .

This edgy need was her new companion. At night, she fell asleep imagining his mouth, his hands. Near him, she all but vibrated, her skin magnetized, drawn to his, singing in his presence. Even now, as he kissed her, she wanted more. What if this hunger never ebbed? What if it could not be satisfied? What if she was broken, somehow, fevered and hopeless of a cure?

He did not seem hurried. He kissed her as though there were no other end but this, to taste her deeply, her lips and cheeks and the hollow where her pulse beat in her throat. When he was done with her, sometimes her knees trembled, but *he* never trembled, nor seemed flustered or startled. Was this so one-sided, then? Sometimes he almost seemed *amused* by the way she trembled for him. He said he dreamed of her, too, but what if this was only a joke to him?

She pushed against him, hoping to feel the proof of his excitement. But before she could find it, he twisted his hips away. When she tried again, he bit her lower lip in punishment, which made her gasp, then tracked his mouth to her ear, nibbling at her lobe.

His hand smoothed over her waist. She wanted it higher—or lower. She caught it, and felt its steadiness as it turned in hers, gripped her, and held her still.

Her breathing was ragged—his, inaudible. Once, she had heard him pant. Two days ago, in the galleries at the Royal Scottish Academy, she had dragged him behind a pillar. After a minute, his hand had slipped beneath her neckline, and as he'd cupped her breast, she'd heard him hiss out a breath.

She carried his hand now to her chest. "Touch me," she whispered.

The edge of his teeth scraped her throat. She heard him swallow, and then, praise be, his hand slipped beneath her neckline, delving under her corset and chemise.

She gasped. It felt better even than it had in the museum. His palm so rough, callused, and hot . . . His thumb found her nipple, chafing her, and her body tightened, her belly twisted, a pulse started between her legs. She arched up and clamped his hand in place, and with her free hand, she swept over his back, down his ribs, to his muscular, flexing buttock.

He went rigid. His pelvis rocked into hers once—yes, at last, there was his desire—before he thrust himself aside, removing his hand from her breast as he went.

He threw himself down beside her, flat on his back, and when, after a minute, he turned to kiss her again, a great pique sizzled through her and she twisted away.

He caught her face and turned it back. "Behave," he murmured, and dragged her into another kiss, not permitting her to struggle.

She had never behaved: he could ask her aunts if he doubted it. Her body was aching, and his hands and mouth were the cure. Did *he* not ache?

She had listened to her married cousins' gossip, late after a night spent drinking whisky and punch. She knew how to make him want her.

She reached down his body swiftly, before he could notice, and grasped the bulge tenting his trousers.

He made a choked noise, then caught her hand and pulled it back up, planting a kiss on her wrist. "Patience," he said roughly.

"Why? Nobody's about—"

"Because I say so."

She yanked free and sat up.

After a moment, he, too, unfolded himself off the floor. Once he was sitting, long legs stretched out and crossed at the ankle, he said, "You're put out."

"You are not in charge of me."

The rain abruptly softened. As the drumming died down, the silence felt shockingly loud between them. He tipped his head as he studied her.

"Fair enough," he said at last. "Is that your only complaint?"

"No."

"May I ask the other?"

"You know it."

"Let me hear it anyway."

"You . . ." Not for the first time she cursed her coloring, which showed her blushes so clearly. "I dislike being the weaker one."

His brows lifted. "Weaker one? In what regard are you weak?"

She blew out a breath. "You're so . . . unmoved."

He stared at her for a moment, and then shook his head, a slight uncomprehending shake. "I am *far* from unmoved. You just felt proof of it."

"And you knocked my hand away."

His mouth opened, began to smile, abandoned the smile, and then closed again. A snort of amusement came from him. "It is my devout wish not to deflower you in a toolshed. I assure you, had I not moved your hand, I might have forgotten that rapidly."

"Then forget it!"

He sat back as though to see her better, his amber eyes wide with amazement. "You wish to—here? Now?"

"I am sick," she said furiously, "of feeling like this— so hot and fevered and . . . *shaky*."

He put his hand to his mouth, staring at her. Then came his laughter, hoarse and soft. "My God. Anna, I do not think you even know how you compliment me. Be careful: my vanity may become unmanageable."

"And now you're laughing," she said, but with less sharpness, for it was impossible to keep her temper when he was looking at her so warmly. "I dislike feeling like an ignorant naïf. Explain the joke, if you please."

He dropped his hand, revealing his grin. "The joke is that I am the luckiest man alive. And the least deserving of it, surely. Lie back, now. I'll cure this fever of yours. But no," he added huskily as he came over her again, "I won't deflower you. For that, I'll need a proper bed—and a great deal more time."

She squinted up at him, suspicious. "Then what—oh," she said softly as his hand closed around her ankle, his grip hot and firm.

"It is a wonderful thing," he said as his hand climbed higher, and his reach permitted him to lie down beside her and speak directly into her ear, "that I might be the one to show you this." His palm massaged her thigh, and her breath caught as he continued. "For now you will think of me whenever you do it yourself."

"Do—" *What*, she was going to ask, but the word slipped back down her throat as his hand found the split in her drawers, and he touched her where even she did not touch herself.

"This," he murmured, his breath hot against her ear. "Practice this when I am not with you." His fingers delved through her folds, finding a spot that made her body clench. "Then, on our wedding night, you can show me what you've learned."

His touch was delicate, light, probing—then, as she gasped, he whispered, "There. Yes?" And at her wordless nod, he pressed his smile into her temple and stroked and pressed more firmly, setting up a rhythm that pitched her fever higher, to a careening, desperate gallop. She twisted, reaching for him—his free hand found hers, clutching it hard, holding it to his cheek as he stroked her, as he whispered words of praise, compliments to her, to the noises she made as she gasped and twitched and arched against him.

The crisis came on her first as a rivulet of sensation washing through her, building, building, and then—climaxing, glorious, glory indeed.

His palm pressed hard into her, holding her steady as she trembled. And then, when the pleasure at last settled and faded, he said, "Look at me."

She found herself unwilling to open her eyes. He was still touching her below. She was wet—she could feel it. It was dreadfully mortifying. She knew she had gone red as a beet.

"Look at me," he said gently. "Anna."

She was no coward. She had asked for this.

On a ragged breath, she rolled her head toward his. His face so close that their lashes tangled, he said, "You are beautiful. And I thank you. I will live on this memory until our wedding night."

Shyness fell away. She clasped his cheek, amazed by him.

"Two weeks to wait," she murmured. "No fortnight will ever feel so long."

CHAPTER TEN

London, 1861

The firm of Kent, Hartsock, and Witt had a blemishless reputation. It had represented Anna's family from her grandfather's time, and Sir Charles Kent had once made the long trip to Edinburgh to draft her marriage contract. But she had never visited his offices.

Thus did she find herself befuddled, on the curb in Lincoln's Inn Fields, by her first sight of the Gothic house. Set somewhat back from the street behind wrought iron gates, the house boasted crumbling iron balconies, a castlelike turret, and an ancient weathervane, which in the sudden strong wind did not swing toward the west so much as lurch toward it, shrieking loudly as decades of accumulated rust forced it to a premature halt.

"You sure this is the right address?" called down Henneage, Lockwood's coachman.

Henneage had driven the horses with such abominable speed that Anna had felt the carriage wheels leave the ground during turns. "Learn to drive," she snapped, and clutched her queasy gut as she stalked into the office.

Inside the small, square lobby, a deep hush prevailed, punctured only by the squeak of Anna's footsteps on the waxed wooden floor. Gentle, lemony light diffused through the tall windows swaddled in yellow silk, casting a cheerful tint over oil paintings of bewigged men in dark court robes.

At the center of the lobby sat a clerk, who stuffed the remnants of a jam pastry into his mouth before linking his hands together atop the polished surface of his mahogany desk, posing like a man who was not trying, frantically, to finish chewing.

Anna turned away, pretending to admire the furnishings, in order to give him a moment to swallow. A faded painting covered the low, domed ceiling: Lady Justice, in Roman stola, holding aloft her scales—and wearing a blindfold.

This sight did not improve Anna's temper. She had not spoken to her husband in two days. Unwilling to surrender his ropes and ties, he had declined to visit her bedroom. At breakfast, she ate alone. Anna spent the evenings with her cousin, lest Lockwood have the opportunity to spurn her for dinner as well.

"May I help you?" came the clerk's inquiry.

She turned back. The pastry had left a jam mustache on the clerk's upper lip. "Yes. I'm here to speak with Sir Charles."

"Appointment?"

"No, but—"

His overloud sigh cut her off. "No admission without appointment. How many times must I say it today?"

The door creaked open behind her. In waltzed a rotund blond man, who doffed his tall hat to etch a sarcastic bow to the clerk. "Hartsock about?"

"Oh, to be sure. In his office."

That did not sound like a man with an appointment. Anna watched him toddle off into the depths of the house before drawing herself straight and facing the clerk again. "You will tell Sir Charles that Lady Forth is here."

The clerk tapped the ledger that sat open in front of him. "It isn't *I* who makes the decisions. This appointment book is what does it. And I see no mention of . . . Lady Forth, was it?" His intonation, paired with the slight lift of his brow, bespoke grave doubts concerning the legitimacy of her title.

"Yes," she said coolly. "The Countess of Forth, to be precise. Sir Charles will be most glad to see me."

"Alas, he can't be disturbed today. I suggest you go home and write a request—"

Here he broke off, for the door had swung open again, admitting a ruddy lad in a rumpled suit, who chewed on an unlit cigar. This man's wink at the clerk caused him to laugh. "What ho, Rollo," the clerk exclaimed. "Back from Margate already?"

"Come to say hullo to the lads," Rollo replied, and shoved his hands into his pockets as he strolled past them.

"So many appointments," Anna said flatly.

The clerk nodded. "Indeed. We're a very great firm, ma'am."

"Your ladyship."

He frowned. "Ah . . . right. Well, as I said, you would do well to go home and write for an—"

She slapped down one of the calling cards she'd had

printed last week. Her hand was shaking, a sight that only soured her temper further. She retrieved her hand and clutched it behind her back. "I will see Sir Charles at once."

The clerk loosed a long-suffering sigh, glanced at the card, then gave her an alarmed second look. Swallowing, he rose and hastened into the hall.

This victory, perversely, only worsened her mood. Lady *Forth* was not worth his time, but Lady *Lockwood* made him jump. Was it Lockwood's title that commanded respect? Surely it was not the man himself.

The next minute, Sir Charles was hastening into the hallway, trim and dapper in pinstriped trousers and a dark morning coat, his silver hair slicked flat against his head—no sign of his useless clerk. "Forgive me, forgive me," he said rapidly. "That boy is new. I'll have a word with him, I promise you."

"It's quite all right," she said stiffly, and allowed him to escort her down the long, dark hall into his office, which offered a handsome view of the small garden that ran alongside the building.

As soon as she settled into a wing chair, she felt herself relaxing. Sir Charles was the very picture of legal authority: painfully erect, magisterially wrinkled. His thick-lensed spectacles magnified the grave and penetrating quality of his gaze, which had held on to hers four years ago without a flicker of surprise or judgment as she'd explained her unusual requirements of a husband.

"I am glad you called," he said as he took his seat. "I had just started a letter to you. Tea?"

"No, thank you." She was not in the mood for any

courtesies. "What was the letter to say? Have the Mac-Cauleys decided to sue for breach of contract?"

"It won't be necessary," he said, beaming.

"You've located Mr. Roy, then?"

"I have put an end to the search."

She stared. "What do you mean? I don't understand."

"Ah. It seems you haven't yet read the *Times* today." She caught the newspaper he slid across his desk. "Top right corner," he said.

It took a moment to understand her eyes.

The Great Western Caledonia Railway—the company that had leased the beach at Clachaig—did not actually exist.

With growing astonishment, she read onward. The land had indeed been leased—its owners, the Mac-Cauleys, described the lessor as a dark-haired gentleman, well spoken, with a city accent. *But we did think it curious when no engineers came to survey the land,* Mr. MacCauley was quoted as saying. *Nor did they ever make good on their promised payment.*

Meanwhile, over the course of the last six months, tens of thousands of shares in the company had been sold to investors—most of them ordinary citizens, driven to high hopes by the grand campaign that had advertised the coastal route.

Sometime over the last fortnight, those shares had been liquidated in secret, the company disbanded. The shareholders now clamored for the return of their money, with little hope of recompense.

She swallowed. "And Mr. Roy . . . ?"

"A false name, so far as I can tell." Sir Charles shook his head, reached for his pipe, then remembered his company and laid it down again. "And to think I'd planned to expand our search into England! We would have been looking for decades."

"How horrible," she said softly. "This journalist writes that a group of widows invested their pensions into this make-believe company."

"Alas, they won't have been the first. I read of similar frauds every month now. 'Railway mania,' they call it. But, on a happier note"—Anna looked up, startled—"your beach is safe."

"Yes." It felt tremendously selfish to call that a blessing. But she would not waste the chance. "Make an offer on the land, please. I would not like the MacCauleys to lease it again."

He smiled. "I've already prepared it."

"And, whatever it costs, please set up an endowment for double that sum to go to these widows."

"Very commendable of you, my lady."

She did not feel commendable. In this plush, comfortable office, with the light fixtures made of brass and her seat of thick rich leather, she felt almost ashamedly fortunate.

"Triple," she said. "Triple the endowment. And please invite applications from any woman defrauded, not just the widows." She rose. "Meanwhile, if the MacCauleys balk, offer anything it takes. I won't be dependent on the goodwill of strangers to reach my island."

"A sound policy." Sir Charles rose, extending his hand to her. But she wasn't quite done yet.

Most women had so few choices. But she was one of the few in this world who had been given the fortune needed to protect herself, and the freedom to act.

"Also, one other small thing." Her throat felt tight.

"These new divorce laws—I gather they have made the matter much easier? No order of Parliament required, is that so?"

Sir Charles had professional expertise in masking his surprise. "I . . . yes, my lady. A special court now adjudicates such matters."

"Excellent. I know the husband must only prove his wife's adultery. And the lady? His adultery *and* abandonment, would that serve?"

"If there is proof, my lady—yes."

She could not imagine that Lockwood had remained celibate these last four years. "Would there be a way to protect a Scottish fortune, should an English husband be found at fault?"

Sir Charles tipped his head. "I am not certain such a case has been tried yet. The laws are very new. But I could look into the matter."

"Excellent." She took a shaking breath. "Please have a dossier prepared on these questions. You may send it to me in care of my cousin Lady Moira Douglas, on Green Street."

"Yes, my lady."

A minute later, Anna passed back through the entry hall, where the clerk shrank into himself and tried to look busy with his appointment book.

Her mood should have been brighter: she had her beach. And provision for ownership of the island required only that a woman be married when she came into possession of it, not that she remain married afterward. Her fortune was Scottish, her lawyer excellent; *she* was in control of her future.

So she smiled at the clerk, a bright, wide smile designed to forgive him and set him at ease.

His relief was almost comical. He nodded gratefully, and bowed from his seat.

Perhaps she had a secret talent for acting, then. She did not feel happy in the least.

That afternoon, an hour after asking the manservants yet again where their master had gone, Anna received a note from her husband, on his club's stationery, informing her of his intention to visit Hanover Square Rooms that evening.

> *I hope this satisfies your continued curiosity*
> *concerning my whereabouts. I enclose a map*
> *of Hanover Square, with my future location*
> *marked by an X.*
> *You are, of course, welcome to join me, if you*
> *wish, though I do not intend to stay for long.*

The hand-drawn map confirmed that his artistic talents had not profited by his journeys abroad. Anna shredded the drawing into small pieces, which she carried into his rooms to scatter across his bed.

After another hour spent fuming, and then a long nap, she decided to write a note to Moira proposing yet another dinner—then remembered, almost too late, that Moira herself was hosting a dinner tonight, for which Anna had claimed to be otherwise engaged. In truth, Moira's husband took these dinner parties as excuses to drone on for hours about his racehorses, while his guests, picked carefully for their keen opinions on racing bills, the Derby, and the Ascot, would no doubt insist on hearing the pedigree of each horse in Anna's stable back to Charlemagne's time.

Hanover Square Rooms sounded preferable.

Anna dressed severely that evening, to show her estimation of her former hopes for marriage: a high-necked dress in a muted olive satin, black lace gloves, and jet earrings and bracelet. If Lockwood noticed the allusions of half mourning, he made no remark when she came down the stairs. "We will be very late," he said as he escorted her to the carriage, his face that of a distracted stranger. Once under way, he did his best to ignore her entirely, his face in profile as he brooded at the sights out the window.

It seemed impossible to believe she had touched that face so boldly at Lawdon. The silence now felt more dreadful for how easily they had laughed together then—and could have done again, she supposed, if only she had not declared against blindfolds and restraints.

But why did he require those props? Was the prospect of looking into her eyes so awful for him? The question swelled in her throat, and she choked it down with the aid of anger. A wife should not have to ask such questions of her husband. Her dignity forbade her to do it. He would be lucky if he remained her husband for long.

But the anger was hollow. Only this afternoon, napping fitfully in the cool of her bedroom, she had dreamed of what he'd done to her. How little she'd cared about the blindfold and restraints, once his lips and hands and body had touched hers.

Dignity? She had none. As the dream had dissipated and her eyes had opened, she'd found herself groping for rationalizations. He had always been unconventional: that was why she'd been drawn to him. That hot current that sang between their bodies deserved something wilder and rarer than convention, did it not? What harm in blindfolds and ties?

Gammon. The harm lay in his refusal to abandon them for *her* sake. In their youth, he had always decided the pace and shape of their intimate relations. She had permitted it, thought it natural, because his experience was greater than hers. But four years of independence had left her with a taste for decision making. And she had not married him to be led, or to have her whims subjugated to his. It would be equality or nothing.

Nor would she let his silence upset her. He was beautiful, with his burnished hair and sun-touched skin and uncanny whisky eyes. What of it? In fact, the purity of his profile, those chiseled lips and hawkish nose, should fill her only with contempt. He looked as though he belonged on some bronze coin cast to commemorate the invader. Men like him had sacked Scotland; why had she not anticipated a similar fate so long ago?

His forebears had needed to crush hers, grind them into the dust for centuries, before her family had at last submitted to English oversight.

She would not be silenced by *him*.

"I do not need to meet your cousin any longer," she said. "If you haven't yet extended an invitation to him, you need not trouble yourself."

He nodded once, but if it occurred to him to wonder at how her problem with the beach had been resolved, he did not ask about it.

Of course he didn't ask. Curiosity would have required that he care.

"How peculiar," she said, her voice cool, as though she had not been stewing for days now, growing angrier and angrier, not only with him but with herself, for still caring a whit. "You seem to have lost the power of speech. Was that my doing? What a talent; I had not suspected it of myself."

He took a long breath, as though it required bracing to turn and look at her. "Forgive me," he said. "My mind has been elsewhere."

How neatly he reminded her of her insignificance. "And where might your mind have gone?" she asked politely. "To all your very important duties, I suppose? The collecting of paintings, and the coddling of artists, and . . ." She had no idea what else he spent his time on. "Brandy at the club?"

The ghost of a smile flitted over his lips before slipping away. "In fact, the club has had a new shipment from France," he said. "Very young, but the red will age well. Fifty-seven was a fine year for the grapes."

He had no shame or even decency. When she remembered the noises she had made in his bed, she felt her skin crawl.

But she was more of an animal than her vanity could bear. She found herself staring at his lips, regardless.

She turned to the window. The streets were gray and wet, and along the curb, the lamplight reflected in the puddles was stippled by light rain. "Yes, well," she said. "You predicted that. About the grapes."

"Did I?" he asked after a moment.

"Yes, that was one reason why you said our first stop should be France." She cast him a taunting glance. "On our honeymoon."

She had thought him relaxed, but for a moment, his

mask slipped, his jaw tightening. He was no happier than she.

The next moment, his expression became opaque again. Aloof and indifferent.

But she'd scented blood now, and her spirits rose at the prospect of petty revenge. "You waged such a great campaign for the wonders of Paris," she said. "I found it very persuasive. Perhaps I'll take advantage of the route from Calais. I hear a lady might have a wonderful time in France, even—or especially—alone."

"You may do as you like," he said casually. "But traveling alone would be foolhardy. Perhaps your cousin would join you."

"Oh, Moira enjoys the season too much to pull herself away. And I would not like a companion—not for the kind of fun I mean to have."

He locked eyes with her. Yes, he had taken her meaning. If *he* would not visit her bed, a thousand other men would gladly serve in his place. "Be that as it may," he said quietly, "you will have a care for your safety. Or your *fun* will be over too soon."

"How good of you to show concern. But I assure you, I've had a great deal of practice in managing on my own. Almost four years, in fact."

He stared at her a moment longer, then turned back to the window. "I am not in the mood to spar."

"That wasn't sparring, Lockwood. It was an expression of surprise at your concern. I suppose you spent your years abroad worrying over me *terribly*."

His laughter did not sound amused. "Christ, Anna. What do you want me to say? That I don't give a damn? That you should run off and get yourself killed, with my applause?"

She fisted her hands in her skirts, where he could not see them. "The truth does less harm than a lie, I believe."

He faced her, his jaw like flint. "I do give a damn: I would prefer you alive. Though perhaps somewhat quieter. Shall we try a gag next time I bed you?"

Horror stole the retort from her tongue. He smiled at her, a slow, dark smile.

"Excellent," he said. "Just like that."

She cleared her throat. "Do you gag all your other women, too?"

He snapped shut the curtain, casting them into darkness. "Only when they annoy me."

Her fists clenched. "Which of them is your favorite? Miss Ashdown? Pardon me—what was her real name? Miss Martin."

His laugh sounded startled. "God save me. I assure you, that lady would not be gagged. Nor would I touch her if my life depended on it."

So Miss Martin would not be gagged, but his wife might? "Ah, *artists* are not subject to your depravities," she said bitterly. "How good to know. I suppose you prefer to hire your companions, then?"

"Christ," he said softly.

"I'm quite sure that God has nothing to do with it."

No reply.

"Prostitutes, then. I should have guessed." The words hurt, as though they cut her from the inside. But she would require proof of his infidelity to divorce him, so this conversation was necessary. "I imagine you *would* have to pay most women to accept such indignities." He paid them with *her* money, of course, for he'd had none of his own. "How much do they charge? Is it piecemeal, or do blindfolds and restraints count as a singular vice?"

"What fevered little fantasies you've been concocting," he murmured. "Alone in your bed—yes, I remember how poorly you dealt with failing to be satisfied. Are you frustrated, Anna? Have you forgotten what I taught you?"

Her blush burned. "I remember everything, Lockwood—including your reluctance to perform. Do you know, I'd imagined it was honor that kept you from bedding me at Muirswood Links! Instead, it was lack of a blindfold. Why . . ." She mimed a gasp of surprise. "Is *that* why you ran off on our wedding night? Too ashamed of your perversity? Poor dear! You should have told me. I'd probably have taken pity on you."

"You are baiting me," he said coolly. "It's amusing. Rather clumsy, but subtlety was never your strength."

Her laughter felt curdled. "Yes, what *was* my strength? For when I look back, all I can see is idiocy. Do you know, I thought you were a good, decent man—I thought you would *respect* me. Can you imagine? But even in this—in wanting a child, in wanting my marital rights—all you do is try to shame me for it."

The silence now felt fraught. She wished she could see his face. She would have known where to aim when she spat.

"You make me feel cheap for wanting to touch you—to *see* you, to behave as a wife to you. I have no notion when you decided to find me repugnant, but I will not be ashamed for—"

He moved all at once—springing from his bench, his

hand wrapping around her nape, his lips crushing into hers.

Shock lanced through her. His kiss was hot and furious, the middle of something rather than its beginning. His tongue lashed hers, his hard body crowding her backward, only the support of his palm holding her up as his weight bore down on her.

This assault should have frightened her: it showed how easily he could overpower her, how indifferent his coachman would be to any sounds of struggle within, how brutally his lips could part hers and take possession.

And yet, after a moment's startled shock, she was not frightened. She was *furious*. Rage swept over her like a hot electric wave.

She clawed her hands into his hair and gripped his head. She crushed her mouth harder into his, and bit his lip until she tasted blood, salted copper, his long overdue debt to her. He made some rough, hot sound in his throat—*encouragement*. His knee came up under her skirts, collapsing her crinolines, pinning her more firmly in place even as his mouth bore down.

They devoured each other, graceless as beasts—she pulled his hair until he growled; he nipped her lower lip and she turned her nails into his cheek as punishment, and still, *still*, she kept kissing him.

She was mad. This was madness. She did not care. He hauled her up, positioning her squarely on the bench as he went down on his knees in front of her. His rough palms trapped her face as he kissed her deeply, angrily.

No. *Desperately.* He kissed her as though she were about to slip away.

That desperation at last penetrated her fury. Her fingers loosened, confused. She licked his lip, a silent apology for her bite. His own mouth gentled, and his grip on her face loosened.

Wait—no. He was going to release her, withdraw. That wasn't what she wanted, either. She was in a misery, her desires tangled and unclear, but he'd been right: she needed satisfaction.

She turned her fingernails into his scalp and kissed him hard again. But it made no difference. He was easing from her grip.

Rage shifted, aimed now at herself. He had made her want him again. "Damn you—"

Her curse broke off on a gasp as his hot, dry hand found her calf beneath her skirts.

"Damned," he said, a hoarse agreement, and laid his open mouth on her throat as his hand slid up, gathering her skirts as it went, yards of heavy cloth.

Hallelujah.

Her head fell back as he sucked at her throat—from beneath her skirts he found her hips and lifted her, pulling her forward to the edge of the seat so her petticoats and crinolines no longer shielded her. He fitted himself firmly against her, rolling his pelvis against hers as their mouths met again. He needed no blindfolds to prepare himself: that was clear. She could feel the full, thick length of him against her.

Insanity. She had just spoken to her lawyer of a divorce! This was reckless, stupid in the extreme. But the way he rocked against her, the hot drugging taste of his mouth, his roaming hands—now slipping between their bodies, finding through the split in her drawers that spot that caused her to clench and moan—these sensations built and built. Reason slipped away.

She *wanted*. It need not be him—this fevered mouth, these clever hands, the feel of this muscled male body. In the darkness, he could have been anyone— more than a man, even; a creature from some hot dream, everywhere at once, manipulating and domi- nating her so skillfully in the dark. Now sucking her ear—now lifting her breast out to suckle rhythmically, unbearably—as below, he plucked and stroked her like an instrument, luring her outside her own good sense, turning her into a twisting, moaning, mindless knot of need.

His fingers pushed into her, a slight, insistent inva- sion; he stretched her with his fingers as he took her mouth again. *Don't stop*—words, thank God, she had no strength to speak. She was afraid he would stop—he had stopped at Lawdon, he could not stop again, she would not bear it—

The head of his cock brushed against her. *Yes.* As he filled her, she heard herself groan. *Animal.* She groped through a foam of silk and lace and linen, skirts bunch- ing between them, blindly hunting for—

His body, his muscular buttocks, heavy and flexing, filled her palms. His hips, pumping against her. She dragged him deeper inside her. She was an animal, who needed more of him—

He thrust deeply, seating himself inside her, and a sigh slipped from her. Now his lips moved softly, tenderly, on that secret spot beneath her ear. "Easy," he whispered, then took up a rhythm, shallow and then deeper, slower and then faster, tormenting her patiently, his discipline infuriating, tormenting, delicious. For long moments—minutes—he teased and bullied her this way, as she began to choke on the urge to beg, sobbing gasps that she would not turn into words, until at last she wrapped her legs around him and said, "*Please*."

He thrust into her deeply and hard, again and again, and she tightened all over, reaching—reaching—

There. Coiled tension burst. Gripping him, her face turned into his soft hair, she shuddered around him, and swallowed her own cries.

The carriage drew to a halt.

From outside came the noises of industry, a crowd: jingling tack, a cabman's shout, the clop of hooves, a burst of distant laughter, the muted chaos of a dozen conversations. The coach rocked slightly as a footman dismounted from his perch.

His cheek against hers felt damp and hot. His breath shuddered across her ear. Then, gradually, he detached from her.

Small movements, slow, as though he feared himself breakable. She watched through the darkness, made lighter by the blaze spilling from the building outside, as he closed his trousers. Righted his waistcoat and jacket. And then, with strong capable hands, ringless and tanned, he took hold of her ankles, one by one. He carried them back to the floor, and fitted her feet into her slippers. She was watching his face, but he did not lift it as he eased back to study her clothing. He would not meet her eyes.

His survey appeared to satisfy him. He took her by the waist and lifted her without warning, knocking down her skirts, smoothing them before resetting her on the bench.

The door shook. It was locked.

"My lord?" came the footman's voice from the curb.

Lockwood sat back down on the bench opposite. His expression was half concealed by shadow, his jaw locked tight.

"I have never wanted to shame you," he said very quietly. "Nor have I ever found you repugnant."

A delicate hope unfurled through her. "Then . . . if I say no more blindfolds, you—"

"I will respect your choice, as I have done since Lawdon. But, no, Anna—barring this exception, the terms have not changed."

Her hands curled into fists. "How much it must mean to you, to have the upper hand."

"I can't deny it," he said flatly.

She turned the lock, allowing the door to be opened.

He descended first, and when he pivoted back to help her down, she shrugged off his hand and reached instead for the footman's.

On the steps up to the concert hall, however, he took her arm without asking, and she would not make a scene. So she tried to ignore how every pore of her skin felt magnetized to his, so close by. How her knees still trembled from what he had done to her. How tears threatened, though she could not say why.

He took care to match his stride to hers. It seemed a mockery of her somehow. Or maybe he was performing chivalry for the sake of onlookers. She did not miss how every woman turned to note his arrival when they stepped inside the hall.

She could smell his skin. Her own seemed imprinted by the scent.

She forced herself to focus on the fine points of the

lobby. Most of it was very elegant, made of paneled pale walls outlined in gilt, lit by extravagant chandeliers. One corner had been blocked off by scaffolding, which was draped in a large canvas sheet. A group of idiots were poking the sheet with their canes, raising a great cloud of dust that caused Anna to sneeze.

"My lord," called a petite blonde from across the room, her voice full of laughter. "Is it not rather late for an entrance? The third act has begun."

"That is Lady Chad," Lockwood told Anna, then called back, his golden voice flexing with charm, "Fashionably late or nothing."

Nobody, listening to or looking at him, would guess he'd just ravished his wife. Clearly it had not moved him.

"Nothing would be preferable," Anna muttered.

"Do try not to be too Scottish, Anna."

She sneezed again. "I *beg* your pardon?"

"Miss Martin," he said as the ladies approached. "Countess, allow me to introduce my sist—"

"His wife," Anna said, sticking out her hand. *Sister!* Now it was clear that he wasn't unmoved: on the contrary, he was trying to provoke her. "Anna Wint—Devaliant, I suppose."

The other two women exchanged a marveling look. Then the brunette, Miss Martin, shook Anna's hand. "I am very glad to meet you, Countess."

So here was the artist whom Lockwood would never gag. What a fortunate woman! Anna beamed at her.

Lockwood made a noise of disgust. "Good God, are you still using that trick?"

She did not bother to look at him. "It's no trick, it's my bloody *smile*."

Lady Chad looked flustered by this curse, but Miss Martin's serene expression did not alter a whit. She had a gentle watercolor prettiness about her, only the vividness of her blue eyes hinting at the passion required to paint such nightmares. Those eyes studied Anna with a cool, unsparing thoroughness.

But the acuity of a woman's gaze would pose no trouble to Lockwood. He would simply keep it covered with a blindfold. "You'll be the artist, then?" she asked. "The one who he's promoting?"

Lockwood's grip tightened on her arm. "Keep your voice down," he said. "That's meant to be a secret."

"Oh, was she unaware she painted?" Anna gave Miss Martin's hand an exaggerated pat. "Do you also suffer from amnesia, then? Forgetting who you are, where you go. My husband knows all about that; perhaps he can suggest a remedy, as he seems to be able to dispel it at will."

"That's quite enough," Lockwood bit out, and pulled her away from the women.

From behind them came Lady Chad's voice. "Do come visit, Lady Lockwood!"

"Can't, I'm off to Paris tomorrow!" Anna called.

"The hell you are," Lockwood snarled.

"Whyever not? *You* set the terms, and *I* have refused them. What cause do I have to stay now?"

Over by the scaffolding, the group of rowdies crowed and hooted. Lockwood visibly startled at the noise, then tossed a furious look over his shoulder at them. The idiots were tugging on the canvas sheeting, buffeting the scaffold and causing it to rock. "You may go where you damned well please," he told her tersely. "I have said from the start that you would do better elsewhere."

He was right. She stopped in her tracks. Her company was a privilege he did not deserve. "Then go ahead without me. I will return home; I am no longer in the mood for music."

"I dismissed the coachman until ten o'clock."

She shrugged. "I saw a cabstand at the corner."

His eyes narrowed. "You will not travel by cab in this city."

"Ah, is that husbandly concern, again? Charming." She started past him, and he caught her elbow.

"This is not Edinburgh. Women are gutted here as easily as men."

"Men, too? How fortunate, then, that you had my escort this evening." She pulled her dagger from her pocket by way of explanation. When he recoiled, she pushed out a mocking laugh. "You've forgotten—I can look after myself. And I never go unarmed, particularly around men who want to tie me up."

A great cheer rent the air—followed a second later by a splintering crash. The rowdies had pulled down the canvas, and the wooden frame along with it.

"Good lord." Anna coughed, waving away the dust. "And to think England considers *Scotland* uncivilized."

Lockwood did not reply. He was staring fixedly at the rowdies, his expression strange—rigid and pale.

"Don't pay them mind," she said.

He turned back to her, but his remark was lost as two guards came running into the lobby. The rowdies scattered, hooting as they swarmed through concertgoers in a race toward the exit. One of them, flying by, slipped on the fallen canvas and smashed directly into Lockwood—who seized the boy and threw him against the wall, pinning him there by the throat.

Anna's wits took a moment to catch up to the sight. The boy made a piteous wheezing sound and groped at Lockwood's hand.

Lockwood did not release him.

"All right, let him go." Lockwood showed no sign of hearing her. She grabbed his wrist. "I said, let him go!"

His forearm was hard as iron, his grip unbreakable. The boy was flushing a mottled red now, his mouth opening and closing in a desperate bid for air.

"You are hurting him!" She dug her nails into his flesh. "*Liam!*"

He recoiled all at once. The boy dropped straight to the floor, then crawled away, casting a horrified glance over his shoulder before managing to scramble to his feet and make a dash for it.

"What on earth is wrong with you?" Anna stared. "You think *me* the odd one, for carrying a knife?"

Lockwood leaned back against the wall, silent as stone.

"What did you mean to do? Throttle him to death?"

He refused to answer, instead staring fixedly at some point in the distance, his breath rasping as though *he'd* been the one nearly choked. She turned to follow his look, but nothing appeared of interest. Fine-dressed ladies and gentlemen were recessing into the assembly rooms, while the mischief makers by and large had succeeded at shoving out the door, past guards who knew better than to manhandle wealthy swells.

Frowning, she turned back to Lockwood. He looked waxen. "What is it? Did you know that boy?"

"No." The word was almost inaudible. He took a deep breath, then used the wall to push himself to his full height. "It's nothing."

His voice sounded unsteady. Perhaps he was shocked by himself. One moment the boy had knocked into him—the next, he'd had the lad pinioned, like a cobra on a mouse.

She started to touch him, then thought better of it. "Your reflexes are superb," she said—trying for humor to defuse his strange mood.

"Yes," he said briefly.

The doors thumped shut behind the last of the concertgoers. Now they stood alone in the entry hall, with only the jaundiced regard of the beleaguered guards to keep them company. A muscle flexed in Lockwood's temple, as though he was grinding his teeth. She had the odd impression that he was fighting some inner battle.

Why this impulse to comfort him? She had spoken to her solicitor of divorce.

And then you let him ravish you in a carriage.

"Are you all right?" she asked finally.

"Yes."

Were these monosyllabic replies designed to irritate her? If so, they began to work. She blew out a breath. "Then stay here all night if you like. I'm leaving."

He caught up with her at the door. This time, as they descended the steps, he did not offer his arm.

She should have been glad. She did not want it, after all.

Instead, she felt a great loneliness sweep over her, with him not a foot away, and the greatest city in the world glimmering around them in the dark.

CHAPTER ELEVEN

A noise awoke Anna.

She sat up in bed, her breath coming quick as some nightmare faded from her mind. The fire in the grate burned low; no noise came from the connecting chamber.

Lockwood had deposited her home, but had not come inside—informing her, with cold courtesy, that he was wanted at the club to discuss some bill. She did not believe him, of course. By the newspapers' accounts, he appeared in Parliament these days only to cast votes for his party, and his withdrawal from his former, more vigorous role in the debates kept everybody puzzled but her.

He was useless now. Living off her money, throwing parties and buying things, and not much else. He had gone to his club to get drunk, no doubt. But the noise that had woken her had not come from his rooms. When she crossed on silent feet to open the door, she found his bed empty, the sheets neatly tucked.

She stood in silence, conscious of the drumming of her heart, until she was certain she had imagined the noise. She turned back for her rooms—

It came again: a distant yell, abruptly cut off. And then, equally dimly, what sounded like cheers.

It was coming from below. Were the servants brawling? She would sack the lot of them, Lockwood's objections be damned. She strode back into her room, taking care not to wake Jeannie in the dressing room as she added a wrapper to her nightgown, and then a heavy cloak over that.

Carrying a candle with her, she made her way down the stairs. In the entry hall, a familiar boy lay snoring on the marble tiles. The reek of liquor wafted up from him.

"Hey," she said, and when that did not wake Wilkins, she gave him an ungentle nudge with her foot.

He jerked awake and leapt to his feet in one simultaneous motion—an impressive trick, but not the reason she stepped backward. His cravat had come unwound. A ropy scar encircled his throat.

Somebody had tried to hang him.

He goggled. "Ain't—ain't it late, ma'am?" He scrubbed his eyes with the back of his hand. "Beg pardon, I didn't think—I was listening, I swear! Had somebody knocked—"

"Enough." Her tone emerged too sharply in her effort to mask her shock. "Regardless of the hour, you are not to sleep on the job. Much less on the floor!"

"I—yes, ma'am." His bow was a respectable effort, but undone by his half-swallowed belch. "I won't do it again, I promise."

She doubted that. But she found herself reluctant to scold him. He looked so remarkably young—nineteen or twenty at most. Yet that scar looked old, silvering. Somebody had abused him terribly when he was but a child.

He shifted, clearly made uneasy by her study of him. "Some warm milk might help," he said. "If you can't sleep. I could go fetch it for you."

"That is not the job of the night porter," she said sternly. "But . . . Wilkins, I do wonder—"

A raucous cheer came from the interior, causing Wilkins to blanch.

"Yes, that," she said. "I do wonder if you might explain it."

"Ah, 'twas probably a dog. Ever so many strays in—"

Another cry interrupted him. A snippet of hoarsely shouted song. Anna lifted her brow, daring him to persist with this nonsense about dogs.

He blew a breath through flattened lips and shrugged. "Some of the staff, ah, they're—given to singing hymns before bed."

"Right." Shoulders squaring, Anna turned for the hall.

"Ma'am!" Wilkins came scrambling up on her heels. "Ma'am, it's no sight for you!"

"Praising our Lord and savior? Nonsense. It sounds quite wholesome." As Anna stalked through the corridor, the sound died away again, the thick Persian leader cushioning her footfalls. The hall was paneled in burgundy brocade, and fitted at intervals with long mirrors that reflected the flickering light of brass candelabra. It felt Gothic tonight.

The first door Anna opened revealed the darkened front parlor; the next, Lockwood's book-lined study. The third uncovered the abandoned gallery.

She turned full circle, frowning. That brawling noise—there it came again, from *inside the walls*.

Ah! There *was* another door, cleverly disguised as part of the woodwork. She hunted for the handle.

"Ma'am, I'm telling you." Wilkins sounded miserable. "It wouldn't be fit for you. He thinks you're asleep, he wouldn't want—"

The door opened, revealing a stone-walled passage that pitched sharply downward, and a set of rough wooden stairs.

Her breath caught as the sound came more clearly now. A man was groaning—in pain.

Someone was being tortured in the cellar!

She was not prone to melodrama. But as she turned to face the alarmed servant, that scar gave her awful ideas. "Your throat," she said tightly. "Who did that to you?"

Wilkins flinched, then groped hastily for the ends of his cravat. She had embarrassed him.

Alas, it seemed more important now to have an answer to the unthinkable question roiling her brain. "Was it my husband who did it?"

He recoiled. "Why—God save you, ma'am, from such a thought!" Head tipping, he gave her a marveling, appalled look. "Lock saved me, he did!"

Lock? What a wondrously informal mode of address for a servant. "Is that so?"

"Aye, that's right, from the very noose itself!"

This notion suggested a dozen equally ludicrous possibilities. "You mean to say that the Earl of Lockwood rescued you from some criminal—"

"He wasn't no criminal. He was the bloody *chief*!"

This outburst clarified nothing. "The chief," she said flatly.

"Aye, of the prison camp!"

"The . . . prison camp." He might have been speaking Greek. That odd accent made him difficult to follow. "What, a—a prison camp in New South Wales?" She blinked. "Do you mean a *penal colony*?"

"Whatever you call it," he muttered. "If it wasn't for Lock, I'd be dead—we'd all be dead by now—"

"You mean to say you met Lockwood in a prison camp. In a *penal colony*."

She expected him to laugh. He was young and had a drunkard's sense of humor: poor, very poor.

Instead, the color drained from his face. He studied her intently, then stepped backward. "I . . . forgive me, m'lady, I misspoke."

"Oh, don't stop now," she said coolly. "I am most interested to hear how the Earl of Lockwood came to rescue you from—execution, was it? In a prison?"

The boy looked hunted suddenly.

"I—I must go watch the door."

He fled the way they had come. She moved to follow him—and the shouts from below resumed, calling her attention back to the ominous darkened stairs.

A pity she'd never had a taste for Gothic novels. She felt certain that they would contain a great deal of useful advice for a woman in her situation. They would probably advise her against walking down a darkened stairway in her deviant husband's house, particularly when it sounded as though someone were being strangled below.

The scientific method, on the other hand, discouraged leaping to assumptions. A theory should be tested before subscription to it.

She exchanged her candle for a nearby candelabra—heavy enough to serve as a weapon, in a pinch—and held it before her as she descended the stair.

It was no cellar at the bottom, but some kind of complex labyrinth of interconnected chambers. A bare and clean-swept hall, lit by gas fixtures set into iron brackets, led past doors that opened onto a series of neat accommodations, more barracks than bedrooms. Narrow cots, walls covered with newspaper cuttings, daguerreotypes and tintypes, rude sketches—the maids and housekeeper were lodged above, so these must be the quarters for the male staff.

Anna's steps slowed. It was not proper for her to tour this area. But there, ahead, through *that* door, appeared to be a small shooting gallery—an odd thing to locate in the staff area. And farther ahead came the source of the noise, which had grown wild, suddenly—grunts and groans and a series of staccato thumps.

"Oh!" cried an unfamiliar voice, young and hoarse and male. "That'll do it!"

She stepped around the corner and beheld a sight of savagery: two men attempting to beat each other to death, ringed by a dozen rapt male onlookers.

For a moment, amazed by the ferocity of their leaping, kicking attacks, she did not register their faces. The next second the taller one pivoted toward her, his opponent's throat locked between his forearm and bicep, and she found herself gasping: it was her husband.

Horror washed over her like an ice bath. She stepped backward. There was no intelligence in Lockwood's eyes. An animal glaze blurred his features. His victim cursed, heels scrabbling for purchase, hands clawing at Lockwood's arm, and Lockwood's grip seemed only to *tighten*.

The hair lifted on her nape, a response to the instinct of danger. The air was hot, moist, scented with sweat and blood. She retreated another step toward the corridor, her breath coming tight and fast. He was killing that man. *He* was the danger.

Someone would die. She had to stop it. "Stop this,"

she said, but her voice was trembling, and nobody seemed to remark it.

Lockwood's opponent found his footing suddenly. He was wolfish blond with cold dark eyes, and moved as fast as a cat: he launched himself backward, slamming Lockwood into the wall, then broke free with a violent twist that caused the onlookers to hoot. Pivoting, he fell into a crouch, his fists lifted. One of the rings glinting on his fingers—Anna squinted—looked to bear a crest.

"Not dead yet, eh?" he said in a mocking Oxbridge drawl. "Try again."

Lockwood wiped sweat from his brow, leaving a smear of blood behind, then flashed a savage grin and came off the wall. The men fell into a prowling deadly dance, circling, feinting and jabbing. Lockwood's fist connected—the blond staggered, then rebounded, landing a solid blow to Lockwood's jaw. Now they clashed, pummeling each other—the blond threw an elbow at her husband's face. Dirty move! Anna choked back a cry of protest when it connected. Lockwood lurched backward, and the rascal swiveled to kick him. How *dare* he! She lunged forward—

A hand caught her arm, gripping firmly. "Patience now," said an old man, his mustache a luxuriant drooping white, yellowed by tobacco at its edges. "They'll be done with each other soon enough."

Lockwood had gotten free of the assault and advanced now with teeth bared.

"Nonsense," Anna spat. The old man looked too respectable to attend this show—his suit was modest but neat, and he carried a top hat crushed under his arm. He looked like someone's grandfather, kind gray eyes and deeply lined cheeks. "Who are you? Why aren't you stopping this?"

"The name's Francis Smith. And why should I stop it?" He quirked a white brow at her, then nudged up his spectacles to take a squinting look. "Here, allow me . . ." He gently pulled the candelabra from her grip. She had forgotten she still held it.

A cry from the crowd jerked her attention back to the fight. Men were a brawling species. In her childhood, Anna had watched her male cousins scrap over any number of stupid offenses. But this was something different. They were *savaging* each other.

"Just a friendly boxing match," the old man said cheerfully.

Boxing! Hardly! Anna knew that sport. It had rules, and a system of point keeping. No scorekeeper would have been able to judge this brawl—nobody was even trying to keep points. Furious, she looked over the crowd. Half of them were strangers—the rest were the same men who slunk about this house at all hours in livery. They were cheering, these hooligans posing as house staff, chanting *Lock, Lock!* as though he were not their employer, but merely their champion, an animal masquerading as a civilized human being—

"Go on upstairs," suggested Francis Smith. "No place for women here."

No place for women? This was *her house*! She had paid for every inch of the interior! "Stop this!" she shouted.

A couple of onlookers casually glanced over, then rapidly looked again, their expressions startled as they inched away from her. One unfamiliar gentleman, lifting a dark brow, offered her a suggestive smile, then a wink.

But the two brawling brutes paid no heed. Their jabbing had transitioned into heavy, deadly blows. Lockwood struck out with an open palm, driving it straight into the other man's nose.

She choked back a cry of shock. The blond stumbled back into the wall, clutching his face, blood gushing through his fingers.

"Oof," said Francis Smith, wincing with sympathy. "Broken nose. Most unfortunate."

But the injury did not give the blond man more than a moment's pause. He lowered his head and charged Lockwood, smacking into her husband with a thud.

"Stop!" she screamed.

The two men grappled, clutching each other as close and fiercely as lovers, their feet clawing for purchase as they turned. They were too well matched. "They're going to kill each other," she whispered.

"Better dead than an easy mark," said Smith.

His lunatic calm snapped her temper. She seized the candelabra and stepped forward, swinging for the blond brawler's head.

The impact jarred her bones. She heard Lockwood's startled curse as the other man dropped to the floor, his dark eyes rolling back, then closing.

The room went silent.

"Well," Lockwood said, on a ragged hoarse laugh. "Victory to the countess, in one."

She glared around the room, taking in each and every face as she set down the candelabra. "Get out," she said. "All of you."

Mutters rose—a dark, unhappy sound. The servants slunk out. Two well-dressed men, one of them the cheeky rogue who had winked at her, came forward to fetch the fallen fighter. "Breathing," said that one. "Smith? You'll set this, I hope."

"Oh, indeed." This remark came from directly beside her. The old man picked up a leather bag—a medical bag, it looked like.

"Are you a doctor?" she asked in disbelief.

"Something of the sort," he said. "But never on Saturdays. Sundays, very rarely."

"And you did not try to stop this?" Her outrage made her voice crack.

"Stop it? Dear, why would I? How else to keep their skills sharp?"

She turned away from him in contempt and dismissal, hot barbs on her tongue for her fool of a husband. But he had pulled himself off the wall. Grabbing his crumpled coat from the corner, he made his way out the door.

She caught up to him in the hallway. He looked barbaric—his hair disordered, his eye already blackening, the smear of blood across his cheek vivid against skin turned parchment pale.

He acknowledged her only with a brief irritated glance. "You should be asleep," he said, and mounted the stairs.

She followed hard on his heels. "You are shameless," she said. "Demented!"

As they emerged into the hall, he seized her by the elbow to pull her aside so his friends could hustle past. His grip caused some electric thrill to dance over her skin. She pulled away, appalled by herself. He smelled of sweat and violence—what a thing to make her heart trip!

"I demand an explanation," she said through her teeth.

Lockwood slammed the hidden door, then leaned his weight against it. "That area below," he said flatly, "does not concern you. Nor does anything that transpires there. Do you understand?"

Her face flamed. "You are brawling for pleasure for the entertainment of your staff. And those other people— who were they? Thugs and goons—"

"A baker," he drawled as he hunted through his jacket. "A butcher, a candlestick maker." Out came a handkerchief, which he used to wipe the blood from his face before tossing both linen and jacket aside. "It does not concern you, Lady Forth."

"*This is my house.* I will not allow—"

"Go back to Scotland if you wish to play the master."

Was this his answer to everything? "I will go in my own good time, and not a *second* beforehand."

"Oh?" He stepped toward her. He was *looming*. Trying to frighten her now!

She straightened her shoulders and glared. Or tried to. But her wayward gaze slipped out of her control, dipping down his body. His linen shirt, sweat soaked, clung as closely as a second skin to his upper body. His pectorals were heavily developed, his abdomen banded with muscle. He looked like a man who regularly had done hard labor.

Perhaps, between the two of them, *she* was the more deranged. For his wildness, the scent of sweat and blood, suddenly riveted her, like a tuning fork calling her baser senses into a sudden ringing clarity. *Here* was the sight she'd been denied.

Without quite knowing what she intended, she pressed her palm flat against his belly.

He flinched. He felt so hot beneath her touch. She

looked up into his face, her own belly turning liquid. His gaze burned as he watched her, a slight cruel smile turning the corners of his mouth.

Her fingers smoothed across his damp shirt, the hard muscle beneath it, and she heard his breath quicken. "I'm not afraid of you," she said softly.

He stepped into her fully, crushing her against the door. "You should be," he murmured.

Her eyes closed. The heat of him seemed to be enfolding her; each breath felt harder to draw. She could barely manage her next words: "I am your wife. Tell me . . ."

But his mouth swallowed the rest of her words. His kiss was punishing, openmouthed, consuming. She clung to his hard waist and kissed him back, tasting the wildness in him, wanting more, more, more—

He ripped free, speaking into her ear: "Here?" His voice was rough. "In the hall? Is that where you would like it next?"

Anyone could come along. She should have felt mortified. But where he pressed against her, she felt the proof of his readiness. It made her knees weak.

"Better here than blindfolded, I reckon." God help her, it was true. She wanted to *see* him, to see what she felt pressed against her now.

His hand caught her chin, tilted up her face so he could take a narrow inspection of her features. "So impatient," he said raggedly. "One wonders if you came to London with something to hide."

She stiffened. The insinuation—that she carried a bastard in her belly, and was looking for a way to trick him into fatherhood—was intolerably offensive.

He saw her temper, and smirked as he released her.

"Wait," she said, "I'm—"

"You will not go into the rooms below again. I will have your word on it."

"You won't have it. I want to look at your head. Is that man really a doctor? He should—"

"I will have your word," he growled, "or set Wilkins to guard you."

"Wilkins! The convict you saved from hanging?"

A flinch moved over his face. She pounced.

"You said you wanted a grand adventure—was *that* your notion of grandness? Sailing to Australia to find criminals to serve as your house staff?"

For a moment, his expression remained so remote that she thought he had not heard her, or had no intention to reply.

But then, all at once, he burst into laughter—laughing so forcefully that he leaned back against the wall to wipe tears from his eyes. As the laughter went on, it became somehow horrible, unnatural.

A chill moved through her. She stepped forward, wanting to touch him, but for some reason afraid now to do so. "Why are you laughing?" she whispered.

He had bracketed his eyes with one hand, which he now lowered to show her his smile—no humor in it, but something sharp and dark and cutting.

"I like this theory of yours," he said. "Very swashbuckling. Let me see if I have it straight: I left you in a temper. I purchased passage to New South Wales. Then I proceeded to go 'round liberating prisoners. Oh yes, quite credible. Pity it took so long to gather them all—I should have placed an order by post."

The ice in his voice stung her. "Have you some other explanation? That man said you rescued him from the gallows!"

"Is that what you want? Will an explanation convince you to leave me in peace?"

She snorted. "A fine start. Then might come an apology—ha! A *groveling* and *extensive* apology, in which you go down on your knees and beg for—"

"No." He spoke flatly. "I will not go on my knees for anyone. But an apology, yes, you will have it. I am very sorry, Anna. I know it must have been shocking to find me gone. What a blow to your vanity. Why, you must have wept for a day or two at least."

She stared at him, a dozen curses on her lips. But all of them were too good for him. "A day or two. Is *that* what you think?"

"Come now. We never claimed to love each other, did we? A marriage of convenience, wasn't it?"

She swallowed hard. "Was it, then? I had begun to . . ."

No. She would not admit that.

His mouth twisted. He looked beyond her, though there was nothing to see. His pupils were dilated, consuming his irises; he looked like a man locked in darkness. "I am sorry." He took an audible breath before meeting her eyes again. "If I could go back in time to change what happened, I would do so."

It was not enough. He sounded indifferent. "I don't accept your apology."

"That is your choice, of course."

She bit her lip, hating the sudden wave of misery that engulfed her. Why should she care? He clearly didn't. He had no interest in her forgiveness; why, then, should she ache?

It was not for *him* she ached, but for the man she'd once imagined him to be. The secret dreams she'd woven around him—those were the losses she still mourned, despite her best efforts to forget.

"Fine," she said. "You have apologized. Now you will explain. How did you end up with a half-hanged servant?"

He stared at her for a long moment. Then he shrugged. "All right. You want it? Here it is: the night we were married, you and I quarreled, and I left the ship."

Her heart tripped. "Yes." He was going to tell her now, at last. "You left. You went to the tavern on the quay."

"I never made it there." His gaze shifted from hers, fixing on a spot just over her shoulder. "They came out of nowhere. Struck me on the head and bundled me into a vehicle."

She blinked. "What?"

"When I woke, I was blindfolded. We were moving rapidly. Then—ether, I expect, something that knocked me out. I have few memories of the journey."

Again with this ridiculous story? "Come now." What kind of joke was this? His delivery was so monotone, his expression opaque. "You're saying you were *kidnapped*."

"Yes."

Her skepticism sharpened her voice. "By whom?"

"Hired men."

She snorted. "Hired by whom?"

His gaze sliced to her, sharp and direct. "Does it matter? I thought you wanted to know how I ended up with convicts as servants."

There was more than one convict on his staff?

She crossed her arms, deeply uneasy now. If this was a prank, he did not seem to be enjoying it. "Go on, then."

He nodded. "When I came to my senses again, I was being loaded onto a ship. A prison bark, bound for the colonies. A man was being removed from the bark—I slipped him my signet ring. I know not what became of it, but clearly he did not take it to the authorities. I found out later I had been traded for that convict, and his name was the one the crew knew me by."

"I don't . . . follow."

He lifted a brow. "Are the words unclear, or the story itself? I am speaking as plainly as I know how."

She felt herself redden. He spoke so coldly, as though every question she asked sank her further into his contempt. "You can't expect me to believe this claptrap."

He shrugged. "Probably not. The crew on the prison bark also found it difficult to believe. I learned quickly to keep my mouth shut, and let them call me whatever name they liked."

She swallowed. That he was not *trying* to convince her made the story more chilling. It almost sounded like . . . truth.

She cleared her throat. "Then what? When did they realize their mistake?"

His smile was faint. "If they did, I was never informed. The journey took six months. It's farther even than Indochina. Very rough seas. And cholera broke out. By the time we arrived at Botany Bay, half the convicts were dead."

This was horrid. Cruel. Anger whipped through her. "Stop this. It's not amusing."

As though released by snapped strings, he turned to reach for the hidden door. Like an automaton, no feeling in him.

She caught his arm. His skin felt as hot as a branding iron. The hall felt icy, but new sweat was beading on his brow. "You must think me mad to believe this nonsense."

His cold gaze dropped to her hand, fixing there until she let go. "You wanted the explanation, Anna."

She wavered, then sank back against the wall. "Very well." How far would he take this dreadful yarn? She crossed her arms again. "Finish it!"

He pivoted back, his shoulders squaring as he stared down at her. "Botany Bay, where the prisoners were unloaded. I spent a handful of weeks there. Then a very few of us were moved farther inland, to a camp called Elland."

"A penal colony," she said, to be clear.

"It was, once." His color looked wan, almost corpselike, his lips taking on the bluish cast of the gaslight. "By the time we arrived there, it had been closed and rehabilitated into a private work camp attached to the local mine. We served as labor in that mine. That is where I spent the next two years."

She opened her mouth once, twice. This was poppycock, of course. "And then?"

"And then the camp came to an end."

"You escaped, I suppose? How convenient."

His smile was cold and brief. "I put an end to the camp."

A tremor went through her. She remembered suddenly how he had looked, boxing downstairs. The animal fury in his face. "Wilkins said . . ." She would not fuel this twisted fantasy he was developing for her. And yet . . . "He said you saved him from the gallows."

He leaned back against the opposite wall, his posture casual as he shrugged. "Every man in this household was with me at Elland." His consonants were beginning to slur—perhaps he *had* knocked his head. "Every man here saved each other, more than once."

She realized that her hands were twisting together at her waist. Her fingers ached from the force of her grip. "You can't expect me to believe this."

He shrugged again, a drop of sweat dripping from his brow, and watched her—levelly, steadily, with an unreadable gaze. His eyes looked so dark, like windows to a nightmare. The wall supported his weight, but did not help his balance: he was swaying slightly.

She had a choice, she realized. She could dismiss this lunacy and conclude he was mad—or else a brilliant and bizarre liar, willing to invent improbable nightmares to avoid telling her his true itinerary over the last few years.

Or . . . she could believe what he said. Nausea boiled through her at the prospect. "If this were true, then you . . ."

Did not abandon me.

The selfishness of the thought made her wince. That was the least of what this story meant.

He seemed to misunderstand her grimace, for he shrugged before wiping his brow. "Yes, precisely. It's pointless."

"I—what? What do you mean?"

"You came here for the man you married. But that man—" His voice cracked. He took a long breath, blinking hard, before continuing. "That man is dead, and I have no interest in resurrecting him. His life—you, the vows we made to each other—I am done with them."

She had no notion of how to decipher such nonsense. She felt as dizzy, nauseated, as he looked. "Liam, I . . ."

He did not wait for her to finish. He opened the door to return downstairs—but did not make it a step before he collapsed.

CHAPTER TWELVE

*W*ilkins was barricading Anna's way into the bedroom. "I tell you, he wouldn't want it! No strangers. Doc Smith is all he needs!"

"That is the rogue doctor," Anna confided to the gentleman beside her—a true medical professional, recommended to her by Moira and Lady Dunleavy both. "Francis Smith. He has been closeted with Lockwood for a day now, but I see no improvement."

"I'm telling you," Wilkins insisted. "This bloke can't help. There's a maid belowstairs that fetched up sick, too. How to explain that? Doc Smith says—"

"Enough!" Dr. Gardener, whom Lady Dunleavy had assured her was a favorite of the Queen, had lost his patience. "What manner of nonsense is this? You are lucky that the countess has not sacked you already!"

"In fact, I would call the police first," said Anna.

This remark had the effect of causing Wilkins to wilt away from the door and slink off, muttering.

Anna followed Dr. Gardener through the sitting room into the darkened chamber where Lockwood lay.

The rogue Francis Smith, she saw with disgust, was snoring in a wing chair, a pot of herbs burning by his feet.

"Repellent," Dr. Gardener said on a cough. "Will you be so good as to ring a servant, my lady, and have them fetch that pot away, and open the windows to air the room?"

There was not a servant in this house whom she trusted. The chambermaids were serviceable, but they skulked about like mice, no doubt terrified of the menfolk who passed out on tables and floors. The men, meanwhile, were lost to hysteria. They had abandoned their duties to take shifts standing guard outside their master's door. Lockwood had a terrible fever, but Francis Smith had filled their minds with some paranoid story about poison.

"I'll remove it myself," she said, and seized the burning pot, placing it in the hallway before returning to the room to throw open the curtains.

The flood of light woke Smith, who jolted to his feet on a protest. "What is this? Who ordered—"

"Out," said Anna.

"Oh." Smith rubbed his eyes. "You mustn't disturb him, dear. He's on the mend now, and—"

"Not in *this* state, he isn't." Dr. Gardener straightened from his patient's side. Lockwood was a tall man, but he looked dwarfed by the heaping of quilts laid atop him, which Gardener now began to strip with violent jerks. "Where did you train, sir? Under whom did you study? This is the grossest malfeasance—"

"I learned my trade when you were still in swaddling clothes," Francis Smith barked. Anna had thought him seventy at the least, but when he puffed himself up in a righteous fit, his belly straining at his waistcoat, her estimation dwindled to sixty.

But Gardener, lean and polished with a beard tailored into a well-groomed point, was not cowed. "And you've not read a study since then, I expect. Overheat a fever! Choke the air with toxic smoke! And is this *laudanum* you've been giving him?" He picked up the bottle between thumb and forefinger. "His respiratory system requires *vigor*, not sedation!"

"For a fever it would," Smith bit out. "What we've got here is a poisoning."

"Poison!" Gardener threw her an astonished look. "What claptrap is *this*?"

Anna sighed. A maid had taken ill after laundering Lockwood's clothing the night of the brawl. Her symptoms followed Lockwood's exactly—a sudden onset of fever and rapid heartbeat; a collapse followed by intermittent periods of muttering confusion. "He took ill very suddenly," she said. "And so did one of the maids. The staff has put it down to mysterious influences."

"Nothing mysterious about it," Smith roared. "He was out at his club, comes back with poison on his clothes, gets sweaty and wipes it into his eyes. A classic technique!"

Gardener snorted. "He leaves, or I do."

"She ain't got the authority," Smith retorted.

Anna smacked her hands together. "Haven't got the authority, you say?" She strode over and seized Smith's cane. "Were I less a lady, sir, I would box your ears, regardless of your age."

A strange gleam entered Smith's watery eyes. "Fine temper," he said. "You're a proper match for him."

"If I want your opinion, I will ask for it. Get out, sir."

"If he struggles again, you give him another spoonful of that laudanum, hear?"

"Out!"

He snatched his cane from her hand and limped for the door.

She called after him. "You might go see to the man whose nose got hurt yesterday. No doubt *he* requires your attentions."

Smith looked back over his shoulder. "'Got hurt,' did it?" He cackled. "Some men catch a cold, Atherton just happened to catch a fist—that right?"

She glared. She would not divulge in front of the Queen's own doctor that her husband had been brawling with the help—and Atherton, whoever he was.

Old Smith read the message in her stare and snorted. "Well, if you're that much the priss, then I take it back: Lock will eat you alive. Good day, ma'am." He tipped an invisible hat to her—for all she knew, the old bat thought he was wearing one—and thumped out.

"Remarkable," said Gardener in tones of pure astonishment. "I will not ask where you found him."

"If I knew, I would put him back," she said. "How does he fare?"

Gardener turned back to the bed. "I must listen to his lungs. If you will assist me?"

She came forward swiftly and helped the doctor strip the sweat-soaked shirt from Lockwood's body.

Together they looked down.

The breath left her.

"Good God," muttered the doctor, then added swiftly, "Begging your ladyship's pardon."

She opened her mouth to excuse him, but could not find her voice.

What in heaven's name had been done to Liam?

She felt the doctor's appalled gaze on her, and realized with a dull start that as Lockwood's wife, she should not look shocked. She should have seen this sight many times before.

But he blindfolded me.

Her heart knocked against her ribs, as though trying to break free. "His lungs." She sounded faint, but she pushed onward. "Shouldn't you listen to them?"

"Ah—yes." The doctor turned away, unbuckling his bag and rummaging through the contents.

She took a hard breath and made herself look at Liam again.

Letters had been burned above his right pectoral. The burn scars were livid and ropy: *WDLL.*

Old scars mottled his ribs and belly. Deep puckered silver slashes—too ragged to have been caused by a knife.

A bladed whip. A cat-o'-nine-tails.

Who on earth would dare flog the Earl of Lockwood?

I learned quickly to keep my mouth shut. So he'd said.

God above. He'd been telling the truth.

Until this moment, distracted by his collapse, she'd not dwelled on what he'd told her. But now the full weight of it descended upon her, made crushing by the proof carved into his body.

She reached out to touch a scar, raised and rough.

He'd bound her so her fingertips would not detect the truth.

Some noise recalled her to the presence of the doctor. She snatched back her trembling hand and fixed her gaze instead on the tattoo, a black snaking design that extended the full length of his forearm, wrist to elbow.

She did not recognize the pattern. It looked to hold no meaning, nor did it resemble any language she had ever glimpsed. It looked like waves—or snakes—or madness, given shape.

Gardener fitted his instrument to Lockwood's chest and listened for several long moments.

"A small amount of fluid," he pronounced at last. He plucked the instrument from his ears. "But this fever . . ." He hesitated before laying a finger to Liam's throat.

That hesitation struck her. Her eyes narrowed as she watched him check the pulses in Liam's body, his touch fussy and delicate at Liam's throat and wrist and groin.

Why should he hesitate to touch the Earl of Lockwood? Did he imagine that scars were catching? A fever might prove contagious. Perhaps that was the cause. But a man afraid of contagion should not have become a doctor.

The doctor now kneaded Liam's belly. "Too warm for my liking," he said, his voice oddly pinched. "But with the fresh air, it should pass." His glance danced down Liam's chest again, his lip curling in distaste. "Has he traveled anywhere unusual of late? In the malarial regions?"

"He has traveled everywhere." Her tone was rude. She did not care. "Far more of the world than you or I will ever see."

He heard the censure in her tone and his own expression smoothed. "Of course," he said, stepping back and bowing shallowly. "Well, you may wish to administer quinine. If it is malaria, you will see an improvement— but the fever may crest again before it breaks. With regular dosing, however, he will be himself in a week. Or he will . . . worsen." He tucked his stethoscope into his bag. "It is up to Providence, my lady."

Dr. Gardener had rushed here without delay, and had promised to stay as long as necessary. But now, all at once, he hurried to leave.

"How helpful you have been," she said contemptuously. She had intended him to see to the maid next, but she would not keep him. There were other doctors in London. "I understand you are helpful to many renowned personages. I expect your popularity is owed to their trust in your *complete* discretion."

The threat was subtle, but his gaze flickered in acknowledgment. "Quite so," he murmured. "I consider myself like a priest in that regard."

She let him show himself out, then rang for a chambermaid and ordered her to send for the other doctor whom Moira had recommended. If that doctor worked a great improvement in the maid, then and only then would Anna risk him seeing Liam. Otherwise, she would not reveal her husband's secrets to a stranger.

She returned to Liam's bedroom, closing and locking the door behind her. Bright sunlight spilled through the window, and a light breeze carried inside the scents of grass and violets and fresh hay in the neighboring mews.

A pitcher of water stood on the dressing table. After a moment, she crossed to it, pulled out a handkerchief, and doused the cloth.

At the first touch of dampness, Liam muttered and pitched himself onto his side. A hissing breath escaped her; her startled fist squeezed water onto the bedclothes.

His back had been lashed even more viciously. His back was a mottled battlefield of scars, raised and pulpy and twisted.

She thought of Wilkins yesterday in the hall, with the rope burn at his throat.

If it wasn't for Lock, I'd be dead.

What had Liam said? *I put an end to the camp.*

Now, the violence embedded in those words gave her a deep vicious thrill of satisfaction.

Good.

She took several long breaths, until she felt calmer. Then she laid the wet cloth to Liam's ravaged back and stroked it slowly, gently, across his skin, hoping it would cool his body, persuade the fever to go.

He had put an end to the camp. But what of those who had arranged for his abduction and transport there? Who had done this to him?

Whomever it was would pay. He was her husband, and he had been stolen from her. Nobody got away with stealing what was hers.

"Please. Please. Please, I beg you. I beg you!"

Anna flew to the bed, seizing Lockwood's shoulders and using her full weight to push him down. "It's all right," she said, but he broke free, springing up with such violent force that she was tossed from the bed, landing on her hands and knees.

Now came the creak of bedsprings. He staggered to his feet—but his first full step failed him, and he fell to hands and knees.

She clambered to her feet and took hold of his arms, but he wrenched free. As their eyes met, an instinctive fear gripped her. His face looked wild, his gaze burning. He was strong—much stronger than she.

"Liam," she whispered. "You're all right. You've a fever, that's all."

She heard him swallow. He looked briefly beyond

her, and then understanding seemed to loosen his features. "Anna." His voice sounded scoured, raw.

"Yes," she said. "You need to—"

"Get out."

Even half dead, he managed to wax autocratic. "You're ill." She adopted a brisk, neutral tone, the address of a nurse, a paid servant, as she reached for him again. "Here, let me help you back to—"

He resisted her grip. "Smith," she heard him mutter.

The staff wanted Smith here, too. The maid was recovering, but with no help from the second doctor Anna had sent for—it was Smith who had nursed her to wakefulness.

Anna had prevented mutiny by promising to follow Smith's orders. But Liam's corpselike immobility, after a dose of laudanum, terrified her more than his delusions. She could barely bring herself to drug him again. "Smith is not here," she said sternly. "Let me help you back to bed, Liam, or *I* will tie *you* there."

The ghost of a laugh scratched from his lips. "God save the world from your temper," he rasped, sounding almost like himself. He reached up to take hold of a bedpost, his bare bicep flexing as he hauled himself to his feet.

As he stood there, balancing with visible effort, a distant part of her marveled at the beauty of his body. Despite the scars, the records of atrocity that stamped his skin, he was a thing of splendor, long and lean and well muscled—enough, even, to give a Scotswoman cause to admire these inbred English ways, if they could produce such a specimen of perfection.

The sane, forward part of her brain snapped at her impatiently as she hurried to assist him into bed.

The top sheets required changing. But when she reached for them, he resisted, grabbing her wrist and clinging so fiercely that she bit back a noise.

"Don't move," he whispered.

"What?"

"There are monsters in the shadows. They are crawling on the walls."

A chill ran through her. "That is the fever." She laid her hand over his. "Let go, Liam."

He remained staring fixedly behind her. On a resigned breath, she used her free hand to reach for the laudanum, clamping the bottle between chin and shoulder as she unscrewed the cap.

Some sudden sharp movement shook the bed. When she glanced up, he was sitting upright, still staring beyond her. Some alert, predatory quality in his posture lifted the hairs on her nape. His hand slipped from her wrist as he stared.

"Liam." She spoke very softly. "It is the fever. That is all." But this was no ordinary fever. She began to wonder if Smith was not right, for all that poison seemed impossible, incredible.

But what was incredible, if Liam's story was true?

"Here." She spilled some laudanum into the spoon and stepped forward, cursing her hand for trembling. "Drink this."

He moved like a snake: his hand suddenly gripped her wrist, his fingers banding like iron as he glared at her.

"I will not beg," he hissed.

"No need," she whispered. "This is medicine, that's all."

His eyes narrowed. The hollows beneath his cheeks, in the half-light, lent him the look of a death's-head, bladed and dangerous.

She shoved the spoon into his mouth.

He choked on it, his eyes flying wide with surprise, and then fell back, sputtering, onto the pillows.

Ah well. Her temperament was not cut out for nursing. But she saw, with some satisfaction, that he swallowed.

He covered his eyes with the palms of his hands, pressing so hard that she feared for his eyesight. But just as she reached for his wrists, he lowered them and pinned her with a steady, sane look.

"It is not safe for you here, Lady Forth."

She held his gaze. "I am the Countess of Lockwood," she said. "This is my place. Now, sleep. Close your eyes."

His gaze moved over her shoulder again, a troubled look cramping his brow. She did not wish to imagine what he was seeing.

"Close your eyes," she said. "Dream sweet things."

It was the wrong thing to say. His mouth abruptly twisted. He clawed his hand through his hair and tried to sit up again.

She shoved him back, the palm of her hand flat against his burning, scarred skin. "Sleep," she said. "No, do not look behind me. Look at *me*."

At last, his amber eyes fixed on hers. A startled, haunted look crossed his face. "You . . ." She forbade herself to flinch as his large hand tore into her hair, scattering pins across his body and the bed. "You are dead," he said raggedly.

"No. I am here."

He blinked, looking doubtful.

But his hand in her hair grew limp, then fell to his side, taking several strands along with it. His lips parted again, but whatever he meant to say was lost as his eyes fluttered closed. Still, his lips moved in some silent recitation—unhappy, she judged, by the tenseness of his features.

She laid her hand on his forehead, cursing silently as she felt his temperature. His hair was silken, very soft. As she stroked it, his body went lax, his expression smoothing.

Recognition struck her, made her swallow some bittersweet lump. Here, at last, was the man she had married: she glimpsed his features, the sweet beauty of the curve of his mouth, only in the sudden absence of the man he had become.

He had not abandoned her, after all.

Grasping that fact felt almost impossible. It made her realize how practiced she had grown throughout her life in being left behind. Her father, a wanderer, had done it regularly. Her aunts had taken her into their homes, but never for longer than a season. She was a trial, a headache, a headstrong and disobedient girl who had never mastered the art of being pleasing. Instead, she had perfected the skill of being left. She had even fashioned a marriage around it. They had agreed to vouchsafe each other's liberties—but they had never promised to stay with each other.

Yet he had not meant to go that night. It had not been his choice to leave. He had been *taken* from her.

And at what cost? When she reflected now on his odd behavior, on his moments of violence and his strange moods, she wondered if there was not a logic to them. His body testified to trials she could not imagine. What toll had they taken, above and beyond the fleshly pains?

Go back to Scotland, he had told her—over and over. But she had practice only in being left. It was not in her nature to leave.

CHAPTER THIRTEEN

*T*he heat is an animal, a wet, smothering weight crouched on Liam's chest, crushing the life from his body. He holds very still, surrounded by raw pulsing earth. Far overhead, weak light filters through the wooden slats, but the light does not reach this depth. The darkness smells like soil and rot, copper and drying blood. It is hot.

If they have forgotten him down here . . .

Stop.

He takes a breath, a careful and shallow sip of air, for the hole is as deep as some mine shafts, and the oxygen won't last. An hour more, or perhaps two—he would know it by the sudden constriction in his chest, the dizziness—is he feeling it even now?

Stop.

Sweat stings his eyes. Sweat is a constant presence, sometimes useful; the sting of it can call one's attention to hidden injuries that should not be ignored. Two days ago he'd found a gash in his leg. It throbs now, insistent as a drum.

Smith, the former army medic, found fresh mud, scraped from beneath the fence at great risk to himself, to pack onto the wound. *Don't scratch at it*, he said.

God, but he wants to scratch. The mud has dried into a makeshift plaster. It, too, is a kind of torture, like the heat, the sting of sweat, the hunger in his belly.

He turns his mind from one small torture to the next, breathing shallowly, letting the ordinary discomforts focus him, while his eyes fix on the light far overhead. The heat is rising with the light and the sun. Sadler was left in this hole to bake to death last week. His body, when they pulled it out—

Stop.

Think of coolness.

Think of England.

He rarely lets himself think of home anymore. Memories pierce the numbness, leave him weak. What happened before is now myth and romance, useless to survival, distracting.

But on rare occasions, those memories might be portioned out, like mouthfuls of water or bread.

He should have kept his mouth closed last night. He should not have spoken up for the boy. But the mistake was made. Now he will bake to death, or suffocate, or be dragged half dead from the hole when the guards remember him. But his mind will be elsewhere, already free.

England. Cool green rolling misty clean soft gentle hills.

Anna, in ivory lace. Bridal, resplendent. Her wry grimace as she scratches her wrist: *nobody mentions how it itches!*

It itches. His calf is on fire. He could knock away the

mud, hook his fingers into the wound, rip himself open to the bone, just to end it—

Stop.

Anna on the island, hair whipping around her face. Her clever fingers tracing his mouth. *I think you will miss me when you go.*

"Do you miss me?"

She is here with him. She cannot be here, but she is standing in front of him, her skirts like ice brushing his knees, blissfully cold, and the scent of her, sea salt and soap and female skin, all around him.

His amazement, his joy, is swift and muscular and gutting. "Anna," he gasps—and then recoils, lashed with horror.

She cannot be here. Huddled into the dirt, bridal gown ragged, she lifts her face, and her eyes are huge and terrified.

"What did you imagine?" Her voice is thin, cold like fog drifting through a graveyard. "Did you think they only took *you?*"

Christ God, no. "You were—" She'd been on the ship when they'd come for him. She'd been safe. "You're not here."

Her smile is a corpselike grin.

Men envision awful things in the hole. He rubs his eyes, but they do not clear. He will scratch them out before he believes them. He looks up for the light, and soil hits his face. Again—and again. Clumps are raining down from above.

They are burying him alive.

His fingers hook into the gnarled root-choked wall. They are *burying him alive.*

He hears taunts from above, snarled curses and

mockery. They are predicting how long it will take for him to die.

With a great cry, he throws himself against the wall and tries to climb. But the wall crumbles beneath his grip. He collapses, breath knocked out of him, and dirt mounds on his back, filling his nostrils, crushing out his breath.

A great boulder of dirt smacks into his back. He is suffocating.

"Last chance!" comes the cry from above. "Beg for your life!"

He will die silent. Pride is all that remains. He will die with his pride intact.

"Help."

This broken whisper cannot be real. It is Anna's voice, choked and struggling. She cannot be here.

"Help," she gasps again.

She is here. She is dying with him.

"I should have told you."

Anna opened her eyes, jarred, confused. Liam was staring at her, his face lost in shadow. She was lying next to him in bed—good heavens, she had fallen asleep beside him.

But he was awake again, praise God! It had been a full day since he'd last spoken. Smiling, she reached out to touch his face.

His skin burned like a brand.

Swallowing her disappointment, she stroked his cheek.

"Long before Paris," he whispered.

More rambling. But something in his presence, in the

clarity of his words, felt different now. He was watching her as though he knew who she was. She studied him, feeling a quick pulse of hope.

"What about Paris?" she asked.

"I should have told you before. The first time I knew."

She smoothed his hair from his eyes. "All right," she said soothingly.

The room was cold. In his fever, he had kicked off the sweat-soaked covers, leaving them both exposed. The chill made her shiver now suddenly.

He felt it. His hand covered hers. "I'm sorry," he murmured. "It would not have made a difference. But I should have told you."

As he shifted toward her, the moonlight slanting through the crack in the curtains cut a pale bar across his face, illuminating the bead of sweat on his brow, the shining fixed quality of his gaze. He was staring at her so fiercely, widening his eyes every few moments, almost as though he were trying not to blink.

"It's all right," she said. How long had she slept? It had been dusk when she'd lain down beside him—it would not surprise her to learn she had slept straight through until the next evening.

His grip tightened suddenly over her hand. "But you knew," he said urgently. "Didn't you?"

"I knew," she told him. "Close your eyes, Liam."

"You knew I loved you."

Her breath caught.

"You felt it. I know you did."

She swallowed, willing herself to remember how ill he was. Perhaps he thought himself looking at someone else.

"I knew that day on Rawsey," he said hoarsely. "It was

too soon—it was impossible. But I could not take my eyes from you. I saw worlds in you. I saw my future."

Her heart turned over. The tenderness in his voice, in his expression, took her four years into the past. Did he speak these words in memory of that time? Or had the fever generated some new narrative, unfamiliar to the waking man, untrue to his experience?

The possibility was too painful to contemplate. She *had* fallen in love with him. But they had never spoken of love. It had not been a part of their contract.

The hardest words she had perhaps ever spoken—but they must be said, for his sake: "Liam, close your eyes." *Keep speaking.* "Go to sleep." *Tell me more.* "You need rest."

He pulled her hand to his mouth, kissing her knuckles with cracked lips, his breath hot. "He said, you will know, all at once. And I did."

She blinked back tears. "Who said that?"

"My father. It was so, with my mother. He told me."

These were the ramblings of a sick man. They could not be trusted. But her heart was so parched. His words, like water, caused it to swell. She would take that nourishment, even from his delirium. "I knew then, too," she said softly. He would remember none of this. "I realized later—I came to believe it later—but that was when I knew."

A faint smile touched his mouth, edged with melancholy. "So why are you here?"

"To care for you. You are ill, Liam."

"But you curse me," he rasped. "Let me die in peace, Anna. Be safe, away from here."

She sat up, looking down at him. "You're not going to die."

He squinted up, frowning a little, as though there was some blazing light behind her, instead of the darkness of the room. "Let them bury me alone."

"No one is going to bury you. You are safe—"

"Shh." He sat up, his hand over her mouth, a hard look overtaking his face. "Don't let them hear you. They are listening."

She laid her hand over his. Where his chest pressed against her shoulder, she could feel the laboring gallop of his heart. He was elsewhere. He looked haunted as he stared upward. He did not see the bed canopy. She could not guess what he saw. Her stomach twisted as she imagined the possibilities.

"You are safe," she insisted again.

"You must go."

He had worked so hard to hide the truth from her. But the man gripping her now was living that truth as he stared up into nothing. He was back in the horror of his past—and she wanted to know, despite her gut-deep, sinking instinct that his answer would be fearsome: "Who are they?"

"They want me to beg," he rasped. "They are listening for it. But I won't do it. I will die first. I will gladly die."

She pulled his hand away, kissed his palm, then urged him to lie back down. "You won't die," she told him. "And you won't beg."

"Will he recover?"

The soft question startled Anna from her reverie. She rose and went to the bedroom door. Anxiety was stamped so plainly on Wilkins's face that she could not scold him for countermanding her orders not to disturb them.

She led him into the hall, where their conversation would not risk waking Liam. "The fever is weakening. He is calmer now when he wakes."

Wilkins slumped a little. "Well, that's good," he muttered. "I'll let the others know."

Only then did she see the small group huddled down the hallway: the footmen, Danvers and Riley and Dunning and Gibbs; the roustabout coachman, Henneage; Hanks, the valet; and even Cook, whose station meant he never should have set foot abovestairs.

For the first time, she wondered what scars *their* uniforms might conceal. She had already seen Wilkins's ravaged throat, which he hid tonight beneath a woven scarf that looked far too fine to belong to a porter.

He noticed her gaze lingering upon it. "Lock gave it to me," he said, groping at the fringe. "It's a fine thing, ain't it?"

"Very fine," she murmured.

"He said he'd stick by us." Wilkins stared intently at the closed door, his jaw tightening. "Once we saw this house, though, what life he was meant to lead . . . well, some said we shouldn't believe him."

She hesitated. "Why would you not believe him?"

Wilkins flashed her a disbelieving look. "He's a nob. But *I* never doubted him. He saved me from the hole— took my place, he did. If he could do that, I said, he'd keep his word on anything."

She felt a stir of dread. The way Liam had looked up at the canopy . . . the words he had spoken: *Let them bury me alone.* "What do you mean, the hole? What is the hole?"

"I . . ." He shook his head as though to clear it. "He's kept his word, is what I mean."

"Tell me," she said urgently. "Did they—did your captors put you underground?"

"They did anything they could." His blue eyes were bloodshot, ringed by shadows. He had not slept in some time—perhaps not since Liam had fallen ill, she thought. "But he was never afraid. Not for himself— only for the rest of us. I reckon he's a rare nob," he said heatedly. "To look out for others, and to keep his word afterward, to anyone."

Belatedly she registered the accusation in his voice. He did not think *her* a 'rare nob.' And why should he? *Every man here saved each other, more than once.* So Liam had told her. And yet, the day after her arrival, she'd tried to sack them all.

"He is an honorable man," she said softly. No matter that she had spent almost four years believing otherwise. Having seen the proof of his story, realizing that he had not abandoned her, and then to have witnessed these men's loyalty to him—could she doubt it?

He was honorable. And *she* had wasted four years embroidering hateful fictions of him, when instead . . .

She should have been searching for him. Raising the alarm and crying for justice.

Staggered, she leaned against the wall. *She* had failed *him.*

Wilkins, misinterpreting her collapse, snapped back into the form she had taught him.

"Forgive me, m'lady. Can I fetch you something? Tea, a meal, a—"

"I've seen to it." This from Cook, who came lumbering toward them, bringing along the reek of his cheap cigars. "Maids are bringing a tray to Lock's rooms for you, ma'am."

"And here's your post," said Henneage, approaching with a handful of notes and cards. "Your cousin called, ma'am, but we told her you was seeing to his lordship. I reckon you'll want to let her know how you fare."

Dazed, she looked between them, these rogues she had disdained so violently. "Thank you." Hearing the break in her own voice, and mindful of the expectant quality of their regard, she swallowed hard and straightened. "Thank you," she repeated more firmly. "As I told Wilkins, his lordship will recover. He is resting more peacefully now."

"Has Doc Smith seen him recently?" asked Riley with a frown. "Because *he* said—" At Henneage's sharp elbowing, he clamped shut his mouth.

"You'll know best, my lady," Henneage said.

But she could see the unease that rippled over the group. She cleared her throat. "Did Dr. Smith leave?"

Riley spoke instantly. "He's below, having a cup of tea. Came to check on Katie."

She was the maid who'd taken ill. "Katie is recovered now?"

"Already on her feet," Riley said pointedly—and then shrugged and added, "Doc says she got less of the poison, most like, what with the water she washed the clothes in."

She nodded slowly. "And Dr. Smith was . . . with you all? In Elland?"

That nobody looked surprised, or hesitated before nodding, broke her heart a little. They all assumed that Liam had told her of Elland from the first—that he had trusted her with the truth as a matter of course.

Perhaps that should encourage her. These men knew her husband better than she did: she could not believe otherwise now. And if they imagined her worthy of Liam's trust, then he clearly had not suggested otherwise to them.

She took a deep breath. Liam trusted them. If Francis Smith was one of their number, then Liam would want him nearby. "Tell the doctor he is welcome to rejoin me, once he has finished his tea."

Relieved smiles traveled the group.

Never had she imagined a day might come when she would feel complimented by the approval of convicts.

CHAPTER FOURTEEN

By the calendar, he'd only lost four days. But the bright midday light showed differently. It lit Liam's face in the mirror and offered a glimpse of his elderly future: hollow cheeks. Ashen bruises beneath his eyes. A marionette's mouth, bracketed by deep lines.

He gazed on himself steadily as he knotted his cravat. The old man in the mirror looked put out. His jaw flexed and hardened, a weakling's sulk, frustration with a cravat that would not cooperate. His hands were trembling too violently to manipulate it.

Liam made a fist, squeezing hard, harder, hard enough to snap his own tendons, to break his own bones.

There. The trembling stopped.

He knotted the cravat tightly. *Choke on it*, he thought.

"Where are you going?"

His wife's startled query came from the doorway. She had forgotten how to knock. She assumed it was her right now to come and go as she pleased. Brazen, entitled, smug little fool. "Out."

"Out, where? You should be in bed. You're—"

He pivoted toward her. His expression caused her to take a startled step backward.

"I have an appointment," he said.

He had tossed her out on waking, four hours ago. She had been sleeping next to him at the time. And beforehand? Watching him, listening to him, undressing him, bathing him, eavesdropping on his dreams, feeding him medicine to keep him weak and careless and exposed. His valet had described these deeds to him in admiring tones, as though they were proof of what a faithful and wondrous boon she was, this wife of his. As though any of it had been her right.

"You nearly just died," she said sharply. She had used these four hours to bathe and refresh herself. Her sacque dress, a russet silk edged in gold lace, had been chosen by somebody—perhaps her, perhaps a cunning dressmaker—to complement the green of her eyes, and to force the viewer's awareness, through the clash of russet and red, to the flaming brilliance of her hair. She looked every inch a countess, fashionable and civilized and impossibly, provocatively beautiful.

He wanted to rip that gown. Rub dirt on her face. Knock the pins out of her complex coiffure. Perfection had no place near him. Her voice droned on, fattened by the authority she mistakenly thought she possessed.

"—no ordinary fever! Dr. Smith thinks someone poisoned you, do you know that? What on earth could be so important that you—"

Words like flies flapping about him. He pushed by them and by her, too, into the sitting room, before her hand caught his elbow.

He turned immediately. "Let go," he said softly.

Her hand detached itself. He took a long breath.

"Very well," she said. "I'm coming with you."

"No, you are not."

"Yes." She moved past him, putting herself in the doorway, barring his way by clutching the doorframe. "You are not going out alone. You have no idea how ill you were!"

He stared at her for a moment. What an absurdity. She knew he could remove her, lift her bodily away, with the barest effort. She did not know how little he trusted himself to touch her at present. If she were a man, he already would have struck her.

The thought felt strange and sickening. He had never understood or appreciated violence before being forced to practice it. He had mastered it *through* practice. Now the skill had become a part of him, an instinct: *destroy*.

"Get out of the way," he said very quietly.

She tightened her grip on the doorframe. "I've spent four days nursing you back to health, and I won't—"

"You overstepped." Words could unleash violence, too. They felt like daggers in his mouth, sharp and murderous to speak. "It was not your place to 'nurse' me. It was not your place even to feel concern."

"How can you say that? I'm your—"

"My wife. My contract wife, whose duties begin and end with the money she provides."

She met his eyes with what she probably told herself was bravery. The noble, stainless heroine, confronting the monster she had married. "You know it was always more than that."

A dull roar rushed into his ears. "I beg your pardon?"

"We loved each other. And had I known then what I know now—"

Pity. She felt pity for him now. He had no interest in what her pity had wrought. "Step aside."

"You're still feverish," she said urgently. "You—"

He grabbed her hand and forced it to his brow.

"I am cold as a stone," he said as he dropped her hand. "And I am sick of you, Anna. Sick of your demands, sick of your good intentions, sick most of all of your prurient little interest in my past. I am leaving—"

"Prurient! Liam, I am telling you I *loved* you. And I . . ." She licked her lips. "And I lost my faith in it only because I thought you had abandoned me. Do you hear me? That love never died. But I thought you had *left* me. Now that I know the truth—"

The truth? She knew only the barest outlines. Would a black-and-white sketch show her the truth of a three-dimensional world? But she *thought* she understood. She thought her pity, her Florence Nightingale ministrations, should *mean* something. He should feel *grateful*, no doubt, to find her willing to look upon him without repulsion—to remember, even, how she had once felt for the boy he'd been.

"I am leaving," he said flatly. "When I come back, you will not be here. Or, if you are, then I will find some other place to lodge. Is that clear?"

She looked astonished. "No, I—are you *angry* with me? Upset that I saw you, is that it? That I know everything now—"

His laughter sliced through her words. "Everything? You know *everything*, do you? And now you love me again. Yes, of course, knowing *everything* has won me your heart. You know, for instance, that I was tied down while some bastard burned my initials into me— because if I wanted to be called that name so badly, I could wear it on my skin. You knew that? And it moved you."

Her lips fumbled around some syllable. Of course she had no reply for him. Unspeakable things had no reply.

But he had survived them. So he could speak them.

"You knew I was whipped bloody," he said, "and salt spread in my wounds. You know I was starved, and felt grateful when Henneage vomited, for the bread came up as soon as it went down."

Her mouth fell open.

"Baby bird," he said. She looked like a baby bird, gaping for a mother's feeding. "Yes, precisely like that."

"God above," she whispered. "I—" She swallowed. "I *want* to know these things, Liam. However horrible, I want to know—"

"How courageous. You'll find the strength to *listen*. Very brave, Anna."

She stared at him, her eyes huge and fearful. An infant, at last beholding light.

But he had more marvels to share. "You'll want to know how I wept like a child as they buried me alive."

No reply for that?

"Two days, I spent buried in the hole. And survived! What a miracle; let us thank God for the miracle. Or do you still want more details? Do you want to know *precisely* how it feels to have soil clog your throat, to turn to mud when mixed with your snot? *That* will inflame your fantasies, won't it? *That* will increase your reborn love. Your husband weeping in terror—you can think of that while you touch yourself."

She recoiled from the doorway. How could she not? She was almost, almost, seeing him clearly now.

"Liam." Her voice sounded broken. "I—I don't—"

"Oh, but that's not all." He heard his own voice, light and casual. He saw her flinch from it. She had no practice at violence. "Later, I begged. I licked a monster's boots. I sucked the dirt off his heels. And I tell myself it was not unforgivable—I tell myself there is no shame; it was for Wilkins's life that I did it. I saved his throat from the noose, so the shame, no, it shouldn't crush me. But here's the truth, Anna: it was not hard by then to bend my knees. I groveled without much effort at all, if truth be told. Go ahead, picture it—hold it in your mind: on my hands and knees, bleeding, licking a man's boots like a dog." He paused, staring at her. His smile made her go paler, it seemed.

"Precisely," he continued. "Now, perhaps you can offer to bathe my brow and tell me again that you love me. *That* will make it all better. Remind me that your heart was broken when I disappeared—what a great tragedy, Shakespearean really! And even now, it makes you weep." For tears were streaming down her face. "Are those tears for you, or for me?"

"For you," she said brokenly.

"Then spare me the fucking sight of them. I cried my fill in the hole. I am done with these goddamned scenes."

He pushed past her.

For once, she had the sense not to pursue.

CHAPTER FIFTEEN

Four years earlier

The ambulatory was made of gray stone, medieval pillars thicker than a man's trunk, supporting archways that opened onto a small walled courtyard. Liam stepped through one of these archways, half expecting to find his path barred by some kilted ghost bearing uplifted claymore, demanding to know his business here.

Marriage, he would say. *I have come here to be married.*

But the courtyard was empty. A damp breeze stirred the branches of the weedy tree growing at the center. Liam took a seat on the single bench and studied his companion. An orange tree, he thought—no wonder it looked shrunken and wistful. It had been bred for kinder climates than this one.

From the other side of the wall came a sudden shout of laughter. Gravel crunched, conversation swelled and dimmed. Guests were arriving, greeting old friends as they processed inside. They would not guess that the groom sat ten yards away, alone, without family to accompany him, or friends to give encouragement in this last hour of his bachelorhood.

Melodrama. He'd left behind several friends in the hot, crowded rectory. Drinking friends, sporting friends, chums from his days at Trinity. In their company, this last hour, he had felt increasingly alone. He needed a moment to remember the people who should have been here in their place.

His father: he could have used his father's advice. His father had known how to keep a complicated woman happy, how to manage the sharp edges of her temper when the world condescended to her, how to keep her laughing, how to provoke and lure her when her quick, changeable interests turned in new directions.

His mother: sharp-witted, strong-willed, restless in her curiosity. Those qualities had proved poorly fitted to what the world wanted of her, but Liam's father had become her refuge, her inspiration, her joy. Liam knew what she would advise him: *Consider your wife your greatest and rarest treasure. Guard her. Protect her. Above all, respect her. For it is a rare treasure that cannot be captured, only coaxed to stay.*

His parents had prepared him well, for all that they had left too soon. Their memories would guide him. He knew they would have approved, and not only because this marriage, his bride's wealth, would save his patrimony. They would have approved of *her*—Anna—his soon-to-be-wife.

He took a deep breath. The salted air tasted like the sea. He had once dreamed only of travel, of adventure. He had not realized that another person could be one's adventure.

He wished Julian were here. Jules would listen to these thoughts calmly, without surprise, but with a dash of wry amusement that would help these feelings seem lighter, easier to bear.

Instead, Julian was in India. Liam had expected a cable from him, good wishes. But none had come.

Some noise startled him. He rose, and caught sight of a furtive movement—a glimpse of ivory lace, retreating behind a pillar.

A disbelieving smile lightened his mood. "Come out," he said.

And his soon-to-be-bride replied, laughing: "It's bad luck. I didn't know you were out here!"

She had plastered herself to the far side of the pillar, but her belling skirts spilled into view on either side—tiers of stiffened satin, gleaming like moonlight, embroidered with seed pearls and fringed in thick lace. "You're superstitious? I wouldn't have—"

"In this, I am! Don't come into view."

"I won't. It's your face I mustn't see—is that right?"

A pause. "I don't think the superstition is specific on that question."

She still sounded amused. "Then stay where you are," he murmured, and reached around the pillar, groping blindly until her hands found his own. Her fingers were warm, soft. As her grip tightened, he felt some last, buried anxiety dissipate. A great peace filled him.

And a jumping, fluttering excitement.

They would be *married*.

As though she heard his thoughts, she whispered, "Tonight, we'll be husband and wife."

"Yes."

They stood for a long moment, the pillar between them, and he listened to the sounds of her: her soft rapid breath, the faint rustle of shifting satin, the scuff of her slippers across stone.

"I have never felt faint before," she said. "But I am

dizzy with it. This time tomorrow, we will be en route to Paris, and married. Together, with nobody to keep us apart."

His thoughts had not gone that far. With his hands pressed to hers, his brain had darted squarely toward tonight, and the challenge this dress would pose. "How many buttons?" he asked.

It took her only a moment to follow his meaning, and she giggled. "Hundreds."

"God save me."

"Your first test!"

They laughed together, and he set his forehead against the pillar, greatly needing the cool reproach of the stone to distract his body. It would not do to go down the aisle in this state.

"Everyone is inside now," she murmured. "I peeked out a minute ago."

"All your aunties?"

"Yes, and sixty or seventy cousins. Are you certain you're all right, Liam? I came out here because this gown weighs three stone, and I needed a fresh breeze. But . . ."

Why are you out here? was her unfinished question.

"I was thinking of my parents," he said quietly.

"Oh."

"This is the happiest day of my life. I only wish my family were here."

She squeezed his hands. "But it is. *I* am here. I'm your family now."

The breath went from him. It took a moment to find his voice again; the words came out hushed, like a prayer. "How fortunate I am."

After a moment, she said, "And your cousin is inside as well. He came alone, I think."

"Yes, his wife took ill, I'm afraid." So Stephen had told him, when they had run into each other on King Street three hours ago.

What a place for a meeting! For half a second, Liam had wondered if Stephen was following him. As young children, they had been close, but once at school, when the difference in their future stations had become apparent, Stephen had grown resentful. Their relationship had come to feel like a competition—one in which Liam's reluctance to compete had only made his cousin angrier. Stephen won handily: he was the superior scholar, the better scripturalist, one of the finest debaters that Eton and Oxford had ever seen.

Regardless, he would never become the earl. And now, in one moment, Liam would also become the wealthier of them—destroying Stephen's only remaining advantage.

There had been an ugly smirk on Stephen's face in King Street as he'd registered the satchel Liam carried and the bank he'd just left. "Counting your chickens?" he'd asked. "I can't blame you."

The letter of credit had suddenly felt heavy and somehow damning.

Liam did not like to imagine that others among the guests might also be smirking, imagining that they perfectly understood the reasons behind this hasty marriage. It was not only about money. Of late, it had nothing to do with money at all. But society would imagine otherwise.

So, perhaps, would she.

"Anna . . ." Adjusting his grip around her hands, stroking her knuckles softly, he wrestled with whether to speak of it. The unusual contract, its peculiar terms, had been agreed on by both of them. But those terms need not dictate their marriage.

"What?" she whispered.

He wished he could see her face. He did not believe he was alone in these feelings.

But what if he was wrong? What if the confession alarmed her? She might fear that he meant to renege on the terms of their contract, and to keep her from her island, her freedoms, which she had declared from the start were all she wanted of a marriage.

Love was the secret around which he danced now as they kissed, flirted, laughed together. Love had not been her aim. But he had fallen in love—and he hoped, prayed, that she had done so as well.

Still, he could not tell her now, when her face was hidden. He would tell her tonight. Or, no—not when hundreds of buttons awaited him. He would tell her in Paris.

From the distance came the swell of the organ. Anna started in his grip. "Goodness! They are starting! And we, out here—"

"Run along," he said, laughing as he released her.

"Don't look at me! Promise you won't! Close your eyes!"

"They're closed," he lied, and watched as she broke away from the pillar, lifting the shimmering layers of her skirts so she might run. The clouds, being wise, suddenly parted: sunlight washed over her figure, calling out glimmers from the seed pearls, the silver embroidery and lace, and drawing fire in the ornate braids of her hair.

Just before she disappeared into the church, she glanced back, and her green eyes widened dramatically as they locked with his.

"Liar!" she called, but she was smiling. She was impossibly beautiful. She was the only sight worth seeing.

"I would be a fool to look away from you," he said. "Even for a moment."

The cabin was palatial: four rooms of velvet and silk, tasseled and carpeted in shades of azure and gold. It would be a very comfortable way to sail to Folkestone, where they would transfer to a steamer bound for Boulogne, and thence to the railway to Paris. Liam opened the door to the balcony, closing his eyes to the cool breeze spilling off the water, carried all the way from the North Sea.

"What did your cousin mean today?"

He turned. Anna had come out of the bedroom, where she had unpinned her hair. It sprawled around her shoulders, roiled in glorious abandon across the pale upper swells of her breasts. She still wore the gown, thank God. He had spent the last hour inventing fantasies of how he would remove it. "What's that?"

"Mr. Devaliant. As we left, he said he was glad that you'd already made your run on the bank, so nothing would keep us from sailing directly."

He caught back his black smile. "He said that, did he?" And here he'd thought Stephen had turned a new leaf. His wedding gift had suggested so—but there was always a catch with his cousin.

"What did he mean?" Anna asked.

He stepped inside, pulling shut the balcony door. "Only what it sounds like. We ran into each other this morning, before I went to the church."

She clasped her hands in front of her, squeezing her fingers, a gesture that looked oddly nervous. "At the bank."

"Yes," he said, trying not to frown. Was *he* the cause

of her uneasiness? Did she anticipate he would jump on her? He took a seat, to allay her nerves. "I had some business there."

"On our wedding day?"

"Yes, why?"

"Oh . . . no reason." She pulled apart her hands very suddenly, then cupped them around her elbows, prowling restlessly around the cabin. "I suppose our mornings proceeded very differently, then. I spent those hours getting plucked and powdered and pressed and curled and sewn into this dreadful gown."

"Far from dreadful," he said. "It's the loveliest—"

"It weighs three stone and it itches. It's a wonder I'm still breathing."

Her quarrelsome tone confused him. But he could not resist the opening she offered. He rose. "Allow me to assist you out of it."

But she sidestepped his reach, fixing her interest on an enameled lamp that stood bolted to the sideboard; with one finger, she traced the raised design. "What business did you have at the bank?"

A sinking feeling came over him. "Nothing of particular interest."

"Oh? Nothing to do with my accounts, then?"

He took a deep breath. "Anna—"

She faced him. "For my accounts are certainly of interest to me."

That waspish tone was not fair. "Our accounts, you mean."

Her eyes narrowed. "Oh, yes, *our* accounts now. For a woman, once married, has nothing to call her own."

He caught himself before he could push out a sharp breath. "Oh, come now. That's dramatic."

"But true."

"Your island, all the lands entailed to the earldom of Forth—none of those are mine."

She lifted her chin, staring steadily at him. "But the money? I assume your business had to do with that."

These delicate little jabs were succeeding: he felt hot now, his temper pricking. "Yes, you're right. The business concerned money. I thought to settle some private debts before we left."

"Private debts? Debts not disclosed to my lawyers, do you mean?"

He felt a twist of shame, which in turn angered him, for he had done nothing wrong. "Forgive me," he said sardonically. "I did not think to submit my tailor's bills to Sir Charles. Would he also like my grocer's address?"

Her lips compressed into a pale, tense line. She bowed her head, her chest rising and falling dramatically, and he knew a sick feeling of having disappointed her—which was not fair, damn it. He'd forgotten a few damned receipts, that was all. "Why so stricken?" Fifty pounds here, twenty pounds there—should he go down on his knees to make requests for each of these payments? Hadn't she known from the start that he'd not had a feather to fly with? "I settled my debts, Anna. Was that not the whole point?"

He regretted the remark instantly when she paled, and the more so when she said, softly and steadily, "Yes, that was the whole point."

For that agreement only made him feel further attacked. "Not the *whole* point, in fact. If I recall, the other point was to secure ownership of your island."

Her cheeks suddenly hollowed. She turned away.

"Tell me, will you wait until after our honeymoon to have the deed transferred?"

No reply.

"You already had it recorded," he said. "The sasine. Didn't you?"

Her slim shoulders lifted in a jerky shrug.

"And when did you tend to *that* business?"

"I didn't tend to it," she said stiffly. "My lawyer did."

"Sir Charles? I saw him in the church. Thought it was rather odd that he'd stayed for the wedding. But I suppose it was business that kept him here."

"He is an old friend of my family," she said flatly.

"I see. Did he go to the General Register before or after we exchanged vows?"

She faced him, her cheeks blazing. "Afterward. The very *moment* we were wed."

Wrong, wrong, to feel a stabbing in his gut—the twist of betrayal, of bitter disappointment. He was a hypocrite, to be sure: he had gone to the bank with their marriage license in hand. Why should her lawyer not have gone to file the sasine the very moment that license was signed?

"Well, then." He took a ragged breath. "You understand why I went to the bank."

"Of course." Her voice was colorless. "We each had business to accomplish. That was the point, as you've said."

But it was not the point. She *thought* it was the point—clearly it *had* been the point for *her*. "Of course, your island could have waited." *No, shut up*, he told himself—but now he could not forget how coldly she'd looked at him a minute ago, as though he were some grubbing charlatan, when she herself had not hesitated to enforce *her* benefits from this marriage. "Your island was not going to drift away, or grow more expensive to keep. But the interest on my debts would have continued to accrue. So I think you'll see it was sound good sense that drove me to act this morning."

"Yes," she spat. "Sound good sense. We are both very *sensible*." She sat down heavily on the bed. "Of course, *I* put the business in the hands of a paid lawyer. *I* spent the morning doing nothing but thinking of *you*."

His laugh felt disbelieving. "My God—that's not fair."

"Quite right, fairness doesn't enter into it. I'm only telling you what *I* was doing, while *you* were paying a call to my bankers to instruct them to divert *my* money south to England."

Her money—again, she said it.

He dragged in a breath, struggling for calm. "Those were the terms on which we agreed. Were they not?"

She tipped back her head to look down her nose at him, mouth twisting with distaste, as though he were an overbearing beggar. "Of course."

He laughed again. This was ludicrous—a fantasy gone wrong in an instant. "I certainly would not have agreed to those terms had I known you would try to shame me with them."

"Shame? Whatever do you mean?"

"What else do you call this?"

She rose suddenly. To his bafflement, tears seemed to glimmer in her eyes. She dashed at them as she hauled open the door to the balcony.

Tears. Shocked, he followed her outside, into a cool night breeze, thick with the scents of fish and salt water and smoke. The twilight glimmered gently over the Firth of Forth, the lanterns on distant sailing vessels winking like stars. "Anna, what is this? What are we doing?" She *was* fighting tears. He felt helpless, confused. "Why are you so upset? I would have told you—I should have told you, but it honestly never occurred to me. This was the arrangement we struck. I didn't think it would . . . distress you so."

"It doesn't." She wiped her eyes once more, then stared fixedly out at the water. "Of course you were right to settle the debts. To act at once, without delay. You were thinking practically. I'm glad of it. It's good to keep one's mind on business, even on one's wedding day. Perhaps *especially* on one's wedding day, when one's marriage is—what ours is."

He felt struck. Why, her distress might bode well for him. Suddenly it seemed the most encouraging sign imaginable: she was upset because she, too, wanted more from this marriage than practicality.

He touched her arm, not letting go when she stiffened. "My mind was always on you," he said urgently. "I wanted to get the business done—out of the way, as quickly as possible. So I would need to think of nothing *but* you afterward."

She nodded once. "And the five hundred pounds sterling on your person?"

He recoiled. "I—" Was he to be interrogated in this fashion, and to submit meekly, like a child accounting for his allowance?

Moreover, how did she *know* about the five hundred pounds? Had she been *spying* on him?

She saw the question in his face, and offered a cool smile. "Your cousin mentioned that withdrawal as well. I found it rather surprising. More so when you let *me* tip the porter, half an hour ago."

He gaped at her, battling a true feeling of outraged

pride, the sorer for how handily his cousin had fooled him again.

No. No. Resist it.

"I had no small change," he said flatly.

That was true: Stephen had only given him banknotes. But it sounded like a petty excuse, and her smile widened, sharp as a blade.

"I see. I suppose you intended that money to defray our expenses on the road?"

"Exactly."

"Yet you also had a letter of credit issued in your name? Not mine. Mine is nowhere on it—I found it in your jacket. You wore it on you to our *wedding*."

"Christ." He stepped backward. "I am not going to defend myself to you. If you think me a swindling con man—"

"I think you an Englishman with little experience of wealth," she said coolly. "After all, your father left you nothing but debts. You'll understand, I hope, if I might wish a *small* measure of oversight as you begin to avail yourself of my—pardon me, *our*—funds."

He turned on his heel.

"Where are you going?" came her demand from behind him.

"Out." Out to wrestle down this furious mood, this dangerous temptation to shove the five hundred pounds sterling in her face, and leave *her* to figure out later that his cousin had lied: Liam had not taken it from her account. It had been Stephen's wedding gift, offered in the church, which Liam had tried to refuse, knowing that nothing from his cousin ever came without strings and hidden blades.

But Stephen had insisted. And *he*, ever the naïve

idiot, had thought that perhaps, just perhaps, his cousin meant the gift as a rapprochement, the mark of a new and more amicable chapter in their relations. He had, after all, spent all day moaning and glooming about his absent family. He'd been ripe for plucking, and his bloody cousin had sensed it.

"Don't hurry back," his wife called as he yanked open the door. "The maid can assist me with the gown."

"I will be back before we sail," he bit out. But he would not stay here and risk saying things he would forever regret. He would go find some peaceful corner in which to get hold of his temper. Then, on returning, he would explain to her calmly what lay between him and his cousin, and why Stephen might have designed this feud to spite him. The ship did not sail until eight o'clock; there was time.

Anna watched the door close. On a great gasping breath, she threw herself onto the bed and let the tears fall, hot and fierce, soaking through her fingers and staining the coverlet.

Stupid, stupid.

What harm if he wanted her money? She *knew* he wanted—*needed*—her money. That was why she had proposed this marriage in the first place. Why blame him now for what had recommended him to her?

But to see the proof of it, so plainly offered—to know that as she'd dressed for their wedding, dreaming of him, aloft on these secret swelling feelings of love, he'd been at the bank, availing himself leisurely of her credit, her cash, her accounts—

It was humiliating.

More humiliating yet, she had no cause to be angry. They had not married for love. Falling in love with him had been *her* mistake. *She* would pay the price for it. *He* should not be punished.

After a few long minutes, she got hold of herself and sat up. The cabin was exquisite. Decked in roses and sateen, ripe for romance. The sky outside was darkening in layers, fading from amethyst to indigo to black.

The mantel clock chimed seven. An hour remained until they set sail.

When he came back, she would apologize. She rubbed her chest, which felt bruised. He would not know how she ached. She would be bright, and apologetic, and cheerful.

She would try to make him love her. But she would not blame him if she failed. If he wanted only a contract marriage, then she would focus on her island, on Rawsey, that gift he alone had given her, the wonder of which would never be diminished even if he broke her heart. Besides, one day—perhaps soon—they would make a child. These were sureties vouched to her by this marriage. She would never regret wedding him, even if this ache in her chest never eased.

But she *could* make him love her. He was close—she knew it. She could not be alone in these feelings. She could have sworn, this morning in the cloister, he had been tempted to speak to her of love. If only she had stepped around the pillar and looked into his face!

She could go now and tell him everything. Confess her heart. Be brave.

She rose, staring at the door, then made herself sit again. She would not chase him. They had promised each other freedom, and she did not break her vows.

But tonight, she would seduce him. She would not call the maid after all—she would wear this dress until he came back. He'd professed himself ready for the challenge of the buttons. And in Paris, as they toured through the artworks he liked best, she would listen closely, and try to see them through his eyes. He had so much to teach her. And she could teach him, too, for her money was not the best thing about her. What was money? It had not persuaded her aunts to keep her, and it had not brought her joy. Joy came from other things, which money could not buy: knowledge and learning, the lung-burning exhaustion of a good walk, conversations with dear friends on cold nights, evenings on the beach at Rawsey, his laughter, his company, *him* . . .

He would come back. And she would apologize and kiss him, and he would smile and apologize, too, and they would fall onto this bed and make a child together. Either way, whether his or the child's, love would be hers soon enough.

She sat, watching the door, and waited.

CHAPTER SIXTEEN

London, 1861

*H*er husband did know his liquor. He kept an excellent scotch at his bedside—peaty, an Isla variety. Anna had been sipping it as she watched the sunbeams intensify and sprawl across the room, then shrink again, until darkness fell.

The air held a chill. A maid had come earlier to start the fire, but Anna had sent her away. An hour ago, the household had settled into a deeper quiet, the servants having retreated to their beds. Now and then, the grandmother clock in the hall announced the time.

He had been gone for seven hours and forty-five minutes. She had not moved, save to refill her glass. She had promised herself that she would give him eight hours to work through his anger and fear. For, yes, it was fear. His anger was simply a mask for it.

She tried not to be angry in turn. Did he truly imagine she would shrink from him, be repulsed by what he'd endured? That he had wept made him human. That he had begged made him practical. That he had survived made him stronger than anyone she knew.

But running out on her—*that* was cowardly. Knowing him no coward, she would give him eight hours to remember himself. Then, and only then, she would give chase. She had learned her lesson four years ago. She had failed to hunt for him then. Tonight, after eight hours, if he did not come home, she would start looking—and she would not cease until she found him, no matter how long it took.

As the clock at last began to toll midnight, she reached for her shawl—then heard the distant commotion of his return, the slamming, far off, of the front door, and an indecipherable exchange between him and Wilkins.

She sank back into the chair. The breath that burst from her seemed to have been pent up since his departure. A brief dizzy relief swam through her, until she inhaled again sharply and willed it away. It felt too close to weakness, and for what came next, she would only need strength.

But oh, God be thanked, *he had come back.*

She bolted the remainder of her glass and filled it from the bottle sitting at her feet. She had been drinking very slowly for hours, on an empty stomach, but her senses felt painfully alert. She heard his footsteps on the stairs—*scented* his approach, the musk of his skin and the astringent soap he used in his hair.

Now came his passage through the sitting room. At the bedroom door, he briefly hesitated. Did he sense her presence? Wilkins would have told him that she had not left the house.

The door opened, the light from the outer room silhouetting his figure and blotting out his features.

"You're home," she said casually. "Good. We will finish our conversation now."

Some slight, abrupt movement suggested his surprise. Perhaps he noticed that she still wore her afternoon dress. Perhaps he smelled the scotch, the decanter uncapped by her foot.

An empty glass sat beside it. She nudged it forward with her stockinged toe. "Have some, if you need it."

He stepped inside, closing the door. With a soft hiss, the gaslights rose.

Wherever he had gone today, he had not gone gently. A smudge of dirt rode his angular cheekbone. His coat and cravat were missing, and mud encrusted his boots. He stared at her for a long moment, his mouth pressed into a hard, flat line, evidently deciding what to do with her.

He did not want to speak of love. He'd made that plain.

Very well, then. They would speak of revenge.

"I thought you'd understood me," he said. "You go, or I do."

She settled deeper in the overstuffed chair, considering this. "No," she said. "That is—you spoke clearly, but not with any clarity. And before either of us goes, there are questions to be settled."

His sigh sounded weary. He leaned back against the door. "Such as?"

"Who was responsible for your abduction?"

"That is none of your concern."

"Wrong. I am your wife. Whoever took you, took you from *me*. It is entirely my concern."

He pushed himself off the door, reaching for the buttons of his waistcoat as he walked to the window. "I am not going to discuss this tonight." He yanked open the curtains. Whatever he saw in the street below did not impress him. He threw his waistcoat to the floor and yanked the curtains shut again. "Get out," he said as he faced her.

"First, we finish this conversation."

He nodded once, curtly, and then strode for the exit.

She waited until he had taken hold of the door latch. "Don't make me follow you, Liam." She said it very neutrally. "I gave you eight hours. That's all you will get."

He pivoted toward her. Even before he spoke, she saw the tack he meant to take in the sneering of his mouth. Viciousness was so foreign to his nature that it transformed his expression entirely. "Poor Anna. Always being left. I thought you had at least grown accustomed to it. Or had more pride than to give chase."

She rose. "*Who did this to you?*"

A beat. Then he shrugged. "He's dead."

Her hands curled into fists. That could not be true. She wanted a pound of flesh—or several. "His name?"

"Harold Marlowe."

She did not know the name. "Who was he?"

"An inventor. He required rare metals for his devices. He purchased several mines overseas, including Elland, which had formerly been a penal camp."

"And? How did he fix on *you*?"

"He used convict labor in the mines," he said in a clipped, bored drawl. "But his overseers' methods did not suit the government. They ceased to supply him with labor. So he found a new source. Rich men paid him to dispatch their enemies, whom he sent to serve as slaves at Elland."

How neatly and coldly he summarized it. Obviously he had practiced this explanation, silently, in his own head. He probably did not know, or had not admitted to himself, that he'd been practicing it for *her*.

But the man who had built that office for her at Lawdon, who had promised her at Muirswood Links that
she would never again be alone if she wished it, and who
had become her family the day of their wedding—that
man had realized that one day, if he survived, he would
owe her a reckoning.

She held his gaze. "You're certain he's dead."

"Yes."

Very well. One down. "And who paid Marlowe to
target you?"

He brushed past her, retrieving a glass and the whisky
bottle. "My cousin," he said, and splashed a generous
amount into the glass before throwing it back.

His reply made sense. Stephen Devaliant would have
had the most to gain from his cousin's death: the title,
at the least, and some of Anna's wealth, too. No wonder
Devaliant had written so many probing letters to her,
anxious to know about the care of the estates, and the
legal entailments of her properties. "What have the authorities said?"

"They aren't involved."

He had dealt with this alone? "Whyever not?"

"There is no evidence," he said through his teeth.

"None? But the letters your cousin wrote me—
he kept insisting that you must be dead. Surely that
proves—"

"It suggests a great deal. It proves nothing. And the
law requires proof."

She understood, suddenly, the dark weight under which
he'd been laboring. To survive, to return to freedom—and
to see one's enemy walking free, without fear. "Then we'll
find evidence."

"A waste of time." He sat in her wing chair and looked

at her, his expression oddly lax, as though drained of all emotion. "There are other ways."

"What ways?"

"Financial destruction, to start." He paused. "Social destruction next. And then I'm going to kill him."

She caught her breath. "You mean you will have justice."

"No," he said. "I mean I will wrap my hands around his throat and choke him to death."

Some restless energy seized her. She paced a circle, stopping in front of him. "Don't be stupid. They hang people for murder here."

He shrugged. "Then maybe I'll hang."

As though it made no difference! Anger blazed through her. "A fine thing to have survived for!"

"Survival doesn't require a reason," he said wearily. "Any dumb beast, from a slug to a roach, will try to persist."

To hear him discuss himself so—to treat his future, his very life, as though it were disposable, to be squandered on his disgusting cousin—infuriated her. "Shut your bloody mouth for once."

That startled him. He lifted a brow. "I beg your pardon?"

She knelt in front of him, gripping his knees hard. "How dare you speak of yourself so. I will not let you do it. You are *mine*, do you hear me? And no one speaks of me and mine that way."

He took a breath—loosed it, then licked his lips. "I don't—how many goddamned times must I say this? I have no interest in being—"

He started to stand. She scrambled up and seized his shoulders, shoved him back into the chair. "Listen to me," she spat. "You wept, Liam. You begged. You were beaten, degraded, you were tortured. Why flinch as I say it? Why recite these things as though they were sins of *yours*?"

"You have no idea—"

"Shut *up*! *Listen* for once! Did you think I needed telling? I *saw* what was done to you—I saw it from every angle. I bathed the scars on your back. I traced the initials on your chest. And you tried to hide them? Why, you should walk naked in the street to boast of what you survived. Other men would learn then what it means to be a man—to survive all that, and to come home *triumphant*."

"Triumphant." The word, spoken against her palm over his mouth, burned like a curse. "Is that what you think?"

"I think you a survivor," she said fiercely. "And I think you *mine*. And I will not let you throw yourself away on that bastard. You are *mine*, and I am *keeping* you."

He was going to throw her off. As his muscles coiled to reject her, she hooked her hands through his hair. When he sprang out of the chair, she yanked him forward, hard, into a bruising kiss.

"Strip," she said into his mouth. "Strip and I'll show you what to do with yourself."

She felt a tremor move through him—and his immediate resistance to it. But she was done letting him set the lead. His cravat and waistcoat were already gone; his shirt must go, too. She gripped the collar and ripped it apart.

He went still, staring at her, his face taut. Now, a moment too late for credibility, his lip curled. He was going to say something mocking, something cutting.

She slammed her palm back over his mouth and put her lips to his throat, letting him feel the edge of her teeth. With one hand on his shoulder, she shoved him back down into the chair.

"Hands over your head," she said.

As he tipped his head back, he regarded her through lowered eyelids, his gaze glittering and opaque. His smirk bloomed, his mask firmly in place. He was silently laughing at her. Mocking her. Between the two of them, *she* was not the expert in this game.

She locked eyes with him. She was a quick learner. So he'd discover.

"Raise your arms," she said.

His fisted hands rested on his broad thighs. He rolled his knuckles, cracking them leisurely against his thumbs.

And then he raised his hands.

She reached for the hem of his shirt. But he moved faster. He caught her by the waist and dragged her down on top of him. A quick, deadly kiss. His tongue stroked the seam of her lips, then broke inside. His hand clamped over the back of her head; he held her gripped, sprawled awkwardly across his lap, as they kissed deeply.

The heat of his palm closing around her ankle called her back to her wits. She knew what he intended. This would be no quick clothed coupling.

She wrested free of him and pulled off his shirt. His undervest now remained. "Get up," she said. "*Stand.*"

A beat of inaction. She found herself holding her breath, her heart pounding. She did not, in fact, have the strength to force this.

But she had other means.

Her sacque unfastened simply, not meant for public wear. With fumbling hands she loosened the ties at her waist, the tapes beneath it. The dress split around her, taking her petticoats with it. She stepped backward, out of it, wearing only her corset and chemise and drawers, and stepped squarely in front of the nearest gas sconce, so the light limned her body through the linen. "Get up," she repeated softly.

His jaw tightened as he looked her over. His nostrils flared.

Then, at last, he uncoiled from the chair—rising as sinuously as a snake, shucking his undervest as he came toward her. Her hands closed on the hot, rough skin of his waist—her fingertips tracing the rough map of scars around to his back. She felt him stiffen slightly, and dug her fingernails into his ribs as she pulled him against her.

Their mouths met again. Yes, kissing was the way, the trick, the magic that made his body loosen and grow limber, molding to her own. He stepped into her, one hard thigh coming between her legs, and held her tightly pinned as he kissed her again.

She pushed him off suddenly, sharply enough that he stumbled. His head came up, his eyes narrow, glittering with animal intelligence as she turned, silently commanding him to unlace her corset.

He pounced, his hands clever and quick with the laces, his mouth hot on the join of her neck and shoulder. He lifted off her chemise; her drawers, too, fell away. His broad palm covered her bare belly and pulled her backward against him, his erection thick and solid against her naked flesh.

No shame: there could be no shame between them. This commandment brought with it a curious and dizzying liberation. She rolled her hips against him and heard him growl into her ear. Her scrabbling hands groped blindly behind her for the fastening of his trousers, and now he worked with her, his own hands taking over, so when he turned her back toward him, their bare bodies pressed together. His grip held her there against him, and she tried twice to pull free before she slapped her hand against his arm, a sound so sharp and furious that it would have shocked her had it not worked to make him let go.

Her mouth fell to his pectoral, to the initials scored into his flesh. She felt him flinch—felt his fingers dig cruelly into her upper arms. He mistook this for pity.

She reached down, closing her hand over the hard length of his cock to show him differently.

His grip loosened.

She kissed her way down his body, in the light of the gas lamps turned high, with the mirror behind him showing her, in brief glimpses, the brazenness of their postures. But without shame, the brazenness became a blessing. Let him look on her—let him stare, his breath audibly rasping in his lungs. She was staring, too— pulling away now to admire the sight of her fingers stretched across the scarred muscled ridges of his abdomen. And her other hand, gripping the jutting length of him, stroking now, at first softly, and then, as his rough noises guided her, more firmly, the length of him.

An idea came to her. He had done similar before. She put her mouth on him and licked him, tasting the salty tip of his cock.

A noise exploded from him. He lifted her underneath the arms, carried her to the bed, and threw her down, coming over her now with no hesitation, his strong hands gripping her face as he kissed her again.

"Always like this," she gasped moments later as he kissed down her throat. "Always in the light."

For the briefest moment, he stilled—stretched over her, leonine, his muscles long and taut, the line of one leg outstretched on the mattress to brace his weight above her, the most glorious line of geometry in the universe. Calf flexing, long foot balanced, thigh sculptured and thick.

And then he kissed her mouth again—gently, so gently. A whisper of lips.

"Anna," he said very softly. "Light becomes you."

The mood changed. Softened. Now his hand combed through her hair, and they rolled lazily over each other as they kissed and stroked each other's bodies. The contrast between the roughness that warped his shoulder blades and ribs, and the smooth hairlessness of his lower back and buttocks, ceased to shock her palms—instead, these variations became fascinating, well worth study.

Pleasure built in quiet, leisurely movements. The lingering stroke of his tongue across her nipple. The teasing play of his hand between her legs, his fingers plucking and flirting with her. She found his cock again, rubbing her palm over the head of it, timing her movements to the music of his breath. And at last, when he fitted himself to her and pushed slowly inside, she felt gentleness swell into something hotter and sharper, an urgent staccato that overtook her hips, and guided his own as he thrust inside her, deeper and deeper, their limbs tangled, his head in her hands, her hair trapped in his, their mouths locked, sealed together, unbreakable.

Pleasure took her first—and a moment later, as though swallowing her cry had overset him, he came as well, shuddering on top of her, then rolling over to pull her atop him, never letting go.

Sweat sealed their bodies together as their breathing slowed. He stroked her hair, untangled it in long, light touches, spreading it in pieces across her back, dropping a kiss now and then on her bare shoulder when she twitched with lingering echoes of delight.

Gradually his hand fell still. The silence grew deep again, pressing on them. But it was a comfortable weight, the respite after a long labor. She felt no need to speak, until suddenly words filled her mouth and pushed out.

"You are mine," she said. "All of you."

His face turned, so his mouth pressed against her temple. But he did not reply.

She had courage enough to speak as long as it took, though. "I mean to keep you. Do you understand?"

The barest suggestion of a smile. Not wide enough to reassure her.

"You vowed to act as my equal, not my better. I mean to hold you to that, too."

Now, at last, he eased away a little, so their eyes could meet. "Your better," he said softly. "God save me. I have never thought that."

She brushed the hair from his eyes, pausing to trace the firm, full length of one dark brow. The shape of his face was beautiful, the bones strong and thick, laid at angles by a masterly hand. "A man is what he makes of himself," she said softly. "Not what is done to him. And so, too, a woman. You know I believe that. Otherwise, I would not have gone looking for a husband four years ago. I simply would have let some man find me. Yes?"

He exhaled. "Yes," he said. "But—"

"No buts. And if there's no justice to be had but Stephen's life, very well. But it won't come at the cost of yours. For your life is *mine*, and *I* won't pay that price."

Some shadow fleeted over his face, gone when she smoothed his brow again. It would be small steps, she understood. But they would not go backward; she would not allow it.

She cleared her throat. "As your equal, I can decide this. And I say, your life is mine, and it will not be risked without my say-so. Do you agree?"

His mouth flattened. She kissed it gently.

"You had best agree," she whispered. "Unless you think my life worth the wasting, too."

He gripped her face and took over the kiss, his tongue inside her mouth, his thumb stroking hard over her cheekbone.

"All right," he said when at last he broke away.

"Carefully," she said, to be sure they were clear. "You will go about it carefully and secretly, if there is no other way."

He lay back again, staring at the ceiling. "I'd have help."

"Who?"

"Auburn. An old friend."

Yes, he had told her of the Duke of Auburn, long ago, in Scotland. School friends, very close. "He knows what happened?"

"Yes. And today . . ." He rolled back toward her, coming up on an elbow, studying her. "Today, I did such a favor for him."

A shock jolted through her. Did he mean . . . ? "Go on."

"Miss Martin was having some trouble," he said. "An

old enmity, from before the war in India. Jules and I . . . ended it."

"Speak plainly."

"Her villain attacked. He is dead. Auburn fired the shot, but my finger was on a trigger as well."

She kept her face carefully blank. He was communicating with her now, and they would not go backward, even if her conscience, shaped by homilies for children, squirmed at these tidings.

"Was that the first time," she asked steadily, "that you found yourself ready to kill?"

He sat up, and for a moment she feared he meant to leave. But, no, he was only taking a deep breath before he faced her. "I have killed before."

The words sounded heavy and dark. He took no pride in them.

She sat up, too. "When?"

"First in Botany Bay. Two men. They wanted me dead. But I killed them first."

"Good," she said quietly, and watched his gaze fall, his downcast lashes veiling his expression briefly. But she sensed his relief, and put her hand over his, squeezing.

"We do what we must to survive," she said softly. "And later? In the camp?"

"It did not end peacefully."

She hesitated. One day, perhaps, he would tell her the whole of it. But now was not the time to push.

The gaslight limned the musculature of his upper body. It gleamed off the thick, solid bunching of his upper arms. He was tense again. She regretted it.

She knew how to cure it.

"Come here," she murmured, and pulled him back into her arms.

He lay down with her again, and delighted her by smiling as she stroked her hand over his waist, then lower.

"Again?" he murmured. "You have quite a thirst for a child, Lady Forth."

"I have a thirst for my husband, and four years to make up for."

"I can help with that," he said, and came over her.

CHAPTER SEVENTEEN

*H*is wife was gambling with criminals—and winning.

"Once more," she crowed, and threw down her cards.

A disbelieving groan traveled the rest of the table. Such was the group's reputation, in this smoky tavern in Tiger's Bay, that the sound of their disapproval sent a visible flinch through the room. Several men standing by the bar began to inch toward the door.

"That's the third game she's won," grumbled Jackson. "If I didn't know you traveled armed, Lock, I might wonder at her honesty."

"But I do travel armed," Liam murmured.

Jackson grunted.

"I have hearing to match my card skills," his wife said sweetly. "And I, too, travel armed. So you may address your aspersions to me directly—although, I confess, I am not in the practice of entertaining complaints from sore losers."

The other men burst into laughter, and after a grudging moment, Jackson grinned, too.

"Well, that's another round on me, then," he said as he stood. "Lads? I know the lady will have another scotch."

"Indeed she won't," Liam said, rising and pulling Anna to her feet. They had already lingered an hour longer than he was comfortable. That she'd managed to convince him to bring her along spoke a great deal of her powers of persuasion, and very little of his good judgment. This was a den of thieves and cutthroats; that she fitted in so well should probably concern him.

"What a pity," Anna said. "Must we go so soon?"

"Unless you mean to bankrupt them entirely, yes. Jackson, will you walk us out? I need a word."

Jackson amiably strolled after them. On the street, Liam handed Anna into the carriage before saying in a low voice, "Any news on how he's still solvent?" Stephen's newest railway company had collapsed in the wake of the new law's introduction, investors losing faith and selling in droves. By now, his financiers should have called in their loans. But no news of bankruptcy had reached Liam's ears.

Jackson frowned, then turned his head aside to spit into the gutter—which, in this corner of London, took up half the street, having not been repaired since a Hanover sat the throne. "Seems a puzzle," he said. "Men come and go, mind you—a hive of industry, over there. But none of them is creditors, by my reckoning, which means he's still got money to pay them somehow, even if by all rights he shouldn't."

A great impatience swelled through Liam. He tamped it down with a full, long breath.

"All right," he said. "You'll let me know if you hear anything."

"The very moment." As Liam turned away, Jackson caught his arm. "Fine piece," he said, nodding toward the coach.

Liam smiled grimly. "Not a piece, Jackson. My wife."

"Ah, like that, is it?" Jackson released him, looking cross. "Right-o. Sometimes I forget, you toffs get quite touchy. Tug my forelock, should I, when I speak to you now?"

Liam paused. These moments, in which his own station intruded into friendships that had been born in blood and dirt—in a time when he'd been a prisoner, same as the others—came more frequently now. And he was not sure what to do. He had straddled two worlds for almost a year now, and until last week, he had not realized the great effort it required.

That evening, Anna in his bed—her mouth on his scars, her forbidding of shame—seemed to have broken whatever scaffolding had supported him. Now, suddenly, he felt the weaknesses trembling through his facade. He did not know how to speak to Jackson anymore. He did not know how to speak to her. He looked in the mirror and no longer knew whether his reflection deserved his contempt—or his forgiveness.

He thought it was possible, perhaps, that this crumbling was the first step toward becoming whole again.

"It's not like that," he said at last, too late. And then he grinned. "Hell, Jackson, you saw her inside—she stomped you at whist. She'd probably take it as a compliment to be called a 'fine piece.'"

The window in the brougham slammed open. "Yes," came Anna's voice. "I would."

The window slammed shut again, and Jackson chuckled.

"Yeah," he said. "I see why you were desperate to make it home." He slapped Liam on the shoulder. "Mad lunatic that you were. Give her my thanks for it. I guess we all owe her a debt." With a nod and a wink, he went back into the tavern.

"You've become an eavesdropper," Liam said as he joined his wife inside the coach.

"Oh, I always was one," she said, twinkling at him. "Auntie Liz tried to break me of the habit, but Auntie May encouraged it—she paid me a shilling for every ill remark that I heard Auntie Liz make about her."

He laughed—without hesitation, genuinely. That reflex had come back almost overnight, it seemed. Perhaps he was indulging it too much; he had a reputation for discerning wit, and would look fatuous now in company.

But the risk did not concern him. It seemed well worth the reward.

In the brief silence, she had turned away to make a study of the sights out the window. On their way here, the poverty in these slums, the broken windows stuffed with rags and newspapers, the ragged children scattering from their games of knucklebone to make way for the coach, had disturbed her. "I have seen this kind of poverty in Edinburgh," she'd said, "but I imagined here, in the heart of the kingdom, so close to the Queen, there might be less of it."

Now, however, her frown seemed to arise from a different concern. "I liked those men very much," she said slowly. "But I don't think I would wish to meet them after dark, if they did not look on me already as a friend."

"They do," he said. "You're my wife. Should you ever stand in need, you may count on them as brothers."

"Yes, but . . ."

He waited uneasily. She was not a woman to guard her words to save offense, which meant she must be deciding whether or not *she* wanted to know the answer to her stirring curiosity.

He was not going to lie to her about anything now. But he still doubted if all his answers would prove acceptable to her.

Better to know sooner than later. "Ask," he said softly.

"I thought Elland a place where rich men sent their enemies. But those men—everyone in that pub knew them. It seemed like they weren't newcomers. Like they had had a longstanding hold on this area, one not strictly . . . legal."

"You're perceptive." Jackson had been transported for attempted murder. Unlike so many others, he'd never bothered to declare his innocence on the charge. "Marlowe's trade in paid abductions didn't keep his mines adequately stocked with laborers. There were legitimate convicts—the ones who caused trouble in their official assignments—who ended up in Elland."

"What a devilish complex operation," she murmured. "It is a pity that Marlowe did not receive the Queen's justice."

The remark darkened Liam's mood. He did not want to dwell on the matter unless some course of remedy was at hand. Anyway, a much more pleasant subject sat across from him.

"Tell me," he said, "was it your aunties who taught you to gamble, or your dozens of cousins?"

"Neither group. I learned that on the island."

"Ah." That made sense, of course. He remembered how friendly, on what intimate standing, she had seemed with the rough-spun Rawseyans. During that brief holiday he'd passed there, while falling in love with her, he'd watched her with amazement. Noblesse oblige had guided many a great lady to condescend to her tenants, but Anna's manner with them had been warm, unaffected—that of an equal.

It occurred to him suddenly that *she* had the skill he was seeking. She moved between worlds, across cavernous divides, without effort.

"What is it?" she asked. "You have a look on your face."

"I'm marveling at you."

She blushed. "A compliment! Quick, has your fever come back?" With a teasing smile, she came onto his bench to check his forehead, and he caught her hand and kissed it, then inhaled her deeply.

Wonder prickled over him. To take her in his arms so easily—to kiss her neck now, that secret spot found only by nudging aside her chignon, so redolent with the scent of her—it seemed bizarre and miraculous that he could do these things, all at once, without feeling a twist in his gut, fear of what she might discover about him. That this gift could be his, that *she* could be his, so suddenly, so completely, when for so long it had seemed an impossibility—

He could not grasp it.

He tried to grasp it as he sucked her earlobe and felt her squirm with pleasure. But on the heels of this amazed happiness, always, chased foreboding.

He tried to ignore it as she turned her face to his and their lips met and her tongue came into his mouth. Stephen had no doubt been behind the attempt to poison him, but that carelessness at the club—handing over his jacket at the cloakroom, when Stephen was about—

would not be repeated. Anywhere Anna went alone, she was followed, unknowing, by one of his men. Stephen, too, was followed. They would not be allowed within a hundred yards of each other. She was safe.

And yet a sense of danger now lived just under his skin, flaring to acuity at odd times. For months, the provocation for it had been sudden noises, or thronging crowds, and once, the flutter of a bird at the periphery of his vision.

But the trigger had changed. The trigger now was this creeping peace, this startled sense of possibility, that came over him in her presence. *She* provoked it, by showing him how much he had to lose.

She tasted the shift in his mood, perhaps, for her mouth eased away from his. "What is it?" she murmured, stroking his hair back from his brow.

He kissed her again. It was not her place to be burdened with this nonsense. She could do nothing to help him dispel it. "Not boredom, I'll promise you that."

She laughed softly. "Yes, with the company you keep, boredom would be a rare blessing."

"Thank you for coming. You fit in alarmingly well."

"And you kept warning me I would regret it!"

"I had no idea that you had such chameleon skills. You must teach me."

She laughed again, and laid her finger on his lower lip, a touch that riveted all his senses, and suggested far better entertainments than talk. "Be born as a woman, then—one of the few with a title in her own right, and a determination to oversee her own estates, and all sorts of masculine interests. That, I fear, is the best way to learn to be a chameleon. I have been called mannish, you know, and sometimes I think it's true."

"Mannish." He pulled her close and spoke into her ear. "I will persuade you otherwise, shall I?"

"Yes, please," she said, and hiked up her skirts to climb on top of him.

No man shows his true face on the honeymoon. So her auntie Liz had once pronounced sourly after quarreling again with her husband. The remark had come to Anna's mind more than once in the last blissful week. It felt to her as though she and Liam at last were having a honeymoon, without ever leaving London.

He did nothing without her; she would not be kept out of anything. If he needed to meet with disreputable friends, fellow survivors, or nervous artists, she went with him. She would know everything, and allow nothing to be hidden. Honesty was the only way to proceed.

And to her surprise, he did not quarrel with her company. He had recovered fully from his illness, that mysterious sickness or poisoning, and carried about him that peculiarly abandoned and merry air of a man who had survived another close call with death.

In the mornings, they breakfasted together and discussed their hopes for the day, and made plans for amusement: the opera, drives through the park, visits to the Royal Academy, where Liam was advising on the upcoming exhibit.

In the late afternoons, when civilized people dressed in preparation for evenings out, they undressed each other, always in the light.

Later they dined together, often in private. Rarely he told her stories of the men in this household, the favors they had done him, the ways they had survived. More often they talked of her life during the past four years. Her labors on Rawsey had grown the community to almost two hundred, among them twenty children, who filled the schoolhouse with song each morning at half past eight. With the aid of new patent manures, the small oat and barley harvests had doubled. In a year or two, should the barley continue to flourish, some of the islanders hoped to create a distillery.

But Rawsey had not kept her entirely occupied; she had also seen to Liam's lands, and not simply for duty's sake. Fertile English soil made an ideal testing ground for experiments in agriculture. Liam listened with fascination as she recounted her trials—some failures, but mostly successes. She had done away with the potato crops, and he agreed to stay that course until five years had passed without further news of blight. Against the will of two of his stewards, Anna had also forced the introduction of a more modern scheme of crop rotation, and she recounted her battles to Liam's amusement.

In these conversations, it began to seem to her that Liam had been a part of her last four years, even in his absence. His estates, the improvements she had made to them, the plans she'd nursed for the future: all of these things she had undertaken in his name, even if she had forced herself not to think of him.

Would an outsider have looked on these evenings with envy? Anna knew that some women would not find romance in the discussion of oats. But what an intoxication to speak of her chemical theories and agrarian strategies to a man who paid rapt attention, and asked intelligent questions that made her pause to think before replying. Oats, it seemed, could form the basis for all sorts of things: jokes, sly repartee, kisses, abrupt excursions to bed . . .

It all felt so easy. Too easy, perhaps. Liam was attentive, kind, ever ready to laugh—but when he imagined her attention elsewhere, she often caught a strange look on his face, distant and evacuated. Wherever his mind went, in such moments, was full of shadows. But he would never answer honestly when she asked about his thoughts. Indeed, his smile appeared so instantly then that she felt unsure if he had abandoned his masks after all.

So, from an instinct of self-preservation, she tried to caution herself as they assembled this new life together. He had not spoken of love, and she would not speak of it again until he did. They shared a bed, and meals, and lovely laughing discussions, and the piecemeal experiences that constituted mundane life. But the specter of his cousin overshadowed them, and after hearing all the measures Liam had undertaken to find proof of Stephen's guilt, Anna began to worry that her own optimism had been ill founded. If no official justice could be had, then a bloodier justice would need to serve. But if he were caught, Liam's execution of his cousin would cost his own life.

No. She would never let that happen—no matter what it took.

In the meantime, she tried to think on anything else. She tried to persuade Liam, with her body and her wit and various amusements around town, that life might be worth living without looking backward.

Perhaps he sensed the nature of her campaign. One afternoon, when she suggested another visit to the Royal Academy, he said, "And what of your interests, Anna?"

What of them? Her interests, her hopes, her anxieties at present centered squarely on him.

But she could not admit so. It might shatter the deceptive serene truce between them. And so, two hours later, she found herself at his side in the lecture hall of the Royal Agricultural Society, listening to a whole lot of nonsense from Sir Montgomery, the renowned chemist.

When her temper had heated to steaming, she leaned over and whispered in Liam's ear, "This is absolute balderdash, I hope you know."

He'd been listening with every sign of congenial interest, but looked over with a lifted brow. "Is it? How so?"

"Monsieur Boussingault has shown it to be nonsense that plants draw nitrogen solely from the air. But perhaps Sir Montgomery does not read French."

"Shocking."

"Isn't it?"

Sir Montgomery opened the room to questions. Narrow eyed, Anna listened to an elderly gentleman rise to praise him, and then a balding young man, who wanted advice for visionaries whose genius was imperiled by want of patronage.

What a uniquely masculine concern, to fear oneself a neglected visionary! Anna's snort drew the censorious looks of two men in the row ahead.

Liam laughed quietly. "Say something."

"What? *Me?*"

"Yes, before you explode."

She looked at him, aghast. "It would cause a furor."

"Good. If he's wrong, he deserves to hear so."

"Of course he's wrong. That's beside the point. Do you note how many women are here today? And how many came alone?"

He glanced around. Three unaccompanied ladies sat in the back rows, each ramrod straight, as though being pricked by pins. They looked neither right nor left, their singular focus, Anna knew, trained sternly lest the gentlemen around them misunderstand their stray glances.

"What of it?" Liam asked. "Surely they'll applaud your temerity."

Perhaps they would. "But the presence of ladies is suffered here," she whispered, "not celebrated. And if a woman today ruins this cheery bonhomie, why, that will be remembered tomorrow—and woe be the women who walk in *then* and feel the chill that greets them."

"Or perhaps they'll feel more emboldened," he countered. "Having seen proof that a woman's question matters."

She hesitated. Some would no doubt feel emboldened. But it was the others—for instance, that young blonde in the back, who had crept in so fearfully—who concerned her. It took courage to enter this room, anticipating the press of male scrutiny, the amusement or even exasperation occasioned by a lady's presence. Any action that would increase that exasperation, or tip it into hostility, would not do women favors, particularly for the less brave among them.

"Anyway," she said, "I've no standing to criticize his work."

He snorted.

"I read the sciences, Liam. I do not advance them."

"And he evidently does not read them, and advances them in the wrong direction."

She bit her lip and said nothing.

"Ah," Liam murmured after a moment. "I see."

"What do you see?"

"You're taking pity on him. Too kind to embarrass him in front of the crowd."

"Yes," she said hastily, "that's right."

But it wasn't true. Even the thought of rising to question Sir Montgomery made her heart pound faster and her face feel warm. Now she thought on it, she had *never* risen to speak at a lecture—she had always waited until afterward, and approached the lecturer for a private discussion. But why?

Another man got up to ask Sir Montgomery's opinion regarding the success at Rothamsted of ammoniated wheat manure.

Anna leaned forward, anticipatory. The crops on Rawsey had profited greatly from that discovery, which in turn suggested a great weakness in Sir Montgomery's theory of plant nutrition.

But Sir Montgomery scoffed, unshaken. "A single field proved unusually abundant: what does this prove, sir, but that nature occasionally showers us with her favors? Mr. Lawes and Dr. Gilbert would have us believe that we can dispense with all minerals save ammonia—"

What a gross misrepresentation of their conclusions!

Anna glanced around, amazed that nobody else looked put out. Ah, but wait—the blonde in the back row was frowning.

Perhaps Anna had misunderstood her timidity. She, too, might be an avid admirer of the new agricultural chemistry, but having no escort, and perhaps no great standing, had no support to speak up and challenge this hogwash.

"Here's your chance," Liam said into her ear as Sir Montgomery announced he would take one more question.

She took a deep breath. She was not shy, not in the least—but she had never raised her voice in a crowd of men who did not know her name and rank. If she stood now, they would see only a woman—one whom they would not know to respect.

Why, was her bravery so fragile?

The realization that broke over her felt unpleasant and disorienting. Perhaps she had not turned down the publishing house's offer four years ago because she'd feared to be known as an abandoned wife. What she'd feared, in fact, had been the contempt of male audiences for her womanhood.

What was that but cowardice?

She shot to her feet.

Sir Montgomery, finger lifting to indicate a gentleman across the room, looked startled by her abrupt movement. A murmur rippled through the hall—masculine amusement and interest. And perhaps, just perhaps, Anna heard a feminine gasp from behind her, a sound of startled delight.

"Goodness," Sir Montgomery said, and retrieved his pointing finger to nudge up his spectacles. "I had no idea my work had received interest from the fairer quarters." Over polite titters, he continued. "You have a question, madam? Some point on which you require clarification, perhaps?"

"Indeed, I do." Her voice shook. She cleared her throat and forced her brightest smile onto her face, which never failed her. Sir Montgomery blinked as if dazed. "First, I wished to observe that nature's favors, while always welcome, do observe a pattern. To wit, my black oats proved far more abundant after an application of ammoniated manure than they did four years ago, when we employed a patent manure based on Mr. Olsen's formula."

Sir Montgomery had endorsed Olsen's formula publicly, and everyone in the room knew it. A murmur rippled through the crowd as his smile faded. "You trifled with the artificial manure, did you?"

Trifled, no. "In fact, I—"

"How charming. I'm very sorry to hear your results did not satisfy you. Alas, the proper application *is* rather complex, and best left to those educated in the relevant techniques."

"Indeed?" Her own smile now felt fanged. "But that is not my question for you. In fact, I wished to ask how you might reconcile your argument for the exclusively aerial origin of nitrogen with Monsieur Boussingault's recent work, demonstrating that plants draw nitrogen from the soil."

The murmurs grew louder. Sir Montgomery scowled out over the crowd, then glared at her. "Boussingault?"

"Monsieur Boussingault," she said. "At L'Institut National Agronomique. In his most recent study—"

"Yes, yes." Sir Montgomery heaved a long-suffering sigh. "Boussingault writes very showily, doesn't he? I'm sure he has persuaded any number of gardeners. But when one understands the science behind it, madam, frills grow less persuasive. And with that, I must—"

"In fact, Monsieur Boussingault was very clear," she said in a carrying voice, which forced him to break off his farewell. "Wheat grown in an atmosphere delimited to—"

"A Frenchman," Sir Montgomery interrupted, then glanced over the crowd with a helpless shrug and laugh, which half the audience reflected back to him, while the other half stared at her, agog. "The scientific method, I believe you'll find, degrades considerably across the Channel."

"No, she's quite right." This from Liam, who rose with an easy smile. "Boussingault's experiment followed a rigorous method, well documented in his work."

Anna knew he had not read a word of Boussingault's scholarship, and crossed her arms, annoyed with his chivalry.

But Sir Montgomery did not know it. He was purpling now. "Alas, I do not make it a habit to follow every piece of rubbish printed abroad."

"Hardly rubbish," came a stranger's voice—a slim, elfin gentleman who rose across the room. "I, too, found myself thinking of Boussingault as you spoke. And may I say, to dismiss sound scholarship because of its origin seems peculiarly provincial."

As murmurs pitched into excited conversation, the lecture's host rushed up to the stage to demand order, and Anna sat back down.

Liam was grinning at her. "Stop that," she said, but the proper sharpness was rather diminished by a swelling sense of exhilaration as she watched Sir Montgomery angrily stumble through an inadequate defense of his own hypothesis. "I did not require your rescue, you know."

He leaned to speak into her ear. "I know," he said. "But I'm a hedonist. I could not resist the pleasure."

CHAPTER EIGHTEEN

*T*hey walked out of the lecture hall into a bright, fresh day. A scudding breeze ruffled women's skirts and lifted the hats off men's heads, carrying them away through the sunshine.

Anna felt electrified, edgy and restless. Two women had approached her in the lobby, offering their cards and thanking her for her incisive questions. "You routed him," the blonde had laughingly told her, but that was not true. Such was his reputation that in a week's time, few people would remember his brief embarrassment.

But Anna would remember how she had spoken, and how concise and informed she had sounded, despite the pounding of her heart and the color in her cheeks. She would not forget that lesson.

"My tigress wife," Liam said as they started down the pavement. He was still grinning. "Sir Montgomery will flinch from the next redhead he sees."

She laughed. "I think . . . yes, I think I will contact that publisher again. The manuscript will require updating, of course—but I think I would be glad now to undertake whatever publicity they might require."

He lifted her hand, delivering a kiss to her gloved knuckles that caused a group of young matrons, passing with their package-laden footmen in tow, to beam at him and then regard her through lowered lashes, appraising, perhaps, what she had done to deserve such gallantry.

What *had* she done? Only been herself—spoken her mind—in public, at last. And her husband rewarded her for it with kisses. Elated, she pulled him to stop by a bench bathed in sunlight. "Thank you, Liam."

The light shaded the tips of his hair to the color of honey and glimmered in the long lashes that framed his amber eyes as he tilted his head. "For what?"

"Accompanying me today. Your presence gave me courage."

With a quick sideways tug of his mouth, he denied it: "Nonsense, you've courage to spare. My presence had no role in that."

It wouldn't, from now on—not now that she had found her voice. But she had needed him by her side today in order to discover it. "No, it's true." She hesitated, feeling suddenly oddly shy as she sat down on the bench. Another gust of warm wind swept over them, fluttering through the edges of his hair, and causing the children playing in the park behind them to shriek with delight. "You make a very fine husband, you know."

The bleakness passed over his face so quickly that someone else might have missed it, or doubted their own eyes, for he recovered immediately, with a swift and lopsided smile. "Oh?" He sat onto the bench beside her. "*Very* fine, you say? And here I'd always thought I'd fumble it."

"I never feared so." She bit her lip. *Before the wedding, before you vanished, before I leapt to the wrong conclusions and cursed you as a wastrel.* "When we met, I had been looking for a husband for two years. Did I ever tell you that?"

"No," he said quietly. She could not see his expression—he had turned away, ostensibly to gaze out at the parade of pedestrians, fresh from the shops on Regent Street. But that sight also made a handy excuse for a man who did not wish to meet his wife's eyes.

What were these moods? Until she learned how to pierce them, she suspected she would continue to find herself suddenly alone, although within arm's reach of him.

"Well, it's true," she continued, pushing the words past the nervous knot in her throat. "Moira warned me that if I didn't lower my standards, I would need to build a man from clay. I had started to fear she was right—and then came the Camerons' party. I had almost declined to attend—did you know that? I wanted so much to be on Rawsey." The memory suddenly amazed her. "Why, we might never have met, had I—"

"Fate," he said flatly.

"Yes, fate."

"Has a rather dark sense of humor, doesn't it?"

She stared at his profile. "I am *grateful* for that fate, Liam." Was he not so? Had everything that come afterward ruined the wonder of what preceded it? "That I met you, that we—"

"So generous." He faced her, his posture somehow braced, as though against a strong wind. "Your judgment is too generous, I think. How many weeks have we spent together, in these four years of marriage? You may wish to reserve your praise until you can be certain I deserve it."

"I *am* certain. Liam, what happened—it does not change who you are."

"No," he said softly. "That isn't true, Anna. I am much changed. You are blind if you deny it."

The hairs lifted at the back of her nape—a visceral response, perhaps, to the shadow that passed over them as a cloud scudded overhead.

"You are changed," she said. "Very well. But I . . ." She could not say she would not have wished it otherwise. "I am tremendously happy with you." That much was true. "That, I *do* know. And you cannot argue with what I feel."

His smile looked effortful as he offered his arm to her. Heart sinking, she let him help her up—but as she rose, a man stepped up to them.

In his pinstriped suit, with his dark hair slicked down, and a gold watch chain snaking across his waistcoat, Stephen Devaliant was dressed for some business appointment and had the harried air of a man who was running late. "What a delightful coincidence," he said.

"Oh, indeed. *Delightful*," Liam drawled, releasing Anna's arm to offer his hand.

She bit back an instinctive protest. She did not want him even to touch his cousin.

Devaliant, for his part, smiled and clasped Liam's hand, though the breeze immediately forced him to let go, in order to catch the brim of his tall hat.

The day would be ruined if they did not walk away. But Liam resisted the subtle pressure that Anna exerted on his elbow. Devaliant, for his part, squared his shoulders and stood tall, as though braced against the buffeting of pedestrians who streamed by them—a young courting couple, an aged matron with a manicured poodle, several plain-dressed clerks marching in single file, boxes in their arms. "I was just thinking of you," he said.

"Indeed?" said Liam. "With so many other matters to occupy you?"

"Ah, if you mean that trifling inconvenience concerning the new law, that is why I employ solicitors. No, I much prefer to think on pleasanter things—good jokes, amusing ironies. You see why you came to mind."

She felt Liam's muted surprise. His cousin's animosity was no longer veiled.

"And Lady Lockwood—a fine surprise to see you in our fair city!" Stephen offered his hand to her, which she pointedly ignored. With a little laugh, he withdrew it. "My wife had mentioned you'd come to town, but I'm amazed you're still here. I wouldn't have imagined there was anything to keep you."

"Oh, I find a great deal to recommend this city— barring the rare blight one might encounter in public."

Devaliant showed his teeth, neat and white. "Yes, quite true. The city feels too small at times, does it not? For instance, I find myself followed everywhere by the same shambling group of hooligans. I think your husband knows them. Associates of his from abroad, no doubt."

He was baiting her, trying to find out what she knew. She kept her cool smile affixed to her lips. "How curious. Paranoia, they say, is a symptom of decline. You might wish to make an appointment with your physician."

"A fine idea," he replied smoothly. "Coz, I'm certain you must have some miracle worker to recommend. You look remarkably well, considering your recent trials."

Anna stiffened. Was that an allusion to the poisoning? Liam obviously assumed so. "I would be glad to recommend him," he said easily. "But even his powers are limited, and I don't think you'll stand in need of him much longer."

In the brief ensuing silence, the two men locked eyes, and Anna began to fear that a public bloodletting was imminent. "Liam," she said nervously, "shall we visit Hatchards before we—"

"By the way," Devaliant interrupted, his pale gaze spearing her. "I do hope you didn't take my wife's rebuff too sorely. Her heart is very tender—I fear she would try to feed every waif who crossed her path. For her sake, I've instructed her to draw the line at dogs and their hoodwinked wives."

She felt Liam's arm harden to iron. "Enough," he growled.

"What was that? Did you bark?"

"Spare us your nonsense," Anna snapped. "We will bid you good day, sir."

"Oh yes, of course, I would hate to interrupt your loafing in the park. Really, coz, I would wonder at you idling here like a common beggar, but I expect the fresh air still seems a novelty to you."

Liam made some violent abrupt movement, which Anna checked by catching his arm again. "Not here," she said urgently. "Not in public."

"Oh, has he told you to expect better in private?" Stephen laughed. "Don't believe him. So far all he's managed is a parliamentary debacle organized largely by his friends. That, and a few rumors that my admirers know better than to believe—and a passel of confused creditors, irritated to find their time wasted when they realize I'm well in the black. I assure you, none of it has spoiled my sleep."

"It isn't your sleep I intend to ruin," Liam said.

"Goodness!" Stephen made a mocking show of ducking, lifting his hands to shield him from some threat overhead. "Not another round of dunning—I couldn't bear it!" Straightening, he grinned. "You could ram a hundred bills through Parliament, Liam—you could rip up every yard of my company track from here to Inverness. You still wouldn't manage to bankrupt me. I recommend you try the old-fashioned route: a bullet, say. But perhaps the floggings crippled your aim?"

The dead look that came into Liam's eyes sent a chill through her. His mouth turned in a slow half smile. "I am going to enjoy this," he said very quietly.

Was Devaliant's aim to bait him into a public murder? Alarmed, Anna said, "Step away from us. *Now*."

"Or what?" Stephen smirked. "Will his knees buckle? My boots *are* rather dusty—they could do with a spit shine."

There was no possible misinterpretation of this remark. He knew the precise details of what had been done to Liam.

As she felt her husband shudder, some queer red cloud enveloped Anna, violent and disembodying. It took control of her, lifted her hand. Her palm slammed into Stephen's jaw, a solid blow that reverberated up through her shoulder.

He caught her wrist, his grip crushing as he yanked her against him.

"Careful," he whispered in her ear. "I enjoy correcting female impertinence."

She tried to yank free, with no luck. Wildly she turned to look for Liam.

He was staring in their direction, his jaw rigid, his

chest rising and falling rapidly. "Liam," she gasped, but he seemed not to hear her. Devaliant squeezed harder, and she swallowed a pained grunt as she shoved the blackguard's shoulder. "Let me go! Let—"

Liam seized his cousin's arm and wrested it off her. Devaliant stumbled back, clutching his wrist and smiling.

"And to think you were once an athlete! I suppose torture does slow a man's reflexes. Or is it your brain that got mangled?"

"I will see you dead," Anna spat.

"You'd have a better chance at it than *he* would." Devaliant's contemptuous gaze flicked to Liam as he wiped his hand on his trousers. "Woof, little coz," he said, etching a mocking bow before he turned and walked away.

Liam stared after his cousin with a strange, stricken look. After a moment, tentatively, Anna touched his arm. He flinched and sidestepped. "Enough," he said roughly.

"Enough of *him*, to be sure."

He looked at her, but his eyes were glassy, and she had the impression that he was seeing something else entirely. "He's right."

"What do you mean?"

"You heard him."

She bit her lip. So, Stephen knew what had been done to him. What difference? Stephen's opinion did not matter a whit. That was what she *wanted* to say.

But in truth, she understood that it did make a difference. To fathom that Stephen knew the details of Liam's degradation, his torture, was a fresh cruelty, salt in an unhealed wound.

"He's loathsome," she said. "Nothing he says is worth—"

"No. You don't follow. He could have . . ." He pushed out a sharp breath. "He could have snapped your neck, Anna. While I stood there, he—" He abruptly ceased to speak. Setting his fist against his mouth, he shook his head once, sharply. His knuckles looked white.

His anguish seemed outsized to the cause. "He was never going to hurt me, Liam. He was only trying to frighten me. I wasn't in any danger—"

His hand slipped away, revealing a horrible smile. "Ask, then."

"Ask what?"

"Ask why it took so long for me to come to your aid."

"I . . ." Remembering his strange, frozen posture, a pit opened in her belly.

No, she did not want to ask about that. "You were wise to hesitate. He was baiting you. He *wanted* you to make a public scene—"

"Stop." His terrible smile vanished, leaving his face stark, his eyes hollow. "Don't take pity on me."

"Not pity." She crossed her arms, miserable. She did not know the right thing to say.

"He is right," Liam said softly. "My brain is mangled."

"Oh, come now—"

"You've seen it before." His voice strengthened. Grew cool and clinical. "At Hanover Square Rooms, for instance. And the first night you came to my rooms—after I bedded you. You saw the start of my panic."

"I . . ." Suddenly fearing what her expression might reveal, she turned away toward the street. He *had* behaved oddly in those instances. But that did not mean his brain was damaged. "You've been through a trial, Liam, and it's no wonder if you need time to heal from—"

His voice came so close by her ear that she jumped. "You did not want a drunkard's child, Anna. Would you want the child of a madman?"

Panic made as sharp a spur as anger. She whirled on him. "I will not discuss nonsense! *Your* child—*that* is the child I will have. Drunk or mad or double headed, it makes no difference. But I won't hear you recite your cousin's words as though they had a lick of truth in them. *Listen* to yourself! He showed his hand today, and all you can talk of now—"

"He showed his hand," he said softly, "and I had always thought that when he did, mine would be ready to strike. Instead, I watched him maul my wife."

"I was not *mauled*." But that was not the right thing to say, either. He was looking past her again, his expression remote.

"You should go back to Rawsey, I think."

And now they were back to *that*? "Don't give him this victory, Liam. *Please*."

He exhaled, glancing back to her. For a moment, as his haunted gaze locked with hers, she thought she would be able to reassure him, after all. "He is nothing," she said fiercely.

But then his gaze seemed to shutter. His expression smoothed, and his lips turned in a false, charming smile as he offered his arm.

"Come," he said. "We'll go find the coach."

His mask was in place again.

His cousin could be vanquished. But his mask, she did not know how to breach.

For the first time all afternoon, she at last felt truly afraid.

CHAPTER NINETEEN

"*W*hat a lovely and unusual room, your grace." This marveling comment came from Liam's wife, who stood in the middle of Jules's drawing room, turning full circle to admire the ebony furnishings and sculptures of sandalwood and marble that sat in niches along the walls.

The early evening light, slanting through the carved wooden screens that shielded the tall windows, cast a bluish cluster of stars onto Anna's bare nape. That line, where her long neck curved into her shoulders, was the greatest wonder in this room of priceless rarities.

He had not touched her in six days.

"Oh, please do call me Emma," said Miss Martin. Or, no—she was the Duchess of Auburn now. Jules had wed her in some abrupt private ceremony a fortnight past. "In fact, most of these furnishings come from the royal family of Sapnagar. They are great friends of Julian's, and sent several new pieces only last week . . ."

He could not touch Anna. He could, at times, barely stand to look at her, for what she saw in him was so clearly a figment of her imagination. She saw some kind of hero. She overlooked the festering flaws that would infect her, too, if she insisted on lingering.

"It is very kind of them," the duchess was saying. "But not the greatest kindness they've ever done us, I assure you."

A pause fell. The newlyweds exchanged a long, intimate look, redolent of private memories.

Some men caused their wives to bloom. The new duchess glowed, her cheeks rosy, her formerly ashen hair seeming to glimmer in the lamplight.

Other men did not have such happy effects on their wives. Liam watched Anna step backward, out of range of the Auburns' entangled gazes, and stare disconsolately at a sculpture of a dancing god. There were shadows beneath her eyes. At night, in her bedroom, she paced more than she slept.

Lying awake in his own room, Liam would listen to her footsteps, slow at first, then faster and louder, as though anger drove her to stalk. Sometimes she knocked at his door, but he never replied. He had no face he wished to show her now. Since their ill-fated meeting with Stephen, the panics had come more often. Perhaps they were fed by his fury with himself. He had let the bastard touch her.

Abandoned, then, she stewed, a trapped animal walking the boundaries of her cage. He listened to her misery in the dark as his own heartbeat escalated, as his breath came short, as a bitter knot choked his throat and brought bile into his mouth.

What a husband he was! Each night he expected to be dead by morning: no man's heart could gallop and stumble as his did, and continue to labor on afterward.

Yet each morning he woke gritty eyed, having fallen asleep at some point before dawn. Still alive, but not relieved by it.

This purgatory in which he now lived was not more bearable than the tortures of Elland. In Elland, only *he* had been at stake. Now, his weakness could cost *her*.

"The entire house is a marvel," the duchess told Anna. "Shall I show you around?"

Liam did not feel insulted by how readily Anna agreed, or with what visible relief she followed the duchess from the room. He, too, felt it easier to breathe when she was gone.

If only she would *go*. Leave London. But she refused. She had made her choice, unwisely and stubbornly, from a surfeit of emotion he did not deserve and would not allow himself to contemplate.

The door closed behind the women. Julian took a seat, his fond gaze lingering on the door. Liam, remembering himself, retrieved his brandy and proposed a toast. "In belated congratulations," he said, with the proper wry cheer that Jules would expect. "And here's my wedding gift to you: I meant to overlook your failure to invite me to the ceremony."

Julian grinned and kicked out his long legs, crossing them at the ankles as he raised his own glass. "We had the footmen for witnesses, no one else. In honesty, I feared she might change her mind, should I hesitate."

That scene with Stephen had snapped something in Liam's brain. It felt rusty these days, as though he were never quite awake. It balked now at the requirement of manufacturing a charming reply.

"No," he said finally. "That's over." Emma Martin, at Liam's first meeting of her, had been ghostlike and withdrawn, hidden behind the shocking camouflage of her vivid and violent artwork. But even then, he had sensed the chrysalis-like quality about her: whether or not she'd known it, she had already been straining toward the light.

That light, for her, had always been Jules, who was looking at Liam now, his head tipped in a quizzical attitude.

"She wouldn't have changed her mind," Liam said. "She always felt you were her . . . fate."

Fate.

Anna had thanked fate for their marriage. The notion made him feel wild and dark.

If fate had brought them together, then fate had also directed what followed. No, he would *not* credit God with that travesty. His soul could not bear it—for he would not worship a god so cruel, nor trust in such a god for future justice.

Julian, frowning, set aside his drink. "All right, what's wrong? I was gladdened when you said the countess would be joining you, but . . ."

But he'd taken one look at them and sensed that their presence would not redouble the lovestruck haze in the air here.

"My apologies. Do I dim the newlywed glow?" Hearing the bitterness in his own voice, the goddamned churlishness, Liam held up a hand—"Forgive me"— and then used it to press his eyes until he saw stars. "I should not have come tonight."

"Nonsense," Julian said sharply. "After all you did for me and Emma—Christ, man, let me return the favor for once. What weighs on you? You got my note, I hope. The Commons appointed a select committee to investigate that railway fraud. Devaliant will be finished soon enough."

"Yes, so I heard." Some make-believe railroad company had bilked investors out of their hard-earned money, and Jules had uncovered proof that Stephen had helped to promote the company, perhaps even to found it.

"Over five thousand investors defrauded, Liam. He could go to prison, as soon as next year—"

"Not enough." He took a breath to dispel the tightness in his chest, to persuade his heart not to pound. "I can't wait any longer."

"Oh?" Julian hesitated. "What changed?"

"He's more ragged than he seems. Coming into the open at last. We had words last week. He all but admitted he knew of Elland."

"Ah." Julian studied him a moment. "Well, good." His smile was hard and unpleasant. "I'm amazed he's still breathing. What happened?"

He opened his mouth to manufacture some story—then abruptly found himself too exhausted to lie.

Julian saw it. "What happened?" he asked more quietly.

Liam had imagined himself intimately familiar with degradation. He'd even believed himself immune to it—inoculated, by a sustained and concentrated dose, to all the other more mundane versions. But this confession felt like a scouring shame. "We met in public. Hanover Square. He grabbed her. And I did *nothing*."

Julian had known him since boyhood. Their friendship ran deep. But even he could not prevent a frown at this news. "Nothing? What do you mean?"

"I mean"—*say it*—"he took hold of her. He could

have snapped her neck. Slipped a knife between her ribs. And I would not have been able to stop him. I simply . . . stood there. Gripped by something."

"Gripped," Julian murmured. "I don't . . ."

"Understand?" The laugh crawled out of him like a worm. "Nor do I. It's a sickness of the brain. Ever since my return, it comes over me at odd moments—a baseless dread, choking, paralyzing."

"You never told me."

A snarl took control of his mouth. "How might I have shared that news? What ho, Jules, I'm losing my bloody mind?"

Instantly he regretted his temper. But Julian seemed not to notice; he steepled his fingertips, frowning. "This . . . grip, as you put it . . . what provokes it?"

He blew out a long breath. "In the early days, I thought I knew. Loud sudden noises, anything that took me off guard. Crowds, sometimes. Dreams of the . . . " *Say it.* "Dreams of the hole."

Julian's face darkened. No doubt he was recalling their conversation at the club, in which Liam had mentioned exactly how Sadler had died in that hole. "Well," he said. "Yes. That makes sense."

Liam's laugh felt harsh. "Sense? What sense does madness make?"

His friend offered a brief, lean smile. "Classic dilemma of the critic: he never excels at self-judgment. You were always mad, even as a boy—I won't argue that. But there's nothing deranged, or even rare, in feeling oneself thrust back into a dark memory."

This felt like kindness rather than honesty. "Don't disappoint me," Liam said. "I have always counted on you for truth."

Julian grimaced, then sat back. Making a fist atop his thigh, he flexed it hard, seeming to study the glint of his own signet ring before he shrugged and said, "All right. At Cawnpore, I witnessed—horrors. Men executed by cannon fire. It took me a very long time, afterward, not to flinch when it thundered. Not to feel my breath come short, and my heart pound. That did not make me mad, Liam. It made me human."

Liam understood the generosity of this admission. Jules very rarely spoke of the Uprising, and then, only in vague detail.

But . . . "I wish to God it were only a flinch. These recent episodes are full-bodied incapacitations. And . . . they're coming more and more often. Every night," he said quietly.

"With no incitement?"

"None." He bit his tongue against the frustrated urge to curse, or to smash something. "Lying in bed, I'll see his goddamned hand on Anna. The next moment, it starts: locked in my own brain, my body beyond my control."

Julian nodded slowly. And then he abruptly shook his head. "On the contrary, there does seem to be an incitement, then: your cousin."

"Of course," Liam bit out. "But—"

"And loud noises, and crowds?"

Liam paused, the question startling him. "No, in fact. I've had no trouble there, recently."

"Then perhaps your cousin has done you a favor. For if he's now the sole cause, then there's a simple solution to it."

Liam allowed himself a brief, dark smile to match Julian's. "To him, yes. But . . ." Throat tightening, he spoke his greatest fear: "For my brain, perhaps not. For I cannot guarantee that once he's gone—"

"Listen." Julian sat forward, eyes narrowed. "I *have* heard of such things. Sometimes, in survivors of violence . . ." He hesitated. "Emma cares for you. She would not mind me telling you this. In the early days after her return, she often had no memory of putting brush to canvas. She painted as though in a wild trance. And afterward, she awoke rageful, in tears. But those episodes did eventually pass."

Liam mulled this. He did not know if Emma wore physical scars. But her paintings were scars; he'd recognized that from the first, and her courage in showing them had called to him. "They went away completely? Even now that she's painting again?"

"Yes. And she says that even the act of remembering— remembering the worst—feels different now. Tranquil, and within her control." Julian tipped his head. "Have you confided in the countess about these moods?"

"She says I only need time to heal."

Julian's expression eased. "Yes. Good. I think she's right."

Liam picked up his drink, took a measured sip. His hand was shaking slightly.

There's a simple solution to that.

Jules was wrong. Ending Stephen would not cure the problem of his brain.

The thought shocked him. It felt odd and electric, like an illicit confession. Liam turned it over in his mind, marveling at how it made his muscles tense, his body brace as though for a violent collision.

Here, he abruptly realized, was the truth he'd not wanted to face—and which he had avoided by refraining from putting an end to the business of Stephen. Ending his cousin would not cure him of all his troubles. He would never again be the man he'd been before Elland. There was no way to undo the changes that Elland had wrought in him.

Yet this insight, as it faded, left a weird lightness in its wake. His hand steadied, and he felt his throat ease. His heartbeat began to slow.

So what if there was no magic cure? It did not mean he was beyond hope.

Neither Anna nor Julian thought him beyond hope. They did not even think him mad. They both believed that healing was possible. Emma was proof of its possibility.

But healing could not occupy him so long as his cousin remained a danger. Stephen had shown his hand in Hanover Square, which meant that he felt desperate or bold enough to do any number of rash and unwise things. Before anything else, Stephen must be handled.

A breath slipped from him. And then came a smile, faint but real. Easy, even. The course was so simple, after all. "It's time to end this."

Julian followed his meaning perfectly. With a swift hard smile of his own, he said, "Only tell me what you need."

"And this is my studio," said the Duchess of Auburn. "Forgive the mess. I had all my paintings fetched over, but I haven't yet uncrated most of them."

As Anna followed her hostess into the spacious white-walled room, a canvas caught her eye. Poised on an easel in the corner, reached by weaving through a maze of unopened crates and boxes, it showed a mundane country scene: a rolling field bounded by a low stone wall, from which a basket of flowers had just been knocked. Both the basket and its contents—a shower of bright flowers—had been caught midfall, as a long, slim hand reached into the frame, unsuccessfully, to catch them.

The subject might have seemed ominous. But the sunny setting, the bright clear sky, and the lush vivid realism of the flowers—their scarlet and saffron petals still gleaming with dew—combined to create a mood of whimsy, even optimism. Things got knocked over. There was beauty in that, too.

"New work," Emma said, joining her side. She made a warm and gracious hostess. When touring Anna through the fine appointments of this house— cunning hallways of inlaid and mirrored paneling, a glass-walled hothouse, paintings by old masters and Mogul portraitists—she had marveled alongside Anna at the fineries, clearly taking no credit for her husband's exquisite taste.

But now, her cheerful serenity fractured. She twisted her hands at her waist as she said, "It's very different from my old style, of course."

Anna had been struggling to keep her manner light; to reflect her newlywed hostess's conspicuous happiness, rather than douse it with her own dark mood. But this remark drew a genuine, amused laugh from her. "Indeed. They could not be more different."

Too late, she feared that her retort would be taken as rudeness. But Emma relieved her by smiling.

"Thank goodness for that. I had begun to wonder if my brush was limited to gray scales."

A proverbial gray scale, Anna assumed. Emma's earlier paintings had not spared the viewer from vivid rivers of blood.

"Well, those fears should be laid to rest now." The flowers were so lifelike that she found herself taking a deep breath, in search of their perfume. "This painting could not be more lovely."

"But is it *good*?" Fretfully, the duchess sat on a nearby stool. "That is what concerns me most. You know that Liam—" She flushed. "Forgive me, I hope you don't mind the informality."

"Not in the least." But it had drawn claws through Anna's gut earlier to watch her husband greet Emma with such apparent and uncomplicated pleasure. A strange poisonous brew of jealousy and despair had coursed through her then. She did not know if she could ever hope to receive such looks from him.

"Liam wishes to mount another show," Emma explained. "For the little season, he says, in December. I told him it was too soon—that I couldn't be sure I would maintain this pace." She laughed. "Happiness—a novel inspiration! I can't trust it just yet. But he insists. And as *you'll* know, one rarely wins an argument with him."

"Yes," Anna murmured. "He is certainly headstrong."

Now that he had decided to entomb himself within his mask, he would not be persuaded or harangued to alter his course. She did not think she had seen his true face since the day of the lecture. He was slipping away to a place she had no skill to reach. Her own panic was strangling her.

She realized that Emma was studying her, those artist's eyes, a strange smoky blue, too perceptive for her comfort.

"I had wondered what kind of woman would be married to Lord Lockwood," the duchess said. "I was very curious to meet you again."

Anna managed a smile. "And do I meet your expectations?"

But Emma did not return the smile. "I don't know if Liam ever told you what he did for me. I was very alone when we met. Hiding from the world. He forced me out into it. He persuaded me to believe in my talent, to believe these awful things I had committed to canvas should—*must*—be seen. And because he showed me a way into the world, I found Julian again." She took an audible breath. "So you see, I'm in great debt to him."

Anna hesitated, uncertain how to reply. "I believe he feels the debt is all his. He thinks the world of your talent. He has always had an eye for genius, but your work—"

"Genius!" Emma pulled a face. "Who knows about that? What he had an eye for, I think, was a fellow survivor." She glanced at the painting, looking pensive. "And enough courage to spare me some of his, when I most needed it."

Anna swallowed hard. How was it that all the world saw Liam's courage, his strength and his worth, save *he*? "You should tell him so. He . . ." She did not want to violate his confidence. But a gut-deep instinct told her that a crisis was upon them. He refused to touch her. They barely spoke. He moved through his own house like a ghost, and when she found him looking at her, he wore an odd expression, remote, as though she were already a memory, lost to him for good. "He would profit by hearing your view of him," she said hoarsely. "Please do tell him."

Emma rose from the stool. "Then I will do. But . . ."

Her hand came gently to rest on Anna's arm. "Why are you crying?"

"Am I?" Appalled, Anna dashed her hand over her eyes. "Goodness." She turned back to the painting, this bright promise that even misfortunes could be beautiful, and tried to compose herself. "Forgive me, I suppose it's your art that moves me—"

"Gammon."

She bit her tongue. The silence extended, becoming conspicuous, uncomfortable. She did not know this woman. She could not unburden herself, and her wits felt too sluggish to compose an excuse for her distress. "Shall we join the others?" she asked at last as she turned.

But Emma stood in her path and did not step aside. "I care for him," she said quietly. "And from the start, I have seen the unhappiness in him. Tell me what I might do to help."

"You can't." The words ripped from her, lent force by her miserable conviction. "He thinks—" Oh, God forgive her. "He thinks his brain is deranged somehow. He was abused, terribly, and he feels he is broken by it, with no hope of healing."

"Ah."

This calm reply, paired with a thoughtful nod, quite disconcerted Anna. And then it angered her. "He is *wrong*, and if you believe otherwise—"

"Of course he's wrong," Emma cut in evenly. "But— shall we dispense with formalities and speak bluntly? Julian told me what happened to him. The broad facts, at least. The kind of violence he survived . . . it leaves marks. It does damage a person. One cannot ever forget what happened, or return to how one was beforehand. But that doesn't mean healing is impossible, or happiness unreachable. Even if one feels unworthy of it—it comes like a gift, if one allows it to approach."

Fine words. Anna had tried to tell him much the same. "He won't believe it."

"With time—"

"He has episodes." She blurted it out. "Moments in which he panics, beyond all proportion. His body fails him. And he blames himself for it. He thinks himself broken."

"Yes." Emma glanced toward a set of crates, still unopened. "All of those"—she waved toward them—"were painted in such states. I don't remember creating half of them."

Anna felt staggered. She sat down on the stool. "*You* had such fits?"

"Perhaps not identical to his. But similar enough to recognize the shape of what you describe." Emma sighed. "Doctors might not agree . . . but I have come to believe that the body remembers grave danger long after it has passed. Strange things, small things, can persuade the body to respond as though one were still in peril."

She did sound as though she understood intimately what Liam endured.

"But . . ." Anna glanced back to the scene of the flower basket, upended—and Emma, following her look, laughed softly.

"Oh, I remember painting that one," she said. "How I cursed when trying to blend that shade of violet! The terrors passed, Anna. They lost their grip on me." Perhaps Anna looked doubtful, for the other woman took her hand. "They were terrible, yes. The doctors could not help me. But then they began to fade." Her grip tightened. "Since the time when Liam persuaded me to put those paintings in the light, I have never had a terror again."

"But he does not paint," Anna whispered. "And I don't know . . ." True justice would help. The thought of Stephen Devaliant bloodied her vision. Oh, Liam would have his justice, she would see to that. But would that be enough to enact an exorcism?

"In such moments," Emma said quietly, "when the terror is upon him—what do *you* feel?"

The question startled her. She pulled her hand free. "What does it matter what *I* feel?" She scoffed. "If you imagine he turns to *me* for comfort—"

"No. He wouldn't. One feels unable to look for help. But I will tell you another fear I had—above and beyond the terrors." Her face open and calm, Emma waited until Anna met her eyes. "I feared that Julian would see me in such a state, and it would replace all else he'd known of me. That he would look at me and see only the darkness in me."

"I would never judge Liam so," Anna said through her teeth.

"No. You love him. You would never judge him so. But *he* doesn't know that. He fears you have no idea who he truly is, and if you were to find out—"

"Rubbish. I know him better than anyone alive."

"Are you certain?" Emma paused. "He's a consummate actor. I have seen him wear a dozen faces in one evening, depending on what was required."

"And I cherish *all* of them, if they are what he requires. But his true face"—she swallowed—"is *mine*. The one he has shown to me . . ." On the cliff side on Ben Nevis. In the great hall at Rawsey. In his bedroom, the night she had forced him to strip. "He is mine," she said in a hushed, raw voice. "And all his faces, too. And his changes. And his scars. And his true face, which I know in my heart."

"Then be his mirror," Emma murmured. "He loves you, I think. Otherwise he would have smiled at you below as easily as he smiled at me. For you alone, his mask threatens to crumble. But if he forgets what lies beneath it, then show him that truth. And never let him turn away from it."

Anna felt abruptly dizzied. So often she fancied herself the sharpest wit in the room. But this woman radiated a serenity and wisdom that she could not find in herself. All at once, she was desperate to believe in it.

"I pray you are right," she whispered. "I won't let him turn away anymore."

Emma looked musingly down at her. "I have not long been a grand lady," she said, "so I hope you'll permit me this." Without further ceremony, she pulled Anna up into a hug.

Anna did not believe in witchcraft. But five minutes after unburdening herself of her fears, she and Emma rejoined the men's company and found the mood transformed. The Duke of Auburn caught his new wife at the door and twirled her in his arms; and as though he had not spent almost a week withholding himself, Liam greeted Anna with a kiss, and then escorted her into dinner with charm and jokes.

Remembering Emma's advice, Anna decided not to question the sea change but to be thankful for it. And so the evening passed delightfully, with good conversation and exquisite French cooking, and plans for supper again next week, this time out of doors, on Auburn's yacht harbored near Greenwich. It was past midnight by the time she and Liam boarded the carriage for the drive home, but it still seemed that they had left too soon.

Indeed, as the coach pulled away from the lamplit curb, casting them into the darkness of late evening, Anna found herself suddenly prickling with superstition—holding her breath, lest the shadows put an end to that warm and celebratory atmosphere that had grown up between them in the Auburns' house.

As though he sensed it, Liam moved off his bench and came to sit beside her. "Cold?" he asked, and did not wait for her answer before tucking the lap robe more closely around her.

Laughing, she shoved off the blanket. "If I'm cold now, then heaven help me when I go back to Scotland. These southern climes will make me soft."

"Oh, *that* cold is bred into your blood, I expect. English winds may chill you—but a good Scottish squall will bring you alive."

She smiled at him, his silhouette amid the deeper darkness, for his fanciful theory charmed her. "The cold does seem different here. Sharper, but less damp. I expect the winters are quite pleasant."

She caught the shine of his eyes as he gently touched her cheek. "And what of a winter in France?"

"France?"

"That honeymoon we'd planned. Better late than never, don't you think? We could reach Paris by the end of July. Remain there through October, then slowly wend our way south to Naples."

Her breath caught. Here was what she'd been waiting for—mention of the future, a future to be spent together. She found herself gripping his hand, holding it in place against her cheek. "Yes," she whispered. "I would like that very much. I still remember—you wanted to show me the Rubens collection in the Louvre, the painting of the two ladies . . ."

"Well, I've a soft spot for a man who admires redheads." His voice was husky, tender with amusement. "But there is more to France than Paris and portraits. We might pay a call on Monsieur Boussingault, who would be very glad, I think, to hear all your tales of ammonia and nitrogen."

She laughed, a sound that struck her belatedly as both giddy and incredulous.

Feeling as though she were coming awake from some beautiful dream, she said, "What has changed, Liam?"

"What do you mean?"

"Your mood, all this week . . . But now, suddenly, you're full of good cheer and plans—"

"Ah. Yes, that." In the darkness, suddenly he was kissing her, a deep and languorous and drugging kiss that lasted long enough to scatter her wits entirely and leave her somewhat forgetful of the subject when he at last lifted his head and continued. "I have been dwelling on the past, haven't I? The past that cannot be changed. But many things still remain in my power. I am no longer constrained. It was my mistake to feel otherwise."

"Of course," she said. "But . . ." She hesitated, not wanting to risk ruining his happy mood with another question.

Yet what kind of marriage would they have if she felt constantly compelled to guard her tongue lest his temper sour?

She needed to understand him. Emma had advised

patience. But patience and probing could go hand in hand. "What made you realize it?" she asked.

"You," he said. "You left the drawing room and took the light with you. Next time, I mean to follow."

She bit down on a happy sigh—amused and a little unnerved by how easily she was flattered. His answer explained nothing, though. "Gammon. Tell me truly what—"

His mouth came against hers again. "Truly, Anna," he said very softly into her lips. "You carry the light with you." His hand slid delicately through her hair, his mouth moving to her ear as he murmured, "Of course, the sun would continue to burn if the planets fell away. But without the sun, the planets would be lost. And I would be a fool to abandon that orbit."

Some vague uneasiness stirred in her belly, at odds with the warmth of her blush. These words, though romantic, did not sound like him. She gently laid her hand across the firm curve of his skull, testing the softness of his hair. Poetry wasn't what she most wanted from him. "I know you've had trouble," she said. "But whatever you feel, Liam . . ."

His lips drew a lazy circle on the sensitive spot beneath her ear, and she had to take a long breath before her next words would assemble.

"However dark your moods turn," she pushed on, "I wish to know them. To see them. *All* of you is precious to me. I know you don't believe this, for you see yourself so differently than I see you." When she remembered how he had spoken of himself, that dreadful day when he'd told her the whole of it, she shuddered to imagine how he saw himself. "You have no clear view—"

"Enough," he said gently. "There's no need for this."

But she would not be silenced. She pulled away to look at him squarely. "But *I* see you clearly. More than that—I also see *myself* clearly, in your company. You fear somehow to fail me, but I tell you, you can't. You are—such a wonder to me, Liam. Such a gift. Never in my life have I felt more *myself* than when I'm with you. And when you tell me to go back to Rawsey—"

"Anna, I shouldn't have—"

"No, *listen*. The only time I was *ever* tempted was the day you woke from your fever, when you stormed out and I feared you would never come home again. *Then*, I longed for Rawsey. And it made me realize—why, Rawsey isn't simply a home for me. It's where I've always gone, I think, to hide."

He stared at her, his expression lost in the dark. He seemed, at least, to be listening.

She took his hand, twining their fingers together. "I told myself I was free," she said softly. "Freer than any woman alive. My birth, my title, my fortune—and then this odd marriage I'd proposed to you, they guaranteed that freedom. But a free woman doesn't require a hiding place." She cleared her throat and forced out the next words, these solid weights now lodged on her heart, for they *must* be spoken. "I should have searched for you, Liam."

He recoiled. "No. Don't—"

But she tightened her grip, holding on to him. "From the very moment you disappeared, I should have raised the alarm. I will never forgive myself for that."

"Stop." His hand turned in hers, crushing her fingers. "Let that go. It was not your fault. None of it was your fault."

"But it *was*. Don't you see?" She blinked hard against

the prick of tears. "I was accustomed to being left. Being left was such a habit, a habitual *humiliation*, that I designed a marriage that would *guarantee* that I was left. Every term of that contract—I said that they were meant to preserve my freedom. But they weren't. They were announcements, to you and the world and to *me*, that you *would* leave, and that when you did, it would be routine—expected—nothing to grieve or surprise me. After all, our marriage had not been designed to keep you. The contract proved it—it showed I didn't expect or want otherwise." She felt her mouth twist out of her control, and lifted their joined hands to her mouth, pressing her trembling lips against his knuckles until she felt able to continue. "But here's the truth, Liam—it was a lie. A lie I constructed to protect my vanity, my pride. My *heart*. Before you'd even signed that contract— before I'd even finished declaring my terms—I knew I wanted you with me always. But I denied it to myself. I was a coward. So afraid of risking hurt. Of facing, again, the fact that I wasn't enough. And so, *yes*—when you disappeared, I wasn't brave. I'd been left again—and instead of asking where you'd gone, I castigated myself for even caring. And I fled to Rawsey then, to hide—from the world, and from *myself*. From this truth that my heart was broken."

She heard his soft exhalation. "Anna—"

"I should have raised the alarm." Tears clogged her voice. With her anger, her fury at herself, she pushed past the tears, spitting out her next words: "I should have searched for you. I should have demanded the authorities hunt for you, in every corner of the world. Instead, I hid, and said nothing, and I *lied* to myself, telling myself I did not care, did not mourn and miss you every minute of every day. I made myself let you go—and that is a mistake I will repent every day for the rest of my life."

His palm, gentle and warm, covered her cheek. "Anna," he whispered. "None of it was your doing. *None*."

Frustration bubbled through her. "And none of it was yours, either." So why did he continue to speak so cruelly of himself for it? Why was his anger so self-directed, when the only proper target for it was his cousin?

"You are better than I deserve," he murmured. "That, I know."

His mouth found hers again, and he kissed her so deeply and thoroughly that the kiss began to feel like an answer somehow—an agreement that she was right, that he would find peace with himself. After a few moments, she forgot their surroundings—forgot everything but the heat and cleverness of his mouth and hands, and the pleasing heavy weight of him against her. It was a shock, then, to realize the coach had come to a stop. They were home—the footman was opening the door.

"Promise me," she said as he pulled away. "Promise me you will try to look on yourself as I do."

He kissed her inner wrist before helping her onto the curb. "Come to my bed tonight," he said into her ear. "Come to where you belong."

CHAPTER TWENTY

*W*hen Anna woke alone the next morning in her husband's bedroom, she did not think much of his absence. Her thoughts were too filled by what had passed between them: long, leisurely, pleasure-swollen hours that still showed in the tangled sheets discarded on the floor. She sat up, blushing as she caught sight of her discarded clothing, now neatly folded and stacked on a nearby chair. The maids had come in without waking her, but they had certainly left with a tale to tell.

Happiness felt rather like a drug. It made her slow to rise, slower to dress; after finding the note from Liam explaining his appointment with Auburn at the club, she found herself mooning at the window seat in her bedroom, watching the breeze play through the nod-ding scarlet heads of the flowers in the window box. At last, finding her own lassitude rather ill-becoming, she bestirred herself to write a note inviting Moira to afternoon tea.

The reply came an hour later, as she paged through a copy of *The British Farmer's Magazine*.

Coz,

I will gladly come to tea, if only to ask you about this mysterious investigation in which the Morning Herald *claims your husband to be a central figure. I confess I am rather sore to be left out of such news, especially when it has now become gossip, of which you know I count myself a superior tradeswoman!*

M.

Anna leapt to her feet and rang for a footman. The first to appear—Riley—did not know where the morning's *Herald* had been laid. He went searching, only to return empty-handed, with Wilkins in tow. Wilkins informed her that his lordship had requested the household's copy of the *Morning Herald* before leaving, and had carried it with him to the club.

Taking a newspaper to a club was rather like carrying coal to Newcastle. Anna could think of only one reason Liam would have done so. He'd not wanted her to see it.

"Find me a copy at once," she said. "Go purchase one—or ask the neighbors, if that is quicker."

Some women, delicate creatures, lost their appetites in anxious times. Her own roared. She sent to the kitchens for a full luncheon, and was digging her way through her second plate of boiled ham and beans when Riley returned with the newspaper.

The story was above the fold.

INQUIRY OPENED CONCERNING DISAPPEARED LORD SADLER

ONCE PRESUMED LOST AT SEA—NOW ALLEGED *MURDERED*
LORD LOCKWOOD TO OFFER TESTIMONY

An astonishing report, confirmed by several personages highly placed in both government and society, comes to light this morning. Stuart Leslie, third Baron Sadler, presumed dead after the disappearance in January 1856 of the SS *Pacific*, on which he was understood to be traveling, now emerges as the victim of a more nefarious tragedy: MURDER. According to certain personages whose credentials amply substantiate the authority of their claims, Lord Sadler was abducted from the SS *Pacific* before departure, and cruelly butchered by none other than the late inventor Mr. Harold Marlowe—whose suicide last year now appears to have been driven by self-horror.

A spokesman for Baldwin & Sons, the insurance company that underwrote the SS *Pacific's* fatal voyage, confirmed that a claim has been paid to Lord Sadler's heirs, and that these allegations, if true, imperil its legitimacy. The company awaits a report from Scotland Yard, which has commenced a closed inquiry into Lord Sadler's death. Their next deposition will take place tomorrow. Lord Lockwood, recently returned after several years' travel abroad, is thought to have some intelligence of a confederate of Marlowe, which will prove useful to the inquiry.

This was bait.

It was bait placed by Lockwood himself—or else, Anna thought on a sharp breath, by the Duke of Auburn. For had not *both* the men's moods been shifted to an extraordinary degree while she and Emma had been touring the house?

The men had agreed on a plan. And afterward, in the carriage, Liam had hinted at it: *I am no longer constrained*, he'd said.

But why hadn't he *told* her outright?

God above, all those sweet words he had spoken to her—that she was sufficient unto herself, her 'own light'—and everything that had come afterward, in the dark of his bed—all of it had been a provisional farewell.

Anger and panic entwined so closely she could not separate them. Her temper fueled her as she strode into the hallway and commanded Riley to assemble the male staff in the dining room.

After a brief excursion upstairs to her rooms, she returned to discover the whole lot waiting for her. Ordinarily, it might have been amusing to watch a group of hardened former prisoners crowd away as she swept past. They expected a scolding, perhaps.

But today she wanted them to forget who she was. She wanted honesty. Drawing up by the foot of the table, she looked them over. "Lockwood went out alone this morning?" she asked Henneage.

"Aye, that's right."

"You dropped him at the club?"

He shrugged. "Had me saddle the roan for him."

That answered two questions: he'd not confided in any of these men, and it was very unlikely that he'd gone to the club.

"Listen to me closely," she said. "I know I have harangued and cajoled you to restrain yourselves in my presence, but this once, I will ask that you speak from your hearts, without care for what I might think. Do you understand?"

"God save us," she heard Danvers mutter. Some elbow nearby jammed into his ribs, and he jumped straight.

"Lockwood has found the man who paid for his transport to Elland," she went on.

The men exchanged uneasy looks. "Aye," said Henneage, "that'll be his cousin."

Of course they would know this. "He means to draw him out today."

This was news. She studied the group's poorly concealed reactions: a wide grin from Henneage, a certain frowning pallor that came over Wilkins, several crossed arms, and Cook's grunting retort: "Long overdue, methinks."

"Perhaps." She placed her fingertips on the table, her weight on her steepled hands. "The catch, of course, is that he has no proof—so if it comes to a killing, he will be hanged as a murderer if he's caught. On top of this, there is no guarantee that *he* will be the one to emerge alive."

"Lock can handle himself," Gibbs said stoutly.

"Could have asked our help," Hanks muttered.

"Aww, your feelings hurt, Poodle?" This from Henneage, sneering.

"His cousin won't play fair," said Wilkins anxiously.

"He don't want our help," snapped Gibbs, "or else he'd have asked."

"Do you *need* his permission to help?" Anna asked.

A startled silence. She looked over the group. "I don't

know where he's gone, or where he intends this meeting to happen. Can any of *you* guess where he would go to meet his cousin?"

A low murmur of discussion broke out. She pulled out the chair and seated herself, her stomach groaning from the weight of her lunch.

"He won't *want* to be caught at it," Wilkins was saying. "So he wouldn't go to the bloke's house. Nor anywhere so public."

"He's stealthy," said Riley. "Remember that guard he took out with a single twist of the neck? You was half hanged at the time, so *you* won't recall—"

"We were all there," Danvers put in. "No need to relive it."

Anna, finding herself the object of several hasty and apologetic looks, forced a smile to cover the nauseated twist in her stomach. "Pretend I'm not here, if it suits you better."

It evidently did. The men turned their backs on her, but did not bother to lower their voices.

"Remember that one tale he told?" This from Wilkins, excitedly. "The first time he realized his cousin did hate him. Where were they then? When his cousin shoved him, and he swore he saw murder in the bastard's eyes."

She leaned forward, biting her tongue to keep from prompting them, her hands twisting together into an aching knot.

"Somewhere private, it was," said Riley. "I remember because he said nobody would have believed it lest they seen it. And then"—he started to chuckle—"he threw ink on the bastard's head."

Henneage cleared his throat. "I reckon we shouldn't

interfere in Lock's business lest he wants it. But he's gone to Lawdon."

Anna rose. "Are you certain?"

"Aye, just about." He shuffled, then sighed. "I asked him where he was heading. He said he'd be there and back by dark."

She started for the door, but Gibbs blocked it, his arms crossed and his chin jutting mutinously. "This ain't right! If Lock wanted us there, he'd have asked."

"He's our *brother*," Wilkins burst out. "It's our duty—"

"He won't like it, is all I'm saying."

"He doesn't need to know," Hanks said. "Does he? That we followed him."

All eyes now turned to Anna.

"All he'll know," she said coolly, "is that I decided to move the household to Lawdon for the week. Step aside, Gibbs."

"Now, wait a second, *you* ain't going—"

"*That* would blow his top off for sure."

"We can manage it, m'lady, wouldn't ever let a thing happen to him—"

"Ain't a lady's place—"

"Gentlemen." She spun back to face them, putting on her best steely look—the very look she'd used on the first morning of their acquaintance with her to evaluate their continued employment in the house.

It took a long moment for silence to fall, but once she had their full attention, she continued: "Do you imagine I love him less than you do?"

"Oof," groaned Henneage. "Now with the water-works—"

"My eyes are quite dry." She reached into her pocket and pulled out her sgian-dubh.

Gibbs snorted. "That'd cut a piece of fruit, maybe—"
He fell silent when she pulled out her pistol.

"I'm an excellent shot," she said. "And a man's flanks, you'll find, pierce as easily as a melon. I invite you to keep behind me for safety, if you like." With that, she shoved past Gibbs and out the door.

The schoolroom stood apart from the main house, in a small limestone building that Liam's great-grandfather had built as a miniature palace for the amusement of his children. The gilt and mirrored interiors, though now chipped and fading, offered a whimsical contrast to the plain wooden floor, the rude desks, and unadorned, child-sized chairs.

On entering, Liam had found himself seized by the uncanny feeling of having stepped back in time. Rows of workbooks still sat on the shelves, thick with the dust of decades. A faded line of Latin could be read on the chalkboard: *Bis vincit qui se vincit in victoria.*

The phrase kept his attention for a long moment. *He conquers twice who, at the moment of victory, conquers himself.*

The ceiling briefly creaked overhead. For a moment, Liam could almost imagine it was the footfall of his old tutor, who had slept in the upstairs apartment. The cunning bat had drilled spy holes in the ceiling so he could nap comfortably while turning an occasional eye on his pupils' industry below.

Liam took a seat at the desk in the corner, which gave him a clear view of the door. Out the windows, a glorious spring day was unfolding, the clear sunlight shining through the green leaves of apple trees. The windows stood closed, but the birdsong penetrated, raucous and cheerful.

At first, at Elland, he had found it difficult to bear such mundane beauty. That the entire world did not suffer alongside him had seemed a sign of God's indifference, or else proof that he mattered not at all. But later, in the hole, he had glimpsed a bird's flight overhead, and had found himself suspended in wonder. Freedom yet existed. He could see it. By seeing it, he could feel it himself. After all, was Rembrandt's work less extraordinary because Liam could not create similar? In the observing, one became a part of what one observed. In the hole, Liam had discovered a kind of freedom within himself, which no man could wrest from him.

It was after he'd left the hole, after he'd won back his objective freedom, that he'd forgotten this lesson. He had become mired then in the trap of his own memories. Claustrophobic, hunted, unable to escape himself.

But if the prison lay within, so, too, did freedom. He sat in this schoolroom where he had first encountered his enemy and breathed deeply, feeling exquisitely calm. Even the rattle of the doorknob, the creak as the door eased open, could not cause his heart to leap.

"I expected you earlier," he said.

"Did you?" Stephen's pale gaze swept the room as he stepped inside. "What a Gothic choice, Liam! The alley behind the club would have served just as well."

"No," Liam said. "Not for a killing."

They locked eyes. Liam felt mild surprise at how relaxed his cousin looked, his pale light eyes steady and focused, his thin lips relaxed. Stephen's courage had never been physical, but the prospect of violence did not frighten him today.

"This is long overdue," Stephen said. He closed the door and leaned against it. He had a hand tucked inside his coat, no doubt gripping a weapon. "I should have done it myself—on your wedding day, when I had the chance."

Liam considered it. "A bullet might have served you better," he said. "But you'd have found it too quick to satisfy. Revenge is better served in portions—slowly, to make the man suffer."

Stephen assessed him with a cold, measuring stare. "Yes, true enough. And you did suffer, didn't you?" His smile spread, slow and ugly. "The grand lordling learned at last what it's like to live as the common folk do."

Liam's own smile felt amazed and very fleeting. "Is *that* what I learned?"

Stephen's glance broke away to rove the room. He shook his head, made a little grunt. "Amazing." His palm ran across the nearest desktop, his index finger pausing over his own initials scratched into the wood. "I'd imagined this place given over to kindling."

"My father was sentimental."

"Yes. I remember."

"You should. You were under his care for five years." Hearing the sharpness in his own voice, his anger on his father's behalf, Liam took a deep breath. "He looked on you as another son."

"A second son," Stephen snapped. "A very great distance from there to the first."

Was that the root of his hatred, then? "There is no time in my memory in which he favored me over you. Every gift we received was equal. Every tutor we had, every trip we took—"

"Oh, he knew the difference." Stephen pulled his

gun into the open, held it loosely at his side. "'Steward-ship of the land is our highest calling, lads.'" Quoting Liam's father, his voice soured. "So he would prate, as though he hadn't mortgaged his acres to hell and back. And then, cursing the bankers who wanted only their due—disdaining the money-grubbers, while telling me all the while what a succor I would be to you once I joined their ranks—as though I had been bred to play the mule, the beast of burden who would haul the Lock-wood fortunes back to greatness!"

Some distant part of Liam marveled at this twisted version of his own memories. "He thought your father a visionary. He was given full custody of your wealth—but never once did he reach into those accounts to ease his own burdens."

"How *honorable*. He refrained from stealing from his ward!"

"A pity his example did not take," Liam said. "You stole a good deal more than wealth from me."

Stephen's eyes rolled. "Poor, put-upon Liam! What a noble victim you paint yourself. Tell me, was familial loyalty *always* such a virtue to you? Did you ever look to *my* comfort? At Eton, while you were off carousing with your friends, did you ever give a thought to *me*, left behind in the dormitories? And later—"

Liam rose, and his cousin made a nervous retreat, lifting the gun to take aim. "You disdained my friends. You called Auburn a—"

"I had no choice," Stephen blazed. "You think we all could prove so tenderhearted? They called you Viscount Sayers. And I? The son of a moneybag!"

Liam stared. "So, childhood taunts drove you to it. Is that what you mean?"

"Taunts? You painted me as *weak*! Telling Darnley to pick on someone his own size—you advertised me as a deficient, something less than a man!"

Stephen had been smaller as a boy. An easy target for bullies at school. "You would rather have gotten thrashed?"

"Yes! Better to be beaten black-and-blue than to receive your *charity*. And later—at university, when you told the Bullingdon Club to invite *me* to join in your stead—another hand-me-down. It was your favorite game—exposing me to the mockery of addled twits!"

Liam felt suddenly awash in exhausted irritation. "Fine," he said. "Let's get on with it."

But Stephen was beside himself now, his pistol sagging as he frothed with rage. "And then, your introduction to Arbuthnot! Who should rightly have favored me all along, for God knows I've more brains in my pinky than you've got in your entire skull. But that sycophant had no interest in real intellect. He was too dazzled by titles to know genius when he saw it!"

Professor Arbuthnot had not kept Stephen on. Liam still remembered his cousin's rage at being transferred to a different tutor. "Oh, but you had your revenge there," he said. "You had me framed as an arsonist and expelled from university. And I never breathed a bloody *word* of it."

Stephen kicked one of the desks, toppling it with a crash. "Another of your favors, eh? All the Bodleian could have burned, and the trustees still would have *begged* you back, if only your father made the request! But, no, Liam—you could not be bothered. For you were *grateful* at being tossed out. You *knew* that you would never top me; there would be no double first for *you.* So you withdrew before I could have my triumph. You fled like a coward—"

"Christ above!" Liam took a hard breath. "Stephen, every sin you lodge against me was done as a kindness."

"I never wanted kindness from you!"

In the ensuing silence, Liam heard his cousin's rasping breath, watched him struggle to compose himself.

"I never wanted kindness," Stephen said more softly. "I wanted *justice.*"

A peculiar calm settled over Liam. He would never doubt his own sanity again. *This* was madness, here in front of him, raving. "Justice—by murdering me."

Abruptly Stephen laughed. "Justice, yes. Even the *word* sounds foreign from your mouth." He paused, looking around again. "Do you know, I applaud your choice of setting. This room—an inspired choice. It was here, you know, that I first noticed it—that difference in our stations, that gap that I could not leap no matter how superior I proved." A muscle ticked in his jaw as he met Liam's eyes again. "And I proved it. In *every* way, I was your better. Intellect, aptitude, character—all of it went to *me.* But after we left this room, none of that mattered. Only a trick of birth—that was all you had over me, but it was everything. So—yes, *this* was the last fair playing field on which we ever met." Stephen took a deep breath, squared his shoulders. "Let us end it here, then." He lifted his firearm once more.

Liam opened his arms wide.

For the first time, a trace of uncertainty disrupted his cousin's countenance. "What—what are you about?"

"End it," Liam said. "You're done anyway. The evidence against you ensures it."

Stephen squinted. "You've got no evidence."

If he had believed that, he would not have come today. "Then shoot," Liam said. "If you feel so certain."

Stephen's finger twitched over the trigger. "I suppose you mean that bloody notice in the papers? I don't care what you've manufactured. There's no proof to be had."

Liam shrugged.

"If there were proof—" His cousin's laughter sounded a little ragged now. "It wouldn't concern *me*. I had nothing to do with Sadler. That was all Davin's doing. The fool *bragged* about it."

"Davin was a fine man. A far better man than you."

Stephen reddened. "Davin, you fool, was the middleman—the one who introduced me to Marlowe. Bragged about how Marlowe had helped him with Sadler! He thought they were friends—another fine brain, almost a match for yours. But Marlowe was a man of business. He was glad to dispatch Davin, for a price. And that was my test, you see. I watched how it worked. And no, *coz*—he left behind no proof whatsoever." He took a large breath. "No, you're bluffing. Davin disappeared cleanly. And so did you."

Liam smiled. "If there's no proof, *coz*, why on earth would I have risked this meeting? Besides, you're about to commit murder—in front of witnesses. That will trump all the rest I have to say."

Stephen cast a startled glance behind him. "You're a lunatic," he said as he faced Liam again. "There's no one—"

"There are witnesses," Liam said calmly. "They are hidden in the walls."

At last, at last, Stephen remembered the apartment above. The spy holes. His gaze flicked upward, and a sharp knock came through the ceiling, causing him to jump.

For the first time, Liam saw fear in him.

"I'm sorry to say, you will *not* become the next Earl of Lockwood," Liam went on gently. "Instead, you will be hanged—for murdering me, or for your confession to murdering Davin. Regardless, your companies and wealth will be confiscated, your wife and children made outcast. Your name will be disgraced, your legacy ruined."

"Hogwash," Stephen bit out, but his voice was now shaking. "Your bloody—"

"Transported convicts are soon forgotten—but your hanging will fill every newspaper. I wonder how your parish will feel, when their churchwarden is hanged as a killer? You'll die infamous, but not celebrated. This will, after all, look like a very stupid way to murder someone—in front of witnesses, staring down from above."

"Shut your lying mouth," Stephen yelled. "Where is your weapon? Pull out your weapon, you coward!"

Some commotion came from outside—shouts in the distance. It caused Stephen to startle and tighten his grip on the gun. "It will be worth it," he said through his teeth. "To see you dead."

"Ask why I didn't kill you," Liam murmured. "This entire year, I could have done it. A *superior* man would have resisted murder—but as you say, I am not superior."

A line formed between Stephen's brows. "Why?" he whispered at last. "Why didn't you do it?"

"The perfect revenge would have been to bury you in the hole at Elland. But Elland is no more. So I settled for what remained: your honor. Your fortune. Your legacy.

Your wife's happiness. Your children's futures. All finished, coz. Your sons will watch you be hanged for your crimes—and they will realize, in the hisses and sneers of their former friends, that it was *you* who destroyed their lives. *You* who murdered their futures. Their father was not a superior man, after all—but a miserable criminal."

Stephen stared blankly, his lips moving but failing to voice a syllable.

"Or you can kill yourself," Liam added casually. "Here and now. And it will be known as an accident rather than a suicide. *That* would be the superior man's course. To save his family, he would shoot himself quickly—for the magistrate is already en route."

He saw Stephen's hesitation, the indecision that contorted his face and caused his trigger finger to twitch. He wanted to shoot Liam first.

"My friend upstairs has a weapon trained on you," Liam said. "But if you manage to shoot me, he will make certain you survive to be tried and strung up by the neck." He came off the wall, continuing in a low, easy voice: "So, decide: are you honorable? Or are you a coward? I give you the choice. Be hanged later, and rot as your family scrabbles to escape the stain of your name. Or die now by your own hand, and be honorably mourned. Your children and wife will remember you fondly. Or they will be reduced to paupers, and they will spit on your grave as they slink past to the workhouse."

Stephen looked very pale now. His gaze broke free, roving once more over the room, the ceiling.

"Make your choice," Liam bit out.

Stephen's gaze dropped, fixing on the chalkboard. *"Bis vincit qui se vincit in victoria,"* he whispered.

The gunfire left Liam's ears ringing. Blood spattered

the chalkboard and walls as the body thumped to the ground.

A mild surprise gripped him, though he was not sure why. He'd seen a great deal of violent death, thanks to the man now lying there dead.

The trapdoor swung open, and Julian dropped onto the floor, landing lightly a few paces from the body. "I nearly shot him." Jules looked tense as he clawed a hand through his thick black hair. "When he lifted that gun again—I felt certain he'd take aim at you. Christ, this was a lunatic plan! I never thought he'd make the choice."

"Nor did I." *There* was the cause of his surprise: in the end, Stephen had not been a coward.

"Well, bully for you," Liam said softly to his cousin. He did not add, *Rest in peace.* He doubted Stephen would have wished for his benediction—and anyway, he was not saintlike enough to mean it.

But he would keep his word. Stephen's death would be known to the world as an accident.

"Bit of a pity," he said to Julian as he pushed open the door and stepped into the bright warmth of late spring. "I'd rather wanted to see him hang."

The gunshot rang out just as Anna caught sight of the schoolhouse. Her heart in her throat, she raced forward—and then cried out in relief as Liam and the Duke of Auburn emerged into the sunlight, intact and unbloodied and hale.

Spotting them, Liam looked profoundly displeased. His scowl was apparent from fifty yards, and as he stalked toward them, he distributed his wrath in pointed glares at his men. "You brought along my *wife*? What in God's name—"

Anna interrupted this nonsensical complaint by pushing past the duke and reaching for him. Liam caught her by the waist and pulled her into his chest, and for a moment, as his hard arms closed around her, she felt reassured by how solid he felt, how steady and strong on his feet.

Then she pulled back, gripping his face. A streak of dust marred his beautiful brow, which she wiped away. "You are an *idiot*," she said. "The men did not bring *me*. I brought *them*."

"And a fine thing she did," Henneage growled. "For I've a mind to have a taste—"

"Hold," Liam called over her head, causing Henneage to abort his rapid advance on the schoolhouse. "No need. He's done."

Henneage pivoted, red-faced. "You might've let us help!"

"Aye," said Danvers, "wasn't very sporting of you."

"Why did you do it without us?" Wilkins cried.

Anna, standing within the circle of Liam's arms, watched his smile grow as he looked over the group of ill-tempered former convicts, all of them scowling at him.

"Because I had to do it myself," he said. "But if I ever require an army—God save the enemy. I could not ask for better friends than you all."

"Wake up, Liam."

A gentle nudge startled him out of slumber. He opened his eyes to a chill salted breeze, and found his wife's arms around him, his head having fallen to rest atop hers, as she nestled into the crook of his shoulder.

"The sun's coming up," she whispered.

"So it is." The light rose over the ridge behind them, spilling all at once across the pale sands. Grain by grain the glimmer rose, until the long rays of light touched the dark waters washing up on the beach. The ocean shushed and sighed, pulling back toward the lingering dark, then charging ahead again toward the light, which began to turn the charcoal waves to a deep and shimmering green.

"You fell asleep," she murmured.

"Only for a moment."

That won him a snort. "You were snoring for over an hour."

"I don't snore."

"Louder than old Murray, in fact."

He laughed, then cast about for the discarded bottle of champagne. "Lies," he said as he wrested the bottle from its sandy berth. "Scottish slander."

The champagne bore the cool chill of the fading night, and washed away the taste of sand in his mouth. When he lowered the bottle, she was watching him, the strengthening light illuminating the shadows beneath her eyes, the fine lines that fanned from the corners. One day they would deepen and crease the tops of her cheeks as well.

Those faint lines struck him suddenly—sank hooks into his chest. He reached out to trace them very lightly with his fingertip. He would be blessed and fortunate to watch them deepen. To know a time when no angle of light would be required to see their shape. To see her aged and weathered, not merely ragged from lack of sleep.

She caught his hand, kissed his fingers. "I'm glad one of us got some rest. I feel dizzy."

This bottle had been three-quarters full, last he'd checked. "The champagne likely didn't help with that."

She grinned, cheeky and unashamed. "I had so much to toast. Not my fault you fell asleep in the middle."

She had such smiles. They took over her entire face, lifting and rounding her cheeks, crinkling her eyes and deepening those lines of fatigue, testaments to how hard and long they'd traveled. They had not gone back to town from Lawdon, accepting Julian's offer to handle the mess.

It had taken thirty-six hours to reach Rawsey. But it felt as though it should have taken longer. He felt as though he were in some new world, unreachable to what had come before.

He was staring too intently, perhaps. She lowered her face, brushed at her hair. "I must look a mess," she said. "I think I fell asleep, too, for a bit."

"You're beautiful."

She flashed him a mocking look. "Did I say I wasn't? Only that I'm tired."

His laughter felt slurred, giddy. He lay back, the thin blanket doing little to cushion the effect of the small coarse rocks that assembled this beach. More rubble than beach, really. But to his bruised body, the small nudges and pokes felt oddly pleasant.

"I look forward," he said toward the sky, "to loving you when you're old."

She lay down beside him, her hair brushing his cheek. "Love me now," she said softly. "Don't wait."

He rolled onto his side to face her. She had been with him through all of it—the interview with the magistrate; the arrangements to transport Stephen's body to London in the false trappings of dignity and honor; the confusion and clamor of his men from Elland, who had wanted to understand better what role Davin had played in the plot—for they had mourned him after his death, and felt confused and betrayed by news of his association with Marlowe.

All the while, through these tumultuous hours of unpleasant business, Anna had stood by him, occasionally taking his hand.

And then the train north—they had slept awhile, and paused at Leeds to dine, adjourning to a room above the tavern for another brief rest, and a strange swift consummation that had had less to do with love than with an animal confirmation of survival.

In silence they had boarded the next train, then the hired carriage to Clachaig. She must have sent news ahead to expect them, for there'd been a boat anchored, awaiting them. But he could not remember their passage over the water, much less how they'd found the champagne.

The stars, though—he remembered how they had dazzled him. In the camp, parched and starving, stars had looked to him like bars in a prison cell, their bright clear numberless abundance and strange orientations announcing how far he was from home, and how alone, and how forgotten.

Here, though, the constellations knew him. He recognized their shapes. And she had lain beside him and they had named those constellations, and he had felt bathed in their light, held in it, and somehow *known*. And then . . .

"I can't believe I fell asleep." Suddenly it seemed very

funny. He began to laugh, though he could not say why the amusement felt abruptly overwhelming. His laughter racked him, and after a moment, she clung on to him and laughed, too, so their exhausted laughter combined in the stillness of the early morning, punctuated only by the steady crash of waves against the sand.

She pushed her face into his throat and he gripped her head, holding her against him as slowly he calmed. Great deep breaths of salt air—the occasional fleck of ocean spray, carried by the light breeze—the warmth and fullness of her body wrapped around his, and the hard discomfort of the grainy sand beneath them; he felt so full of sensation he was not sure what to do with himself. Sleep, a minute ago so seductive, now felt impossible.

"I think I'm with child," she whispered.

His hand clenched on her hair. It understood before he did.

He exhaled slowly. "You . . ." His mind clicked into gear, and he pulled away from her, sitting up. "And you came to Lawdon?"

She pushed herself upright, already frowning. "Yes, and I came to Lawdon."

He opened his mouth, then bit down on the urge to speak. Instead he rose, dusting off the sand, and stared down at her, wrestling with emotions too mixed and violent to parse.

She blew out a breath. "It does happen, you know, when a man and a woman lie together. Even if blindfolds are used."

If that did not invite a curse in reply, then nothing did.

Instead, with remarkably commendable calm, he

said, "You went to Lawdon, knowing what would happen there, knowing you might carry our child—"

"Knowing our child's father was risking his life." She stomped to her feet. "Risking his life with extreme recklessness, without having bothered even to tell me so, and without regard for *my* welfare or for this child's. And knowing myself your *equal*, regardless of whether I am a mother as well. Or does my life mean more, suddenly—or my mind and my will mean less—now that I carry your child?"

"No." This he spoke instantly. "No, your life is . . ." He cleared his throat. "Immeasurably precious, Anna. Nothing changes that. Or alters it by a whit."

"Well, good, then." But then she bit her lip, seeming somewhat at a loss, hunting in her skirts for pockets that did not apparently exist, for her palms then fell to hang by her sides, her fingers flexing on air. "I am glad to hear it," she said, turning to look over the water. "But I . . . I confess I did not even think on it. If I had a babe in arms, I would not have brought *her* with me."

Her. Amazement leapt through him. A child, a new life, both of them combined. He stepped closer. "You have a feeling? A feeling it will be a daughter?"

She slanted him an impatient look. "*One* of them will be, surely. We can try again if it doesn't work out this time."

Now he laughed again, from sheer amazement. The thought of a daughter like her—burnished hair, and a spiked tongue—but their daughter would never want for a steady home. Nor for a father.

The thought chilled him a little. This strange endless day, now forty or fifty hours old, had left him somehow drunk, perhaps too optimistic. Stephen was finished, all the mysteries solved, but his own brain could not be fixed so easily.

"I will be a good father," he said slowly, to himself as much as to her. "No matter what goes on inside my head, I will never show her—".

She took his arm, squeezing hard. "Inside your head is the part of you I love the most. I won't let you deny our children that."

The sun was high now. Beginning to blaze. It had wiped away all signs of her exhaustion. She looked young and fierce and determined, no trace of age on her face. They had time ahead of them—so much of it. They had all the time they needed, perhaps, to live happily, joyously, and forget what it meant to feel otherwise.

He pulled her into a kiss. She tasted like champagne; she smelled like the sea. The blood quickening to a throb through his body, the call of a seabird passing overhead, the sudden whip of the wind and crash of the waves—this was life, *his* life, like a gift delivered unto him, which he would guard henceforth for her sake, for their family's sake, for his *own* sake. This was his.

"I love you," he said into her mouth.

He felt her lips turn into a smile. "I know you do," she murmured. "You're a man of good sense, after all. One of the reasons that I love you."

EPILOGUE

Isle of Rawsey, 1869

The blindfold became her husband, accentuating his broad, angular cheekbones and the firmness of his jawline. Anna watched his throat as he swallowed, then found herself distracted by his lips, full and wet and gleaming.

"Mossy," he murmured.

"Go on," she murmured back.

"Nutty. A touch of the sea." His lips curved into a smile. "This batch is ours. From the spring water, not the loch."

"By Gad, he does it again!" The stool thumped as Iain MacDougall jumped to his feet. Anna, reminded abruptly of the company, applauded with the others as Liam pulled off the blindfold.

"That's eight for eight," MacDougall crowed. In his excitement, he had clawed his bright blond curls into an ecstatic halo and knocked his spectacles askew. "You've a talent, m'lord. We could market your services, I'll wager, if only you weren't known as an Englishman!"

Liam laughed. "His services are not for sale," Anna

said, but she was smiling—as were the rest of the men and women in this small room off the distillery. The floor was packed earth, the roof overhead thatched tight against the falling rain, and the long wooden table, solid enough to dance upon, held a variety of whiskies from all over Scotland—among them Rawsey's, in two varieties stamped with the seal that young Mariah MacKay, not yet sixteen, had designed last year under the supervision of one of Liam's visiting artists.

"However," Anna added, "I believe Lord Lockwood accepts tips for his services, in the form of a dram for his wife."

Laughter traveled the room, notes of relief uppermost. For five years, as the whisky had aged in oak barrels, the islanders had been anxiously awaiting this day, when the first batches would finally be tested. What dreams they had spun for this fledgling industry! And now, today, those dreams seemed closer than ever, for the whisky was more than fine. It had the robustness of the Islay, the complex flavor of the Speyside, and all the heat of a Highlands batch, thanks in part to the excellence of Rawsey's barley—which had flourished due to Anna's patented blend of ammoniated manure.

MacDougall, who had overseen the production, held up the two bottles, both single malt, one made with the peaty water of the loch, and the other from the fresh, clear springwater on the northern end of the isle. "Would you prefer homegrown, m'lady, or an Islay for your—"

"Oh bosh," she said. "Homegrown, of course! But none of these foreign interlopers must go to waste. Indeed, we must get rid of them before the journalists arrive from Edinburgh." It transpired that the oversight of an earl and countess did much to promote a newborn distillery; the newspapers had clamored to be invited to the formal inauguration of the business, and so, in turn, the islanders had quickly organized one—to occur the day after the *true* event. "Perhaps you might call in the others to help with drinking all this?"

Soon enough, the doors were thrown open, admitting the pearly gray light of the damp afternoon. The rest of the islanders, who had been patiently awaiting the verdict from the distillery's board, took turns pushing inside for a taste.

Thomas Wilson had brought his fiddle, and his wife, Tammy, a flute; soon, with glasses in hand and bottles passing regularly, the crowd spilled back out into the rain, stomping and turning reels in the mud. Inside, the heat grew and the air rattled with happy chatter. Iain MacDougall, returning to the table after a triumphal procession through the crowd, fell into a seat beside Anna, interrupting her inappropriate and entirely whisky-fueled massage of her husband's thigh beneath the table.

Happily, MacDougall was too distracted to notice this mischief. "Now," he said to her husband, who took a deep breath, ostensibly to inhale the fumes of his glass—but perhaps, in reality, to collect himself, for beneath the table, his thigh pressed hard against Anna's— "you didn't say much of t'other one, from the loch. I had some fears over it."

"Also superior." Amusement flavored Liam's voice. It had become a joke on the island that he, the only Englishman in residence, should prove the sharpest and most gifted taster of whisky. "Harsher, to be certain— but complex, with an aftertaste that continues to develop for minutes afterward."

MacDougall nodded, looking satisfied. "Peaty, you'd say?"

"Certainly. But foremost, smoke—and beneath that, fruit: apricot, dried plum, cherry. A smooth, lingering finish to it—coffee, I'd say, and a touch of chocolate."

MacDougall slapped the table, causing Anna to jump. "Chocolate. Aye, precisely!" He leapt to his feet and hurried down the table to share the news. "Very peaty," Anna heard him pronounce, "but complex—smoky; his lordship called it so. A toast, lads and ladies, to the future of whisky!"

Laughing, Anna raised her glass again, touching it to Liam's. As his own smile faded, something soft and tender entered his expression. "Shall we walk?" he said.

"Indeed." She rose, looking fondly over the islanders, now plotting boisterously how they'd make use of future profits to expand the distillery's production. The operation was wholly theirs: she had signed a document putting the distillery and its profits into the perpetual custody of the people of Rawsey. "Those journalists may see the proof of our whisky," she murmured in Liam's ear, "in the great number of headaches they'll encounter on arrival."

"We'll feed everyone well tonight," he said, grinning, "and then dispatch them to sleep it off."

"Oh goodness! I forgot to check on the kitchens." She had meant to do so before coming down to the distillery, but had been snared into a game of hide-and-seek with Robert and Ada. "Did you—"

"All in order," he said. "Ada reminded me, before she set off to find you for a game."

Anna laughed as she took his arm. They fell into step up the winding path toward the manor house, the rain a gentle light patter against her skin, cool and salt scented. "What a little manager she is. Mrs. Dawson"—their housekeeper in London—"says she would fear for her job, if Ada entered the competition."

"Her capability is terrifying," Liam agreed. "She takes after her mother, I believe."

That deserved a kiss—and here, on Rawsey, Anna felt able to turn to him in public and give him one, for the islanders' regard was ever only kind.

He caught her head to hold her to him, releasing her with obvious reluctance when a shrill girlish cry came from the direction of the house: "Papa! Mama! Robby is drawing on the walls again!"

Anna sighed and picked up her skirts to speed her pace. "Your fault," she remarked to Liam. Robby had inherited an artistic talent from some unknown forebear—a talent nurtured, in turn, by the succession of artists whom Liam hosted at their many properties, and, of course, by his godmother, her grace the Duchess of Auburn.

"Entirely my fault," Liam said, not even attempting to sound repentant. "Wagers on what he drew?"

"Sheep."

"That was last month's obsession. Horse, is my guess."

"A unicorn!" announced Ada crossly as she stomped toward them. "But he gave her two horns! I told him that a unicorn has only got the one. It's in the *name*, isn't it? But then he told me I was wrong, and *then* he added *wings*!"

"Appalling." Anna scooped up Ada with an effort that made her grunt. A shocking thought occurred: one day soon, Ada would be too heavy for her to carry like this. A bittersweet pang tightened her belly; she pulled her daughter's red head against her, breathing deeply of Ada's sweet scalp. "You're growing so big, sweetheart."

"I'm nearly eight!"

Anna laughed. "Another ten months. But yes, soon enough."

"When I'm eight, I can come on your tour! You said so!"

"Yes, so you will. But there won't be another tour for some time, sweetheart." Anna had yet to complete the draft of her next manuscript, a new set of science stories for children. The last tour had been lovely—a great success, the publishers said, which had sent her second book into eighth and ninth printings. But the entire time, she had longed for her children. She would not tour again until they were old enough to accompany her.

Liam opened the door for them and she stepped into the vestibule. The savory smells of the coming dinner, a celebratory occasion for the entirety of the island, made her stomach growl.

She set Ada down. "All right, where did Robby draw on the walls?"

But before Ada could answer, Nanny came charging in. "Forgive me, m'lady! He got into your rooms somehow—I swear I was watching him—he sneaks off, I don't know how he does it—he's a proper escape artist, that lad—"

"Like his father," Liam said with a smile.

That smile was wondrous to Anna. For a time, after his cousin's death, she had wondered if the darkness would ever release him completely. Stephen Devaliant's suicide had released him from his panics, but on occasion, she had still caught him brooding, shadows in his face as he looked at her, heavy with child. He had confessed that he feared some new trapdoor might open in his mind, and make him unfit to be the kind of father that he himself had been blessed with.

But after Ada's birth, he had taken to fatherhood with an ease and open affection that acted like a tonic, washing away his anxieties. And nowadays, the darkness was such a distant memory that he could even occasionally make these glancing references to that portion of his history—references that others would find unremarkable, but that Anna considered precious proof of his wholeness. He could smile as he spoke of his talent for escape.

Glancing over, he caught her watching him. His smile shifted, into something hotter and more private, not intended for others' eyes.

"Where is Robby now?" he asked Nanny, without removing his eyes from Anna.

"Oh, he's back in the nursery. I would have had the mess cleaned up, but I thought first I should tell you—"

"We'll manage it," Liam said. "Will you take Ada up as well? We'll come fetch them in an hour for dinner."

"I don't want to go!" Ada said. "I wanted to play hide-and-seek again—"

"After supper," Liam said. "First I have some private business with your mother."

Arm in arm they mounted the stairs, Anna turning her head now and then to inhale the scent of him through his woolen coat. His hand around hers drew secret patterns on her palm, his thumb rubbing lazily over hers, a small subtle movement that caused her breath to shorten and her knees to turn weak.

There were many miracles between them. What happened between their bodies was no less miraculous than the rest.

When he opened the door and ushered her inside, she turned immediately, lifting her face for a kiss.

But instead, he burst into laughter, then turned her by the shoulders to see for herself.

Robby had indeed drawn a winged unicorn—hovering aside the edge of a mountain, poised to catch the two stick figures falling from the cliff. Beneath this tableau, in the broken handwriting of a six-year-old, he had handily labeled the scene: BIN NEVUS.

"You told him that story?" Anna gasped.

Liam's mouth touched her ear. "Of course," he murmured. "He asked why men and women got married. I explained that it was to have someone to catch you when you fall."

She turned. "Catch me, then," she said, and threw her arms around him, laughing again when he picked her up and carried her to bed.

Find your next read at

XOXO *after* DARK

Join us for the best in romance,
ebook deals, free reads, and more!

Because the best conversations
happen after dark...

XOXOAfterDark.com
f / XOXOAfterDark
🐦 @ XOXOAfterDark

57916

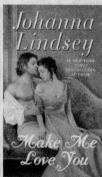

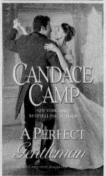

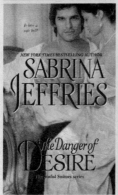